n Territories

Osgard

Tarsepolis

Floating
Gardens

Great Steps
of Charis

Guardians
of Justice

Charis

S E A

Lighthouse
of Nazirah

Nazirah

KINGDOM
OF
HERAT

Al-Khansa

u Steppe

Tel Amot

Red Gate
of Mercy

Behezda

Seti Desert

SOUTH
SEA

INTO THE
DYING
LIGHT

INTO THE
DYING
LIGHT

AN AGE OF DARKNESS NOVEL

KATY ROSE POOL

Henry Holt and Company
New York

Henry Holt and Company, *Publishers since 1866*
Henry Holt® is a registered trademark of Macmillan Publishing Group, LLC
120 Broadway, New York, New York 10271 • fiercereads.com

Library of Congress Cataloging-in-Publication Data
Names: Pool, Katy Rose, author. | Pool, Katy Rose. Age of darkness novel ; book 3.
Title: Into the dying light / Katy Rose Pool.
Description: First edition. | New York : Henry Holt and Company, 2021. | Series: The age
    of darkness ; book 3 | Audience: Ages 14–18. | Audience: Grades 10–12. | Summary: The
    ancient god has been resurrected and sealed inside Beru's body, but both of them are at
    the mercy of the Prophet Pallas, who wants to subjugate the Six Prophetic Cities; but the
    god grows stronger and far away Anton is learning to harness his powers as a Prophet, and
    planning to lead Jude, Hassan, and Beru's sister, Ephyra, on a desperate quest to destroy the
    god and Pallas, and save the world from darkness—even if it requires an unbearable sacrifice.
Identifiers: LCCN 2021008644 | ISBN 9781250211798 (hardcover)
Subjects: LCSH: Gods—Juvenile fiction. | Cults—Juvenile fiction. | Magic—Juvenile fiction. |
    Prophecies—Juvenile fiction. | Prophets—Juvenile fiction. | Quests (Expeditions)—Juvenile
    fiction. | Fantasy. | Young adult literature. | CYAC: Gods—Fiction. | Cults—Fiction. | Magic—
    Fiction. | Prophecies—Fiction. | Prophets—Fiction. | Fantasy. | LCGFT: Fantasy fiction.
Classification: LCC PZ7.1.P6435 In 2021 | DDC 813.6 [Fic]—dc23
LC record available at https://lccn.loc.gov/2021008644

Our books may be purchased in bulk for promotional, educational, or business use. Please
contact your local bookseller or the Macmillan Corporate and Premium Sales Department at
(800) 221-7945 ext. 5442 or by email at MacmillanSpecialMarkets@macmillan.com.

First edition, 2021 / Designed by Mallory Grigg
Printed in the United States of America
10 9 8 7 6 5 4 3 2 1

For all who have braved their own Age of Darkness

I

THE KEEPER
OF THE WORD

1

BERU

BERU GAZED OUT AT THE WITNESSES GATHERED BEFORE THE ALTAR, A SEA OF black and gold. Pallas's palm rested gently on her shoulder, a reminder to the Witnesses, and to Beru, who was in control here. Her skin crawled. The god was restless, bristling beneath Pallas's hand, straining against the Four-Petal Seal that kept it bound inside her.

She could feel the god's vitriol, the ever-present desire to strike Pallas down, a low hum in the back of her mind.

"Today," Pallas intoned, "is a day of glory. A day of divine judgment, where the wicked are punished and the worthy rewarded."

His long fingers dug briefly into Beru's shoulder as he nodded at Lazaros. The Witness slunk like a shadow toward her, his Godfire scars gleaming in the torchlight.

His hands were cold as they unlocked the Godfire collar that circled Beru's neck. As the metal drew away from her skin, Beru felt the sudden jolt of the god's power flowing through her. It was almost painful.

WE COULD STRIKE HIM DOWN, the god whispered in her mind. WE WOULD BE FREE.

Without the collar to contain it, the god's hatred seeped through Beru like acrid poison. She closed her eyes against it and stepped up to the edge of the altar, raising her hands. She could feel the invisible currents of *esha* that reverberated throughout the temple, and with a twist of her wrist she tugged on them, flinging the temple doors open. Bright white light flooded the sanctum. The revelers gasped in awe.

Pallas's voice echoed through the chamber. "Who among these faithful will be the first to receive revelation?"

The crowd parted, and a Witness dressed in black and gold robes marched toward the altar. A woman in chains stumbled along behind him, her dark hair lank and loose around her shoulders. She looked frail and dirty, a trapped, half-starved creature, but there was a ferocious gleam in her eyes.

"Immaculate One," the Witness said, bowing to Pallas as he reached the altar. He turned to Beru. "Holy Creator. I seek revelation, and I bring you this unholy sinner to receive your judgment."

The chained woman trembled as she stood before them, but her gaze didn't falter.

Beru felt sick. She used to score her body with alchemical ink—one mark for every murder her sister had committed to keep Beru alive. She bore no physical marks for the people whose Grace she had stolen over the past two moons, yet she knew her count far outnumbered Ephyra's. Her horror never abated; each was as awful as the first had been.

"Come forward," Pallas said, stepping aside to let the Witness and his captive onto the altar.

The Witness knelt at Beru's feet. The captive resisted, standing tall, until a violent yank on the chains sent her stumbling to her knees with a sharp cry.

Beru knew what Pallas wanted her to do, the role he wanted her to play. And she knew, too, that she would play it. But she would make him wait, first. Make him wonder if maybe this time, she would refuse. Maybe this time, she would decide this game wasn't worth playing any longer.

Maybe this time, she would strike.

Every order Pallas issued was a careful calculation. What would he ask her to do next? Would it be awful enough to make her hesitate? To make her refuse? Open defiance from Beru would mean punishment for Ephyra, whom Pallas had locked in the citadel. But Pallas didn't know what Beru's limit was.

Beru didn't know, either.

She raised her hands, the god's power surging into her palms and fingertips like cold fire. The captive stared up at her, mutinous. Beru made herself take in the woman's face, her wide brown eyes and the stern set of her mouth, as she reached with the god's power and grabbed hold of the pulsing warmth of the woman's Grace. The captive let out an anguished cry as Beru spread her fingers and pulled against the woman's Grace, unraveling it thread by thread from her body.

Beru closed her eyes against the horrific sound of torture. That sound would ring in Beru's head, joining the other screams and shrieks that haunted her. In a moment, it was over—the woman collapsed, her Grace ripped out of her.

"The abomination has been cleansed," Pallas intoned. "And now the righteous rewarded. What was corruption has been purified, transformed into a blessing for the faithful few."

The Witness kneeling at Beru's feet rose.

Beru extended her hands again, and the bright, shivering Grace she'd ripped out of the captive swirled around the Witness as Beru carefully knitted it to his *esha*. The Witness cried out, falling to his knees.

Before Beru knew what was happening, she was whirling around toward Pallas, Godfire leaping from one of the torches and into her hands. Pallas froze, his blue eyes wide. The god's vicious satisfaction oozed through Beru as the crowd behind them gasped.

Beru slammed her eyes shut, heaving in a breath as the god wrestled for control. She could feel it, like a dark fog invading her mind.

She reached for a memory to drive it back.

When I was seven, I found a bird with a broken wing beneath the acacia in the yard, she thought. *I brought Ephyra to it, and she healed it.*

She saw the memory in her mind, holding on to it tight. The way the bird's little feathered chest had trembled when Ephyra touched it. The way it had hopped away from them, shifted its healed wing. The little warble it had made when it flew away, joining the other birds high up in the branches of the acacia.

The details of the memory grounded her. Reminded her of who she was and what she could feel. She let those feelings fill her like light, breaking through the fog.

YOU WANT TO, the god said, pushing against the seal. I CAN FEEL THE DESIRE IN YOU. YOU WANT TO END HIM AS MUCH AS I DO.

Between one breath and the next, she considered it. Killing Pallas. Letting the god go free.

But she couldn't. As evil as Pallas was, the god would be worse. If she set the god free, then there was nothing to stop it from wreaking total devastation upon the world, the way it had in Behezda, with Beru just a passenger inside the beast.

She felt a presence at her side. Lazaros hovered behind her, ready to restrain her with Godfire chains if need be.

She dropped her hands, letting the Godfire extinguish, and turned back to the Witness and the chained woman on the altar. The Witness groaned and climbed to his feet.

"Behold!" Pallas said, stepping smoothly out in front of Beru as if nothing was amiss.

The Witness took a lurching leap, his newly stolen Grace launching him farther and higher than an ordinary human could manage. It was a clumsy and somewhat inept demonstration, but he would learn to wield his Grace in time.

Beru met Pallas's icy gaze. Dread pooled in her gut. Though she'd managed to stop the god, the damage was done. And Ephyra would pay for it.

———————

That night, they returned to the Archon's residence in the citadel, and Beru to her collar. She was used to the slight sting of the collar by now, and it was a relief not to feel the god's emotions encroaching on her mind like storm clouds.

Beru took a seat by the fire, and Lazaros lurked by the window. Lazaros was her own personal shadow—standing guard to ensure that the god inside Beru was under her control and that Beru herself didn't step a toe out of line. For as much as Pallas seemed to enjoy ordering Beru around in front of his followers, he did not elect to spend any time alone with her. He knew very well how the god longed for his death as much as it longed for freedom.

Beru found Lazaros unsettling. The Witnesses flocked to Pallas for a variety of reasons, but Lazaros's devotion went above any of them. He'd burned out his own Grace just to prove it. That kind of devotion defied explanation—Beru had sensed that even some of the other Witnesses were wary of Lazaros.

Even after two months, she had not quite gotten used to his watchful gray eyes, the jagged pattern of scars that crisscrossed his face, or the careful way he held himself. But what unnerved her most was the way he stared at her so reverently. To Pallas, she was a tool, but to Lazaros she was something to worship. She didn't know which one she hated more.

As the sky darkened outside Beru's window, a knock came at the door. Lazaros slunk over and opened it.

Ephyra stalked inside, flanked by two other Witnesses. Godfire cuffs encircled her wrists, although unlike Beru's collar, they were never allowed off. Beru noticed a fresh welt across Ephyra's cheek, and the stiff way she walked hinted that there were more injuries Beru could not see.

Beru rose from her seat and went to her sister, embracing her.

"Thank you for delivering her," Beru said to the Witnesses in a clipped tone. "You may leave now."

They hesitated as Beru stared them down, casting their gazes over her shoulder, where Lazaros skulked. Only when he signaled did they retreat.

"Bring us some supper," Beru called after them.

"And some wine!" Ephyra added.

The second the door clicked shut, Beru seized her sister's chin to get a closer look at the welt.

"I'm fine!" Ephyra huffed, batting away Beru's hand and flinging a nervous glance at Lazaros.

"I'm sorry," Beru said plaintively. The welt seemed to shine on Ephyra's face, a reminder from Pallas that it was Ephyra, always Ephyra, who would suffer for Beru's disobedience.

These meetings with her sister were part of the negotiation between Beru and Pallas, but it was not lost on Beru that they provided Pallas with something else to use against her. A gift offered that could easily be revoked if Beru disobeyed.

"Don't be," Ephyra replied, a hint of pride in her voice. She reached into the fold of her jacket. "Brought you something."

Lazaros shot toward them. Ephyra rolled her eyes but dropped the proffered item into his hand. It was just a seashell, collected from the cove that the Archon Basileus's residence perched over.

Once Lazaros was satisfied with his examination, he held it out to Beru. When she opened her palm, he pressed the shell into it. His touch was always cold, like Godfire. Beru suppressed a shiver and drew her hand away.

"Thank you," she said to Ephyra, and went to put the shell with the others on the windowsill. "Come on, let's sit."

Together they returned to the fire, letting it warm their hands. A chill was beginning to take the air in Pallas Athos as the hot summer months turned over into fall.

Servants, holdovers from the Archon Basileus before his arrest, arrived a few minutes later with their supper—a stew of lamb, walnut, and pomegranate pillowed on a bed of saffron rice, with a jug of wine to wash it down.

Beru and Ephyra were both so used to surviving on scraps and living in hovels that they'd had to adjust to the newfound abundance of this place. There were other things to get used to, too. Like the soft, searching looks Ephyra sent her as they ate. Like the guilt gnawing at Beru's heart as she tried not to think about the faces of all the people she'd tortured today.

There had been eighteen of them, more than usual. She didn't want to think about what that meant—that Pallas's message was spreading, that more and more people were taking up his cause, going out and finding Graced to capture and mutilate.

"I'm sorry," Beru said suddenly, setting down her fork.

Ephyra touched the welt on her cheek. "Beru, I already told you—"

"Not about that," Beru said. "Or—not just about that. I'm sorry that I never understood until now what it was like for you. All those years, killing people just to—I'm sorry."

"Beru, that was *never* your fault," Ephyra said, staring at her intently.

"I called you a monster," Beru said, her throat heavy with tears.

Ephyra looked away. "Maybe I am one."

"Then what does that make me?" Beru asked. "Those people today, in the temple . . . I'm a hypocrite. I blamed you for everything you did for me. But now that I'm in the same position—"

Ephyra clamped a hand down on Beru's, a storm roiling in her dark eyes. "You could never be a monster. You're my little sister. And we'll—" She cut a quick glance at Lazaros, and Beru understood what she had stopped herself from saying.

We'll find a way out of this.

"It's going to be all right," Ephyra said. She patted Beru's hand with a wan smile.

Beru turned her palm up and squeezed Ephyra's hand once, willing her to understand the dangerous words she left unsaid.

There was no way out of this. Not for Beru. Because with each passing day, the balance of power tipped—not toward Pallas, and not toward her, but toward the god. Its will grew stronger, and Beru didn't know how long she had until it wrested control from her completely.

And then they'd all be doomed.

2

HASSAN

HASSAN PUSHED OPEN THE DOOR OF THE ROOM HE SHARED ABOVE THE THREE Palms Taverna, exhaustion and anger turning his limbs to lead.

The sea air, sticky with salt and brine, puffed through the open window. Sprawled across a mattress, Hector lifted a hand in greeting. Hassan noted the other already held a cup of wine.

"Jude's not here?" Hassan asked, kicking the door shut and swallowing down the hot anger crawling up his throat. Jude and Hector usually got off their shift at the docks at the same time, several hours before Hassan's work at the ledger's office ended. But Jude seemed to be constantly disappearing, to Hassan's growing frustration.

"I need to tell you something," Hector said in a low voice, sitting up. He blinked, taking in Hassan's expression and visibly dour mood. "What's wrong? Did someone spill ink on the ledgers again?"

Hassan let out a breath, collapsing onto the bed across from Hector's. "There were even more Witnesses in the square today."

"Ah," Hector said knowingly. "Let me guess—they're blaming

Behezda's destruction on the Graced? Telling everyone that Pallas the Faithful is coming to save them all?"

After the destruction of Behezda, thousands had fled the ruined city and made their way to Tel Amot. Some had boarded ships bound for Charis and Pallas Athos, even as far as Endarrion, but many of them had stayed in the port city like Hassan, Hector, and Jude had. With the refugees had come the Witnesses, taking advantage of their desperation to recruit them. It made Hassan seethe just thinking of it, and he couldn't help but remember the Witnesses who had terrorized the Herati refugees in the agora of Pallas Athos.

"The sooner the Archon Basileus gets back to us, the better," Hassan grumbled. "Then we can finally get to Pallas Athos and *do something* about the Witnesses."

Picking up jobs at the docks and the ledger's office had been more than just a way to keep themselves afloat in Tel Amot while they considered their next move. As a bookkeeper in the ledger's office, Hassan had access to information about shipments coming to and from Pallas Athos. He'd been able to smuggle messages to the Archon Basileus in Pallas Athos via special ordered shipments of palm wine to the Archon's estate. It had been a gamble, but Hassan had known in his gut that the Archon Basileus would oppose the Hierophant's takeover of Pallas Athos and that he'd do what was in his power to stop him.

It had taken a month of smuggling messages back and forth for Hassan to convince the Archon that he was worth helping and to formulate their plan to get into Pallas Athos without being detected by the Hierophant. And now Hassan was just waiting for the final piece—a ship sent by the Archon that would get them safely into Pallas Athos's harbor.

He'd been waiting on it for almost two weeks, and his patience was beginning to dwindle.

"About that." Hector cleared his throat. "Something's happened."

Unease prickled over Hassan.

"There was a ship in today from Pallas Athos," Hector said. "The crew said the Archon Basileus was arrested by Pallas's men."

Hassan's stomach dropped like a stone. "What? That can't—Tell me you're joking."

But by the grave expression on Hector's face, it was clear he wasn't.

Six weeks of planning down the drain. Hassan felt breathless with anger. The Archon was their *only* ally in Pallas Athos, knocked off the board by the power-hungry Hierophant. Hassan should've known the Archon wouldn't be able to cling to power for much longer. They should have moved faster.

"We'll figure it out," Hector said feebly.

"*How?*" Hassan exploded. "Without the Archon's help, we won't even make it past the harbor. The Hierophant has the city too tightly controlled."

They would have to start completely from scratch, this time with no help from anyone within Pallas Athos.

"I don't know!" Irritation crackled through Hector's voice. "There must be *someone* who can help us."

Quietly, hesitantly, Hassan said, "Well. There is one other place we can turn."

Hector groaned, heaving himself off the bed and scratching at the scruff of a beard he'd stopped bothering to shave. Six weeks of labor at the docks had thickened the cords of his muscles, but now he seemed to shrink in on himself. "Please don't start with this again. Not until I've had more to drink."

"We need allies," Hassan said tersely. "And the Order of the Last Light, no matter your issues with them—"

"They're *not* our allies," Hector said, heat creeping into his voice.

"Hassan, come on. You pretended to be the Prophet, Jude disappeared with the *actual* Prophet, and I broke my oath. On the list of people they want to ally with, we're ranked pretty low."

"Not lower than the Hierophant," Hassan replied stubbornly. "We should at least *try* to contact them. We're out of options."

"What about the Lost Rose people?" Hector asked. "Still no answer from them?"

Hassan shook his head.

"So their whole plan of guarding the Relics failed and now their worst nightmare is unfolding and they're—what? Off touring the islands?"

"I don't know," Hassan replied. The only reason he even knew the Lost Rose existed was because he'd found a scroll in the Great Library in Nazirah, hidden there by his father. A covenant that had said the Lost Rose were protectors of the Four Sacred Relics, the origins of the Graces.

Maybe it was just wishful thinking on his part, the idea that this secret network of guardians could come to their aid. Maybe it was the fact that his father had been connected, somehow, to these people, that gave him a glimmer of hope. And when Jude had told him that he'd met their leader in Endarrion, that she'd returned the Relic of Heart and helped lead them to the Relic of Sight—it had felt like a sign that the Lost Rose was out there somewhere, guiding them. But Hassan felt foolish, childish, when he let himself think that way.

No one was coming to fix this for them.

"Maybe . . ." Hassan trailed off with a glance at Hector. He wasn't sure he should finish the thought, but he pressed on anyway. "Maybe I should go back to Nazirah."

Hector's eyes widened.

Hassan had made his choice—two months ago, when they were

still picking up the pieces, cobbling together some semblance of a plan out of the wreckage of Behezda. Hassan could have gone back to Nazirah, to join back up with Khepri, Zareen, and the others against Lethia, now that she was weakened without the Hierophant's presence in Nazirah.

He hadn't. He'd stayed, alongside Jude and Hector, for a chance to stop the Hierophant—Pallas. For a chance to help them rescue Beru, the girl with the power of a god. He thought it had been the right choice at the time—save the world to save his people.

Now, he wasn't so sure.

The door creaked open again, and Jude shouldered into the room, his gaze pinned to the floor and his whole body pinched with weariness. A terse silence descended, one that seemed to grow more pointed each time the three of them were in a room together.

"There's food downstairs," Jude said tonelessly as he stripped off his threadbare jacket.

"Ate already," Hector said.

Hassan said nothing, watching Jude cross the room and yank open their shared wardrobe, hanging the jacket inside with short, stilted movements.

"The Archon Basileus was arrested," Hassan said to the tense line of Jude's shoulders.

Jude didn't turn around. "I know. I was with Hector when we found out."

"And what exactly was more important than coming back here to tell me our entire plan is ruined?" Hassan demanded, rising to his feet.

"I was out," Jude replied curtly. "What does it matter?"

"It *matters* because we have been in Tel Amot for six weeks now and you've barely lifted a finger to help us come up with a plan to stop the Hierophant. *I* came up with the plan. *I* got in contact with the Archon

Basileus. I don't even know where you are half the time! Do you even *want* to go back to Pallas Athos?"

Jude finally whirled on him. "Do *you?* Or do you want to run back to Nazirah?"

So he'd heard that. Hassan wasn't surprised—he was used to living with two people with superpowered hearing by now.

"I want to go to Pallas Athos," Hassan said heatedly. "I want to stop the Hierophant. I want to rescue that girl from him and stop the god like we *planned.*"

Jude stared at him mutely. He'd never answered Hassan's question.

Hassan took a steadying breath. "We're supposed to be in this together, but sometimes it's like you're somewhere else entirely."

Jude met his gaze, and the shadow of a pain too terrible to name overtook his face. Hassan had seen it lurking behind Jude's eyes ever since that first week in Behezda when they'd picked through the ruins searching for some sign that the Prophet, Anton, still lived. They'd found nothing. On the road back to Tel Amot, it was like Jude had shut his pain away, locked it up tight somewhere, as though he could deprive it of air and suffocate it. But Hassan could see that it was suffocating *him.*

He knew Jude was barely sleeping, staying up until the wee hours of the morning and tiring himself out with hard labor at the docks before he'd finally pass out from sheer exhaustion. He trained compulsively with Hector, sparring and practicing his koahs with a fervor bordering on obsessive. And sometimes, he simply shut down for seemingly no reason—like the other night, when Hassan had suggested they blow off some steam down at the Three Palms card tables. Jude had stormed out of the room without a word, not returning until the following morning.

And there had been an incident, about a month ago, that had resulted in what could only be described as a street brawl. Jude, against half a dozen Witnesses. They'd been no match for him. One, he'd almost killed. It had taken Hassan and Hector together to pull him back.

Hassan recognized that rage too well. Hector did, too. They all knew it for what it really was—grief. The kind that could tear you apart if you let it.

"He's gone, Jude," Hassan said firmly. "And the best way to deal with that is to keep going. Finish what you started with him. Stop the Hierophant."

"He's not—" Jude cut himself off, jaw clenching as he looked off toward the window. "If you want to give up, then fine. Go back to Nazirah. I'm not stopping you."

Before Hassan could summon a reply, Jude stalked back out of the room.

Salt air swept through the window in his wake, chilling Hassan as he sank down onto his bed.

"You're not really going back to Nazirah, are you?" Hector asked into the long silence that followed Jude's departure. "What about the Hierophant? What about *Beru?*"

Hassan lifted his gaze to meet Hector's. Hector had told him, one night when he'd been too deep in his cups, what the girl really meant to him. The revelation had struck Hassan hard—a little too hard. Because it had only made him think of Khepri and what he'd left behind in Nazirah. Despite the lies and broken trust between them, he missed her so much he could hardly breathe sometimes.

"Our plan fell apart," Hassan said. "We've run out of allies, and I can't sit here and do nothing, Hector. Not again."

It felt too much like those first weeks in Pallas Athos after the Hierophant had taken Nazirah. Sitting in Lethia's villa, *waiting*. Desperate for any scrap of information, for *any* way to make himself useful.

"Just . . . give it a few more days. One more week."

Hassan was caught off guard by Hector's soft, beseeching tone. He swallowed the objections on the tip of his tongue. Maybe there were stones yet unturned.

"I'll talk to Jude," Hector promised. "We'll figure this out. A smuggler who will take us, or—or we can stow away—"

"A week," Hassan agreed. A deadline made him feel better. More in control. He could give Hector another week. He owed that much, for the role he'd played in unleashing the god on the world. The role they'd all played in putting that god in the hands of the Hierophant. "But one way or another, when the week is out, I'm leaving Tel Amot."

3

EPHYRA

WHATEVER BERU HAD DONE—OR HADN'T DONE—THIS TIME, IT MUST HAVE been bad.

That was Ephyra's first thought when the Witnesses dragged her out of her room for the second time in as many days. Usually, they doled out their punishment right there, but perhaps this time it wasn't enough to simply let Beru see the evidence in the bruises they left. Maybe this time they would make Beru watch.

Ephyra tried not to think about it as they made their way through the unfamiliar residence of the Archon Basileus of Pallas Athos. The huge, sprawling villa, which sat on the cliffs overlooking the sea, was so grand it almost felt like a castle. To Ephyra, it felt more like a prison. She was allowed only in the room where she slept, the adjoining courtyard that faced out to the sea, and of course, Beru's room, where they ate dinner together every night. Wherever the Witnesses were taking her, she'd never been before.

They arrived at a grand set of double doors that opened to reveal a lavish room decorated in gold and white. A marble desk faced out from a row of shelves filled with books and decorative plaques and vases. It looked like an office of some sort—perhaps where the Archon Basileus had once conducted his official business, before the Hierophant had put him in chains.

At the back of the room, against a pane of windows filtering in bright light, stood the Hierophant himself. With his crisp white robes and the golden sunlight haloed around him, Ephyra could almost understand why the priests of Pallas Athos worshipped him.

As the Witnesses shoved Ephyra into the room, she realized the Hierophant wasn't the only person inside. Illya Aliyev leaned against the desk behind him, arms crossed over his chest, managing to look at once elegant and nonchalant.

Ephyra wanted to kill him.

His gaze flicked over her, snagging on the thin chains encircling her wrists. Ephyra could read nothing in his expression. She looked away abruptly, before their eyes could meet.

She had seen glimpses of him over the past two months, from across courtyards and down hallways—enough to know he'd wormed his way back into the Hierophant's fold through his usual combination of charm, a lack of moral code, and willingness to do whatever repugnant thing was required of him. But this was the first time they'd stood in the same room together since that day in Behezda.

The Hierophant's other favorite lackey, the one with the Godfire scars, was nowhere to be found, which meant that Beru wasn't here.

"Please," the Hierophant said to Ephyra softly. "Have a seat."

As if Ephyra had acquiesced to this meeting. As if she was a guest here and not a prisoner.

"I'm good here," she replied, not moving.

"I'm sure you're curious why I summoned you."

She *was* curious. She'd barely even laid eyes on the Hierophant since they'd arrived in Pallas Athos. He seemed content to keep her locked up, bringing her out only when he could use her to control Beru.

This felt like something else. She just didn't know what, and not knowing made her more nervous than if he'd simply brought her here for another beating.

"Illya tells me this isn't your first time in my city," the Hierophant went on. "You killed a priest here not long ago, didn't you?"

Not long ago. Had it been four, five months since then? It felt like a lifetime.

"You had quite the reputation, didn't you?" the Hierophant asked. "In this city and others. The Pale Hand. Killer of the wicked."

Ephyra eyed him, wondering what he was after. A confession?

"What do you want?" Ephyra asked, irritated.

The Hierophant didn't seem angered by Ephyra's outburst. He let the silence linger, let it punish Ephyra as she waited to see how he would react.

"I want you," he said slowly, "to continue your work here."

"My work?"

"The Archon Basileus is currently in the citadel, awaiting his death," the Hierophant said. "I would like for you to be the one to deliver it to him."

Ephyra was stunned silent for a moment. The Hierophant wanted her to kill for him?

"Why me?" she said at last. "You have a pet god, don't you?"

The Hierophant did not reply. He didn't even look away. His expression was as unreadably placid as ever, betraying nothing.

But Ephyra knew. She knew because she was Beru's sister. And no matter how much power Pallas had over Beru, there were some things he couldn't threaten her into doing. Not even to protect Ephyra.

"I felt you would be best suited for this role," the Hierophant replied at last.

It was a deflection, but he was right, in more ways than one. He'd referenced her reputation, the mystique of the Pale Hand and the fear it inspired, especially in this city, where she'd killed not just an average scammer or brute, but a priest, someone meant to be untouchable. And now she was under the Hierophant's control, just like Beru. To him, she was an untapped source of power—her actual power, yes, but also the power of showing the world that someone like her was under his control.

"Perhaps I should give you time to think it over," the Hierophant suggested. "Tonight, in solitude."

She saw the game now. He would keep her from seeing Beru until she said yes. Each sister the perfect pawn to use against the other.

Ephyra had never had much of a mind for tactics, but even she knew they were helplessly outflanked.

"Or perhaps . . . Illya," the Hierophant said, without taking his unsettling gaze off Ephyra. "You've spent quite a bit of time with our murderess, haven't you?"

Ephyra had been doing a good job of pretending he wasn't in the room, but now her gaze darted toward him unbidden. He rapped his fingers against the desk, looking bored, like he had much better things to do.

Ephyra knew, in the pit of her stomach, exactly how the Hierophant knew enough about her and Beru to play them so easily. This whole arrangement had Illya's mark all over it. It was what he did—manipulate, exploit whatever weaknesses he could find, and steer people where he wanted them to go. And even when you saw it coming a mile away, you still fell for it.

"Yes, Immaculate One," Illya replied, a smile curling his lips. "Quite a bit of time."

She wondered, sometimes, what Illya had told the Hierophant about her, about *them*. This—the curl of his lips, the glimmer in his eyes, the suggestive lilt—felt like an answer. An angry flush rose to her cheeks.

"You're pathetic," she said to Illya. "All that shit in Behezda you said about making amends, cleaning up your mistakes—but the minute the tide turned, you crawled back to the Hierophant like an obedient little dog."

Illya just smiled blithely.

Ephyra wanted nothing more than to wipe the expression off his face. To hurt him, just to know that she still could. She took a threatening step forward, uncaring of the Hierophant's piercing gaze fixed on her. "I'll make you pay for this. If it's the last thing I do, I'll make you pay."

Illya looked past her, to the Hierophant. "See? I told you it would take more than a few bruises to break this one."

It took every shred of Ephyra's self-control not to lunge across the room and throttle him. If she didn't have the Godfire cuffs on, she would have. As it was, she just stared at him, radiating fury.

"All that power," the Hierophant mused, his gaze running over Ephyra. She shivered, despite herself. "It does make you wonder what that power could do in someone else's hands. The *right* hands. Perhaps . . ." He moved his gaze back to Illya. "Yours?"

Horror flooded her. She knew what the Hierophant was having Beru do—taking Grace from those that opposed him and giving it to the Witnesses. Was that what Illya wanted? To have Ephyra's Grace transplanted in him? After all, that was what had attracted him to her in the first place. Her power.

"To be able to raise the dead," the Hierophant said. "To kill with a single touch. To live—if not forever, then for a long, long time. You'd make much better use of that Grace than she does, wouldn't you?"

"I would," Illya agreed, stalking toward Ephyra with a predatory gleam in his eye. "For one, I would learn to control it. Something she's never been able to do."

"It is so often the case that those who are given these gifts lack the control to properly wield them," the Hierophant replied.

She held herself still, ignoring every instinct that told her to attack, even when Illya reached out and took her wrist in his hand. Her skin burned beneath his touch.

"The Pale Hand is just another in a long string of those who seem to have power but are truly weak inside," Illya said. "A killer who can raise the dead, who can bring back a god, but doesn't even know how to heal."

His eyes met hers, his expression unchanged as he tucked his thumb beneath the slender Godfire cuff around her wrist, pressing against her pulse for the barest second.

"She never learned how. Ironic, isn't it?" He dropped her wrist and turned back to the Hierophant.

Ephyra didn't breathe.

"That's a shame," the Hierophant replied, sounding almost amused. "Though I suppose we all have our weaknesses."

His bright gaze lingered on Illya for a half second longer, and when he flicked his eyes back to Ephyra she scrambled to smooth her expression into something like fear, or fury, instead of the helpless confusion churning through her mind. Her pulse pounded where Illya had touched her.

Because once again, she had underestimated him. Once again, he had tricked her, pulled the wool over her eyes and ripped the floor out from beneath her. How many lies had he told her, starting from the first time they'd met, here in Pallas Athos? She didn't even know. He was a liar; she'd always known that.

And he had just lied to the Hierophant.

4

JUDE

ANTICIPATION THRUMMED IN JUDE'S CHEST AS HE DUCKED INSIDE THE slyhouse, steeling himself against the sweet-smelling smoke and perfume. In the front room, the slyhouse's workers slunk around in gauzy shifts, perching on the cushions and low couches spread out around tables. Just inside, a courtesan held court with a small group of well-dressed men, their laughter loud and raucous. Behind them, a boy plucked the strings of an instrument Jude didn't recognize, playing a lilting tune.

A girl with a serving tray sidled up to Jude. "See something that catches your eye?"

"I'm here to see Zinnia," Jude replied.

The girl narrowed her eyes, the look of cloying welcome sliding off her face. "She doesn't take walk-ins. Appointment only."

"I have an appointment."

The girl looked unconvinced, but she just said, "Have a seat."

She handed her tray off to another server and disappeared behind the curtain.

Jude sat stiffly on an open cushion.

"Hi there," a voice said to Jude's left.

He turned and saw a boy sprawled languidly beside him, dimpling a smile at Jude. He looked a little younger than Jude, with fair hair and hazel eyes, a pearl glittering in one ear.

"You waiting on something?" the boy asked, leaning toward Jude. The sweet scent of jasmine teased Jude's nose. "I can entertain you while you wait, if you like."

There was a gleam in the boy's eye, a coy curl to the corner of his lips that suggested a very particular kind of entertainment.

"No!" Jude blurted, flinching back. "I mean. That's quite all right, thank you. I'm fine."

The boy shrugged one shoulder, his bare skin golden in the low light. "Suit yourself."

The gesture reminded Jude so viscerally of Anton, it stole the breath from his lungs.

"So *this* is where you've been going off to?" a familiar voice said incredulously.

Jude leapt to his feet as Hector shouldered his way through the front doorway.

"This really isn't what I was expecting." Hector's gaze swept the room with suspicion. A girl draped over the windowsill flicked her eyes back at Hector with interest.

Jude's jaw clenched. "What are you doing here? Did you follow me?"

"I was worried," Hector replied, striding toward him. "And I have to say, if this is what you've been up to, I think I'm right to be."

Jude flushed. "You don't know what you're talking about."

A few of the others, who weren't otherwise engaged, snuck not so subtle glances, clearly amused by whatever drama they assumed was unfolding.

Hector seemed to realize the notice they'd garnered and lowered his voice as he stopped in front of Jude. "Look, I'm not judging you. I get it. Sort of. Grief can make you do things you usually wouldn't—"

"It's really not what you think," Jude replied, desperate not to let Hector finish that thought. "Just—I'll explain later, all right?"

"So will it be the two of you, or . . . ?"

A girl appeared from behind the curtain, leaning against the doorway with one hip cocked, eyeing Hector and Jude. She was dressed in far plainer clothes than the others, simple gray trousers and a pale blue tunic. Jude watched an uncharacteristic blush spread across Hector's cheeks.

Jude wished dearly to bury himself in the earth. Suddenly the prospect of Hector learning the true reason he'd come here didn't seem so bad.

"For Keric's sake," Jude muttered, rubbing his temple as he made up his mind. "Come on, then."

"What?" Hector balked, his voice going high and strained. "Jude, I don't—"

"Just—come with me. You want to know what I've been up to? I'll show you."

Hector still looked extremely wary, but Jude blustered past him, nodding at the girl who turned and led him through the satin curtains. A moment later, Jude heard a low curse followed by Hector's hurried steps behind him.

They clipped down a hallway bordered by archways, some curtained off and some that opened out into more private versions of the front room, with people in various states of undress. There were also closed doors, behind which sounds emanated that made Jude blush despite himself. A few of the slyhouse workers passed them in the hallway, greeting the girl—Zinnia—cheerfully.

"Why do you work here?" Jude asked as they turned down another hallway.

"I like the ambience," she replied flippantly. "Why? Does it offend your sensibilities?"

"No," he said, his blush betraying him.

"What's your type, then? Boys who blush as prettily as you? Girls who know how to take control?" She glanced back to Hector. "Tall, broad-shouldered, dark-eyed men?"

Hector coughed awkwardly.

"You know that's not why I'm here," Jude said darkly.

"Maybe it should be," Zinnia replied. "You look like you need to learn how to relax."

Jude didn't bother to dignify that with a response, clenching his jaw as Zinnia pushed open a door near the end of the hallway, revealing another sitting room, with a low couch slouched behind a table set with a silver tray, crystal glasses, and a decanter full of dark red wine. The girl sauntered over to the table and motioned for them to take a seat on the couch as she poured a glass. Jude sat, but Hector remained hovering just inside the door.

"So," Zinnia said, offering him the wineglass. "Jude Weatherbourne. What can I do for you?"

Jude waved off the offered wine. "I don't—wait. You know who I am?"

She shrugged, taking a sip of wine. "I'm good at my job. That's why you're here, isn't it?"

He nodded slowly.

"I also know that you've already hired six different bounty hunters in the past month," she went on. "They all told you the same thing. So what makes you think I'm going to have a different answer for you?"

"They say Mrs. Tappan's Scrying Agency is the best," Jude replied.

"So you want to pay five times the price to hear the exact same answer?"

"Wait," Hector spoke, coming away from the door at last. "Bounty hunter? We're at a slyhouse looking for a *bounty hunter?*"

Jude ignored him. "I want to hire you to do what those other bounty hunters couldn't."

Zinnia chewed her lip, shaking her head. "The person you're looking for is dead."

Jude touched the scarf that lay folded against his breastbone. He could still remember finding it in the wreckage of the tomb of the Sacrificed Queen. How it had looked, bright blue against the crumbling red rock, and how Jude's heart had clenched tight as a fist when he'd pulled it free. How he'd dug and dug there for another sign of Anton. But there was only this—a scrap of cloth he could tuck beside his heart. Nothing else.

He could feel Hector's gaze on him. This was why he had kept this from Hector. He couldn't stand the pity in his eyes. He thought Jude was a fool for holding on to hope this way, but Jude would rather be a fool than give up on Anton.

"He's not dead," he said evenly.

"Jude," Hector said softly. Jude still refused to look at him. "We looked for him in Behezda. For *weeks.*"

"He's alive," Jude said sharply. "I know he is."

He could not explain why he was so *certain.* Even with the world falling around them, somehow Anton had survived. Jude *knew* it. Because if he'd gone from the world, his body returned to the earth, his *esha* released into the air, then Jude would have felt it. Just as he'd felt it the moment Anton had entered the world, all those years ago.

Anton was the Prophet. He couldn't be gone, because if he was, it would mean there was no hope left.

"You should listen to your friend," Zinnia said, her voice softening. "When six scryers try to find someone and not a single one succeeds, it can only mean one thing."

"So you don't want the job?" Jude asked brusquely, heading back to the door. "Come on, Hector. We're done here."

"Hold on just a *second*," Zinnia said, sounding amused. To Hector, she said, "Is he always this surly?"

Hector barked out a laugh. "These days, definitely."

Jude spun back to them, glowering.

"I may have something else for you two," Zinnia said. "As it so happens, I've been expecting you."

"What?" Jude asked, his heart thudding as he exchanged an alarmed look with Hector. *It's a trap. The Witnesses, Pallas—They're here.* "What do you mean?"

Hector's hand snapped to the hilt of his sword as Jude pulled himself taut as a bowstring, ready to flee or fight at the slightest provocation.

"Mrs. Tappan said you would stop by," Zinnia said with a wave, entirely unconcerned with their obvious apprehension. "She sends her regards."

"I've never met her," Jude replied flatly.

"Yes, you have," Zinnia replied confidently. "She lent you her ship."

Jude's tension gave way to sheer bafflement. "Lady Bellrose?"

Zinnia smiled. "One of her many aliases."

"Who?" Hector asked, glancing between the two of them.

"She's a collector," Jude said. "Or she posed as one." Anton had said she was a bounty hunter. And she'd called herself the leader of the Lost Rose. He looked at Zinnia. "How did she know I'd be here?"

She shrugged.

Lady Bellrose had been something of an enigma when Jude met her in Endarrion, but everything she'd told him had turned out to be true.

She'd known that they needed to find the Four Relics to stop Pallas, that the god's *esha* had been sealed in the Red Gate—she'd even known why Jude's Grace had been damaged and what he'd needed to do to restore it.

"But then . . ." Jude paused, pieces slotting together in his mind. "You're—the Lost Rose?"

Zinnia smiled. "You're a lot smarter than you look."

"Wait—the Lost Rose?" Hector echoed. "As in, the secret organization that Hassan's been trying to contact?"

Zinnia held out her arms. "And here we are, answering. You're welcome."

"We could have used your help six weeks ago!"

"Hector," Jude warned.

"We've been busy," Zinnia replied. "What with the god you and your friends unleashed on the world."

Jude flinched. "That wasn't our fault."

"Wasn't it, though?"

Jude fell silent. They'd all played a role in the god's resurrection, whether they'd meant to or not. They were all part of the last prophecy.

"Why are you reaching out to us now?" Hector asked, suspicious.

Zinnia rose to her feet. "We have a message for you."

Despite his wariness, hope leapt in Jude's chest. If Lady Bellrose and the Lost Rose were getting in contact with him, that meant they had news. News that, he hoped, would help lead him to Anton.

"How do we know you're telling the truth?" Jude asked carefully. "About the Lost Rose and Lady Bellrose? How do I know you're not actually working for the Witnesses?"

Zinnia smiled slightly, as if the idea were amusing. Instead of replying, she circled around to a marble chest that sat in the corner. She muttered a string of words, too quick for Jude to catch, and the chest opened, allowing her to pluck something out. She returned, tossing the item down on the table in front of them.

Hector and Jude both leaned forward, peering at the copper sphere that rolled across the wooden table before coming to a halt. It was the size of Jude's fist, with intricate swirls etched into it, forming a dizzying pattern that Jude almost recognized. It was a moment before it clicked—this sphere looked just like an oracle stone, which the Prophets had used to record their prophecies.

Jude glanced up at Zinnia. "What is this? What does it say?"

She shrugged.

"Stop with this cryptic horseshit," Hector demanded.

"I'm not being cryptic. I really don't know. The message will only reveal itself to one person." Her eyes met Jude's. "You."

Jude's gaze slid back down to the sphere as he carefully picked it up. The moment he touched the cool surface, the sphere began to glow. He nearly dropped it in surprise.

"Hello, Jude," a familiar voice echoed out from the sphere. "I'm glad you could finally make it."

Lady Bellrose. She really *had* been expecting Jude, then.

"I wish we could speak in person, but I have some other urgent business that needs attending to," she continued. "So I hope you'll forgive the impoliteness in coming to you in this manner. But I need your help. Or, I suppose, you could think of it the other way around—I am here to help you."

Hector and Jude exchanged a glance. This was too good to be true.

"I know that you seek a way to return to Pallas Athos," Lady Bellrose went on. "And perhaps more critically, a way to free the girl, Beru, from Pallas's control. As it so happens, I can offer you both. Listen closely. The Archon Basileus of Pallas Athos has recently been arrested by Pallas's men. His execution is scheduled for the autumnal equinox.

It is the perfect opportunity to get to Beru, as we'll know exactly where she'll be and when. The Lost Rose will help you as much as we can, but the task of her rescue will fall to you.

"I can offer the following—a ship, currently docked here in Tel Amot, that can take you to Pallas Athos. Forged documents that will get you inside the city without detection. Once you're there, I have the name of a trustworthy ally with valuable knowledge of the citadel's inner workings, and an alchemist with ties to the Lost Rose who can aid you with whatever you may need."

Jude glanced at Hector, who caught his eye with an expression of disbelief.

"I hope all of this will be of use to you," Lady Bellrose said. "I wish there was more I could do. As for what to do with the girl—and the god—once you have them, well—let's just say I'm working on it."

The glow of the sphere faded as the room was plunged back into silence.

"What," Hector said after a long moment, "just happened?"

Jude palmed the sphere, eyes flicking back to Zinnia. "Can I take this?"

"All yours," she replied. "Oh, almost forgot."

She went back to the chest, picking something else out of it. When she returned, she held out her hand. A gold ring sat in her palm, with the symbol of a compass rose carved into it. "Show this to the captain of the *Longswallow*."

Jude stared down at the ring, feeling overwhelmed. He'd come to the slyhouse with one purpose: find Anton. But instead, he had all of this dropped into his lap. A way into Pallas Athos. The beginnings of a new plan to get the god out of Pallas's control.

It was exactly what Hassan had been desperately trying to find since they'd arrived in Tel Amot, while Jude had been spending his time trying to track down any sign of Anton. He should be glad. He should be thankful for this, for a plan, for something to do. But all he could think about was what it would feel like to get on that ship and sail away from any last hope of finding Anton.

"Thank you," Jude said uncertainly, tucking the ring and the sphere away.

She tipped her wineglass toward him. "Hope it works out for you."

She said it so casually, like they were discussing the outcome of a game of cards rather than the fate of the world.

"Yeah," Jude replied. "Me too."

———————————

"So do we trust them?" Hector asked the moment they stepped outside the slyhouse and into the cooling evening. "This Lady Bellrose person? The Lost Rose?"

Jude shook his head. "I don't know."

"I mean, I guess Hassan does," Hector said. "Since he's been trying to contact them this whole time. Maybe it's a sign—a good one. We could use one of those."

"Maybe," Jude said. But his mind was not on the Lost Rose and Lady Bellrose. It was on the first thing that Zinnia had said to him—to give up on Anton. Hector fell silent as they trudged through Tel Amot's red light district toward the ocean and the sun fading behind it.

"All right, are we going to talk about it?" Hector asked at last as they began to descend the wide steps down to the harbor and the Night Market.

"Talk about what?"

Hector took hold of Jude's elbow, wheeling him around. "You've hired—what was it, six bounty hunters to find the Prophet? You could have told me what you were doing. I would've understood. You know that. I've been down this road before. The first time I left the Order, I searched for almost a year to find the Pale Hand. Threw away everything to do it."

"This isn't the same thing," Jude replied hotly, jerking away from him. "How?"

"Because your family was already dead!"

For a moment, Jude thought that Hector might hit him. His hands tightened to fists, his eyes going cold and deadly. Jude wasn't entirely sure he wouldn't have deserved it.

But then Hector let out a breath and slumped.

"Hector, I'm—I'm sorry," Jude stuttered.

Hector waved him off. "Don't. Like I said, I get it. I've said worse to you—done worse."

Jude's gaze dropped. He knew they were both recalling it—how Hector had left Jude bleeding in a burned-down ruin in Pallas Athos. For a long time, Jude had thought that would be his last memory of Hector.

But here they were. Working together, sparring together. Trying to heal together. The break in their friendship, the cracks it had stemmed from, still stood between them some days, a chasm they might never completely cross.

"You didn't tell me why you returned," Jude said quietly, lifting his gaze back to Hector's. "To Kerameikos. After you went searching for the Pale Hand."

Hector drew a knuckle across his mouth. "I don't really know why I did it. I guess I was just tired of it all. Tired of my search. Tired of being by myself. I missed you."

"I missed you, too," Jude said. He still remembered the cold dread that had gripped him when he'd arrived back at Kerameikos Fort after his Year of Reflection to find that Hector had not waited for him.

Hector offered a tight-lipped smile. "Not like you miss him, though. The Prophet. Anton."

Jude turned away, back toward the sea. It hurt to even hear his name. He closed his eyes. "I've been having these dreams. Half the time I can barely remember them. Just . . . just him."

That wasn't entirely true. Sometimes Jude woke and it was like Anton had just been beside him, his warmth and his scent lingering. Sometimes the dreams were slow and sweet, the honeyed light of late afternoon warming them as they kissed. And sometimes Anton stood out of reach, calling to Jude. *I'm here. It's me. I'm right here, Jude,* and Jude would wake, gutted, furious, certain that there was no crueler torture.

He'd never been a good sleeper, and now it was worse—staying up for days on end, staving off sleep however he could so he wouldn't have to see the specter that haunted him so sweetly, before giving in, tumbling into sleep and into Anton's arms again because there was nothing he wanted more.

"I used to dream about my family." Hector reached for Jude's shoulder. "My parents, my brother . . . every night, it felt like. If you let it, it'll consume you."

Jude looked at Hector's hand, recalling a time when he'd been the one to reach out in comfort, to offer futile words of reassurance.

He shrugged Hector's hand off. "Maybe it should. Maybe I deserve it."

"It wasn't your fault."

Hector didn't understand. Jude hadn't been able to protect Anton when it mattered most.

"I failed," Jude said abruptly. "He's the Prophet, the one destined to stop the Age of Darkness. How are we supposed to do it without him? How am I—" He cut off abruptly. His words teetered too close to the heart of the matter, and Jude didn't know if he could survive it.

"I don't know," Hector said, his gaze locked on Jude's. "But we have to. Somehow, we have to."

Hassan looked distressed after they replayed Lady Bellrose's message for him in the privacy of their room.

"So, she just . . . gave this to you," Hassan said slowly. "It was just . . . waiting for you?"

Jude nodded. "She also gave me this."

He held out the ring.

Hassan took it, inspecting it. "That's their symbol. The compass rose. I saw it at the Great Library, when I found the covenant. If they gave you this, that must mean they trust us."

"But do *we* trust *them*?" Hector asked. "Doesn't this whole thing seem too . . ."

"What?" Hassan asked. "Easy?"

Hector gave him a wry look.

"I didn't trust Lady Bellrose at first," Jude said. "But she did lead us to the Relic of Sight. And she was right about the god and the Hierophant."

She'd been right about a lot of things.

"And my father was part of her organization," Hassan said. "He must have trusted her."

Jude glanced at him. It was so rare, lately, for the two of them to agree on anything.

"This execution she talks about," Hassan continued, "of the Archon Basileus. It sounds like the opportunity we need. I say we take it."

Hector's gaze moved from Hassan to Jude. He looked thoughtful. "All right. If you two trust this, so will I. Anything that gets us closer to Pallas."

To Beru, he didn't say, but Jude saw the unspoken words in his eyes. They hadn't exactly discussed everything that had happened in Behezda, but Jude knew Hector, and he knew that he cared about the girl—the revenant—and wanted to save her.

It was a strange thing to realize, especially because when Jude had last seen Hector in Pallas Athos, he'd been planning to kill her. He'd been convinced she was the last harbinger of the Age of Darkness—and as it turned out, he'd been right. But then neither of them had realized just how complicated the prophecy, and their mission, really was.

"So I guess this means we have a ship," Hassan said, ticking off a finger. "We have a plan, or the beginnings of one. And we have allies. There's nothing stopping us now. Right, Jude?"

Jude caught Hassan's pointed look. There was nothing stopping them. And that was more terrifying than anything else. Jude had spent the last month and a half thinking he had to stay in one place so Anton could find him. He had felt like leaving this awful, crooked town was the same as giving up hope.

He met Hassan's gaze with a nod. "Right."

Jude's hope, his faith, wasn't in Tel Amot. It lived inside him. Even when he left—even when he got on that ship to sail across the sea—it would still be with him. His path was leading him away from Tel Amot, but someday, somehow, it would bring him back to Anton.

It had to.

5

ANTON

ANTON SIGHED CONTENTEDLY AS JUDE DIPPED TO KISS THE FRECKLE ON HIS JAW.

He didn't know how many minutes—hours—they'd lost to this gentle exploration, but an awareness crept over him that he wasn't supposed to be here. He let Jude kiss him for several more seconds before gently easing away.

"We shouldn't be doing this," he said. "I didn't even mean to come here."

Jude frowned at him, sitting up. "Where?"

They were lying in the grass below the pavilion in the Floating Gardens, dressed in the clothes they'd worn to the Nameless Woman's party.

"You're dreaming," Anton told him. "This is a dream."

A crinkle appeared between Jude's eyebrows. "This can't be a dream. I'm not asleep."

"You are asleep," Anton said. "But I'm not. I'm in your dream."

"You're not making sense."

This was a conversation they'd had too many times to count, ever since Anton had first mastered dreamwalking. Sometimes, like now, Jude seemed to have forgotten they'd been separated two months ago in Behezda. Other times, he did remember, holding Anton close and whispering apologies against his skin.

But more often, Anton didn't try to explain anything, letting the dream play out.

He didn't know whether these nighttime visits made things harder or easier. He wasn't sure he cared. Not enough to stop, anyway.

He drew his knees up to his chest. "I know it doesn't make sense. I just . . . I'm not strong enough to stay away."

Jude smiled at him. "Why would you want to stay away?"

"Because," Anton said. "It just makes it worse."

"Makes what worse?" Jude asked, concern creeping into his voice.

Anton reached up and combed the hair off Jude's forehead. "Being apart from you."

Jude frowned. "We're not apart. We're together."

Anton sighed and leaned his cheek onto Jude's shoulder. "You're right," he said, his voice muffled. "You're right, of course we are. I'm just being foolish."

Jude laughed, and the sound tore clean through Anton's chest.

Anton opened his eyes to the dawn twilight over the steppe, Jude's laughter still ringing in his ears.

He and the Wanderer needed to get on the road before the sun had fully risen. He knew she was already waiting for him, but he let himself lie there a little longer, imagining he could hear Jude's soft breathing beside him, the way he had every night they'd spent in the mountains around Kerameikos. Maybe Jude was awake now, too, gazing up at his own patch of sky, watching the stars fade beneath the first rays of sun.

Anton felt that familiar tug, the desire he'd wrestled with for two months, to go to a scrying pool and cast a stone and whisper the name Jude Weatherbourne into the ripples. To know where he was, to see it on a map and draw his fingers across the distance between them. But the temptation would be too strong. He had to stay focused on the journey ahead. On the impossible task before him.

When he felt he could put it off no longer, Anton rose to get dressed. As he pulled on his worn riding leathers and a rough-hewn shirt, the tent flap fluttered open and a familiar chiming *esha* filtered over him.

"If you came to fetch me yourself, I must be really late for breakfast," he said, spinning around to face the Wanderer.

"You need your energy," she said. "We're headed through the Black Snow Pass today."

Once they made it through the pass, they would reach the Bay of Tarsepolis, where a ship waited to take them across the Pelagos, back to Kerameikos, the former stronghold of the Order of the Last Light. It was not a place Anton was particularly thrilled to return to, but it held the key to his plan.

Anton followed the Wanderer out of the tent and toward the smell of cooking meat. Ziga and Tomo waved Anton over to the firepit. The two of them, along with three others from various Inshuu tribes, had agreed to guide Anton and the Wanderer over the Inshuu Steppe.

After the destruction of Behezda, when the Wanderer had found Anton crouched in the rubble of the tomb, they had sailed up the River of Mercy to the Inshuu Steppe where they had taken refuge in a place that Anton thought only existed in legends.

The Wandering City.

While there were only six Prophetic Cities, this place belonged to the Wanderer. It was where she had hidden after the other Prophets turned their backs on her. Pallas had made sure that no monuments would be built in her honor and no city would bear her name, but there was still this—a city that wasn't a city, a city that existed in the hearts and minds of thousands of different tribes in the Inshuu Steppe, carried with them wherever they went. A city that came into being when they put the call out to the steppe.

It had been centuries since the last time the Wandering City had gathered. They hadn't needed it, not until now. Not until the destruction of Behezda, the resurrection of the ancient god. The Age of Darkness.

Anton had needed it, too. The Wandering City had sheltered him, given him a place to regain his strength over the past two months, and offered time for the Wanderer to make good on her promise to train Anton in how to wield his powers as a Prophet.

His first lesson had been one of necessity—learning to shield his *esha* from anyone who tried to scry for it. It had kept them safe from Pallas for the past two months. From anyone who might be trying to find him.

"What say the Prophets?" Ziga asked, passing Anton a bowl as he sat down beside the warmth of the fire. "Will the first snow come today?"

"That's not really how it works," Anton said, taking a bite of thick rice porridge.

"Ah, well, it was worth a try," Ziga said.

Anton was itching to get to Kerameikos, but a part of him would miss the steppe. Its wide-open sky, the pace of a life lived wandering, even the people who, despite himself, he'd begun to care for.

Illya had once told him that their mother was a daughter of the steppe, a descendant of the tribes that had been taken over by the Novogardian Empire at its peak. He didn't really know if that was true—if he shared kin with these people, if part of him recognized them. So much of his past was lost to him. His grandmother had only ever talked about Emperor Vasili and the legacy that guided their lives.

Thinking of Illya made Anton's stomach clench, the prospect of breakfast suddenly unappealing. But Illya was a world away from him—in Pallas Athos, with Pallas, likely worming his way back into his good graces.

Pallas was another problem that needed solving. While Anton was growing stronger and learning greater control of his Grace here in the Inshuu Steppe, Pallas was using his control over the god—over Beru— to bend the world to his will.

But when he'd brought it up to the Wanderer, she'd just told him to stay focused on his mission. Get to Kerameikos.

"I'll take care of the rest," she'd said. "Well, not me. But I have my best people on it."

Probably more members of the Lost Rose, then. That was good— they could keep Beru safe and the god contained until Anton secured the weapon he needed to kill it.

"Did you sleep all right?" Tomo's voice asked softly to Anton's left.

Anton thought about the soft rumble of Jude's laughter and felt himself heat. "Yes. I mean. Fine."

The Wanderer leaned toward him. "Let's not get distracted now, Anton."

Anton looked away. She could always tell when he'd been dreamwalking.

A week into their time in the Wandering City, he had come to her, asking her to teach him how to walk into someone else's dream, the way she had once entered his. It had taken her all of two minutes to figure out why he wanted to learn, and two days for him to persuade her.

She'd known what he wanted to do—tell Jude where they were. She had been cautious, explaining gently that once Anton knew the full truth, once he saw what she planned to show him, he wouldn't want Jude there anymore. Anton hadn't believed her, hadn't thought it possible. Since that day on the lighthouse, he'd never imagined that he would have to do any of this—be the Prophet—without Jude.

But now he understood that the only way to keep Jude safe was to leave him behind.

"You haven't changed your mind, have you?" the Wanderer asked.

Anton shook his head. He wouldn't tell Jude where they were heading, no matter how much he wanted to. Anton had only learned to dreamwalk so that he could tell Jude that he was alive and safe. Somehow, though, it had turned into these near-nightly visits, where Anton lost himself in Jude's closeness, only to wake missing him more than ever.

It was a new sensation, to miss someone like this. He'd protected himself against it for so long that he couldn't help but feel angry—at himself, at Jude—for letting cracks form in the walls around his heart.

"You know how that all ended for me," the Wanderer said to Anton.

"Dreamwalking?" he asked, being purposely obtuse.

She gave him an indulgent smile. "The other thing."

She meant love.

And he did know how that had ended for her. He knew because she had shown him. Because his third and most important lesson had been how to reach back into the past and see with his own eyes who the Seven Prophets were and the mistakes they had made.

The Wanderer had shown him everything he'd wanted to know. But the answers he'd gotten from the past weren't the answers he'd wanted.

"Well, I won't let it end like that for me," Anton said firmly. He would do everything in his power to ensure history didn't repeat itself. It was the very reason they were on this journey. Why they'd left the Wandering City, bidding the people who'd sheltered them farewell and journeying half a world away, to Kerameikos. To find the only other people who knew how to defeat the god.

BEFORE

THE SKY SHIVERED WITH COLOR. GOLD AND PINK AND VIOLET LIGHTS CHASED one another across the stars. The air seemed to pulse with it.

And then, as Pallas watched from the steps of the Temple of the Holy Creator, six drops of light fell to the earth. Pallas alone could hear the words ringing from the sky, the message of the Creator.

"AS THERE WAS ONE PROPHET TO DELIVER MY MESSAGE, SO NOW THERE WILL BE SEVEN. SEVEN PROPHETS TO HEAR MY WORDS, CHOSEN FOR THEIR VIRTUES. NAZIRAH THE WISE. KERIC THE CHARITABLE. ENDARRA THE FAIR. BEHEZDA THE MERCIFUL. TARSEIS THE JUST. AND ANANKE THE BRAVE."

Pallas entered the temple and lit a prayer candle at the altar.

"Holy Creator," he said. "I have been your most faithful and obedient servant. I have delivered your message to your people. I have had temples erected in your name. Why, then, have you spurned me? Why have you created more Prophets?"

The shadows on the altar flickered.

"Answer me, Holy One," Pallas pleaded. "Tell me what I have done to displease you."

A fierce wind blew through the sanctum, and the flame of the candle flared brighter.

The god answered, but not in words. Instead its answer came through the vibrations of *esha*. And Pallas knew that he had angered it. That he had been presumptuous.

Pallas bowed his head. "I beg your forgiveness, Holy One."

A vision came to him—of himself, stripped of his power. Left without the divine word of his god. Deaf to the *esha* of the world.

Pallas shuddered. "It is true I am not worthy of your divine words. But please—let me remain your faithful servant. I will never question your will again."

The shadows receded, creeping back into the darkness.

The six new Prophets stood in the Temple of the Holy Creator, facing the Prophet Pallas.

Everyone in the Pelagos and beyond knew Pallas the Faithful, the only person in the world who could speak to the Creator god. Until now.

"You have been chosen," he told the new Prophets. "As the first and most faithful of the Prophets, it is my duty to teach you to carry out the will of the Holy Creator. We serve our god—not man. It is for that reason that you must renounce your loyalty to your kings and queens, renounce your ties to your tribes and families. Such attachments will cloud our faith and render us unfit to deliver the holy message."

The Prophet Ananke raised her head to Pallas. "And what about love?"

"Love," Pallas repeated disdainfully. "Our hearts belong to our Creator. That is the only love that matters."

———————————

Ananke the Brave heard Pallas's words, but she did not heed them. She had a love, a childhood sweetheart called Temara, a girl whose beauty and skill with the sword was known throughout the land. Temara joined Ananke's Order, becoming one of her acolytes to stay close to her.

But their relationship was forbidden by Pallas the Faithful, and so they hid it from him.

For six years, the Seven Prophets served the Creator god, receiving its visions and sharing them with their people to guide them to their destinies. As a symbol of their devotion to their god, each year on the summer solstice, one of the Prophets chose a life to sacrifice to the Creator.

On the seventh year, Pallas was to choose a sacrifice.

The Seven Prophets and their acolytes gathered at the Temple of the Holy Creator. Pallas knelt at the altar. "Holy Creator, we humbly offer you one of our own. We offer you the life of a mortal as proof of our devotion to you. Our lives belong to you. As do our hearts."

It was then that Ananke knew what Pallas was about to do.

"Holy One, the life of Temara, acolyte of Ananke the Brave, is yours."

Three of Pallas's own acolytes marched Temara from the crowd and up onto the altar. Temara's sword was at her hip, but she did not fight back.

Instead it was Ananke who leapt upon the altar after them and drew the blade from her beloved's sheath. Ananke who held the sword and put herself between Temara and Pallas.

As Ananke stood there, holding the sword with the point at Pallas's throat, a roar of thunder filled the air and the skies opened up.

"Choose another," she demanded. "You cannot have her. Choose another."

"You would defy me?" Pallas whispered. "Defy the Creator?"

"Yes," Ananke said. "I would rather spit upon the holy altar than hurt the one I love. I would rather the Creator doom me to an eternity of suffering than to see her suffer."

"This is a test of your faith, Ananke," Pallas said. "And you have failed."

"Then let the Holy One strike me down," she replied. Thunder cracked across the sky, but Ananke did not waver.

She turned to Temara. "Will you go with me?"

Temara didn't answer. Instead, she took the sword from Ananke's hands, and with the strength she was known for, she cleared a path out of the temple, into the storm that raged beyond it.

Temara and Ananke ran to the very edge of the world, a land formed by fiery eruptions and cut by ancient glaciers. A land so strange and remote that even the god had forgotten it existed.

For eleven months, they hid. Ananke did not dare use her powers, lest the others find her, but at night she dreamed of the destruction wrought on the rest of the world. Fires, famines, and plagues beset the Pelagos. Pallas and the other Prophets sacrificed one, five, a dozen acolytes, but the god would not be placated. Ananke's defiance had upset the balance between the god and its creations.

Guilt ate at both their hearts.

"How can I be worth this?" Temara asked her when Ananke woke up from yet another dream.

"You are worth everything," Ananke replied, kissing her palm. "Before the Holy Creator claimed me, I was yours. And you were mine."

But in the spaces of their silence, guilt grew between them.

And then, in the twelfth month of their exile, Ananke and Temara were found.

6

EPHYRA

PALLAS'S OFFER HUNG IN EPHYRA'S MIND LIKE A SPECTER, HAUNTING EACH moment of her confinement. For six days, she'd had nothing else to do except stare at the walls and ponder how to get a message to Beru. Servants brought her meals twice a day, and every night a Witness knocked at the door and asked Ephyra the same question.

Would she become the Hierophant's executioner?

Every night, Ephyra gave them her answer.

Tonight's messenger was a woman, barely older than Ephyra herself, with a sharp face and an intense gaze.

"I want to see Beru," Ephyra told her.

"Very well," the Witness replied. "You only need to say the word, and I'll take you to her myself."

"Take me to her now, and I'll think about it," Ephyra countered.

The Witness smiled thinly. "We'll try again tomorrow."

She turned back toward the hall.

"Wait," Ephyra said, the command escaping before she'd thought it through.

The Witness paused, expectant.

Ephyra swallowed. She missed Beru like a limb. And she hated being alone, she always had. After six days of it, she felt like tearing through the walls.

Pallas's offer taunted her. The thought of using her Grace to kill at his command made her skin crawl. But what difference did refusing really make? Whomever Pallas planned to execute would be killed anyway, whether it was by Ephyra's hand or someone else's. And her hands were already stained. What did a few more deaths matter?

She met the Witness's gaze. "Can I get some more firewood? This place is freezing."

The Witness's eyes narrowed in irritation before she turned and swept through the door without another word.

"I'll take that as a no!" Ephyra called after her. The door clicked shut, locking Ephyra inside.

She slumped back against the edge of the bed with a shiver. She hadn't been joking about the cold. Summer had turned over rapidly into autumn, and what were once balmy nights had slipped into the kind of chill Ephyra could feel in her bones.

Heaving a sigh, she crossed the room to the hearth, brushing away the ash of last night's fire. Something lay crumpled in the cinders, and it took Ephyra a moment to realize it wasn't just detritus from the fire. It was a long, thin strip of paper.

Ephyra froze, her heart in her throat. A message from Beru—it had to be.

She reached for the paper with shaking hands. But when she unraveled it, she knew immediately that someone else had left this for her. Because this message was coded, the exact same way the location of Eleazar's Chalice had been coded. And the only other person here who knew that cypher was Illya.

Distantly, she registered that somewhere in the back of her mind, she had been waiting for this. For Illya to reach out after their brief but strange meeting with the Hierophant. Ephyra had tried to shove that conversation into the dustiest corner of her mind, but to her irritation, she'd returned to it countless times in the past six days.

She could not deny what she'd heard—Illya had outright lied to the Hierophant. He'd said that Ephyra didn't know how to use her Grace to heal, even though he was living proof that she did. Three distinct possibilities had sprouted in her mind.

The first, that for some reason Illya didn't want the Hierophant to know that Ephyra was, in fact, capable of healing.

The second, that Illya had lied to the Hierophant knowing Ephyra would recognize it as a lie, in the hopes of conveying some sort of message. What kind of message, Ephyra hated to even consider. She felt like a fool, entertaining the possibility that Illya had been trying to show her he was truly on her side and always had been, or something equally asinine.

And then there was the third possibility, the one that was easiest to believe—that it was a setup. That he was trying to trick her into trusting him again.

She thought about how he'd touched her, just a tiny graze of his thumb against her wrist. Like it could have been an accident. But she was sure it *hadn't been*. She just didn't know what it meant.

And now this. A message written in a code that only the two of them would understand.

Cursing herself, she searched the room for something Illya might have used to make his code. Several stout candles sat on a table beside the bed. There were probably candles exactly like them in every room in the villa. She picked one up and wrapped the strip of paper around it, lining up each edge until the letters spelled out a message along the length of the candle.

Meet on roof.

She raised her eyes to the ceiling. The message, and the fact that Illya had left it in the fireplace, meant one thing—Illya knew that Ephyra had discovered a way to sneak out of her room.

Yet, he apparently hadn't ratted her out to the Hierophant.

She looked back down at the note. She couldn't trust him. She knew that. She tore the paper into tiny scraps, scattering them back in the fireplace.

She didn't want to fall into another one of Illya's traps. But she was tired of sitting in her room, doing nothing. And she couldn't deny that she was curious.

Taking care not to alert the guard outside her door, she padded over to the fireplace and climbed onto the grate. Rubbing ash onto her hands to make them dry, she scaled the chimney and emerged out into the night. It reminded her of being the Pale Hand—staking out victims, racing through the streets of whatever city she and Beru had found themselves in. She almost missed it.

Illya loomed over her as she pushed herself up to sit on the edge of the flue.

"You sure took your time," he commented as she climbed to her feet. "Is this a family trait? I've been standing here for hours."

She wished she'd made him wait even longer. She brushed the ash from her pants instead of letting herself look at how the moonlight fell across Illya's aristocratic face, how the sea breeze ran its fingers through his fawn-colored hair. Even with his features pinched in irritation, he was starkly handsome.

With a curt nod, she led him to where the pediment would

hide them from view should anyone happen to glance up at the rooftop.

Unfortunately, the hiding spot forced them into very close proximity. Closer than Ephyra would've preferred, close enough that she could feel the heat radiating off him.

"Talk," she said. The quicker he explained what he was doing, the quicker she could get away from him.

"I have a plan to get you out of here."

She stared at him, uncomprehending. "What?"

"I should say *we* have a plan," he amended. "Beru and I."

Every thought in Ephyra's head came to an abrupt halt. "My *sister*, Beru?"

Illya rolled his eyes. "Obviously."

"What are you doing planning with her? What are you doing even talking to her? You—You *stay away* from her, or I swear I'll—"

She hadn't realized she'd gotten in Illya's face until he grabbed her wrist, stilling her. Her pulse thundered under his thumb, and she could feel his breath against her cheek.

He didn't seem to notice. "You really think I pose some kind of threat to a girl who has an all-powerful god trapped inside her? You must have a high opinion of my capabilities."

Ephyra wrenched her arm out of his grasp, glowering. "Don't talk about your *capabilities* and my sister in the same sentence. Actually, just don't ever talk about—or to—my sister ever again."

He huffed indignantly. "She's worried about you."

The idea that Beru would confide in *Illya* made Ephyra so furious, it took all her willpower not to push him off the roof.

"Listen, we don't have a lot of time." Illya's gaze was intent on her. "You need to agree to the Hierophant's offer. If you do, I can get you out."

It all pieced together in her mind. This was what he wanted.

Her suspicions had been spot-on. It was another scheme, a ruse to get her to say yes. Pallas must have been running out of patience. A part of Ephyra felt comforted by the fact that Illya was once again trying to con her. At least she'd seen through it this time.

"Yeah, right," she said, turning abruptly to retrace her steps back to the flue.

"You don't believe me, do you?" he said, following.

"Do you ever get tired of asking me that?" she shot back.

"If you want to go back to your room so you can sit there being utterly useless, then go ahead," Illya called after her. "But I am telling you the truth."

Ephyra stopped. "Then prove it." She turned to face him. "Take me to see Beru."

A breeze ruffled past them, teasing the curls of Ephyra's hair and the edges of Illya's coat. The shadows on his face shifted as he dropped his gaze.

"I can't," he said at last. "It's too dangerous."

"That's what I thought," Ephyra said. "You're all talk, but once there's a real risk, once you actually have to put yourself on the line—"

"I meant dangerous for you," he cut in. "And for her."

"Sure you did," Ephyra replied, spinning back around and swinging her leg over the edge of the flue.

"Why did you come up here if you think I'm lying?" he asked. "If you didn't think there was a chance I'm actually on your side?"

Because I'm an idiot, she thought bitterly. Because she still remembered kissing him, and how good it had felt. Remembered those weeks when he'd been the only person who hadn't abandoned her. And even after he'd stolen the Chalice from her, she'd still wanted to save him.

Even now, even after he'd betrayed her *yet again*, she wanted to believe that it had all meant something to him. That *she* meant something to him.

But she'd rather be trapped inside her room for the rest of her life than admit that. So she didn't answer, just dropped back into the flue, leaving Illya alone on the roof.

Ephyra didn't risk climbing up to the roof the next night, just in case Illya was lurking there. She stayed in her room, fuming and furiously recounting everything Illya had said to her. Had she made a mistake in walking away? Had she missed her only chance of freeing herself and Beru from Pallas?

The door to Ephyra's room swung open abruptly, interrupting her spiraling thoughts. She leapt to her feet as a Witness swept inside.

"Come," the Witness said, her expression stone-faced. "You've been summoned."

It seemed a bit late for the Hierophant to summon her, but then again, who even knew if he slept. She supposed he was getting impatient for her answer. Maybe he thought he could catch her off guard, scare her into agreeing to be his executioner.

Part of her wondered if maybe he was right.

They rounded a corner of the corridor, and Ephyra's heart sank when she spotted Illya in a doorway up ahead.

"I'll take her from here," he told the Witness.

The Witness hesitated.

"Trust me," Illya said. "You don't want to bother him right now."

The Witness reluctantly handed over Ephyra and turned back

around. Ephyra waited until she was out of earshot before whirling on Illya.

"What are you doing?" she demanded.

"In a second," he said, taking hold of her wrist and hauling her down the corridor after him.

Too startled to do anything else, Ephyra followed. "The Hierophant didn't actually summon me, did he?"

"Of course not," he answered, pushing open a door that led out into a courtyard. "I just needed to get you alone. This seemed like the most expedient way to do it."

Ephyra told herself it was just the night breeze that made her shiver. Her wrist felt warm in Illya's long-fingered grip. "What is this, your idea of a romantic moonlight stroll?"

Illya glanced back at her with a barely realized smirk and then dragged her between a tall bush and a wall. "Here we are."

"Are you going to tell me why you just pushed me into the bushes?" Ephyra asked, leaning back against the wall.

"Give it a moment," he replied.

She heard the sound of running water from within one of the rooms above the bushes, and then a window pushed open.

Ephyra startled, certain they were about to be caught, but Illya looked utterly unconcerned.

"My deepest thanks for being punctual for once in your life," Illya said drolly.

Beru dropped to the ground between them. "I'm sorry, am I cutting into your busy schedule of snide remarks and—Ephyra?"

Ephyra blinked at her sister, who looked equally shocked to see her.

Beru recovered first, surging toward Ephyra and pulling her into a hug. "You're all right!"

"I'll leave you to it," Illya said.

Ephyra could hear him walk away, but her focus was entirely on Beru and her sister's fierce grip.

"I was so worried," Beru said against Ephyra's shoulder. "I didn't know why they stopped you from coming to see me. I had no idea what they were doing to you. And then Illya told me—"

"Illya," Ephyra repeated, pulling back. "You two are actually working together?"

Beru nodded.

"Why? *How?*"

"It's a little hard to explain," Beru hedged. "I know you think you can't trust him—"

"Because I can't!" Ephyra said. "*We* can't. Beru, you don't know him like I do."

"Maybe not," Beru agreed. "I'll admit, I was skeptical of his motives at first. But—"

"But nothing," Ephyra said. "Whatever he said to get you to trust him, it's a lie."

"He didn't say anything," Beru replied. "He risked a lot by even meeting with me. By bringing you here tonight. And if you can't trust him, you can at least trust me. We have a plan to get you out of here."

"Get me out of here?" Ephyra repeated, incredulous. "Beru, I—I can't leave without you."

"You have to," Beru said firmly. "Ephyra, don't you get it? If you're gone, the Hierophant will no longer be able to use you against me."

Ephyra wasn't a fool. She knew that what Beru said made sense. But the thought of escaping without her made Ephyra want to burn the entire citadel to the ground.

"I won't go without you," she said. "Either we both get out, or I stay."

Beru looked away, her face crumpling. "You should have let me go." Her voice cracked. "Why couldn't you just let me go?"

Did she mean at the Red Gate? Or after she'd killed Hector? Or maybe she meant the first time, in Medea, when Ephyra had woken up to find Beru dead beside her.

"Listen to me." Ephyra grabbed Beru by the shoulders. "I will never give up on you. *Never.*"

Beru shook in Ephyra's hands, tears finally spilling over.

"We'll find a way, all right?" Ephyra said. "We always do."

Beru closed her eyes, and more tears streaked down her cheeks. "I have to go back now. Otherwise he's going to notice I'm gone."

Ephyra knew she meant the scarred Witness, Lazaros. She swallowed, wrapping her arms around Beru tightly, not knowing when they'd see each other again.

Beru slowly disentangled herself, wiping at her eyes. "Please—at least consider my plan. *Please.*"

Her gaze held on Ephyra, eyes bright and glimmering with tears as Ephyra answered only with silence. Then with a bitter shake of her head, Beru turned and climbed back through the open window.

Ephyra closed her eyes, wincing at the sound of the window clicking shut. She stayed hidden behind the bushes a moment longer, dabbing at her eyes before she emerged back into the courtyard. Illya waited on the other side, leaning against a pillar with his arms crossed over his chest.

"So?" he said as she approached. "You believe me now?"

Ephyra didn't reply as she swept through the doors that led inside. He kept pace with her down the corridor to her room.

Illya had done what she'd asked. He'd taken her to see Beru. And for some reason, Beru seemed remarkably sure of Illya's intentions. So much so, it drove a spike of doubt through Ephyra.

Of the two of them, Beru had always been better at reading people.

While Ephyra was quick to assume the worst of almost everyone, Beru was evenhanded in her evaluation. She saw the good in people—or rather, she saw the truth of them, their intentions, what drove them.

Growing up, Ephyra had always let Beru take the lead when it came to dealing with people. The night she'd brought Anton back to their hideout in Pallas Athos, all those months ago, it was Beru who had persuaded him to help them.

Maybe somehow, she'd managed to do it to Illya, too. Maybe she'd figured out the key to win him over. Illya was compelled by power, and now Beru was powerful. More powerful than Pallas. More powerful than Ephyra.

"Why did you want me to agree to be Pallas's executioner?" she asked, rather than answering Illya's question.

He looked surprised by the question. Instead of answering, he reached for her wrist and touched one of the cuffs around it.

And she understood. If she said yes, if she agreed to be Pallas's executioner, then at least for a few brief moments, he would have to remove her cuffs. She'd be free to use her power.

"I can't kill him," Ephyra said. "Pallas. If I kill him, then the seal breaks and Beru—"

"I know," Illya replied. "I had a different idea."

"You really have a plan?" Ephyra asked carefully. "A way to get me out of here?"

He nodded, his golden eyes pinned on hers, his hand still touching the cuff, but not the skin beneath it.

She sucked in a breath, gathering herself. "Then I'll say yes. When Pallas summons me again, I'll agree to be his executioner. But your plan—you need to get me *and* Beru out of here. Or I won't do it."

She expected him to protest, to argue and tell her it couldn't be done, it was too risky.

But he just drew back his hand and dipped his head, as if he'd expected it. "All right."

They reached the door to Ephyra's room. Instead of pushing it open, Ephyra turned back to him. "What did she offer you?"

"What?"

"You would never risk yourself like this," she said. "Not unless the reward was worth it. So what is it? What did she promise you?"

His throat bobbed as he swallowed, his golden eyes dimming with something like guilt, or regret.

"It's Grace, isn't it?" she said slowly. "She's going to give you someone's Grace if you do this."

A muscle in his jaw tensed. "Good night, Ephyra."

He turned and left her standing in the doorway, alone.

7

ANTON

THE DREAM CAME TO ANTON IN FRACTURED PIECES.

Jude on his knees in an unfamiliar room, his face a patchwork of bruises and fresh cuts.

The sharp tang of blood and the harsh, staccato rhythm of Jude's breath bursting from his lungs.

A voice rasping through the air like wind through dead leaves. "Where is the Prophet?"

Jude didn't answer. Someone struck him across the face, and Jude's neck snapped to the side. He stared up defiantly as blood trickled from the corner of his mouth.

"I'm prepared to kill you if you don't give me what I want, Captain Weatherbourne," the same voice said, mocking now. "Where is the Prophet?"

Anton woke in a tangle of sheets, cold sweat matting his shirt to his back.

He kicked off the sheets and scrambled to his feet. The whole room seemed to lurch with him. After a moment of blinking in the darkness, he remembered he was on the Wanderer's ship. Anton swayed, feeling like he might vomit.

Air. He needed air.

He threw open his cabin door and stumbled down the corridor.

"Anton?"

A light flickered behind him, and Anton turned to find the Wanderer opening the door of her own cabin. In her thin cotton nightdress, her hair braided simply over one shoulder, she looked more human than he'd ever seen her before.

"What's wrong?" she asked.

He dragged a hand over his face. "Nightmare."

The dream clutched at him like the cold fingers of a corpse, and the hair on the back of his neck stuck up. It hadn't felt like a nightmare. Not how they usually felt to him. It had felt . . . real.

He sucked in a steadying breath and asked, "How do you know if something's a dream or a vision?"

Her dark eyes met his. "You think you had a vision?"

He nodded. "It's happened before. I dreamed of the Hierophant, the night you told me to go to Endarrion. But it wasn't a dream. And I don't think this was, either."

"What happened?"

Bile rose in his throat as the image of Jude's bloody face flashed through his mind. "It's Jude. Something's wrong. He's hurt. I saw— there was blood and they were interrogating him—they were looking for *me*."

Anton blinked and a second later the Wanderer was right beside him, holding him up.

"You need to breathe," she said soothingly.

It had been a long time since his panic had gripped him so tightly, but he knew the signs. He gasped for air.

"Just focus on me," she said. "Focus on my voice. Can you count your breaths?"

Anton nodded, but his mind was consumed by the horror of his dream, by Jude's pale, bloody face.

"Come on," the Wanderer said, pressing him closer to her and helping him up the stairs. "Let's get some air."

They wobbled up to the main deck, and as they emerged into the open, Anton closed his eyes and felt the wind blow over him. He breathed it in deeply, and then let it out, pressing his fingers below his jaw to feel the tap of his pulse. He counted each tap as he breathed, until he felt calm enough to open his eyes again.

"Can you tell me what happened?" the Wanderer asked. "Or can you show me?"

He shook his head. Whether vision or dream, he couldn't bear to see it again. He would have to tell her.

"I saw Jude being . . . tortured," he said. "I don't know if it's happening right now, or it's going to happen or—"

Or if it had already happened, and Anton was too late.

No. It wasn't possible. He would know if Jude was gone. He would know.

"You said you wanted to stay away from him." It had been her suggestion at first, but in the end she had left the decision to Anton. And this was what he had chosen—to go to Kerameikos alone. To leave Jude out of it in order to keep him safe.

But if Jude was already in danger, then Anton had chosen this loneliness and this longing for nothing.

He met her gaze. "I need to know that he's all right."

"You should save your strength," she said gently. "I can scry for him."

"No," he said quickly. "I mean . . . I need to do it. I need to be sure."

She gave him a tight smile and he knew that she understood. It wasn't about not trusting her. It was about knowing that the only way to quell the shaking in his bones was to feel Jude's *esha*, safe, for himself.

He closed his eyes and summoned his Grace, sending it out in ripples the way he'd been aching to do for over two months, searching for that stormlike *esha* that was as familiar to him as his own.

He felt his Grace brush up against it. Unmistakable. Like a beacon lighting in his mind. He hadn't let himself do this for *months*, but it still felt as easy as breathing.

He pressed in toward his sense of Jude's *esha*, using his Grace to peer past the endless, intricate patterns of energy that made up the world and resolve it into an image that his mind could process as if he were truly seeing it. Another trick the Wanderer had taught him.

He found himself in a familiar room. It took him a moment to understand *why* it looked familiar. It was almost identical to his cell in the citadel of Pallas Athos, when he'd been kept prisoner for a night.

Jude sat hunched against a stone wall, eyes closed. He was as real and vivid as he looked when Anton walked into his dreams. Maybe more so. And his face was unmarred—no bruises, no cuts. Anton longed to reach for him, to smooth a thumb across the line that creased his brows even in sleep.

But just as he moved toward him, the image flickered and vanished.

Anton opened his eyes.

"What did you see?" the Wanderer asked, her tone urgent, her face pinched in concern.

"He's . . ." Anton swallowed. "He's imprisoned in Pallas Athos. In the citadel. I don't—What is he doing there?"

The Wanderer's expression darkened. "Pallas has him."

There was such certainty in her voice, like she understood something that Anton did not.

But Jude was supposed to be *safe*. He wasn't supposed to be in Pallas Athos.

There was only one reason, really, he would have gone there.

"He . . . he must have been trying to rescue Beru," Anton said slowly. "To get the god out of Pallas's control."

He glanced back at the Wanderer, and she seemed to avoid his gaze. Her words came back to him.

I have my best people on it.

Not the Lost Rose. Jude.

"*You* did this," Anton said incredulously. "You sent him to Pallas Athos."

"No," she said. "I didn't send him anywhere. He was already planning to go there. I just offered him help."

Anton backed away from her, horror and betrayal thundering through him. "How could you? How could you do this and keep it from me?"

"Because I knew you'd react like this." Her voice was tight with agitation. "You have your own mission to fulfill. Your own plan. A plan *you* came up with, need I remind you?"

"He could be killed because of you!" Anton said furiously. "And if I hadn't seen it in my dreams, then I would have never known. If you were wondering, *this* is why I don't trust you. This is why it took me so long to let you teach me how to use my Grace. Because you are always, *always*, playing your own game. I'm sick of it."

Her dark eyes narrowed, flashing like steel. "I was trying to make this easier for you. For both of you. There was no way to stop Jude from going to Pallas Athos, so I helped him. And yes, I kept it from you. But what would you have done about it, had you known?"

"I would've stopped him," Anton growled. "I *will* stop him."

"You'll go to him?" the Wanderer asked. "And then what? He won't let you go after that. And you won't be able to walk away, either."

Anton glared at her, fury and helplessness rioting in his chest. She was right. He knew she was right, and it just made him angrier. "Maybe it was a mistake to try in the first place. Maybe I need him for this. For all of it."

"You'll tell him the truth?"

Anton clenched his jaw. She knew what she was doing by prodding him. Anton couldn't tell Jude the truth. That was why he'd needed to stay away from him. But staying away hadn't protected him, so there was only one option left. Find him. Save him.

Lie to him.

"I have to go," he said to the Wanderer desperately. "I have to help him. You know that I do."

She pursed her lips. Anton's heart hammered under her assessing gaze. What would he do, he wondered, if she refused him? If she insisted they ignore his vision, the churning fear in his gut, and stayed the course?

He didn't know. And he didn't want to find out.

"We'll need a plan," she said at last.

Relief ballooned inside him, so expansive he felt almost untroubled by the task that now lay ahead. "A plan. Right."

They'd have to figure out how to get into the citadel. Anton remembered very little from his own time there, when he and Ephyra had been taken in, ostensibly for temple robbing. His stay had been brief but horrible—one night of cold, clawing fear before Hector had arrived and offered him a way out.

An offer that, looking back, had changed the course of Anton's life. Had led him to Jude.

"The Sentry are loyal to Pallas," the Wanderer said. "I'm not sure a simple bribe will do the trick."

Anton snorted. A bribe was most likely how Illya had gotten past the guards to break Ephyra out.

The thought struck him sideways, and Anton had to steady himself against the gunwale.

"Oh no," he said out loud. "Oh *no*. I think I have a really terrible idea."

The Wanderer peered at him curiously.

"But I think it might work." He met her gaze and said simply, "Illya."

She considered this. "Why would he help you?"

"He might not," Anton admitted. "That's why I said it was a terrible idea. But he's opportunistic. Remember in Behezda when he gave the Chalice to the Necromancer King? He was happy to turn on Pallas for the right price then. And now, he's probably running low on currency with the Witnesses."

"Which could mean he'd take the opportunity to use *you* as currency," the Wanderer said. "Deliver you to Pallas to earn back his favor."

"That's a risk," Anton agreed. "But this is the only idea I have. You don't have to do this with me. When we get to Pallas Athos, you can wait on the ship. If it comes to it, I know you don't want to risk facing Pallas."

The Wanderer looked away, gazing out at the black sea surrounding them. "Do you really think me such a coward?" There was no bite to the question, no recrimination. She sounded like she wanted an honest answer.

"No," Anton said. "But you showed me what he did to you. And if it were me, I'd do everything I could to stay away from him."

"If it comes to it," she said. "I am not afraid. Perhaps it's finally time I face him again."

BEFORE

"HOW DID YOU FIND US?"

Pallas the Faithful stood before Ananke, on the threshold of a hut at the edge of the world.

"It was not easy," he said. "It took nearly all my strength."

And indeed, he looked frail.

"May I come in?"

Ananke didn't move.

"I am not here to hurt you," Pallas said. "Nor your beloved."

"Then why did you come?"

"To offer an apology," Pallas said.

"I don't believe you."

Pallas sighed. "I am sure you have seen the destruction the god has wrought on the world since your defiance."

"Of course I have seen it," Ananke said. "Every night when I close my eyes, I see it."

"The blame does not fall solely on your shoulders, Ananke," Pallas said. "I was the one who chose Temara as a sacrifice. I wanted to test your faith, and I should have known that you would fail."

"If that is what you came here to say, leave now," Ananke said. "You claim you know about faith, but you have none. You were the first of the Creator's Prophets, but you weren't enough, were you? The Holy One had to create six more, to make up for your failure. And now you show up here, preaching to me about faith?"

Pallas stared at her, his bright blue eyes penetrating. "Perhaps coming here was a mistake."

"Perhaps it was," Ananke agreed, moving to close the door on him.

"I was wrong to test your faith by telling you to sacrifice Temara," Pallas said, stopping the door.

There was something about his tone that made her pause.

"I have had much time to think on what you did," Pallas continued. "*Why* you did it. And I wonder—Would a just god demand a sacrifice in the first place? If the Creator made us with love in our hearts, why then ask us to betray that love?"

"I have never believed the Creator to be just," Ananke replied.

"Then perhaps it is time the world has just rulers," Pallas said. "Faithful rulers. Wise rulers. Merciful rulers. Brave rulers."

"What are you saying?" Ananke asked.

"That we need your help, Ananke."

8

HASSAN

HASSAN AND HECTOR WENT OVER THEIR PLAN ONE FINAL TIME, PICKING AT THE last of their rations in Hassan's old sitting room.

Lethia's villa, abandoned after her return to Nazirah, had become their base of operation in Pallas Athos. It seemed when Lethia had left, she hadn't intended to return—furniture had been removed, her personal effects were gone, and even the shelves of the library had been stripped bare. No servants had remained behind to maintain the grounds, and in the past three months, the gardens had begun to grow parched and overtaken by weeds.

"Time to get dressed," Hassan said once they'd finished breakfast. He tossed the Sentry cadet uniform to Hector before disappearing into his old closet.

The uniform had been provided to them by the Lost Rose's ally, the former captain of the Sentry. He had resigned the minute the Hierophant took power, and much of their plan today depended on the old man and the information he'd supplied them. Hector and Jude had been inside the citadel of Pallas Athos once, but their knowledge of the place was limited. They'd met the former Sentry captain once, too, when the Paladin Guard had first arrived in Pallas Athos.

"Honestly, I'm pretty sure he didn't like us," Hector had said of the meeting.

"He didn't seem to like much of anything," Jude had added. "Not us, not the Order, and definitely not the Priests' Conclave."

He also hadn't seemed to like the three of them when they met in Lethia's villa a week ago.

"*You're* the ones who are supposed to fix this mess?" he had asked, his voice laced with skepticism.

Hector had looked ready to reply with some choice words, so Hassan had hastily cut him off.

"Do you see anyone else lining up to save this city?" he'd asked, leveling the captain with his most authoritative stare.

The Sentry captain had looked from Hassan to Jude and back before finally throwing up his hands. "Well, I guess you can't make things much worse."

He'd spent hours going over the layout and the day-to-day operations of the citadel. The Archon's execution, he told them, would take place in an amphitheater perched at the very edge of the cliff overlooked by the prisoners' tower. That was where Beru would be.

Hector had suggested that they could smuggle themselves into the execution along with the public, but the Sentry captain had shot down that idea. The execution wasn't for the public to witness—it was for the priests and the other leaders of the city. A reminder of what would happen to them if they followed the Archon's lead in defying Pallas.

"There won't be a single soul there that wasn't chosen to attend by Pallas himself," the captain had said. "There'll be no blending into the crowd."

"What about a way to sneak in?" Jude had asked. "A secret entrance or something?"

"There's only one way in, through the main gate. And as for sneaking, you'll be far too conspicuous. Especially you," the captain had added, with a glance at Hassan. "You're very recognizable."

It was that comment that had given Hassan the idea. If they tried to sneak inside and someone recognized him as the prince, his whole cover would be blown.

Unless, of course, being the Prince of Herat *was* his cover.

"Huh," Hector said, when Hassan emerged from the closet dressed in an elaborately cut emerald brocade overcoat embroidered with gold thread and fastened with a row of gleaming buttons. A silver sash and delicate gold chain around his neck completed the ensemble. He looked exactly like a spoiled prince.

"What?" Hassan asked peevishly.

"No offense, those clothes make me feel like punching you," Hector replied. He looked thoroughly believable as a Sentry cadet, filling out his light blue uniform emblazoned with a white olive tree.

"You should," Hassan said, realization striking.

"What?" Hector looked briefly scandalized.

"Well, it should look like I put up a fight, right?" Hassan pressed. He raised his chin. "Come on. Hit me."

Hector looked extremely unconvinced. "All right. But just remember, you *asked* me to—"

"Just hit me already—" Before Hassan knew what was happening, Hector's fist cracked across his face. Hassan let out an involuntary whimper of pain.

"Oh, that looked like it hurt."

"That was *way* harder than it needed to be." Hassan glared, holding a knuckle up to his now-bleeding lip. "Behezda's mercy."

"Sorry."

"Did you hit Jude that hard?" Hassan asked, wiping off the blood.

"He didn't ask me to," Hector replied defensively, a shadow of worry crossing his features.

Hassan gripped Hector's shoulder comfortingly. "Jude will be fine. As long as we stick to the plan."

"I know. Hard not to picture him locked up in that cell all alone, though."

"Yeah, well, that will be our fate if we don't pull this off, so save the worrying."

"It's not just that," Hector said. "It's also . . . seeing Beru again. After all this time."

Hassan understood. He felt a pang, imagining how he would feel if he knew he would be coming face-to-face with Khepri for the first time in over two months. Even more nervous than Hector was now, undoubtedly.

And there was another reason to feel uneasy about seeing Beru. They had no idea what state the girl would be in when they found her. No idea how strong her control over the god was. Hassan could still feel the terror of watching the entire city of Behezda crumble to the god's will. It seemed impossible that one girl could control all that power. And even if everything went smoothly today, even if they did manage to wrench the girl—and the god inside her—from the Hierophant's control, what then?

One problem at a time, Hassan reminded himself. First they had to rescue the girl.

They left the villa, winding down the road and into the second tier of the High City. Even from here, it was possible to see the citadel perched high on the cliffs that overlooked the sea. Somewhere behind those high, white walls was the Hierophant. Hassan's blood burned hotter just thinking of him.

Once the towering limestone gates were in sight, Hassan held out his hands and let Hector chain them together.

"This might be the most foolish thing I've ever done," Hector said.

"It's not even top five for me," Hassan assured him.

Hector's lips quirked in a smile before he smoothed his expression and grabbed the back of Hassan's shirt, marching him down the long esplanade bracketed by massive columns and lined with silver-leafed olive trees. They were at least a hundred paces from the gate when two Sentry approached.

"Cadet!" the older of the two called out to Hector. "What are you doing out-of-bounds? Who is this?"

"Sir," Hector said deferentially. "My apologies. I was patrolling the perimeter when I spotted this boy trying to breach the walls."

Hassan held his breath as the two Sentry came closer.

"Very well," the older one said. "Take him to the holding cells."

"Sir," Hector said, grabbing hold of Hassan's face and turning it toward the Sentry. Hassan made a show of struggling against his hold. "I think you're going to want to tell the Prophet about this. Directly."

The older Sentry squinted at Hassan's face, and then his eyes widened in shock. "It . . . it can't be."

"I wasn't sure at first, either," Hector said. "But look at him. Unmistakable."

"Fuck you," Hassan spat, trying to shake him off. He threw his head back, smashing it into Hector's jaw. Hector grunted in pain, his grip tightening on Hassan's shoulder in warning. Hassan wasn't too concerned—it would sell their act further, and Hector frankly deserved payback for hitting Hassan so hard earlier.

"Save it," Hector barked.

The second, younger Sentry looked on in confusion.

"Stavros," the older Sentry barked. "Go to the Prophet. Tell him we have the Prince of Herat."

The younger Sentry blinked in surprise and then departed hastily.

"Cadet," the older Sentry said commandingly. "Why don't you hand our prisoner over to me?"

Hector's hand tightened a minuscule amount on Hassan's shirt. "I'm not sure that's a good idea, sir."

Hassan's pulse hammered in his throat as the Sentry eyed Hector. Did he suspect that he wasn't who he said he was?

"You and I both know that the Prophet will want to hear exactly how I found him," Hector continued. "I wouldn't want to get caught trying to deceive him, would you?"

The older Sentry narrowed his eyes at them. "What's your name, cadet?"

"Kostas, sir," Hector replied without missing a beat.

The older Sentry nodded. "You're a very good cadet, Kostas. Trustworthy. Smart. It was very fortunate you were able to capture the prince under my orders."

He held Hector's gaze, and Hector nodded hesitantly, catching on. "Very fortunate, sir."

Hassan resisted the urge to roll his eyes, relief coursing through him. The Sentry wasn't suspicious at all—he just wanted credit.

Stavros appeared at the gate again, racing toward them. By the time he reached them, he was panting.

"Sir," he said, addressing the older Sentry. "The Prophet has requested that the prince be brought to him immediately. He said—" He cut himself off for a moment, his eyes darting to Hassan nervously. "He said they're about to begin the execution. And there's time for one more."

Hassan resisted the instinct to catch Hector's gaze, cold dread seeping through him. They'd banked on the fact that the Hierophant would want Hassan brought directly to him. But an execution? That wasn't part of the plan.

"Well?" the older Sentry said with an expectant look at Hector. "What are you waiting for? Let's go."

"Of course, sir," Hector said, nerves threading through his voice.

Hassan took a stumbling step forward at Hector's prodding. The older Sentry led them through the gates at a brisk clip.

"Time for one more?" he hissed under his breath. "Hector—"

"Be quiet," Hector barked loudly, still playing his part. Lowering his voice, he whispered, "We'll still get to the amphitheater. This doesn't change anything."

Hassan fell silent, but he couldn't calm the sick lurch of dread in his gut as they entered the citadel.

9

BERU

THE EYES OF THE SENTRY FOLLOWED BERU THROUGH THE CITADEL'S CENTRAL courtyard.

Lazaros had told her nothing when he'd come to collect her from her room this morning. He'd just waited while the servants dressed her in yards of white robes, threaded through with intricate gold and silver. Robes fit for a god.

She had waited there for Lazaros to remove the Godfire collar that kept the god, and Beru's access to its power, subdued. But this time, he'd left it on.

The Godfire collar twinged now as they crossed through the courtyard, beneath a broad walkway and into a tunnel that penetrated the cliff itself.

"Where is Ephyra?" Beru asked. "Just tell me they aren't hurting her."

"I could tell you that, if you'd like," Lazaros said in his quiet, whispery voice. "But it could easily be a lie, so what would be the point?"

"I don't think you'd lie to me," Beru said. He looked, for a brief moment, surprised. She pressed the advantage. "Don't you have any family? Someone you'd do anything to protect?"

His gray eyes were intent and unsettling on her face. "I had parents."

"Had?" she repeated. "Did they die?"

It was another long moment, their footsteps echoing quietly through the tunnel, before he replied. "The man who sired me and the woman who birthed me are still alive. But their son is long dead."

Beru shivered.

"We—" He cut himself off, his eyes flicking away from her for the first time.

"What?" she asked sharply.

"We're the same," he said quietly. "I know what it is to be destroyed and made into something new. Something pure."

She stared, swallowing down her revulsion. "That's what you think I am? Pure?"

He met her gaze again, his gray eyes shining. "You are the vessel of the Creator. That makes you holy."

He was so *certain*. She almost envied him that belief.

IF HE WANTS TO WORSHIP ME, HE CAN START BY FREEING ME, the god said.

Beru ignored it.

"And the Hierophant?" she asked. "Pallas? Is he holy, too?"

"Of course," Lazaros said swiftly. "The Immaculate One—"

"He lied to you. He's a Prophet," Beru hissed, and she knew it was her own voice, her own words, but it felt like the god was speaking through her. "He killed it—me—in the first place. Is that holy?"

Lazaros hesitated. She could see on his face that it wasn't the first time he'd been confronted with this idea. But it was perhaps the first time he'd heard it spoken aloud.

"A necessary sin," Lazaros said at last. "There must be darkness for there to be light."

She stared at him a moment longer, wondering at how easily he could arrange his own beliefs to justify his master. Wondering what was inside him that made these ideas grow like a weed, taking over everything. A belief that was almost cannibalistic, eating itself until there was nothing left, no truth, no sense, just the Hierophant.

She would never understand it.

The tunnel spat them out at the top of an amphitheater bracketed by the edge of a cliff. The sea roiled below, filling Beru's ears with the roar of the waves crashing against the rocks. The stands of the amphitheater were crowded with people—from their intricate robes, Beru guessed they were the Priests' Conclave, as well as a group of Sentry in light blue uniforms, and a smaller cluster of swordsmen in darker blue cloaks.

Dead ahead, Pallas welcomed Beru and Lazaros onto the amphitheater's stage, magisterial in his white and gold robes, a shining beacon against the gray sea beyond the cliff. At his side, Ephyra rose to her feet, coiled tight like a spring, her gaze fixed on Beru.

Beru's heart plummeted into her stomach.

She'd done it, then. Ephyra had agreed to be Pallas's executioner. Beru darted a glance around the stage, for any sign of Illya. She hadn't seen him since he orchestrated their courtyard meeting and had no idea whether he'd managed to persuade Ephyra to follow their plan. Or whether Ephyra's distrust and refusal to leave Beru behind meant their plans were over before they'd begun.

But Ephyra had said yes to Pallas. Why would she agree, if not to escape?

A treacherous part of her recalled that Ephyra had chosen this path before. She had chosen, in Behezda, to kill, to become the Pale

Hand again. Beru hadn't allowed herself to think too deeply about why Ephyra had made that choice. To wonder if maybe some part of Ephyra *enjoyed* it.

Wind buffeted Beru as she reached Pallas's side, gazing at the limestone walls of the citadel looming above them, the prisoners' tower stretching up against the gray sky.

"Bring the first prisoner forward," Pallas said, his voice ringing out across the stage. A group of Witnesses descended from the stands, dragging a figure in chains between them. The prisoner struggled, but the Witnesses forced him to his knees.

A breath punched out of Beru's chest as she stared at the prisoner.

"Illya Aliyev," Pallas intoned, grasping Illya's chin between bony fingers for the crowd to see his face. "You may not recognize this man, but he once pledged himself to me. Before he betrayed me for his own gain. Let it be known here and now that I, Pallas the Faithful, can see through the deception and lies of each and every one of you. I know the truth of your hearts, and if you try to deceive me, you will end up just like him."

No, Beru thought, panicked.

Illya was her only ally. Her only chance of getting Ephyra out of here. How could he have been found out? *How?*

As Beru gazed at Illya's grim face, she felt like the floor was dropping out from beneath her. THIS IS WHAT COMES OF PUTTING YOUR FAITH IN WEAK MEN, the god said.

Shut up, she thought fiercely. *You want out just as badly as I do.*

Beru looked over at Ephyra, whose gaze rested on Illya, her expression closed off. Did she know? Or was she as surprised as Beru?

"I am sure," Pallas said to the crowd, "that you have all heard of the Pale Hand of Death."

A murmur rippled through the onlooking priests. They surely remembered one of their own falling to her hand.

Pallas waved two Witnesses forward, and they went to Ephyra, uncuffing her as Pallas spoke to the crowd.

"The Pale Hand seeks out the wicked," he continued. "Rooting out the corruption of our society. Her justice is dispensed on behalf of our Creator. She is the instrument of his judgment, the Hand of God. And she will dispense the fates of these liars and apostates."

Pallas let his gaze fall on Ephyra.

"Pale Hand, take the first of your victims."

He indicated Illya, his expression placid. But Beru knew this was a test. He must know something of their past together—that Ephyra had once trusted Illya. That perhaps she did again.

Ephyra prowled toward Illya, her face carefully blank.

Beru's chest tightened. Ephyra was going to do it. She was going to kill him—for Beru. She felt Pallas's eyes on her and knew why he had summoned her. It wasn't just for the spectacle in front of the priests and Sentry. It was for Beru to see what he could do. To show her that even now, after all this time, she was still turning her sister into a killer.

Pallas had both Beru and Ephyra clutched in the palm of his hand, and there was nothing either of them could do.

"Don't," Beru gasped, her voice swallowed by the wind. She took a step toward Ephyra. Then another. Lazaros gripped her arm in warning. "Ephyra."

Standing over Illya's kneeling form, Ephyra met Beru's eyes across the platform. She shook her head minutely, and then wrapped her hand around Illya's throat, her eyes falling shut.

Beru trembled. She had never seen Ephyra kill before, not really. The only times she'd been there for it, she'd been too weak to track what was happening. But here on this platform above the bleak sea, she saw everything. She saw the breath that rose and fell in Ephyra's chest as she pulled Illya's *esha* from his body. She saw how her hand tightened over his throat. She saw Illya's eyes fall shut, his body relaxing, his chest going still.

A scream tore from Beru's throat, and only Lazaros's iron grip kept her from flinging herself across the platform as Illya collapsed, a pale handprint almost glowing against his skin.

"No," Beru croaked, straining against Lazaros's hold. "*No.*"

He was dead.

Tears stung Beru's eyes as Ephyra stepped back from Illya's body. She felt numb, horror pitting her stomach.

This murderous, cold-blooded killer—How could that be her sister? How had Beru let her become this?

Another group of Witnesses appeared on the platform, with a wheelbarrow at the ready to transport Illya's body. Beru watched, her heart thumping hollowly, as they carried him away.

"And now," Pallas said, when they were finished. "It is time for our second sinner to meet his fate."

The Witnesses dragged out another prisoner, this one an older man, tall and balding.

The Witnesses shoved him to his knees in front of Pallas.

"I am sure you recognize the former leader of this city," Pallas said, touching the man's shoulder gently. "His reign was marked by weakness and avarice. And when your glorious Prophet, Pallas the Faithful, returned, this man tried to defy me. For his role in defying the Creator's plan, he must die."

The Archon's face twisted in utter terror. Ephyra stared back, impassive.

Beru wanted to hide her face. She couldn't watch again. But she made herself. Ephyra had only become this rotten creature because of Beru. *For* Beru.

Ephyra stepped up to the Archon, quicker this time. Pallas moved to step away, but Ephyra grabbed a handful of his white robes and yanked the Prophet toward her.

Pallas took a stumbling step, his eyes wide with shock as Ephyra twisted around and wrapped her hand around his throat.

The crowd around them erupted with gasps and confused chatter. Someone screamed.

"What are you doing?" Pallas demanded, the usually gentle lilt of his voice gone harsh and clipped.

"Me?" Ephyra asked, her hand tightening around Pallas's throat. "I'm dispensing the Creator's judgment, like you said."

"Stop her!" Pallas barked, his gaze darting toward his Witnesses, not daring to make any sudden movements lest she kill him just as easily as she'd killed Illya.

"Take a step toward us and your delightful little Prophet dies," Ephyra warned the Witnesses who approached.

Beside Beru, Lazaros went rigid.

"She won't do it," Pallas said, his voice forcefully calm. "She won't risk freeing the god."

"Won't I?" Ephyra asked, baring her teeth. "I'm not sure you want to find out, actually."

Pallas seemed to freeze for a moment, deciding whether or not he could call Ephyra's bluff.

WHAT IS SHE DOING? the god demanded. SHE SHOULD KILL HIM.

Beru feared that she *would*. That this wasn't a bluff.

The Witnesses hovered, tense, waiting for their orders.

"S-stand down," Pallas choked out at last.

"You," Ephyra said, looking at Lazaros. "Let go of Beru."

Pallas jerked his head. "Do as she says."

Lazaros stepped away from Beru, and for a moment Beru thought she might collapse without his support. She swayed on her feet.

"What are you doing?" she asked faintly. The wind picked up, howling over the cliff, drowning out their voices.

"I told you," Ephyra said. "I told you I wasn't giving up. I told you I'd find a way."

A hysterical cry rose in Beru's throat. "But this, Ephyra? *Illya?* You *killed* him! What are you—"

"You have to trust me," Ephyra pleaded. "As your sister, as the person you used to run to when you had nightmares, *trust me.*"

Beru could recall a time when her trust in Ephyra had been automatic. Above reproach. When Ephyra was her big sister, who made everything all right just by being there.

When had she lost that? When was the first time she'd looked at her sister, the only person in the world who truly loved her, and wondered whether a monster stared back at her?

She studied Ephyra's face now. The desperate gleam in her dark eyes. The scar that sliced down the left side of her face, a reminder of what she'd done to Hector.

"Beru," Ephyra said. "Please."

Maybe Ephyra was a killer. Maybe there was a monster inside her, as sure as there was one inside Beru.

But she was still her sister.

Her cheeks wet with tears, Beru nodded her assent and darted toward Ephyra.

"Clear the way!" Ephyra yelled to the crowd.

People dove to get out of their way, as if afraid that Ephyra would suck out their *esha* the way she had Illya's.

Bile rose in Beru's throat at the thought of him, but she gritted her teeth and forced it down. Ephyra shoved Pallas, her hostage, in front of her as she made her way across the platform. She reached back for Beru with her other hand.

"Come on," she said. "I'm getting us out of here."

Trust Ephyra. Beru stumbled to her side and took her sister's hand.

10

JUDE

JUDE WAITED UNTIL THE MORNING GUARD SHIFT CHANGE TO MAKE HIS MOVE.

It had been a brutal four days in the prisoners' tower, imprisoned alone with nothing to distract him from his thoughts. He'd run through their plan so many times he was sure he could recite it without missing a beat.

The first step, getting himself into the prisoners' tower, had been easy enough. He'd entered the citadel dressed in a Sentry uniform, and then changed back into plainclothes and locked himself inside a holding cell. The next morning, he'd staged a breakout, and they moved him into the more securely guarded prisoners' tower.

Jude could only hope the rest of the plan went as smoothly. He palmed the small vial that Hector had slipped into his dinner the night before. A thimbleful of dark green, viscous liquid sloshed inside. The Lost Rose's alchemist had sworn it would be enough.

Holding the vial as far away from his body as he could, Jude uncorked it and splashed it onto the far wall of his cell. The liquid immediately began chewing through the stone until it formed a hole about one arm span across, through which Jude could see gray sky. The edges of the hole were smoking slightly.

Jude laid down the thin blanket provided to him and leaned out of the gap. His cell was on the side of the tower that faced away from the amphitheater, where Beru was supposed to be. All he could see when he looked down was the ocean, lapping up against the cliff a hundred feet down.

Jude remembered being perched on the top of the lighthouse of Nazirah with Anton and the long fall into the sea that had followed.

He shook away the memory, swinging his legs through the opening and lowering himself against the tower's outer wall. The masonry of the tower made for fairly good toeholds, and with his Grace increasing his strength and balance, it was an easy climb around the side of the tower despite the wind driving cold stiffness into his fingers.

When he reached the other side of the tower, he finally caught sight of the amphitheater, filled with hundreds of tiny figures too small to make out. He began to descend, pausing at the halfway point of the tower, where one of the stones was marked with paint. He pressed a palm to the stone, and it shifted slightly. Jude pushed it all the way in and then swung himself into the opening it revealed.

He got to his feet in yet another cell, empty save for the supplies Hector had stashed here. He changed into the sturdy clothes Hector had provided and strapped one sword to his belt, the other to his back. He longed for the familiar weight of the Pinnacle Blade, but he had lost it when he'd handed it over to Pallas in Behezda, along with the other Relics. They were no doubt hidden away somewhere—Pallas needed the ancient, Grace-imbued remains to maintain the seal that bound the god's will inside Beru.

Jude picked up a glass orb filled with bright, iridescent liquid and tucked it into his cloak pocket, then slipped back through the opening of the tower. Keeping a firm grip on the masonry with one hand, he smashed the orb against the tower wall. The liquid glittered as it splashed against the stones.

Jude knew very little about alchemy, or any of the trades of the Grace of Mind, but he had to assume that the alchemist who'd created this tincture, along with the one he'd used to escape the cell, was a genius. The iridescent liquid, when exposed to air, would create a flash of blinding light that would blanket the entire area between the prisoners' tower and the watchtower across from it. But the real brilliance was that the reaction was delayed by ten minutes. Enough time for Jude to get in position.

He climbed hastily down the tower until he could hear the voices of the crowd carrying over the wind. As he clung to the tower wall two stories above the amphitheater, he realized the crowd was no longer seated in the stands, but on their feet, pouring toward the exits. The stage, in contrast, was empty.

Where was Beru? Where was Pallas? He scanned the crowd for them, eyes darting over priests in long sweeping blue robes and Witnesses in black and gold. At the edge of the stage closest to him, his eyes caught on Hassan and Hector, back-to-back, surrounded by gleaming silver swords.

Jude didn't think before he started moving. He summoned his Grace, braced both feet against the stone wall, and pushed off as hard as he could, flipping in a graceful arc to land gently on his feet behind the group of swordsmen that surrounded Hector and Hassan.

Voices cried out indistinctly as Jude unsheathed the sword at his belt. The swordsmen closest to him turned to face him.

Jude froze, his eyes locked on the swordsman. He *knew* him.

Yarik. Annuka's brother, a member of Jude's Guard.

"*Oathbreaker*," Yarik snarled, his blade gleaming in the gray light.

Like the others, he wore a deep blue cloak—but only now did Jude register the seven-pointed star brooch pinning his cloak to his shoulders.

Jude was rooted to the ground. These were not just swordsmen, they were *Paladin*. His mind refused to make sense of what he was seeing. These people—*his* people—under the command of the Hierophant.

And then Yarik was on him, his sword slashing out wide, forcing Jude to parry. The wrongness of this fight, of facing off against his own people, knocked Jude breathless.

But Yarik didn't seem to have the same reservations. Didn't seem to care that he was attacking his own captain, his own Keeper. He barreled toward Jude, his blade a silver blur. Jude was the faster fighter, always had been, but Yarik was a good deal stronger. And Jude didn't want to hurt him. Even knowing Yarik had allied himself with Pallas, Jude couldn't bear the idea of harming a member of his Guard.

Jude evaded and blocked, spinning out of the way of another strike.

"Jude!" Hector's voice cried out.

Over his shoulder, Jude could see Hector and Hassan battling their way through the group of Paladin. Jude angled himself toward the two of them, and as he blocked Yarik's next strike, he leapt back toward them.

Hector grabbed Jude's arm, yanking him out of the way of another Paladin's attack.

"We have a problem," Hector said as he released him to fend off another Paladin.

"I can see that," Jude said faintly, parrying a strike from one Paladin and then another.

"Not the Paladin," Hector grunted, forcing another attacker back. His gaze caught Jude's through the fray. "It's Beru. She's gone."

11

EPHYRA

EPHYRA KEPT HER GRIP TIGHT ON PALLAS AS SHE HUSTLED HIM AND BERU through the tunnel that fed into the innermost hub of the citadel. Instead of emerging into the central courtyard, Ephyra took a hard left onto the path toward the infirmary, pressing close to the inner wall to avoid straying into sightlines.

Keeping pace beside her, Beru was silent.

"Help me find something to tie him up with," Ephyra said, her hand locked around Pallas's arm like a vise, reminding him how easily she could kill him.

Beru nodded, and without a word darted off.

"This is futile," Pallas said imperiously, his bright blue eyes flashing. "And it will only make things worse for you."

"Not sure they can get any worse, actually," Ephyra replied.

"Here," Beru said, reappearing around the side of the building, a coil of rope slung over one shoulder.

Ephyra pushed Pallas up against one of the columns that lined the walkway and looped the rope around him and the columns as many times as she could before tying it off.

"Where will you go?" Pallas said, his voice still infuriatingly, intractably calm. "You won't make it out of the citadel, much less the city."

Ephyra ignored him as she grabbed the rope and tugged, testing its strength.

"Good enough," she decided, turning back to Beru. "Come on."

"You know this is foolish, Beru," Pallas chastised. "You know that I am the only thing keeping the god from overtaking you. You need me. You—"

Ephyra grabbed Beru's arm, pulling her away from Pallas and his desperate threats.

It would only be a matter of time until one of the Sentry or the Witnesses found him. They had to be long gone by then.

"Ephyra, can you *please* tell me what we're doing?" Beru asked as they raced toward the infirmary. "How are we going to get out of here? We can't escape through the gate. There's no other exit."

"Actually," Ephyra replied. "There's one other way out."

"Where?"

"A place like this needs a way to dispose of dead prisoners without contaminating the rest of the citadel," Ephyra explained. "There's a tunnel that runs underneath the perimeter wall from the infirmary where they can remove the dead without dragging the body through the citadel. But it stays locked, unless there's a body to dispose of."

"So we're going to unlock it? How?"

"We're not going to," Ephyra said. "Illya will."

"But you just killed him!" Beru said, her brow creasing. Then her expression darkened. "Wait. Don't tell me you're going to *bring him back*."

"Not exactly," Ephyra replied, dropping into a crouch and skirting around the infirmary wall. "He's not dead. I drained most of his *esha*. Not all of it."

"But the handprint," Beru said. "That would only show up if you killed him."

Ephyra flexed her hand. "Alchemical ink. Invisible unless it reacts with a certain agent. Illya had the agent. I had the ink." She clapped her hands together to demonstrate. "And thus we had another victim of the Pale Hand. But not really. All I have to do is revive him."

And she'd have to hurry. The tunnel led to a crematorium where the bodies were disposed of, and if Ephyra didn't revive Illya in time . . . well, he'd be disposed of, too.

"I need you to keep watch while I revive him," she told Beru. "Then we'll sneak around to the tunnel entrance, and by that time he should have it open."

The wobble in her voice betrayed how nervous she was about the plan. When Illya had first presented it to her, she'd been very skeptical about pulling it off. She'd been skeptical of just about everything Illya had to say. She'd spent much of the past two days on the verge of calling it all off.

But she hadn't. Because for once, Illya *was* putting himself on the line. He'd asked Ephyra to trust him, but their plan didn't work unless he trusted her, too. Trusted her to nearly kill him. Trusted her to revive him, afterward. Trusted that she *could*.

They had practiced, numerous times, in the dead of night, with Ephyra draining Illya's *esha* and reviving him from farther and farther away, until she was able to do it from inside her room while he was on the perimeter of the Archon's residence grounds. She could tell after these sessions how much nearly dying took out of him, his face drained of color, his hands shaking, but he never once complained.

"I know you wanted me to get out of here without you, but I couldn't do it," Ephyra said. "I couldn't leave you here with Pallas."

"I know," Beru said, a note of sadness in her voice.

"And Illya . . . he figured out this plan. A way to get us both out." Ephyra shook her head. "I hate to say this, but you made the right decision to trust him. I wouldn't have done that."

If they pulled this off, she would owe him. On top of whatever it was Beru had already promised him in exchange for his help. She almost wanted to ask her, but maybe she was better off not knowing.

"Well," Beru said, a hint of humor in her voice. "I didn't have a lot of other options."

"You always see the best in people," Ephyra said, meeting her gaze. "Even me."

"Ephyra . . ." Beru said softly.

A shout split the air. "They went that way! Find them!"

Witnesses. Or Sentry. Either way, if she and Beru were found, their plan would fail—and Illya would truly be dead.

"This way," Ephyra said, ducking around the corner, away from the sightlines of the watchtower that flanked the front gate, Beru's hand clutched in hers.

There was a flat pavilion roof ahead. If they could climb up, they'd be hidden from anyone passing by below. Ephyra raced toward it, Beru on her heels.

Then, from nowhere, a high-pitched screech shattered the air. The world exploded into white.

For a moment, Ephyra was certain she was dying. She couldn't hear anything, couldn't see anything, could only feel Beru's hand clutched in hers. A second later, her hearing wavered back.

"Ephyra," she heard Beru say, her voice sounding far away. "Ephyra, I can't *see*."

Ephyra couldn't see anything, either. She was completely blind, drowning in bright light.

"There! It's them!" she heard someone call.

"Where? I can't see anything!" another voice answered.

At least they weren't the only ones running blind. Ephyra tugged Beru, and they both stumbled forward, in what she hoped was the direction of the pavilion. But before she could take another step, someone seized her by the arms.

"Cuff her!" someone called out.

Whoever had taken her arms wrenched them behind her back.

"I'll kill you," she snarled, thrashing in their hold. "Let go of me or I'll kill you."

She started to draw the *esha* from her attacker, felt his grip weaken, and then she felt someone else slap a cold cuff around her wrist. Fire and ice shot through Ephyra's veins as her Grace strained against the Godfire cuff.

"No," she whispered. "No."

She still had to revive Illya, or his body would be taken to burn. She still had to get them all out of here.

"Take them to the courtyard," a voice ordered. "And round up the others."

Others? What others?

She felt someone press her into the ground and heard Beru's panicked breathing as the Witnesses dragged them away.

12

HASSAN

"CLOSE YOUR EYES!" HASSAN CRIED OVER THE SHRIEK OF THE FLASH BOMB.
Behind his eyelids, the world was lit in white.

He felt Hector—he assumed it was Hector—reach out and grab
his shoulder as the flash bomb faded. Hassan blinked open his eyes and
saw the surrounding Paladin shielding their vision against the fading
blast. But it was too late for them—the flash bomb had done its job.
Even with their Graces, the Paladin couldn't see as long as the flash
bomb's effects lingered. It would buy Hassan, Hector, and Jude a few
minutes—long enough to flee the amphitheater.

"I don't get it," Jude said, looking around. "Beru was supposed to be
here. Where did she go?"

Hassan shook his head. "I don't know. We need to get out of here
and come up with a new plan."

"You!" Hector cried, striding over to one of the Paladin who was
stumbling to his knees, clutching his face in horror. Hector grabbed
hold of his collar and jerked him back to his feet. "Tell me where she
went."

"Oathbreaker," the Paladin spat. "What did you do to us?"

"Tell me where the girl is, or I swear on my broken oath I'll throw you into the sea."

"I would never tell *you*," the Paladin snarled.

Without missing a beat, Hector shoved him toward the edge of the cliff.

"Wait, wait, wait!" the Paladin said, stumbling, hands grasping out into nothingness. "She and the Pale Hand escaped. They took the Prophet hostage."

Hassan glanced at Jude, who looked just as confused as Hassan felt.

"Let's get to high ground," Hassan said. "Maybe we can spot them."

Jude and Hector sheathed their swords, and Jude led them up through the stands and into the tunnel that connected the amphitheater to the central hexagonal courtyard of the citadel. Hector and Jude took up the front as they hustled through, on the lookout for more Sentry and Paladin.

"Stay here," Hector said to them. He sprinted past the mouth of the tunnel and bounded smoothly up onto the wall that surrounded the courtyard.

"Wait, Hector!" Jude cried.

Hector froze on the wall and Hassan spun to see what Jude had spotted. Down the walkway that branched out from the courtyard toward the citadel perimeter, a group of Witnesses strode briskly toward them, flanked by more Paladin. Cuffed between the Witnesses was the god-girl and her sister.

Jude seized Hassan's arm, dragging him back into the tunnel, out of sight. He unstrapped the sword across his back and handed it to Hassan.

"Be ready," was all he said, before he disappeared around the corner.

Hassan waited in tense anticipation, clutching the sword tight.

A moment later, he spotted a blur of movement and heard the scrape of a sword unsheathing. Jude.

Hassan raced forward, unsheathing his own sword.

"Get them!" someone cried as Hassan launched himself into the frenzy of Witnesses. Jude and Hector were barely visible, just blurs of movement, their speed enhanced by their Graces.

But very quickly, Hassan realized they weren't the only ones using enhanced speed. The Witnesses were, too. As if, somehow, they were Graced.

A Witness seized hold of Hassan. Hassan stumbled back, jerking to break his hold. With a flick of his arm, the Witness tossed Hassan back against the wall with unnatural strength.

Hassan collapsed, the wind knocked out of him. There was no mistaking it—the Witnesses *were* Graced.

The Witness didn't bother with Hassan again, instead whirling off to where Hassan could see Jude and Hector fighting their way toward the god-girl and her sister. A circle of bloody Witnesses surrounded them.

Hassan stumbled to his feet, still dizzy from the impact, and raised his sword as he launched himself back into the fray. He ducked under another Witness's attack and parried a blow from a Sentry before skidding to a stop in front of Jude and Hector, who had finally reached the sisters.

"Hector, what are you doing here?" the god-girl demanded as Hector rushed toward them, letting Hassan and Jude take point against the Witnesses still closing in.

"Rescuing you, what does it look like?"

"We didn't need you to rescue us," said the god-girl's sister, Ephyra. "We have a plan."

Hector glared. "Yeah, and how's that going?"

"We need to move," Hassan cut in tersely. "We're exposed here, and the flash bomb has already worn off. They'll be sending in reinforcements."

The Paladin in the amphitheater wouldn't be far behind.

"Flash bomb?" Ephyra demanded. "That was *you?*"

"We had a plan," Hector said.

"*We* had a plan," Ephyra spat. "And you messed it up."

"Stop it, both of you," the god-girl chided. "We still have a way out."

"If someone will get this stupid thing off me!" Ephyra cried, shaking a metal cuff on her wrist.

Hassan glanced at Jude, and Jude gave a slight nod before lunging to drive back another Witness. Hassan retreated toward the girls, and Hector wordlessly took up a wider perimeter, buying them time. Hassan seized Ephyra's wrist, turning the cuff over.

"It needs a key," Ephyra said, gritting her teeth, "which we don't have. You're going to have to break my thumb."

Hassan blanched at the prospect. "Maybe if we—"

"Ephyra," the god-girl said in a concerned tone.

"There's no time—just do it!" Ephyra demanded hurriedly. "I can heal. Get it off me, and we can get out of here."

Out of the corner of his eye, Hassan spotted more Paladin choking the entrances of the courtyard. They were surrounded by enemies, and escape was seeming a more and more distant prospect. Ephyra gripped her sister's hand with her uncuffed one and held the other out to Hassan.

"Do it!" Ephyra yelled, panic making her voice brittle.

Hassan seized her thumb and wrenched it toward her palm.

Ephyra let out a shriek of pure agony that rattled Hassan's bones.

Cringing, he tugged the cuff off as quickly as he could. Ephyra shouted a very long expletive as the cuff pulled free. She stumbled, as if she was about to collapse, and her sister caught her around the waist.

"I'm fine," Ephyra wheezed, sounding very much not fine. She breathed out hard, eyes still closed, and went still, her uninjured hand curling into a fist.

Hassan glanced at her sister. "Is she all right?"

Her sister shushed him. "Give her a moment. She needs to concentrate to revive him."

Revive whom? Hassan wondered. But this was not a time for more questions. He whirled back to the encroaching Paladin, flinging himself into the fray to help Jude and Hector defend their position.

But if Hassan had struggled against the newly Graced Witnesses, he was no match for experienced Paladin. They were on Hassan before he'd even realized what had happened, three Paladin surrounding him. Hassan dodged one strike, spinning to parry another—leaving him completely open to his third opponent.

"Hassan!"

Before he could blink, Jude was there, blocking the blow. Heart thumping wildly, Hassan felt someone seize the back of his coat, tossing him to the ground with ease. He hit the stones hard, and with a sharp grunt he swung wildly, desperate to defend himself. The Paladin kicked the sword from Hassan's hand, and then all Hassan could see was the swordsman's dark blue cloak and his menacing eyes as he drove the point of his blade toward Hassan's chest.

"Stop!" a cold, authoritative voice echoed through the courtyard. The Hierophant's voice.

Hassan let out a shaking breath as the Paladin's sword stopped inches from Hassan's chest.

He followed the voice up to the perimeter wall and saw the

Hierophant flanked by six Witnesses, including the one who had burned out his own Grace.

"Lower your weapons," the Hierophant commanded.

To Hassan's surprise, it was the Paladin who obeyed, stopping where they were and turning to face their master.

Hassan's head pounded. What was the Hierophant up to? He glanced at Jude and Hector, who held themselves taut, ready to fight or run.

"You have foolishly tried to defy me," the Hierophant said, his tone seeping with disappointment rather than outright anger. "You will surrender now, or your friends will pay the price."

From behind the Hierophant, more Witnesses arrived, dragging prisoners with them. They shoved the first of them up against the parapet. It was a boy who looked even younger than Hassan, his dark hair mussed and his face bloodied. Hassan didn't recognize him, but he heard Jude's sharp intake of breath.

The second prisoner was shoved against the parapet, and Hassan felt the blood drain from his face. He knew those eyes, deep golden brown and shining with defiance. Those slender fingers had touched him, those bloodied lips had kissed him.

"No," he heard himself say. "No, no."

It wasn't possible. Khepri was—She was in Nazirah. She couldn't be here.

But the truth was in front of him. Khepri had never escaped the ruins of the lighthouse. When the Hierophant had taken Hassan and Arash, he must've taken Khepri, too.

This whole time she'd been a prisoner. And Hassan hadn't even known.

His shock sharpened into terror as he noticed the blade against Khepri's throat.

"Surrender," the Hierophant commanded again. "Or they die."

Khepri's gaze met Hassan's, fear and ferocity in her eyes. The blade bit into the underside of her jaw, drawing blood so bright Hassan could see it from twenty paces off. She shook her head. But Hassan was already raising his hands in surrender.

Ahead of him, Jude laid down his sword.

Hector glanced at the two of them, and then back to the Hierophant and his hostages. Blowing out an enraged breath, he let his sword clatter to the ground, too.

Hassan felt someone grab him from behind, yanking his hands behind his back and securing them. One by one, the Witnesses led them out of the courtyard.

13

ANTON

"ARE YOU CERTAIN THIS IS THE CORRECT PLACE?" THE WANDERER ASKED skeptically as Anton led her to the low, squat building at the end of a dirt path.

"Yes, I'm sure," Anton replied, irritated. The hollow scrape of Illya's *esha* rattled faintly around him. It always set him on edge, but this time at least he was seeking it out. "Why?"

"Because this is a crematorium," the Wanderer replied.

Anton startled. What was Illya doing in a crematorium?

"Come on," he said impatiently, crossing the dirt path toward the building.

"Do we knock?" the Wanderer wondered.

He gave her an annoyed look. She'd never broken into anything before.

"If it's a crematorium, then there's gotta be a chimney," he said, circling around the building and climbing atop a stack of crates. He was just barely able to grab the edge of the flat roof, heaving himself up and scrabbling against the sides of the building.

"I'll just wait out here for you, shall I?" the Wanderer said. "Keep watch."

"Just go to the door," Anton replied, still annoyed, and then darted over the roof. Sure enough, there was an opening on the roof just large enough for Anton to slip through. Below he could see a pile of wood, where they burned the bodies. It would cushion his fall, a little.

He dropped down, the woodpile clattering loudly enough that someone was sure to come running. But the building was silent. He waited a moment to be sure and then struggled to his feet and opened the latch on the door.

"It's empty," he told the Wanderer as she strode past him.

"Good," she replied.

"As in, no Illya," he clarified.

"Not good," she amended. "Look, there's a stairwell over here. Maybe some kind of basement?"

Anton searched the room for a lamp but found nothing. They would have to brave the dark.

He led the way down, the Wanderer at his heels. The light grew dimmer the deeper they descended, and Anton felt a chill run down his spine as they were let out into a dark, airless room with a low ceiling. It smelled vaguely of earth, and each side was lined by what looked like wooden cribs.

Not cribs, Anton realized with a start. They were *caskets*. Filled with bodies.

His hair stood up on end, and he froze as the Wanderer inspected the row of caskets.

"Anton," she said, her voice carefully controlled, her gaze pinned on one of the caskets.

He knew what she was going to say before he even went over to her.

Anton had spent so long being terrified of his own brother's face.

But now, looking down at it, still and placid as he lay inside the casket, Anton didn't feel fear. He felt hollow, like he had lost something he hadn't even realized he had. Illya's eyes were closed, his face strangely boyish without the usual cruel curl of his lips, the malicious gleam in his golden eyes. He looked almost small. Human. Not the monster from Anton's nightmares—just a boy.

And on his throat, Anton saw a pale handprint.

He took an unsteady step back. Ephyra? Had she killed him?

But he could still feel the faint thread of Illya's *esha* reverberating in the room like the sound of breaking glass.

"He can't be dead," Anton said, raising his eyes back to the Wanderer. "You can feel his *esha*, too, can't you?"

She reached into the casket and held her fingers against Illya's jaw, checking for a pulse. "He is alive. But barely. What do you want to do?"

This was *Anton's* plan. His stupid idea.

They needed another way to get inside the citadel. A new plan.

But before he could come up with one, Illya's eyelashes fluttered. Anton froze, certain it was a trick of the light, but then Illya gasped, his eyes flying open.

Anton reeled back, his heart pounding so hard he thought it might burst from his chest. He tripped back against another casket and went toppling to the ground.

"I'm not dead!" Illya shouted, gripping either side of the casket and dragging himself up to a sitting position.

"Clearly," Anton huffed, his heart still hammering as he climbed back to his feet.

Illya's gaze landed on him, his whole face scrunching up in confusion. "Anton?"

"Surprised to see me?" Anton asked, dusting himself off to avoid looking at Illya.

"If you're a hallucination brought on by me nearly dying, then no," Illya replied. "But if you were a hallucination, you'd already be listing every terrible thing I've ever done to you, so I'm guessing you're real."

"Maybe we'll have time for that later."

Illya started to climb out of the casket and then paused, looking at the Wanderer. "Who are you?"

"She's with me," Anton answered. "Want to explain why you're in a crematorium, practically dead?"

"If you must know," Illya replied, straightening his clothes primly, "I was just executed by Pallas. Well. He thinks so."

"Excuse me? You don't *look* like you just got executed." Anton narrowed his eyes, taking in Illya's washed-out face and shaking hands.

"Yes, thank you, that was the point," Illya replied, licking his thumb and swiping it across the pale handprint on his throat. To Anton's astonishment, the mark of the Pale Hand wiped off. "It's part of the plan." He eyed Anton. "*You* were not, however. And I'm expected elsewhere so maybe we can have this reunion later?"

"What *plan*?" Anton asked. "What are you up to?"

Illya didn't reply, he just turned on his heel, retreating deeper into the chamber.

"Where are you going?" Anton called after him. He shot a confused glance at the Wanderer, who all but shrugged.

"There's a passage that leads into the citadel," Illya replied. "Aha. Here it is."

"Why are you going into the citadel?" Anton asked, drawing up beside Illya at the mouth of a tunnel, which was lit intermittently with incandescent lights.

"To rescue Ephyra and her sister," Illya replied, as if it were obvious.

Anton laughed. Illya just stared at him coolly. "Wait. You're serious?"

"Of course I'm serious," Illya answered. "As long as Pallas still has control over that girl, he has the god's powers at his disposal. We get them out, and he'll lose his one source of power."

Anton gaped at him. "Do you *really* expect me to believe you've turned on him? After what you did in Behezda?"

Illya gave him a familiar look of disdain. "What I did in Behezda got me a position in Pallas's inner circle, which is what allowed me to do all this."

"You must think I'm really stupid, huh?"

"I don't really care what you think at the moment," Illya replied. "You are free to wait here, or come with me if you like and see for yourself. But I'm going."

"Right," Anton said. "You probably want me to come with you so you can deliver me straight to Pallas."

"I just said I don't care whether you come or not."

"Well, as it happens, I need to get into the citadel, too," Anton said. "So we are coming with you. And you're going to take me to Jude."

"Jude?" Illya echoed in confusion. "You mean that swordsman who's hopelessly in love with you?"

Anton flushed.

"Why would I take you to him? I haven't the faintest idea where he is."

"Don't lie to me," Anton replied fiercely. "I know Pallas has him locked up. I *saw* it."

Locked up and maybe being tortured. Anton swallowed down his fear.

"I have absolutely no idea what you're talking about."

This was stupid. He didn't need Illya to find Jude. He was a Prophet. He closed his eyes, searching for Jude's *esha* again. He let it pull his mind away from the crematorium, from Illya, from his own body, and carry him through space, until he could see it, see *him*.

Jude knelt in a grand foyer, his back to one of the walls. Tall windows stretched above him, letting in the gray light of the sky. He wasn't alone—Hector knelt beside him, along with the Prince of Herat, Beru, Ephyra, and a Herati girl Anton didn't recognize. With a jolt, Anton realized the boy beside her was Evander.

They were all bound, surrounded by a dozen Witnesses, and, strangely, a few Paladin, held at attention in front of a mezzanine balcony, from which Pallas gazed down at them. Anton couldn't hear what was being said—everything came to him indistinct and blurred, like he was listening through a thick glass pane. But then two of the Witnesses seized Jude and dragged him away from the others.

"*No!*" Anton cried, and the image dissolved. He was back in the tunnel with Illya and the Wanderer, his hands curled into tight fists.

"Anton?" the Wanderer said, her hand on his shoulder. Even Illya looked spooked.

"Pallas has them. All of them." He looked at Illya. "Beru and Ephyra, too."

Illya let out a soft curse. "Where?"

"I don't know, some kind of foyer," Anton replied. He tried to recall. "It had tall windows and a balcony overlooking it."

Illya spun on his heel and entered the tunnel.

"Where are you going?" Anton called after him.

"The room you saw is in the Archon's residence," Illya called back. "This tunnel will lead us to the infirmary inside the citadel, so we just need to sneak back to the residence. Although I'm not exactly sure how to get through the citadel without being seen—oh! We can find some Sentry uniforms in the infirmary and disguise ourselves."

"And then what?" Anton demanded.

Illya paused, looking off into the darkness. "I think I might have a plan," he said slowly. "Unfortunately for you, it means you'll have to trust me."

Anton recalled the look on Jude's face as the Witnesses had dragged him away. That grim determination, fire and steel in the face of fear. Whatever Pallas was planning to do with him, he wanted to break him. Kill him, maybe.

"Fine," Anton said, reluctantly pushing the word out. Illya's eyebrows shot up in surprise, as if he hadn't expected Anton to actually agree. "I'll do it."

"You'll trust me?" Illya asked, his golden gaze careful on Anton's face.

Anton felt the Wanderer's curious gaze on him as well. He wrapped his arms around himself, staving off the chill that suddenly staked through him. "No. Never. But I'll go with you."

Illya peered at him through the dark, silent and unmoving for a long moment. Anton could not read the expression on his face. Finally, he nodded. "Then let's not waste any more time."

He started down the tunnel, and after a beat, Anton followed, the Wanderer beside him. He'd risk her life and his own to save Jude. He'd do anything—even follow Illya straight into the jaws of his enemies.

BEFORE

IN THE END, IT WAS THE FEAR OF WHAT THE GOD MIGHT DO TO TEMARA THAT persuaded Ananke. She kissed Temara goodbye in the hut at the edge of the world and went with Pallas.

Their journey lasted many weeks as they sailed across the Pelagos Sea and marched far into the Seti Plain. Ananke spent much of that time dreading what the other Prophets would say when she arrived. She was at turns sorrowful, repentant, and furious at their betrayal.

The other Prophets met them on the banks of the River of Mercy, on the outskirts of Behezda's city.

"We don't have much time," Pallas warned them. "Once the god senses that Ananke has returned, it will come for her."

"Then let's be brief," Nazirah agreed.

"Wait," Ananke said. "I—I need to tell you how sorry I am for causing all this."

Behezda put a hand on Ananke's shoulder. "What you did was foolish. But we would be fools not to see that this is our only option."

"There will be time for recrimination and redress later," Tarseis replied. "Pallas, tell us what we must do to destroy the god."

"The god speaks to us, and only us," Pallas said. "We alone can hear the holy words of our Creator. Not the words of human speech, but the powerful voice of the god that would drive any other person mad. We alone can understand the language of *esha*."

"And so?" Keric asked. "How do we defeat it?"

"By speaking back to it," Pallas replied. "In each of us, there is a piece of the god's *esha*. Alone, that piece of the god's *esha* gives us the power to understand its message. But if we were to combine our powers, we could speak the language of *esha*—of the god—ourselves. Our *esha* could combine to speak a word that could destroy it."

"Speak a word of god," Nazirah repeated, shaking her head. "That is a dangerous plan, Pallas."

"It is our only path if we want to save the world from the god's wrath," Pallas replied.

Uneasily, the others nodded their agreement.

The Seven Prophets let their *esha* call out into the world around them. Each one rang at its own divine frequency, and as the ripples of their *esha* spooled out, they began to layer together, resolving into a single wave of power.

A word that spoke in the voice of the god, the language of its creations.

The Sacred Word called out from the Prophets.

A dark shadow covered the sun. Wind whipped through the plain.

Shadow and light coalesced into a swirling mass.

The god had come.

It roared over the land, descending upon the Prophets like a great, unknowable beast.

And the Seven looked up. Saw the god's destruction coming for them.

They reached up. And with the Sacred Word reverberating between them, they touched the god.

Light and fire.

Pale flames crackled through the air as the pattern of the god's *esha* ripped apart. Its body, built of light and shadow, fell to the earth.

14

BERU

BERU KNELT ON THE COLD MARBLE FLOOR BESIDE EPHYRA.

"I'm glad you attempted to rescue your friends," Pallas said, walking slowly down the line of prisoners. "Now I have more valuable hostages. The Prince of Herat." He touched his palm to the back of the prince's head, just firmly enough to push it down. "And the boy with a curious connection to my favorite pet."

Beru hated the idea of Pallas using Hector against her, almost as much as she hated how he used Ephyra. But they were all at his mercy now. The Witnesses had already dragged the other swordsman, Jude, away. Beru feared to think who might be next.

She glanced at Hector as Pallas stroked his fingers over the back of his neck. Hector shuddered, straining against the Godfire chains on his wrists. A wave of fear and fury washed through Beru. She realized she had missed feeling Hector's emotions, which had been absent these past few months. Their connection strengthened the closer they were to each other.

She'd gotten so used to feeling the god's emotions instead. But

Hector's feelings were different—they didn't feel unnatural, obliterating, absolute. Instead, they were steadying. Familiar. She took in his profile, the stiff set of his jaw, and focused on his feelings as the god's voice rang in her head.

LITTLE MORTAL, the god hissed. NOW IS YOUR CHANCE. STRIKE HIM DOWN.

I'm bound, she reminded it. Her neck stung beneath the cold metal of the Godfire collar.

NO, I AM BOUND, the god replied. YOU COULD BE FREE, IF YOU WEREN'T SO AFRAID. CHAINS CANNOT HOLD A GOD FOR LONG.

Beru shivered. She knew the god spoke the truth, and while it meant the collar, the same was true of the seal binding. It wouldn't hold the god's will forever.

YOU LET THEM CONTROL YOU, EVEN WHEN WE ARE SO MUCH MORE POWERFUL THAN THEY CAN IMAGINE, the god taunted. YOU CONDEMN YOUR FRIENDS TO SUFFER BECAUSE OF YOUR OWN WEAKNESS.

"And you," Pallas said, cupping Ephyra's face. "I think you need to learn your place here."

"Don't," Beru said. "Don't punish her. Punish me. It was my plan."

"Oh, but I am punishing you," Pallas said. He had never made her watch before.

"Wait!" Beru pleaded. "I'll do whatever you ask. Just don't—don't hurt her. Don't hurt any of them."

THERE IS ONLY ONE WAY TO SAVE THEM. KILL HIM.

Beru squeezed her eyes shut, trying to block out the god's thoughts.

KILL HIM AND SET ME FREE, the god commanded. I WILL BE MERCIFUL. I WILL ALLOW THESE OTHER MORTALS TO LIVE, IF YOU LIKE. I WILL PROTECT THEM.

No. She still remembered what it felt like, to be trapped in her body as the god rained destruction down on Behezda. It was a terror she had never known, and it haunted her still. The deep, unfathomable ocean of its rage. Her own utter helplessness, not knowing if the god would smash and shake the world until it broke apart completely. Until everything and everyone she loved was dust beneath the god's limitless power.

No. She wouldn't kill Pallas, wouldn't set the god free. Not for anything.

"You will do exactly as I say, or I will kill each and every one of them," Pallas said. "Just like I killed Illya. I knew you were conspiring together."

Beru stared hard at the floor, willing herself not to look at Ephyra. Illya. He was still out there, somewhere. Had Ephyra been able to revive him before they were captured?

Just as the thought entered her mind, the great doors opened, spilling light into the foyer.

But the person who ascended the grand front steps wasn't Illya. It was a woman who Beru didn't recognize.

But the god clearly did.

BETRAYER, the god spat. THE SEVENTH PROPHET. THE ONE WHO BEGAN THIS.

The woman strode coolly through the doors. She was dressed in a simple dark blue dress, her hair pulled into a sleek knot, yet she was the most elegant woman Beru had ever seen. A chill prickled through Beru as the woman stared down Pallas. There was something about her dark eyes, something piercing about her gaze that was so like Pallas, and yet not.

THE WANDERER.

Beru stared at the Wanderer in shock. Another Prophet? She didn't know why it hadn't occurred to her—that if Pallas still walked the earth, so could any of the other original Prophets.

Beru had seen a lot of impossible things in her life. Her own resurrection. Hector's. The Necromancer King, alive after five hundred years and imprisoned in an oasis in the desert. The return of a murdered god in the ruins of Behezda.

But still she was astonished to see the Wanderer, one of the Seven Prophets who had slain a god and given Grace to humanity, walk casually into the foyer.

The Wanderer's gaze found Pallas's. He stared back, almost expressionless, the stern lines of his face locked into place.

"Pallas," the Wanderer greeted. "It's been a while, hasn't it?"

"Over a hundred years," Pallas agreed. "I assumed you were afraid to face me."

"Me, afraid?" the Wanderer said, a hint of humor in her musical voice. "I'm not the one who forsook my name and took on a new identity just to hide from the others."

"Not that you had a name to forsake."

"You saw to that," the Wanderer replied with a hint of a smile. "A long time ago."

Beru glanced between the two Prophets, unsure what to make of their exchange. Were they allies? Enemies?

"So have you finally returned to bargain for your life?" Pallas asked. "You must know how very long I've waited to kill you."

"No, no," the Wanderer laughed. "I'm afraid you'll have to wait a bit longer. I've come to offer you something you desperately want."

"And what's that?"

"Me," a new voice rang out through the cavernous foyer.

Beru swung her gaze to the balcony above, where a lone figure stood, bathed in the light streaming through the stained-glass windows. Anton.

She heard Hector's sharp intake of breath, and the prince's low murmured, "It's not possible."

A ripple of whispers went through the Witnesses and the Paladin.

"Seize him," Pallas commanded the Paladin. "*Now*."

Anton calmly raised his hands as the Paladin mounted the stairs, surrounding him on the balcony. He gave a slight nod, barely a tilt of his head, and then Beru felt someone behind her. A voice whispered, "Don't react."

Beru held perfectly still.

"I'm going to unlock the collar," Illya said in hushed tones. "Use your power to get everyone else free. There's a ship down at the wharf."

She understood what he was asking. Could she use the god's powers to snap everyone out of the Archon's residence, out of the citadel, and to the ship? And could she do it without unleashing the god entirely?

She wasn't sure. She could feel the god pressing up against the bars of its cage, shaking the seal that kept its will trapped inside her. Using its power would feed it, make its will stronger.

But before she could weigh this danger against the possibility of freedom, she felt Illya's fingers at the back of her neck as he unlocked the collar. It dropped into his waiting hands. The dull pain of the Godfire metal ebbed. In its place, the god's emotions battered at her. Anger and excitement twisted up with her own relief and fear.

"Now," Illya urged. "While the Paladin are occupied."

COME, LITTLE MORTAL. LET'S SEE WHAT YOU CAN DO.

Beru hesitated, panic flaring hot and sharp inside her.

YOU AND I BOTH KNOW I'LL BREAK FREE, ONE WAY OR ANOTHER, the god said. YOU MAY AS WELL SAVE YOUR FRIENDS WHILE YOU CAN.

Beru looked at Ephyra and Hector, who were both staring at Anton up on the balcony, unaware that Illya already had a rescue underway. If Beru was brave enough to do her part.

Beru took a breath and pushed to her feet. With a simple flick of her wrist, she snapped the others' chains.

Pallas's gaze tore back to them, and Beru thought she saw a hint of fear.

In a blink, Khepri and Hector had the two Witnesses beside them pinned to the ground. The others weren't as quick to act—Ephyra and Hassan struggled against three other Witnesses in a flurry of movement. Two more advanced on the Wanderer in the threshold of the foyer.

"Kill them!" Pallas hissed. "If she will not obey me, then kill the others."

No.

Without thinking, Beru threw out a hand. The god's power surged. The Witnesses and Paladin froze, their limbs locking into place. Some of them toppled to the ground, unable to catch their forward movement. Beru realized *she* had frozen them.

Pallas's eyes widened, his gaze locked on Beru. The god's delight hummed through her. Finally, *finally*, they had the upper hand against Pallas. Finally, he was afraid of what they might do next.

A flash of movement caught her eye, and she spotted Anton breaking away from the frozen Paladin, turning on his heel to race away from the foyer and into the corridor.

"Where is he going?" she heard Ephyra ask.

"To find Jude," Illya said from behind her.

Automatically, Beru found Hector's gaze. Fear and ferocity drummed through her, and she knew what Hector wanted to do.

She gave him a slight nod. "Go."

Hector nodded back before sprinting after Anton.

Beru refocused her attention on Pallas.

KILL HIM, the god demanded, its voice a roar in Beru's ears.

She stared into Pallas's cold, blue eyes and felt the god's hatred well up inside her. With it came the desire to use the god's power against Pallas, the way she'd been forced to use it *for* him so many times.

She could feel her control slipping. By the fear in his eyes, she knew Pallas could see it, too.

"Beru," Illya said, his voice nervous behind her.

The wharf. The ship. She had to get everyone there. But inside her, the god's will raged, flooding her with the crushing desire to break Pallas's neck. It would be so easy.

Squeezing her eyes shut, Beru slackened her grip on the god's power so it could not overwhelm her.

The Witnesses and Paladin broke free, suddenly able to move again.

"The Godfire chains!" Pallas barked. "Quickly!"

The Witnesses and Paladin leapt back into action, surrounding Beru and the others. They were weaponless. Defenseless.

Beru was their only chance of making it out.

You are Beru of Medea, she told herself, reaching for the god's power again. The floodgates opened, the god's will storming through her body. *You are Beru of Medea.*

She reached for something, anything, to ground her, and conjured a memory from some sheltered part of her mind. Hector's face in the dark. *I forgive you*, he'd said. *I don't want you to die.*

Beru held the memory in her mind, gripping it like a lifeline as she reached again for the god's power, bracing against the fury that came with it. She threw out a palm and a force burst from her like a wave, crashing against the walls of the foyer and shattering the windows.

She seized the glass shards in midair, suspending them in place, sharp points trained on each Witness and Paladin.

The god's will shrieked in her head, threatening to engulf her. Across the room, Pallas's eyes blazed with fury.

NOW! KILL HIM!

Beru pitched forward, her hands on the cold marble floor, every inch of her screaming to reach out and tear Pallas apart. All she could do was hold herself still on the floor and fight.

"Illya," she gasped. "The collar."

"What?" He dropped to a crouch beside her.

"When I say," she said, and then reached out with the god's power to grab hold of each of her friends and *pulled.*

The world spun. Sand flew into Beru's face. The crash of waves and shouting voices swirled around her. But she couldn't move, could barely think beyond the roar of the god. It flooded her body, bleeding through Pallas's binding and seizing control. And Beru was helpless to stop it.

15

JUDE

BLOOD DRIPPED LIKE RAIN ONTO THE RUG OF THE SITTING ROOM WHERE JUDE knelt. Already he had lost count of how many times the Witnesses had sliced into him. His jaw bloomed hot with fresh bruises.

The scarred Witness held a poker over the flames of the crackling hearth across the room. Jude remembered meeting those cold gray eyes over the clash of their swords. And he remembered seeing him heaped in a bloody mess in the ruins of Behezda the last time they'd met.

It seemed the Witness remembered it, too, judging by how he appeared to relish Jude's pain. Turning slowly, he stalked back to Jude, swinging the hot poker leisurely. "Tell us where the Prophet is."

Jude's vision blurred, the scarred Witness swimming in and out of focus. "I don't know."

His voice sounded very far away.

"You expect me to believe that?"

Jude flicked his gaze at the other Witnesses looming over him. "Why don't you use your stolen Graces to tell if I'm lying?"

His teeth chattered as he spoke. When none of them answered, he choked out a laugh, thick with blood. "Or let me guess—you don't know how, do you? Just because a god ripped out someone's Grace and gave it to you doesn't mean you know the first thing about—"

A roar of pain erupted from Jude's chest as the scarred Witness pressed the red-hot iron against his sternum. It sizzled against his skin, lacing over the old Godfire scars. Jude could barely breathe through the pain. Blood coated his mouth and bile crawled up his throat.

"Keeper of the Word," the scarred Witness said musingly. "You're his protector. His servant. Tell me, Keeper, does your service to the Prophet extend to his bed? Some of the Paladin here seem to think so."

Anger whipped through Jude, swift and white-hot. How dare these Paladin, who had so flagrantly betrayed their duty, turn Jude's devotion, his love, into something base. *They* were the ones who should be ashamed, not Jude. Never again, and never for that.

The scarred Witness pressed the hot poker against his sternum again. A terrible, animal cry burst from Jude's throat, pain seizing his senses.

"I wanted to simply kill you," the scarred Witness said, grabbing a fistful of Jude's hair and wrenching his head back. "But the Immaculate One says you must know where the Prophet is. If I tell him that you don't, do you think he'll let me slit your throat?"

Jude fought for breath, his whole body trembling so violently he felt he might be ripped from his skin. His pulse strained weakly, and he reached for the relief of unconsciousness. Anything to escape the pain.

His eyes fluttered closed. Maybe it wouldn't be so bad. To let go. To stop. Maybe it would be like falling into a dream, like the dreams he had of Anton. He didn't want to die, but that didn't seem so bad.

The closer he floated to unconsciousness, the duller the pain felt. It was already ebbing away.

A clamorous bang cracked through the room, but Jude heard it as if from under water. He was already so far away. It couldn't possibly matter. None of it could.

"Get out of our way," a voice growled. It was familiar—Jude felt a warm flicker of comfort at the sound.

"*You*," the scarred Witness snarled.

More commotion filled the room, flashes of movement and sound. Jude floated above it, a splintering boat tossed by a raging sea. Time seemed to pulse and contract, and Jude didn't know if it was seconds or hours later when a single voice rose above the din, calling out his name.

"*Jude!*"

Hands clutched at Jude's shoulders. He didn't even have the strength to jerk away.

Jude forced his eyes to open. Anton's face, lovely and familiar, swam before him, as if Jude had conjured him. He couldn't help the smile that lifted the corners of his mouth.

Vaguely, he puzzled over why he didn't feel the least bit surprised to see Anton here. And then he realized: This was a dream. He had already slipped into unconsciousness.

"Jude, Jude, we have to go," the specter said hurriedly. Jude felt the chains around his wrists fall away and without thinking, he raised a hand to touch Anton's face.

The specter stilled.

"I dreamed about finding you," Jude said hazily.

The specter let out a shaking breath, its dark eyes wide. Its hand cupped Jude's, holding it against its cheek. "I know you did, Jude."

The crash of steel rang out around them, and the specter blinked.

"Can you stand?"

Jude felt pressure at his side as the specter tried to lift him to his feet. Jude stumbled, his arms wrapped around the specter's waist, staring up at it.

"Hector!" the specter cried, and a moment later there were more hands hauling Jude upright.

"He's really out of it," the specter said. "I think he lost a lot of blood."

"Anton," Jude said. There was something important to tell him, something Jude needed to say. He grasped for the words, but they dissipated like smoke.

He opened his eyes. For a moment Jude thought he was back in the burned-down mausoleum, abandoned by Hector, waking to find the most beautiful boy he'd ever seen kneeling over him.

"Hey, hey, don't do this," Anton's voice said, close by Jude's ear. "Stay awake, Jude. Stay with me."

Tears spilled from Anton's eyes as Jude reached up to touch the freckles scattered like stars across his cheeks.

And then Jude closed his eyes again and let everything slip away.

16

EPHYRA

THE SEA WIND HOWLED OVER EPHYRA AS SHE PICKED HERSELF OFF THE SAND and took stock of her surroundings. She was on a small strip of beach, surrounded by Pallas's other prisoners—there was Prince Hassan, being helped to his feet by the Herati girl, and just beyond them the fearful boy with blue eyes was sprawled in the sand beside the woman Ephyra had once known as Mrs. Tappan.

Down the beach, Ephyra spotted Beru. Heart leaping into her throat, she sprinted across the sand.

She'd done it. She'd gotten them all out of the citadel.

But something was wrong. In her relief, Ephyra hadn't realized, but as she neared Beru, unease pitted her gut. The way her sister held herself, the blankness of her expression—Ephyra recognized it from that day in Behezda. From those first, terrible moments after she'd realized that she'd resurrected a god inside her sister.

The same fear and despair clutched at her heart now, only it was darkened by the knowledge of exactly what the god was capable of.

In front of her, Illya lay unmoving in the sand. With careful, measured motions, the god who wore Beru's face raised a hand and lifted Illya's limp body into the air.

"No. No, no, no," Ephyra gasped. Illya remained suspended before her, his head lolling back, something clutched in his hands.

The Godfire collar.

Ephyra could feel the others behind her tense as they all came to the same realization—that once again they were at the mercy of a vengeful god.

Beru opened her mouth, and that ancient, terrible voice came out. "YOU SHOULD HAVE TAKEN MY OFFER WHILE YOU COULD, LITTLE MORTAL."

It sounded as if it was talking to itself. To Beru.

"I WOULD HAVE SPARED YOUR FRIENDS."

Ephyra went cold as the god slowly closed Beru's fist. Illya's body jerked in the air. His eyes flew open as he let out a terrible choking sound and began to thrash.

"No!" Ephyra cried, fear pumping through her blood as she reached out instinctively to Illya.

The god's gaze snapped toward her.

"Beru, it's me," Ephyra said. Her voice shook, but she held her ground. "You have to fight it. You *can* fight it."

"YOUR SISTER IS NOT IN CONTROL."

"I know you can hear me, Beru," Ephyra said. She darted a glance behind her at the others, willing one of them to understand what they needed to do. Get the Godfire collar while the god was distracted. "I know you're in there, fighting."

The god's hand dropped. Illya plummeted back down into the sand. The god went still, Beru's face warped as if in pain as she collapsed in on herself, trembling.

It was *working*. Beru was fighting, pulling at the god's will to regain control.

"Listen to my voice," Ephyra instructed. From the corner of her eye, she saw Hassan darting toward Illya's crumpled form. "Listen to me."

The god let out a terrible roar and waved a hand, batting the prince down into the sand.

"*Hassan!*" the Herati girl shrieked.

"YOU WILL NOT BIND ME," the god raged. "I WILL NOT BE PUT IN CHAINS AGAIN."

Ephyra trembled. "Beru—"

"SILENCE!"

Ephyra opened her mouth to speak again, but no sound came out. She tried to scream, but the god had taken her voice.

"Beru!"

It was Hector's voice, calling from the top of a rocky outcropping that overlooked the strip of beach.

Ephyra turned and saw him lurching over the rocks toward them, Jude slumped between him and Anton's smaller frame. The trio stopped, taking in the scene before them. Hector foisted Jude onto Anton, who stumbled under the weight, and took a careful step toward Beru.

And suddenly he was jerked off his feet, up into the air. Ephyra winced, waiting for him to be tossed to the ground as the prince had, but instead he hung there, suspended. Beru crumpled, hands clenched into fists, shaking.

"I can feel you in there, Beru," Hector said, his voice rising above the wind. "I can feel you fighting."

He dropped suddenly, plummeting toward the sand. Ephyra stifled a gasp, but before his body hit the ground, he stopped, hovering a few inches in the air.

"It's all right," he soothed, his tone smooth and even despite the pallor of his face. "You can do this. You can fight it."

The god let out a chilling sound, a groan like the earth shifting.

Ephyra knew her window of action was small. She bolted across the sand to Illya. He was lying on his side, his hands tucked beneath him. Ephyra took his shoulder, turning him over. He groaned, blinking open his eyes.

There was something soft and hazy in his expression as he looked up at her. "Ephyra?"

"The collar," she replied.

She stole a glance back at Beru. The god was on its knees now, Beru's whole body clenched tight like a fist. Hector was on his feet again, approaching slowly.

"Quickly," Ephyra urged. Illya shifted, rolling over and holding up the Godfire collar. Ephyra had the strangest urge to kiss him, but instead she just took the collar and climbed to her feet.

Hector was right beside Beru now, a hand clutched at her shoulder. Whatever he was doing, it seemed to be helping Beru seize back control.

But who knew how long it would last?

Ephyra sprinted across the sand toward them, gripping the collar tight. Hector's gaze caught hers over Beru's crumpled form.

This close, Ephyra could hear the sounds the god was making—little choked-off moans of agony, its whole body trembling.

No, not the god. It was *Beru*.

"Hector!" Beru cried, and then bit off the sound into a high shriek of pain.

Ephyra threw herself to her knees, cradling Beru's head in her lap.

"I've got you," Ephyra said soothingly as she lifted the collar to Beru's throat with shaking hands. "We've got you."

At last the collar fastened around her neck. Beru let out a gusting breath and then went still.

Ephyra raised her eyes to meet Hector's. "What did you do?"

He shook his head. "I'm not sure. I just—I felt her in there. Her feelings, her *esha*."

Ephyra was aware of the strange connection between Hector and Beru. The result of how she herself had killed him all those months ago. The memory of that day hung heavy in the silence between them.

"Not to interrupt what I'm sure is an emotional moment," Illya's voice cut in drily from behind them, "but I'm pretty sure those are Paladin heading our way."

He was sitting up in the sand, clutching his ribs and staring down the beach. She followed his gaze to find more than a dozen swordsmen dressed in dark blue cloaks trampling over the beach toward them, unnaturally fast.

"All right, everyone up and onto the ship," the Wanderer called out, strangely chipper.

Hector gathered Beru in his arms and lifted her easily. Ephyra and the others followed, stumbling away from the Paladin closing in. The Wanderer led the way to the dock. Ephyra didn't dare glance behind her as she trailed the others over the rickety wooden planks to board the ship that floated beyond.

"We'll be setting sail immediately, if you don't mind," the Wanderer said mildly to one of the ship's crewmen as they boarded.

"Aye, aye," the sailor replied, and strode off barking orders to the others.

"Let's get her inside," the Wanderer said, turning to Hector and Beru. She glanced over her shoulder at another sailor. "Take them to the infirmary." She indicated Hassan and Anton, who had Jude's unconscious form propped between them.

Hector turned to Ephyra. "You need to go with them."

"With them?" she repeated. "But Beru—"

"Jude needs you," Hector said. "He's in bad shape. You need to heal him."

Ephyra gritted her teeth. The swordsman didn't matter. Beru did.

"You owe me," Hector said darkly. "Heal Jude and consider it a debt paid."

She let out a breath and gave one short nod. She *did* owe Hector. For more than just taking his life. He'd also saved hers in Behezda. And she owed the rest of them, too. Hassan, Jude, Anton. Even Illya. Despite how disastrous their help had been, they had ultimately freed Ephyra and Beru from Pallas.

"Fine," she said, and with a last glance at Beru, she hurried after Hassan and Anton.

As Ephyra entered the infirmary, Anton looked up, wild-eyed and frantic. Ephyra recognized the expression, had felt that same delirious panic herself. His arms and chest were wet and dark with blood. Jude's blood.

The swordsman lay in a ragged heap on one of the thin, narrow beds. His arms were torn up and bloody, his face a mess of bruises. Burned skin blistered his neck and chest, and one particularly deep gash down his torso continued oozing blood. Ephyra had grown used to death, but her kills were always clean. Nothing like the ruin that the Witnesses had made of Jude.

"Can you heal him?" Anton asked, voice shaking, hands balled in the sheets beside Jude.

Ephyra knelt at Jude's side, breathing through the nausea that gripped her stomach. She wasn't really made for healing. Killing came more naturally. She looked up at Anton, throat tight. Jude was minutes from bleeding out on this table if she couldn't heal him.

"You can use my blood," Anton said. "My *esha*."

Ephyra shook her head. "The amount that I would need to use . . . it could kill you."

"I'll risk it," Anton replied brusquely.

"I want to do this right," she said, realizing the truth of those words as she said them.

"It doesn't matter if it's *right*. It just needs to—" He didn't finish, but Ephyra got what he was trying to say.

"Trust me," Ephyra said, meeting his furious gaze. "It matters."

Pushing down her own fear and panic she got up to rummage through the infirmary's stores of dried plant cuttings until she found a few jars of macerated leaves and cactus flesh. Ephyra was not well versed in the different kinds of cuttings healers employed for different purposes, but *esha* was *esha*, and any kind of plant had at least some that she could use.

She worked quickly, silently, pressing the dried cuttings to Jude's bare skin. She didn't know the patterns of binding that the other healers used to guide *esha*, so she just put the paste on Jude's pulse points— wrists, throat, heart.

Closing her eyes, she focused on Jude's pulse as it pumped blood through his body. She tried pushing the *esha* from the cuttings into Jude, but she couldn't grasp it. It was like water running through her hands.

Anton glared at her as she struggled, and Ephyra could practically taste the anxious energy coming off him.

"Can you possibly go loom somewhere else?" she asked irritably.

"If this doesn't work—" Anton said.

Jude would die. She could feel his *esha* seeping out of him, helpless to staunch it.

She met Anton's gaze and could see in his exhausted eyes what it would do to him. She knew that kind of grief. She had lived it.

"She can do it," Illya's voice spoke quietly from the doorway. "Let her."

Ephyra and Anton both whirled to face him.

"What are *you* doing here?" Anton demanded.

Illya lifted one shoulder in a lazy shrug. "You were so worried about your swordsman earlier. I just wanted to make sure he was all right."

"Liar," Anton spat. "Get *out*."

Illya held up his hands and started to back out the door.

"Wait," Ephyra said. "Don't—don't go."

Only after the words left her lips was she able to look at him. His face was a facade of calm, but there was a glimmer of curiosity in his golden eyes. He tilted his head slightly, and she could almost see him thinking, solving the puzzle of why she wanted him to stay.

"I need your help," Ephyra said in a low voice, gaze dropping to her own hands, clutched in the bloody sheets. "Like you did at the Red Gate."

He looked, for one brief moment, earnestly surprised. Then he smirked. "I had no idea my encouragement meant so much to you. You should've said."

Irritation crackled under Ephyra's skin, but before she could answer, Anton pushed away from Jude's bedside, prowling toward Illya. "Help her, or I will throw you off this ship. Understand?"

Ephyra blinked, oddly impressed. She'd never seen Anton threaten anyone, and she still remembered the first reunion he'd had with Illya, how fearful he'd been.

Illya looked a little impressed, too, but he just shrugged again and brushed past Anton to kneel beside Ephyra.

With surprising gentleness, he placed Ephyra's hands on Jude, one hand over his heart, the other at his wrist. "You can do this." His voice was soft in her ear. "You healed me. You can do anything."

Ephyra released a shaky breath, closing her eyes as she focused on Illya's voice and the gentle pressure of his hands on hers, swallowing down her annoyance at how effective he was at calming her. She felt focused, more sure as she curled her hands around Jude's wrist, sensing the fluttering pulse beneath her fingertips.

And then she felt it. The *esha* from the cuttings brushed against Jude's *esha*. Ephyra didn't try to pull at the energy, didn't force it the way she had so many times before. She just held it gently, guiding it, opening up a new pathway and letting the *esha* flow into Jude, mixing with his, spreading through each vein and capillary. Soon it was like the *esha* was guiding itself, Ephyra just a conduit, directing it to soothe and repair the damaged flesh. She felt Jude grow warm beneath her hands, and distantly she heard a soft gasp from Anton.

She opened her eyes. Jude's wounds were closed, only the blood left to show they'd been there at all. His bruises were faded. Color had returned to his face, and his breath came slow and even.

She sagged backward, exhaustion and relief suddenly hitting her like a bag of rocks. Illya, she realized, had already moved away from her. "He just needs rest now."

"When will he wake up?" Anton asked, moving forward to take Jude's limp hand.

"I don't know," Ephyra said. "Hours? Days? He'll live, though. His wounds are healed, but his body is still reacting to the trauma." She shrugged. "I'm sorry. I'm really not an expert at this."

Anton nodded, his gaze returning to Jude, something soft in his expression that was hard for Ephyra to look at.

"Thank you," he said quietly, touching his thumb between Jude's eyebrows. "Thank you for saving him."

Ephyra didn't know what to say. She gave a stilted nod.

"I can take you to see Beru now," Illya offered.

Ephyra let him lead her down the corridor. A strange sort of tension grew between them as they walked in silence.

Illya had come through for them. He'd put his life in her hands. And he'd helped her, again, just now in the infirmary.

Despite all that, she still didn't know if she could trust him. There was a persistent question still nagging at her, one he'd never answered.

"Why are you helping us?" she asked as Illya started to climb the stairs up to the next deck.

He paused, looking over his shoulder at her.

"I just don't get it," she said.

"No," he agreed. "You wouldn't."

He resumed climbing the stairs. Ephyra followed.

"Did Pallas do something to you?" Ephyra asked. "You want revenge or something?"

He didn't answer.

"Is it guilt?" she asked. "Because of what you did to Anton?"

He gave her a wan smile that did not reach his eyes. "Beru is right down the hall."

She searched his face, but found nothing, no crack in the facade that would tell her whether she was getting close. He wasn't going to answer her.

Without another word, Illya turned and descended back down the stairs.

Ephyra took a breath. Beru was here, safe. Everything else could wait.

Her heart tripped in her chest as she approached the door. Before she could knock, it swung open and Hector stepped outside.

They stared at each other.

"Jude?" he asked, slightly desperate.

Ephyra nodded. "He'll be all right. He's resting."

He gave her a jerky nod. "Thank you."

He stepped aside, and Ephyra rushed into the room without a backward glance.

She was greeted by the sight of Beru sitting peacefully on the bed, collar firmly back on.

Ephyra threw her arms around her, breathing deeply for what felt like the first time in days. "We did it. We really escaped."

Beru pulled back, a familiar shadow of worry on her face. She shook her head. "We almost didn't."

Ephyra took her hand, pressing it between her palms. "But we *did*."

Beru dropped her gaze. "The god—It's getting stronger. When it took over just now . . . I didn't think I would be able to overpower it. Every time I use its powers, its will gets a little stronger. We're running out of time."

Ephyra brushed her fingers through her sister's hair and patted the side of her head. "What's new? We're always running out of time, aren't we?"

Beru let out a rueful smile. She picked at a loose thread of her sheets. "I suppose that's true."

"We'll find a way," Ephyra promised. "Whatever it takes."

17

ANTON

EIGHT HOURS HAD PASSED, AND JUDE STILL HADN'T WOKEN. ANTON CLUTCHED his limp, feverishly hot hand, watching the rise and fall of his chest as he breathed. A plate of food sat by his elbow, ignored.

"Anton?" Evander's hesitant voice called.

Anton tore his gaze from Jude's unmoving face to take in Evander, looking frail and lost in the doorway, his usual cheer and effervescence dimmed.

"Are you all right?" Evander asked.

Anton reached for a reassuring smile. "I'm all right. Are you?"

Evander approached slowly, sitting tentatively beside Anton, facing Jude. "You don't need to worry about me."

Anton recognized a deflection when he heard one. "Why did the Hierophant have you? What were you doing in Pallas Athos?"

Evander blinked his wide blue eyes at Anton. "After you left Endarrion, a group of Witnesses turned up, looking for you. I guess some of the people at Lady Bellrose's party remembered you two and remembered that I was the one who'd brought you."

"And they sold you out to the Witnesses?" Anton guessed.

Evander nodded. "They . . . once they knew Pallas had returned, most of the city declared its allegiance to him and Pallas Athos. Endarrion merchants like my father rely heavily on trade with Pallas Athos. I guess they all decided profit was worth more than my life. And more than the Graced in Endarrion, too."

Anton let out a heavy sigh. "I'm sorry, Evander. I'm sorry we ever got you involved in all this."

Evander's face twisted into a frown. It wasn't an expression Anton was used to seeing on him. "I don't blame you. Not a bit. I just wish that there was something I could do to help you."

Anton looked at his clear blue eyes and messy, dark hair, and felt that perhaps he'd never really been fair to Evander. He'd thought he'd known everything there was to know about this boy with all his beautiful clothes and frivolous stories, but there had always been more beneath the surface that Anton hadn't bothered to examine.

"You helped me," Anton assured him. "Before, in Endarrion, you helped us get Jude's sword back. And before that, you were always a good friend to me. I'm just sorry I was never a very good friend to you."

Evander looked a little hopeful and a little sad. "I always knew you were holding yourself back from me. When we first met, I liked you so much and there were times when I felt like you liked me, too, and then there would be this—this *wall* that you put up. Even when you were vulnerable it was . . . I don't want to say it was an act, because I don't think you were lying. But you only let me see that side of you when it suited you."

Anton felt himself go a little stiff, realizing now for the first time that Evander hadn't been as oblivious as he'd seemed and that Anton had been so transparent.

"I do care about you, Evander," Anton said. "I did back then, too. I think I didn't even realize how much at the time. I'm sorry."

Evander shook his head with a little smile. "Don't be sorry. Just . . ." He took a breath, nodding his head toward Jude's sleeping form. "Try and do better this time."

Anton followed his gaze, curling his fingers into the sheets. There were things he couldn't tell Jude, things he had to keep from him, but he'd already decided the minute he'd seen him, bruised and broken in his dreams, that he was done staying away.

A knock sounded from the doorway, and Anton and Evander both turned to face the Wanderer.

"I hope I'm not interrupting," she said mildly. "Some of the others are waiting on the upper deck. They have a lot of questions. I thought maybe they would want to hear answers from you."

The idea of facing everyone when Jude was still unconscious, still vulnerable, made Anton feel sick. "Can't you talk to them?"

The Wanderer just gave him a look that was all too easy to interpret. *This is your responsibility now, Anton. This is what being a Prophet means.*

"I can stay with him," Evander offered gently. "So he won't be alone."

Anton swallowed down his protests and gave Evander a brusque nod before pushing himself to his feet. With a last, lingering look at Jude, he followed the Wanderer through the corridor and up the stairs to where the others waited in a sitting room.

Ephyra leaned against the wall in one corner, arms crossed tight over her chest. Hassan sat beside Hector at the table. And to Anton's displeasure, Illya sat across from them. All four of them turned to look at Anton and the Wanderer as they entered.

"So," Ephyra said, breaking the silence. "What's the plan? I'm assuming there is a plan. Because we've spent nearly two and a half months under Pallas's control, and while I'm very excited to be free, we have another huge problem to deal with."

"The god," Illya said, unnecessarily.

A thick silence filled the room, and Anton knew he wasn't the only one remembering Behezda.

"We have to kill it," Hassan said bluntly. "I mean, it's the only way, right?"

"The Hierophant said it took Seven Prophets to kill it," Hector replied. "I think we're a few short."

"He was right," the Wanderer said. She looked at Anton.

Anton took a breath. "That's why we're going to find the other Prophets."

Silence descended on the room. Just a few short months ago, the idea of any one of the Seven Prophets still walking the earth would have sounded absurd. But now they were sitting right in front of one. And had just escaped from another.

"Well, where are they?" Hassan asked finally. He looked to the Wanderer. "You're one of them, aren't you? You must have some idea where the others are."

The Wanderer shook her head. "Unfortunately, I don't. There were . . . far more issues between us than we ever let on to you mortals. They all believed I meddled too much in human affairs. One of their many grievances against me."

"Can't you just scry for them?" Ephyra asked, waving a hand vaguely.

"It's not that simple," Anton replied. "Prophets can hide their *esha*. It's how we've avoided being found by Pallas this whole time. How we're continuing to hide from him now—and hiding you all, too."

"So *that's* why Jude couldn't find you," Hector said, almost to himself.

Anton turned to him, startled. "What?"

"Jude hired these bounty hunters to track you down and . . ." He trailed off. "You know what, never mind. How do we find the Prophets?"

Anton paused, his gaze still locked on Hector, already knowing what he would say the moment Anton brought up Kerameikos.

"There's a certain place," Anton said carefully. "It has . . . echoes of the Prophets' Graces. We think if we scry *there*, then we might be able to sense a trace of the Prophets' *esha* and use it to track them down."

Hector was shaking his head before the words were fully out of Anton's mouth. "No. No, no, no. We can't go there."

"We don't have a choice," Anton replied testily. "The Circle of Stones is the only place that will give us a chance of finding the Prophets."

"The Order of the Last Light has decided that Jude and I are oath-breakers," Hector replied. "Kerameikos is too dangerous—and not just for the two of us. We have no idea if the Paladin there are loyal to Pallas."

"The Guard wouldn't turn against—" Hassan began.

"Yarik did," Hector said darkly. "And even if the rest of the Guard is in Kerameikos, even if they haven't joined Pallas, Anton and Jude abandoned them in the middle of nowhere. I wouldn't exactly count on their support."

"Well, it sounds like we don't have a choice," Ephyra said.

Hector pushed toward Anton, beseeching. "Come on, you know how much this puts Jude in danger. You're willing to risk that?"

Anton looked away. He *wasn't* willing to risk Jude. And that was exactly why they needed to go to Kerameikos. But he couldn't tell Hector the truth—not without revealing the real reason he wanted to find the Prophets, and what would happen if they failed. "I won't let anything happen to him."

"You're going to protect him?" Hector asked disbelievingly. "Against a hundred Paladin?"

"Yes."

"You two don't even need to come off the ship," Hassan interjected. "We can go in alone."

"No."

Anton's breath caught in his throat at the sound of Jude's voice. He released it shakily, heart pounding, before he turned toward Jude, who hovered stiffly in the doorway, his gaze locked on Anton.

"If you're going into Kerameikos then I'm coming with you."

Anton's stomach swooped at the sight of him, whole and healed. He couldn't speak, rooted to the spot, overwhelmed with the realization of how much he'd missed him. How much it had cost Anton to stay away.

"It's good to see you back on your feet," Hector said warmly, breaking the tense silence.

"Thank you," Jude replied, flashing him a brief, tired smile. "If it's all right with everyone, I'd like to talk to Anton alone."

Anton heard the others filter out of the room, but his gaze remained trained on Jude. The moment felt fragile, like a snowflake that would melt on Anton's fingers if he tried to touch it. Every part of him longed to cross the space between them. Yet he couldn't move, couldn't trust himself to take those last few steps without collapsing.

Hector lingered in the doorway, glancing at them warily. His hesitation rankled. Anton was grateful that Hector had helped them escape the citadel, but now part of him resented the fact that Hector was right back at Jude's side, after everything he'd done to him. Even if Jude forgave him for it, Anton certainly hadn't.

With a last warning glance, Hector retreated from the room, closing the door behind him.

The sound of the door closing broke Anton's last shred of self-restraint. Between one breath and the next, he flung himself across the room, wrapping his arms around Jude and burying his face against his neck. He let out a shuddering breath. Jude was warm and solid in his arms, more intoxicating than any dream. Anton felt drunk with desperate, terrified relief. He'd known that Jude was all right after Ephyra healed him, but knowing it and *believing* it were two separate things. Only now, with Jude's breath tickling his ear, did he feel the worry seep away.

"It's *you*," Jude said at last, his arms stiff at his sides as Anton clung to him. "It's really—" He cut himself off with a ragged breath. "I thought I was dreaming."

His voice sounded quiet and far away, like it had when Anton had found him being tortured by the Witnesses. He still hadn't moved, hadn't returned Anton's embrace, and for the first time since laying eyes on him, broken and bloodied on the floor, doubt crept behind Anton's ribs.

He pulled back, searching Jude's face. "It's really me."

Jude didn't meet his gaze, his brow furrowing. "I knew you were alive. I—I felt it. Hector and Hassan didn't believe me. Hector said . . ." Jude stopped, seeming to gather himself. "He said if you were alive, that you would've found us. Scried for us—for me."

There was hurt in his voice that he wasn't even trying to mask, and Anton understood suddenly, painfully, why he was so reluctant to reach for Anton the way Anton had reached for him.

"I did scry for you," Anton said. "That's how I knew Pallas had you. That's why I came for you."

"Two months, nine days, and four hours." Jude's voice was so quiet, Anton wasn't sure he'd heard him correctly.

"What?"

Jude looked up, and the tempest of his gaze knocked the breath from Anton's chest. "*Two months*, nine days, and *four hours*. I had no idea where you were. You were just gone and I—I dreamed of you. And I *hoped* and I—"

"They weren't just dreams," Anton said as steadily as he could. "That was really me. I walked into your dreams and told you . . . as much as I could tell you."

Jude's mouth fell open as he took a floundering step back. "You . . . walked into my dreams?"

Anton nodded. "The Wanderer taught me how. I wanted to tell you that I was safe, that you didn't need to worry. I never knew if you believed me so I just . . . I kept coming back. Every night, nearly."

"Every—" Jude cut himself off, hiding his face in his hand. He looked overwhelmed, angry. A little mortified. Anton wanted to take him in his arms again, to soothe him, but he couldn't make himself reach out if there was even a chance Jude might rebuff him.

"It was torture," Jude said at last, his voice muffled in his palm. "Seeing you and thinking it wasn't real. Like my own mind was taunting me."

Anton's chest lurched with guilt. He had known what he was doing to himself, going to Jude in his dreams. He hadn't even thought about what he was doing to Jude. "I couldn't stay away. I didn't—I didn't know it would be like that."

"What do you mean?" Jude asked.

Anton's lips parted as he tried to put into words how agonizing the past ten weeks had been. But how could he describe something he'd never, in his seventeen years, felt before now? A ceaseless ache, like someone had reached inside him and pulled out a piece of his heart. He'd never let himself miss anyone before, but with Jude it hadn't been a choice. It had just been *there*, the fixed point around which the rest of his thoughts turned, the rocky shore that his heart crashed into again and again.

He shook his head. Even now, standing inches away from Jude, he felt that same longing pull at him.

The storm in Jude's eyes returned. "I would have gone with you. Wherever you needed to go, whatever you needed to do, I would've—"

"I know," Anton said. "But there was something I needed to do, and I needed to do it alone."

Pain blossomed on Jude's face like a bruise. Anton remembered what he had said to Jude the night they'd left the Guard. *I can't do this without you.* Maybe it was cruel to take that back now, but Anton would rather be cruel than tell Jude the truth.

"If you . . ." Jude's voice shook. "If you really didn't need me . . ."

Anton couldn't stand the hurt in Jude's eyes, knowing that he was the one who'd put it there. But neither could he explain that he *did* need Jude. More than he'd ever needed anyone. And that was exactly why he'd had to stay away from him.

"It was just . . . a Prophet thing," he said. "The Wanderer was teaching me how to use my powers, to control them. It wasn't that I didn't need you, Jude, it was just that I needed to . . . focus."

Jude's brow creased. "And I'm what—a distraction?"

"Yes, actually." Anton reached up and brushed a strand of Jude's hair away from his face. "You were all I thought about as it was."

Jude flushed a lovely pink that made Anton lose all sense and lean in to kiss him.

With a sharp noise like a breath being punched from his chest, Jude caught Anton's wrist, reeling back. "You still shouldn't have left me."

I had to, Anton didn't say.

"I haven't forgiven you."

"Oh," Anton replied. "So you don't want to kiss me."

Jude's gaze dropped to Anton's mouth. "No."

A smirk tugged at the corner of Anton's lips. "Haven't I told you you're no good at bluffing?"

"Anton," Jude said, sounding pained.

Anton softened. "I'm sorry. I mean it. I know that I hurt you and if you can't forgive me or if you need time . . . I'll be here. I promise."

He held Jude's gaze, hope welling in his chest despite himself. When Jude didn't reply, Anton swallowed down his disappointment, mustered a rueful smile, and started to retreat.

And Jude, at last, reached for him. It was just a hand on Anton's elbow, but it settled the unease that had gnawed at him since the moment he'd decided to go after Jude. Or, if he was being honest, since the moment he'd decided to stay away from him in the first place.

"I do," Jude said haltingly, tense with the thrum of nervous energy.

"You do what?" Anton asked, heart leaping into his threat. *Forgive me? Need time?*

"Want to kiss you."

Anton's chest fluttered at the simple admission, and the raw desire on Jude's face. Without thinking, he leaned in again, and this time Jude let him. His mouth was soft and sweet, and Anton had missed it more than he thought possible. All those dreams had been nothing but a pale shadow.

But even as Anton reveled in the kiss, he could feel how careful Jude's touch was, like if he held too fast Anton might slip through his grasp.

Or maybe Jude was only responding to Anton's hesitation. Because as much as Anton wanted nothing more than to sink into the warmth blooming between them, he couldn't quiet the thought that festered inside him like an old wound, scarred over. The thought that said that anything worth having could be taken from him. That it was better to have nothing at all.

———————————

Anton knocked gently on the doorframe of Beru's cabin, peeking through the half-open door.

"You can come in, Anton," Beru called from the bed, where she sat with her knees tucked against her chest.

She watched him with careful eyes as he entered. After what Anton had seen on the beach, he would be lying if he said he wasn't a little apprehensive to be in a room alone with Beru, but he was determined not to put off this conversation.

"How is he?" Beru asked. "The swordsman?"

"He's fine," Anton answered. "Ephyra healed him right up."

The rest of their reunion had been cut short when Jude's stomach had insistently reminded him that he'd spent the last four days locked in the prisoners' tower. Anton had taken him to the ship's mess hall, offering to meet him back in their cabin when he was done. Anton took it as a good sign that Jude had readily agreed.

"I'm glad," Beru replied. "Ephyra told me how worried you were."

"And you?" Anton asked. "Are you all right?"

Beru let out a long exhale. "I'm . . . better."

Anton hesitantly sat beside her on the edge of the bed. A smile crept onto her face, and she shook her head.

"What?"

She laughed. "I believe the last time we spoke, you were a server at a taverna and I was squatting in a crypt. Now look at us."

Now they were two of the most powerful beings in the world. When Anton thought about it like that, it seemed absolutely absurd. He cracked a smile.

"I trust you, Anton," she told him. "I did back then, too. I don't really know why, but I . . . I think I'm right to trust you."

"I trust you, too," Anton said. The first time they'd met, Beru had offered him nothing more and nothing less than the truth of her worst fear. The past she and Ephyra had every reason to conceal. She had asked only for his help in return.

This conversation felt a little like that one.

"The god is getting stronger," Beru said. "Every day it takes more and more out of me to keep it shackled. Pallas's binding won't last forever, so whatever it is you're planning, you need to do it fast."

"Do they know?" he asked. "Hector and Ephyra. Have you told them, or anyone else?"

"They know," Beru said. "But they don't—They'll probably try to convince you that there's some way to stop the god without hurting me. So I'm asking you—because I *do* trust you, Anton—not to listen to them. Kill the god however you can, as quickly as you can. Whatever it takes."

Her brown eyes met his, and Anton saw all her fear and grief. She would sacrifice herself, if it kept the world safe.

"Promise me," she said.

Anton swallowed. He couldn't promise, not this. He couldn't face her, couldn't see how selfless, how brave she was, how she'd stared down death again and again and didn't flinch. He could only see his own selfishness reflected back at him.

She was waging a war in her own body, keeping the god and its destruction at bay with every breath she took. All she wanted was for it to end.

And Anton couldn't give that to her. Not now. Not yet. Not without giving up the only thing he couldn't stand to lose.

"All right," he said, knowing it was a lie even as he said it. "I promise."

BEFORE

THE GOD LAY DEAD BEFORE THE SEVEN PROPHETS, BUT THE SACRED WORD remained. They could each feel its power, calling out across the plain in echoes.

"We must destroy it," Behezda said.

"No," Nazirah argued. "What if the god returns? We should keep it."

"It is too powerful," Tarseis said. "We must hide it. Bury it."

"How?" Endarra asked.

"We must put it into a vessel," Pallas said. He flicked a hand, and out of the shadows of the ruins, a group of his acolytes appeared. Bound between them was Temara, straining against their grasp.

Ananke froze. "What is this? What is she doing here?"

"This girl is the reason we are here," Pallas said. He spoke not just to Ananke but to the other Prophets, too. "Perhaps the god needed to be slayed. But your disobedience cannot go unpunished."

At the sight of Ananke, Temara redoubled her struggle, fighting hard to get to her.

"What are you doing?" Ananke demanded. "Let her go at once!"

Pallas waved a hand. Glowing, white light spilled from it.

Ananke felt a tug on the power of the Sacred Word. Pallas was drawing it out of her, out of the other Prophets.

The light circled around Pallas's hands for a moment before surrounding Temara. She fell to her knees as the acolytes released her. The pale light grew brighter until Ananke could no longer see Temara.

"What are you doing to her!" Ananke demanded, hot tears racing down her cheeks. "Let her go!"

She realized one of the others—Tarseis—was holding her back. A low hum filled the air as the pale light contracted into Temara, and instead of the dark, sea-green eyes Ananke loved so much, all she could see was white light.

And then the light vanished and Temara collapsed.

"Temara!" Ananke screamed, and with all the strength she had, she wrenched away from Tarseis and raced over to Temara.

"She is perfectly fine," Pallas said. "Her *esha* has been knitted to that of the Sacred Word. Should we ever need it again, it will be a simple matter of unlocking it from her—or from her descendants, I suppose, as she is not immortal as we are."

Ananke threw herself to the ground beside Temara, cradling her carefully. She could see the rise and fall of Temara's chest, could feel the aching vibrations of her *esha*, now fused with something that howled and shook Ananke like a storm. The Word.

"Of course, unlocking the Sacred Word will kill her," Pallas said. "But that is a price that we will have to accept, should the need arise."

Ananke wept, burying her tearstained face in Temara's hair.

"Pallas, surely we don't need to do this," Behezda began. "Surely there is some other way to protect the Word."

"It is done," Pallas said, in a tone that made it clear he would not discuss it further. Ananke could hear his footsteps approaching, standing over the two of them.

"Give her to me," Pallas said softly.

Ananke looked up at him through her tears. "Why did you do this?"

"Because you must learn," Pallas said. "Just because the Creator is dead does not mean our hearts are our own. *We* are the gods now, Ananke, and we must remain pure and unshackled to the mortals we rule."

"I don't want to be a god," Ananke said through tears.

"Then leave us," Pallas said coldly. "Deny your right to rule. I will have your name struck from the world, and no person in our Prophetic Cities will ever speak it again. No city will bear it. You will live an immortal life, the same as the rest of us, but you will be a ghost."

"And Temara?" Ananke asked.

"Temara has a duty, even if you refuse yours," Pallas said. "She is the Keeper of the Sacred Word. And her child will be Keeper of the Word, too. And their children. She was meant to be a sacrifice to the god. And now her sacrifice will be our safeguard should the god ever rise again."

II

THE EDGE
OF THE WORLD

18

HASSAN

HASSAN COULDN'T SLEEP. IT HAD BEEN TWO DAYS SINCE THEIR ESCAPE FROM Pallas Athos, two days of being trapped on a ship with a creature who could end each and every one of them with a snap of its fingers. Though the god had been subdued, every time Hassan caught a glimpse of Beru his blood turned to ice and all he could think about was the fathomless power locked inside her, waiting to burst free again.

And then there was the guilt. He had barely spoken two words to Khepri since the escape, but when he wasn't worrying about the god, he was thinking about the months Khepri had spent at the Hierophant's mercy.

It was *Hassan's* fault. He was the one who'd tried to make a deal with the Hierophant back in Nazirah. The one who'd gotten Khepri captured. The one who hadn't even realized she was still a prisoner.

Guilt and fear chased each other in circles until finally Hassan sat up in his bunk, rubbing his face. In the bunk across from him, Hector snored peacefully.

Hassan got out of bed, pulled on his clothes, and crept out of the cabin. Normally on nights like this when he couldn't sleep, he would hole up somewhere with a book. So when he strode down the corridor past a half-ajar door and caught a glimpse of bookshelves, he found himself stopping to peer inside.

The room appeared to be empty, with a few plush chairs, a single low table, and a bookshelf that stretched all along the back wall. He drifted inside, letting his fingers trip over the leather spines. There were volumes of history, collections of poems, and the writings of dozens of acolytes. He paused on one with flaking gold lettering that read *Origins of the Seven Prophets*. As he reached to pluck it off the shelf, the sound of someone clearing their throat came from the open doorway.

"Behezda's mercy!" Hassan swore, fumbling the book off the shelf.

"Behezda would say you got what you deserved for snooping."

Hassan turned and was met with the sight of the Wanderer sauntering into the room, a small smirk on her lips.

"I wasn't snooping," he said, unable to hide the thread of nervousness in his voice as she approached. Her presence made him feel strangely small and a little dizzy—as if his mind could not properly reconcile the idea of the mythical Wanderer and the woman standing in front of him.

She stooped to pick up the book, looking down at the cover. "An interesting choice for late-night reading. I'm afraid it's not terribly accurate, though." She set the book back on the shelf and moved toward a cabinet on the adjacent wall. "I've something that might help you get to sleep more easily."

She unlatched the cabinet doors, revealing bottles of rich, dark alcohol, and a few crystal cups. She poured a glass and held it out to him.

Not knowing what else to do, Hassan took it. As she withdrew her hand, Hassan caught sight of her ring, and the distinctive seal it bore: a compass rose.

"The Lost Rose," he blurted. "You're—You're one of them?"

She raised her eyebrows. "Jude didn't tell you?"

He shook his head mutely.

She turned back to the cabinet, pouring another drink. "I created the Lost Rose. After the other Prophets and I slew the god, I made sure its *esha* was sealed away. That each of the Relics was protected and would continue to be protected over the centuries."

"So then . . . *you* were the one that helped us get to Pallas Athos?" he asked. He had *known* her voice sounded familiar when he'd first heard it in the foyer of the Archon's residence.

She tipped her glass at him. "You're welcome."

"My father," Hassan said, before he could stop himself. "He was part of the Lost Rose, wasn't he?"

The Wanderer inclined her head.

"So he did know about the Relics," Hassan said. He had guessed as much when he'd found the covenant of the Lost Rose hidden in the Great Library in Nazirah and when his father's compass had led him to the Crown of Herat beneath the lighthouse. But somehow hearing it from this woman—a *Prophet*, no less—made it feel more real.

"He knew some," she replied. "The way that I designed the Lost Rose . . . each member had their own crucial secret to keep and pass on. But I am the only one who knew how the pieces added up and what we were truly protecting."

"Did you know my father?" Hassan asked, a little desperate.

The Wanderer took her time in replying. "I met him only once. He was young—a little older than you are now. It was just after his mother had named him heir and passed down the secret of the Relic of Mind to him. He took his newfound responsibility very seriously. He was . . . compelled, I think, by the idea of this secret knowledge, meant only for him and his descendants. Eager to protect these secrets, and with them, the world. You remind me of him at that age quite a bit."

Hassan felt laid bare by her words. It was all he'd hoped for once—that someone might see his father in him. That Hassan could live up to his example.

"We kept in touch after that," the Wanderer said. "Particularly once his mother passed. In fact, your father was the first one to tell me about the Hierophant. He didn't know, of course, that it was Pallas, but he told me of the reports about the Witnesses and their leader, and all the rumors surrounding them."

"You could have warned him what was going to happen," Hassan croaked. "The covenant of the Lost Rose—that was the reason that the Hierophant came to Nazirah in the first place. My father died protecting *your* secrets."

The Wanderer bowed her head, staring down at her drink. "I may be a Prophet, but I can no longer see the future. I didn't know what Pallas would do to Nazirah or your father. I wish I had."

Hassan clenched his jaw, pressure building behind his eyes. He'd only cried over his father's death once—that one desperate night he'd spent as a prisoner in his own palace. He felt like crying again now.

"Your father knew there were aspects of the Lost Rose and the Relics that I never told him. But even without that knowledge, he understood the importance of his duty and he dedicated himself to it wholeheartedly, knowing that he was protecting the future of not only his own kingdom, but the whole world. And I think you understand that, too, don't you, Hassan? That's why you're here, isn't it?"

Hassan's voice caught in his throat. During those six weeks in Tel Amot, he'd come so close to giving up and returning to Nazirah, turning his back on everything to do with the prophecy, the god, and the Age of Darkness.

"I thought I was here because it's my destiny," Hassan replied.

A destiny he'd never asked for. Just like his father had never asked to be part of the Lost Rose, entrusted to protect an ancient secret and bear a burden that was so much greater than just his own kingdom. But he had done it anyway.

"You could go back to Nazirah," the Wanderer said. It sounded like a genuine offer. "You could go home."

He could. He could leave Jude and Hector and Ephyra and Anton to handle all this. Leave it all on their shoulders and go back to worrying about his own people.

"What do you think I should do?" Hassan asked.

"I think," she said, "you should finish your drink and go back to sleep."

Hassan found Khepri the next morning at the stern of the ship, holding on to the railing and looking out at the rocky coastline as they neared the inlet that would lead them up the river to Kerameikos Fort.

His heart beat unsteadily as he approached. It had taken him this long to summon the courage to talk to her, and he knew what to expect—anger, certainly, at what he'd done in Nazirah and how it had led to her capture. Relief, perhaps, that he was alive.

He let his gaze linger, studying all the ways in which she'd changed since the last time he'd seen her in Nazirah. She was thinner, the muscles of her arms less defined, and her usually glowing bronze skin seemed sallow and anemic. Even her eyes were different—that spark he usually saw there, that fire and steel, had dimmed.

"I'm so sorry," he said, before she could speak. "Khepri, I—I don't even have words for how sorry I am."

She shook her head. "I've had weeks—*months* to think about nothing except why you did what you did. Why you lied to us, lied to *me*. I know you were just trying to protect Herat but I still—" She bit her lip, cutting herself off.

"You still what?" Hassan asked, heart fluttering in his chest.

Her amber-gold eyes caught on his, and he watched pain flicker there. "I still can't forgive you. I can't *trust* you."

His heart sank. He had wanted to hear her say that she did—that she still loved him, that she understood why he had done what he'd done. That they could move past this.

"But I'm so glad you're alive," she said in a rush, tears brimming in her eyes. "The whole time the Hierophant had me prisoner, I was terrified. I thought that he must've captured you, too. Or that you were . . . that he'd killed you. But now . . ." She brushed a tear from her cheek. "Now we're both free, and we can go back to Nazirah."

Hassan looked into her eyes, guilt pulling at his gut. He wanted to give her everything she wanted—to return to Nazirah. To begin to win back her trust in him.

Instead, he shook his head. "I'm not going back to Nazirah, Khepri," he said as gently as he could.

"What?" she said sharply.

"I *can't*."

Her eyes went flinty and hard. "I know you feel bad about what you did, Hassan, but you can't just run away."

"I'm not running away," he said, although the pang in his chest told him that wasn't entirely true. "Look, there's a lot you don't understand."

"Hector told me everything that happened in Behezda," Khepri said.

"Hector did? Why didn't you—"

"Ask you? I wanted answers, and you were avoiding me," Khepri replied. "So I went to someone else who would tell me the truth."

"Then you know why I can't go back," Hassan said, frustration breaking through his voice. "The prophecy, the god, the Age of Darkness—this is bigger than Nazirah. It's bigger than Herat, than Lethia, than all of us."

"But it's not on *you*, Hassan," she said. "Let the Prophets and the Order of the Last Light and—and whoever these Lost Rose people are worry about the world ending. We need to worry about *our* people."

He shook his head. "I'm a part of this, Khepri, whether I like it or not. I'm a harbinger, and I was *there* when the Red Gate fell, so I don't get to just turn my back and return to Nazirah."

"This isn't about the prophecy." She stared at him, anger still burning in her eyes. "Hassan, you are *choosing* to be part of this. What about Zareen and my brothers—"

"They'll be fine," Hassan said. "They survived without us before. And once we stop the god and stop Pallas, we'll take Nazirah back. Just like we planned."

"I don't like this," she said. "It feels wrong."

"Well, we don't have much of a choice anyway," he said. "This ship is heading to Kerameikos. So unless you want to swim all the way to Nazirah . . ."

She snorted, and almost cracked a smile. It felt like a burst of sunlight in Hassan's chest.

"Look," Hassan said, more gently. "Once we get to Kerameikos, if you still feel this way and there's a chance to go back . . . I won't stop you."

"But you won't go with me," she said, finishing the thought he hadn't said aloud.

He gave her a weak smile.

She sighed, loosening some of the tension in her body and flopping forward against the rail of the deck. "So. The Order of the Last Light to the rescue again, huh? You think they'll really help us after we lied to them and said you were the Last Prophet?"

"Honestly, no," Hassan replied. "They have plenty of reasons not to. And it's not just me, either. We've got two oathbreakers, a renegade Prophet, three harbingers, and someone who used to work for the Witnesses and betrayed the Hierophant."

She glanced at him sharply. "What?"

Hassan rubbed the back of his neck. "Yeah, well, allies are thin on the ground."

"But you trust them." It wasn't quite a question.

He nodded, surprised to find that it was true, that he didn't even need to think about it. As much as he and Jude had fought over the last two and a half months, as much as the Wanderer and the Pale Hand remained mysteries to him, he trusted them.

"Right now," he said, "we're all we've got."

19

BERU

TIME PASSED SLOWLY ON THE JOURNEY TO KERAMEIKOS. BERU SPENT MOST OF her days out on the deck, feeling the cool rush of the wind on her cheeks and trying to ignore the god's voice in her head.

It had been even angrier since Beru had managed to subdue its will on the beach. Baffled might have been a better word—and Beru couldn't help but feel a little baffled, too.

Some part of her had thought that using the god's power would consume her entirely. But something had happened on the beach. First, when Ephyra had spoken to her—pleaded with her. Focusing on her sister's voice had anchored her, kept her from slipping beneath the consuming tide of the god's wrath.

And then, when Hector had shown up, she'd felt it. His fear, his relief, his hope sparking to life in Beru's mind. A lifeline, something to hold on to as she pulled herself from the depths of the god's will.

Now, with the Godfire collar back on, its emotions were more muted—she could feel them bleeding through sometimes, but there was always a sense of separation. Somehow the persistent awareness of herself remained, a will the god could not wholly conquer.

But the Godfire collar could not block out the god's voice in the same way, so Beru was stuck listening to it air its grievances in every quiet moment.

I don't know what you're so upset about, Beru chided, leaning her face out toward the wind as the god subjected her to its latest rant against the Prophets. *We're free of Pallas, now. You should be happy about that, at least.*

HAPPY? the god echoed blankly.

You wanted to be free of him, and now you are. That's a good thing.

I WANTED PALLAS DEAD. HE IS NOT DEAD. THAT IS NOT "GOOD."

Beru let out a sigh. There was a time when she'd been afraid of the god's thoughts. But more and more often, she felt tired of its single-mindedness, the way it seemed to have such vast knowledge of the world, of creation, and yet seemed to know so little.

So just because things didn't go exactly the way you wanted, you throw a fit.

LITTLE MORTAL, YOU WOULDN'T UNDERSTAND, the god said. I MADE THIS WORLD. IT EXISTS BECAUSE I EXIST. IT IS MINE. IT IS *ME*.

Beru considered this. She'd thought the god almost petulant. But it wasn't that, exactly. The god could not be satisfied by small victories. It had only ever existed in a state of omnipotence before. If it had wanted Pallas dead, then Pallas would be dead and there was nothing to be happy or angry about. It just *was*, because the god had decided it.

But not anymore.

EVERYTHING IN THIS WORLD WAS OF ME, the god went on. AND YOU HUMANS WERE OF ME, TOO. UNTIL YOU BEGAN TO CHANGE. TO CHOOSE. TO . . . LOVE. THERE WAS NO GOING BACK, AFTER THAT. YOU WERE NO LONGER ME. THAT WAS WHY I CREATED THE PROPHETS. ONCE HUMANS WERE NO LONGER OF ME, I WAS CUT OFF FROM THEM.

SO I GAVE A LITTLE OF MYSELF TO A FEW OF THEM, SUCH THAT THEY COULD TELL THE OTHERS.

Tell them what?

MY MESSAGE. MY LAWS. MY EDICTS. WHAT THEY WERE TO DO AND WHAT THEY WERE NOT TO DO. BUT UNRULY BEASTS—THEY WOULD NOT DO AS I SAID.

So you punished them?

PUNISHED? The god did not seem to understand this, either. THE ONES WHO FOLLOWED MY LAWS WERE ALLOWED TO CONTINUE. AND THE ONES WHO DID NOT WERE ENDED.

Beru shivered. The god thought only in absolutes. Nothing was justified, because there was no need for justification. It was chilling to consider the world that way. To realize that the god's wrath was not borne of callousness and cruelty, but utter ignorance of even the concept of empathy. Of self and other. Of love, and pain, and suffering.

Perhaps it was fruitless to try to explain to the god the truth of its creations. Maybe a creature like this, something so vast and limitless, wasn't capable of seeing the world the way humans did.

That is what punishment is, Beru said. *You hurt them because they disobeyed you.*

I FIXED THEM.

You made them suffer.

"Beru, isn't it?" a voice said, jolting Beru from her thoughts.

She attempted a polite smile as the face of the Herati Legionnaire girl swam before her. She hunted around in her mind for the girl's name.

"It's Khepri," the girl said, clearly interpreting Beru's blank smile correctly.

"Sorry," Beru said.

Khepri waved her off. "It's fine. I know you probably have a lot going on in your mind."

Beru's smile turned a little brittle.

"That came out wrong," Khepri said. "We haven't really spoken before and here I am—all I'm saying is, I know you've been through a lot."

"We all have," Beru said, tucking a wayward curl behind her ear. "You were held captive by Pallas, too, weren't you?"

Khepri glanced back at her, considering. "Pallas, huh. I still don't quite believe it. The Hierophant is a Prophet. It figures, though. He always seemed like he was way too used to having people worship him. That must warp you a little bit, don't you think? Certain people . . . must be easy for them to get obsessed with keeping that power."

Beru thought of the god, and its need to shape the world precisely to its liking.

"There's a reason you came over here to talk to me, isn't there?" Beru asked.

Khepri's lips curled into a rueful smile. "No point in pretending otherwise, I guess. Hassan told me not to."

"Not to talk to me?" Beru asked. Khepri didn't seem afraid of her—maybe a little wary, but not *afraid*. Beru supposed it would be hard to believe that in her body lurked an ancient being so powerful it could reduce an entire city to rubble unless one had seen it for themselves. "He told you I was dangerous, didn't he?"

Khepri nodded, and Beru had to appreciate her forthrightness. "I guess I find that hard to believe, too."

"Well, he's right," Beru said, curling her hands around the gunwale. "I *am* dangerous."

"Dangerous enough to take over the Six Prophetic Cities," Khepri said. "That's what the Hierophant was doing with you, isn't it? Using you to subjugate the other cities. I guess Nazirah wasn't enough."

Beru felt a hot pulse of anger, and in its wake a sick lurch of guilt. Khepri was right. She'd let Pallas do all that.

"I know what happened in your city," Beru said. "You were fighting Pallas before any of us."

Khepri's expression sprang open in surprise. Then she swallowed, looking solemn. "That's right. And so were the people of Nazirah. My brothers, the Scarab's Wing . . . they've been fighting Pallas this whole time."

"And you want to help them."

"I want *you* to help them. I saw the way you broke our chains with a flick of the finger, the way you stopped a whole—" She cut herself off, shaking her head. "You have all this power inside you. Don't you want to *use* it?"

"I can't," Beru said. "I'm sorry. I wish I could. But I can't."

"Why *not?*" Khepri demanded. "You could do something *good*, to make up for the things that the Hierophant made you do for him. You could save my people."

Beru turned so she wouldn't have to see Khepri's face, anguished and in pain.

SHE'S RIGHT, the god said. YOU COULD. *WE* COULD. YOU WANT TO.

Beru gazed at the horizon. The god was right. There *was* a part of her that wanted to be able to wield this power for good. To help Khepri, to help anyone and everyone who knew suffering.

But she knew how that would end.

"I can't use this power," she said, forcing herself to look Khepri in the eye. "It isn't *mine*. And the thing that it belongs to . . . if I let it out . . . if I let it *free* . . . you saw what happened on the beach. That was just a small taste of what it's capable of. If I saved your people, it would doom the entire world."

Khepri held her gaze for a long moment.

"I'm sorry," Beru said again. "I truly am."

Khepri shook her head, looking out toward the horizon. "I guess I seem pretty selfish, asking you this while you're trying to save the whole world."

"Nazirah is your home," Beru replied. "Of course you'd want to do anything you could to protect it. Maybe that is selfish, but it's also human. And that means it's worth holding on to."

———

The only person aside from Ephyra, and occasionally Anton, who sought Beru's company was Evander, the merchant's son they'd rescued from the citadel. Despite what he'd endured at the hands of the Witnesses, the boy was the friendliest person on the ship and didn't hesitate to talk Beru's ear off about whatever topic struck his fancy. Frequently, it was to bemoan the shortage of nice clothing available to him, sometimes to gossip about the others (he was, she'd learned, shockingly perceptive despite the oblivious airs he often adopted), and occasionally to speculate about what awaited them in Kerameikos.

Beru didn't mind the constant chatter. She found it soothing, Evander's voice drowning out the god's in her head.

This afternoon, the sixth of their journey, Evander was recounting every outfit he'd worn to the five-day wedding celebration of the archduke's daughter in Endarrion while Beru dozed lightly in her bunk.

"Do you hear that?" Evander asked suddenly, in the middle of musing about the benefits of Endarrion-style jacket laces.

"Hear what?" Beru asked.

"It sounds like someone's pacing outside," Evander replied, getting to his feet to investigate.

He was right. There was a rhythmic sound of footsteps that, at first, Beru had simply attributed to the rocking of the ship. Her stomach clenched with nerves.

Evander poked his head out the door and then immediately shut it and turned back to Beru with a mischievous glint in his eye. "It's that handsome swordsman. Should I let him in?"

He could have meant Jude, but Beru knew instinctively it was Hector. The nervousness she'd felt had come from him.

"I'll go out there," Beru said, slipping off the bed. "You stay here."

It took her a moment to summon the courage to open the door.

Since their arrival on the ship, Hector had kept his distance. Beru didn't know what she'd been hoping for—he'd seemed so relieved, so terribly, achingly pleased to see her in the citadel. But since the escape, he hadn't sought her out. She must have frightened him, with all that had happened on the beach.

Or perhaps, he hadn't been glad to see her at all. Perhaps, once again, Beru's own feelings of relief at seeing *Hector* had been projected onto him through their strange connection.

He doesn't really love you, she reminded herself. He only thought he did, because Beru had let her own feelings spill over to him, warping him.

She felt ill just thinking about it. But she forced the feeling down as she wrenched open the door and stepped into the corridor.

Hector's back was turned as he paced, but the minute he heard the door open he whipped around to face Beru.

They stared at each other for a long, awkward moment.

"Um," Hector said at last. "How—how are you?"

It took Beru a moment to answer. "Better than I was six days ago, I suppose. I never thanked you—you and Prince Hassan and Jude—for rescuing us."

"You were actually the one who got us out of there," Hector replied.

And the god had almost killed them as a result.

"We should talk about what happened on the beach," Hector said abruptly. "I didn't imagine that, did I? I did something to you. To the god."

He looked so uncertain, almost frightened, and for a long moment Beru wasn't sure what to tell him.

"It's . . . When I use the god's power, the god's influence over me gets stronger," Beru began. "I fight it by grabbing a piece of myself—a memory or a feeling—and holding on. But on the beach, it wasn't my own feelings I was grabbing hold of. It was *yours.*"

"You mean . . . because of the connection between us," Hector said haltingly.

Beru nodded. "Sometimes . . . I feel my own emotions and thoughts get overwhelmed by the god. But yours . . . they came through so clearly."

Hector's dark gaze flicked away from her. Beru felt something like shame welling up in her throat, but she wasn't sure if it was coming from Hector or herself.

"I'm sorry," she said at last. "I know that's a lot to put on you."

He shook his head, scratching at his light scruff and Beru realized—he *was* embarrassed. "No, it's—it's a good thing, right? I mean, I'm glad I can help."

It was strange to see Hector like this. So unsure. So *nervous.* The opposite of everything he usually was. Maybe it was the god—maybe Hector didn't know how to act around her because of the dangerous creature that lurked inside her.

It hurt, a surprising amount. After everything they'd been through, Hector still saw her as this strange, alien thing. It felt like a return to the start, when Hector had first found out she was a revenant, when he'd looked at her with fear and horror.

But he wasn't looking at her like that now. He wasn't looking at her at all.

"Hector," she said carefully. "What's wrong?"

"It's just . . ." He paused. "All this stuff about the connection between our *esha*—it's all because the Necromancer King brought me back from the dead, and I don't even know *why*."

Beru *did* know why. Or at least she knew some of it. "It was a favor. He told me, back at the oasis, after you left."

"You never told me that," he said, betrayal straining his voice.

She looked him in the eye. "You never asked."

He looked cowed by the reminder that he'd been avoiding talking to her alone. He swallowed. "A favor for *who*?"

"For me," a voice spoke from the end of the hallway.

Beru and Hector both turned to face the Wanderer, who stood illuminated in a doorway, as beautiful and inscrutable as ever.

"Your life for a debt owed," she continued.

"What kind of debt?" Hector asked. "What did *you* want me alive for?"

She returned his heated stare placidly, and Beru had the distinct sense that they were each trying to outlast the other.

"I found your body in Medea, where I also found Ephyra. I surmised what had happened and knew that if Beru was destined to become the vessel of the ancient god, then your resurrection would become a weakness to the god. And I was right, wasn't I?"

"You mean the connection between us," Hector said. "That's the reason I'm still alive?"

The Wanderer's gaze focused on him, almost calculating. But Beru detected a hint of something else, something akin to sorrow. "I suppose there was another factor, too. I suppose I . . . felt a little guilt. At contributing to your demise."

Beru stared at her. "What are you talking about?"

Hector looked equally baffled.

"Everything that was set in motion," the Wanderer said, "it was due to my . . . well, meddling, I suppose Pallas would call it. I set you all on a collision course."

Beru thought back, realization dawning. "You sent Ephyra and me to find Anton. And then Anton and Ephyra wound up imprisoned in the citadel, where Hector found them."

"I gave you a little nudge, here and there," she said. "So that you all might find one another."

"So you knew this would happen?" Hector demanded. "All of it?"

The Wanderer pointed at herself. "Prophet. Remember?"

They stared at her.

"Of course, it's a little more complicated than that," she said with a wave. "I can't see the future anymore. None of us could, after our final prophecy. But after two thousand years of watching prophecies unfold, my best guess is pretty good."

"So you pushed us toward one another," Hector said. "Why?"

"'To bring the age of dark to yield,'" she replied. "I believe in you. In all of you. And I believe that you will right the mistakes of the past. My mistakes."

"You think you can just—just move us around like game pieces?" Hector said, his fists clenched at his sides. "We're not cards in a hand of canbarra. We're people with our own lives, our own *wills*."

"You're right," the Wanderer said. She almost sounded sad. "In fact, that was something I used to say to the other Prophets. For centuries, I argued that our power of prophecy wasn't helping the world. That, in fact, we were harming it. Setting people down paths they never would have taken otherwise. People made choices, to love or to hate, to harm or to heal, based solely on the stories we told them. Empires rose and fell, wars were lost and won in accordance with our words. I never thought it should be so—I resisted doing what the others had done, establishing a place for myself to impart my visions on subjects. And now I have found myself doing exactly what they did, guiding you toward an end that we predicted. The irony is not lost on me."

Beru thought about this. For so long she had felt bound to a destiny, one she didn't even understand, just the feeling that she was *meant* to die in the village of Medea. And later, she believed she was meant to bring darkness to the world. And now she was living with a god shackled inside her head. Was that what it had all meant? That her purpose was to become a vessel of destruction?

"So bringing us all together," Beru said. "Bringing Hector back from the dead . . . that was all so we could fulfill our destinies? To stop the Age of Darkness."

"That is what I hope, yes," the Wanderer replied.

"And what if you're wrong?" Beru asked. "You say you can't see the future anymore, so what if we only make things worse? What if none of this would have happened without your—your meddling?"

"That is always the danger of prophecy," the Wanderer replied. "But I only brought you together. It was your choices that got you here. And it will be your choices that determine the fate of the world."

20

JUDE

THE SHIP PULLED SMOOTHLY INTO THE RIVER HARBOR AT KERAMEIKOS FORT.
Seeing the signs of destruction sent Jude's heart buzzing in his chest.

The Temple of the Prophets still stood, a rotunda perched over a
cascade of waterfalls, but half of its exterior wall had crumbled. Some
of the gates seemed to have been damaged in the siege, but most of
the structures, with their delicate, vinelike pillars and rails, were still
intact.

It was decided that the others would remain on the ship with
Hassan's countrywoman, Khepri, to protect them. Hector had insisted
on disembarking with Jude, refusing to let him bear the brunt of the
Order's ire alone. Jude hadn't had the strength to refuse the offer, particularly after the grueling argument he'd had with Anton over whether
he would be coming with Jude.

"We have no idea who's taken charge of the fort," Jude had said. "We
don't know if they're loyal to Pallas, and if they are we can't let them
know you're here."

"And I can't let you face them alone," Anton had argued. "*I'm the* reason you walked away from the Order, and if they want to punish you for it—"

"Then I'm sure you can storm in dramatically the way you did at my Tribunal sentencing," Jude had said, a blush threatening to creep up his neck when he thought back to the Tribunal. It was, looking back, the moment he'd realized that the magnetic pull he'd felt toward Anton had begun to grow into something more.

"I don't like this," Anton had replied, glowering.

"You don't have to."

Strangely, arguing with Anton felt like safe ground. They'd been tip-toeing around each other since that first conversation after Jude woke up, fumbling through being together again after months apart. Jude sometimes caught himself longing for that first, unguarded night they'd spent together on the road to Behezda, after abandoning the Guard, when Anton had asked him *what do you want*, like it was that simple.

Now, returning to Kerameikos after all this time, with Hector of all people at his side, things had never felt more complicated and Jude had never felt less certain. They didn't even know who it was that waited for them in the fort. Whether they were friend or foe.

"Ready?" Hector asked as they pulled up to the dock.

Jude lifted a shoulder. "As I'll ever be, I suppose."

They stepped out onto the dock, where four sword-wielding Paladin waited to greet them.

"You are not authorized to dock here," said the Paladin in front. Jude recognized her vaguely—she had short, dark hair and a smatter-ing of freckles on her cheeks. "Take one more step, and we'll draw our swords."

Jude and Hector exchanged glances. They couldn't surrender them-selves, in case these Paladin were working for Pallas. But neither did they want to risk a fight, in case they *weren't*.

"Under whose command is Kerameikos?" Jude asked.

"That is no business of yours," another one of the Paladin, a younger man, said acidly. Then his eyes widened as he took Jude in. "You're . . . you're the Weatherbourne heir."

The dark-haired Paladin glanced at her companion sharply, and then looked back at Jude, her eyes flinty. "Oathbreaker."

The fury in her voice stole the breath from Jude's lungs.

"Both of them," said another Paladin. This one Jude did know—as did Hector. His name was Ariel, and Hector had once started a fight with him over something Jude could no longer remember. The fight had ended when Jude had broken it up. "That's Hector Navarro."

The dark-haired Paladin's eyes narrowed. "Go get the captain. Now."

Ariel strode away. Jude kept his gaze pinned to his retreating back. The captain? Hope glimmered in his chest for a moment as Jude imagined they were fetching his father. As if somehow he was alive, he'd survived the Witnesses' attack after all. He quickly extinguished the thought as fear took its place. Whoever their captain was now, they could very well be under Pallas's command.

"What are two oathbreakers doing on our shores?" the dark-haired Paladin demanded. "You should have known you wouldn't be welcomed here. If I had to guess, I'd say you had a ship full of oathbreakers and you've come here to reclaim Kerameikos." She turned her head to call over her shoulder. "Search the ship."

Jude stiffened as the two Paladin advanced.

"Move aside, or I will strike you down," one of them said, when Jude didn't move.

"Then strike me down," Jude replied levelly, his hand going to the sword at his hip. He didn't know what the Paladin woman meant by oathbreakers. Those who had joined Pallas? Or those who hadn't?

The Paladin in front of Jude unsheathed his blade. A split second later, Hector's sword scraped free of its sheath, the tip of the blade pointed at the Paladin's throat.

"I wouldn't do that if I were you," Hector said, an edge of amusement in his voice.

"Hector," Jude warned.

"Stand down, oathbreaker!" the dark-haired Paladin ordered. A flurry of scraping metal rang through the air as the other Paladin drew their own swords.

"You're outnumbered," the dark-haired Paladin said, her sword pointing at Hector, but her eyes on Jude. "Surrender and submit to our search."

"I'm very sorry," Jude said, "but I can't let you search the ship."

"You have not the means to stop us," the Paladin replied. "And if you *think* about drawing your sword—"

Jude didn't draw his sword. Instead, he breathed in and summoned his Grace, the way he had in Behezda when he'd faced the scarred Witness. It came to him easily now, so easily he didn't need to move through a koah to channel it, swelling like a building storm. Power surged through him, until the very air around Jude caught with it. Water from the river sprayed and leaves whipped around him.

"What are you doing?" the Paladin asked, her eyes growing wide and alarmed.

Jude didn't answer, just let his Grace flare inside of him, bolstered by the strength of his intention, the oath that was now bound to his *esha*.

"S-stop this!" the Paladin cried, now panicked, one arm thrown up over her face to protect against the gale. "How are you doing this?"

"Stand down!" a new voice cried from the top of the fort's outer wall. "Stand down at once!"

Jude glanced up and caught sight of a familiar figure, her copper braid coiled close to her head, her silver torc gleaming in the sunlight.

Startled, Jude let go of his Grace and felt it ebb away, the wind subsiding.

"Penrose!" He could not help the jolt of relief and joy he felt at seeing her here, though he knew her reaction was probably quite different.

She leapt down from the wall, advancing on the group slowly, her jaw set and her eyes locked on Jude. There was no hint of warmth or welcome in her expression.

"Captain Penrose!" the Paladin woman said, snapping to attention. "We were questioning the oathbreakers as to their motives in coming here."

Captain Penrose. Jude tried not to show how rattled he felt.

Penrose leaned toward the Paladin woman, whispering something that even Jude's Grace-enhanced hearing couldn't catch. The woman cast a glance back at Jude and then hurried away.

Penrose and Jude stared at each other across the dock for a long moment.

Then Penrose nodded to the Paladin who still had his sword out in front of Jude. "You. Search the ship."

A wave of hurt hit Jude as he took in the hard expression on Penrose's face. He hadn't expected this reunion would be a happy one, but he also hadn't thought her trust in him had broken so deeply.

But he still trusted her. So when three of the Paladin moved to go past him onto the ship, Jude stepped aside without a word. He may have betrayed Penrose, let her down too many times to count, but he knew who she was. He knew her heart. And he knew she would never follow the Hierophant, even if he had turned out to be a Prophet.

She just stared him down, steely-eyed, as they waited for the

Paladin to complete their search. Very quickly, Jude heard the sounds of a scuffle that told him they'd found Khepri, and sure enough a moment later, two of the Paladin emerged onto the deck, dragging the struggling Legionnaire between them.

Penrose's eyes widened. "Khepri?"

Hassan sprinted across the deck after them.

"Prince Hassan?"

Hassan stopped, leaning over the ship's railing, looking down at Penrose. "Khepri, stop. It's Penrose."

Khepri ceased her struggle immediately, letting the Paladin lead her onto the dock.

"Captain Penrose!" the third Paladin called out. "They have the Prophet."

A moment later the Paladin emerged, dragging Anton by the arm, and by the expression on Anton's face, none too gently. Jude felt his Grace flare inside him again on instinct, an almost primal urge to defend Anton rising in him.

"Let him go," Penrose commanded, and when Jude's gaze found her again he could see the disquiet in her probing stare. He knew her heart, and she knew his as well. "Let them all go."

"But Captain—"

"I said let them go," Penrose repeated, her tone allowing for no argument.

The Paladin released Khepri and Anton. On the ship behind them, the others had stepped out onto the deck. Penrose's gaze tracked Anton as he went to Jude's side.

The words of the scarred Witness rang in Jude's head, ugly. *Does your service to the Prophet extend to his bed?*

He shook it off. The other Paladin might not understand, might think Jude nothing but an oathbreaker, debasing their Prophet with his weakness, but Jude knew the truth, and he wasn't going to hide it any longer. He met Penrose's gaze.

"I know you have no reason to trust us, after what we did," he said, keeping his voice as even as he could. "We abandoned you and the rest of the Guard."

"You abducted the Last Prophet and put him in harm's way," Penrose corrected sharply.

Anton opened his mouth, looking like he was ready for a fight, but Jude quieted him with a touch to the back of his wrist.

He inclined his head to Penrose. "You're right. I didn't trust my own Guard. I cannot apologize for making the journey to the City of Mercy to try to stop the Hierophant, but I do regret that we parted as we did."

"And now?" Penrose asked. "Now that a god has been resurrected and Pallas is using it as a weapon to subjugate the Prophetic Cities you've come here for what? To hear that you were right, and we were wrong?"

Jude heard the pain in her voice.

"No," he replied. "We came here because we need your help."

"So let me get this straight," Penrose said as they sat around the table in the tearoom with the remaining members of the Guard—Petrossian, Osei, and Annuka, who Jude was grateful and relieved to see had not followed her brother to join Pallas. Jude, Anton, and the Wanderer were the only ones Penrose had allowed inside the gates, which was perhaps for the best. She seemed barely able to look at Hector.

"You're actually a Prophet?" Penrose pointed at the Wanderer, who nodded. "You all have the god with you? And you brought it *here?*"

"Beru isn't dangerous," Anton assured her.

"We've seen what the god has done," Petrossian interrupted darkly. "Tearing out Grace and giving it to Witnesses."

"That was Pallas controlling her," Anton replied. "Beru is . . . she's *good*. I know it's hard to believe, but she's helping us. She wants the god gone just as much as we do, and she's willing to do whatever it takes."

"And so you two need to use the Circle of Stones to find the other Prophets?" Penrose asked. "You don't know where they are?"

The Wanderer sighed. "When the final prophecy came to the seven of us, we went into hiding. The prophecy had essentially stated that our time—the Age of Prophets—was coming to a close. We felt it safest to disappear, as we could no longer wield any influence over the world. The thought was that once the Last Prophet was born, we could return to help teach him."

"But the others didn't return," Jude said. "Why not?"

The Wanderer shook her head. "I don't know. In the intervening century, Pallas turned against this plan, obviously. He returned to the world in secret. But the others . . . they could be, quite literally, anywhere, masking their *esha* from scryers."

"Which is why we need to use the Circle of Stones to scry for them," Anton added. He looked at Penrose. "Remember before the Witnesses attacked Kerameikos, how the Order wanted me to scry to prove I was the Last Prophet? This is exactly the same thing."

Penrose bit her lip. "I don't know if I like this."

"If the Prophets haven't returned, it must be for a reason," Osei agreed. "We must trust that they know what is best."

The Wanderer laughed, a pleasant, wind chime of a sound. She stopped abruptly when she realized no one else had laughed with her. "Oh. You actually mean that."

Penrose stiffened. "We must trust in the Prophets."

"I *am* a Prophet," the Wanderer said, her eyes flashing. "So is Pallas. I know the Order of the Last Light has sworn oaths to serve us, but it's not that simple. Even back then, relations between the seven of us were . . . complicated."

Jude eyed the Wanderer curiously. She'd spoken very little about the other Prophets and their past together. Her relationship with the others had been strained, that much he knew. But she seemed reluctant to divulge how that tension had come to be and what had made Pallas turn against the others.

"The point is," Jude said, redirecting their attention from what he knew would be a fraught topic, "we need to find the Prophets."

Penrose looked wary. "I don't know about this. I need to think it through."

"Actually, we really don't have—" Anton began.

"That's fine," Jude said, cutting him off. "But before you make a decision, you should know the risks, too."

Anton sent him a warning look, but Jude ignored it. Penrose might be furious with him, but he still trusted her. He refused to involve her and the rest of the Order without telling them the whole truth.

Anton sighed and answered for Jude. "The other Prophets will feel it when we use the Circle of Stones to scry for them, as if we were sending up a beacon. Which means . . ."

"Pallas will know where you are, too," Annuka finished darkly. She'd been quiet until now, not that she'd ever been the most talkative to begin with. But Jude could sense the bitter loss and betrayal radiating off her at the mention of the Hierophant. He could barely fathom the pain it must have caused her when Yarik had forsaken the Order to join Pallas.

Jude nodded. "Everyone will have to leave Kerameikos before we do this."

"Leave Kerameikos?" Penrose echoed. "We've only just gotten it back. Some of our people lost their lives retaking it from the Witnesses."

"Pallas is going to do whatever it takes to find us and get Beru back," Anton said.

Penrose looked like she was going to protest again.

"Penrose," Jude said gently. "We wouldn't ask this of you if we didn't think it was the only way."

"You can't just waltz back here after everything you did, Jude," she said sharply. "You can't just make these outrageous demands and expect us to go along with it. You left us, Jude. When we needed you the most, you abandoned us. And do you know what happened? Other Paladin lost faith. They broke rank. The Order is not what it once was, and it's your fault. Our people left! *Yarik* left to follow Pallas because you and the Prophet weren't here to lead us. Pallas convinced him that you had turned your back on us. And he was right, wasn't he?" She punctuated that with a swift look at Anton, making her meaning clear.

Jude felt his own anger rise up in his chest. He turned to Anton and the others. "Could you give us a moment?"

The Wanderer retreated toward the door with a mild look, the rest of the Guard filing out behind her. Anton hesitated, gaze trained on Jude, before following.

Once the door shut, Jude turned back to Penrose. "I know about Yarik," he said unsteadily. "I saw him in the citadel, following Pallas's orders."

"You are the Keeper of the Word, Jude," Penrose said. "And when you disgraced yourself, you disgraced the entire Order. It wasn't so long ago that we worshipped Pallas, and the fact that you weren't here to stand up to him made it all too easy for some of us to return to him."

Guilt crawled up Jude's throat. There was some truth in what Penrose said, and there was even a part of Jude that understood what

Yarik had done. Jude had been told his whole life to follow orders. Told not to question the Order or the Prophets. That was what had stopped him from stepping out of line for so long. The fear that if he didn't have the Order's rules, he would have to make his own choices.

And for some of the Paladin, that fear had led them to follow a man like Pallas rather than face a world where they had no one to guide them.

Jude met Penrose's gaze. "Do you think it was easy for me to come back here?"

"Well, it was easy enough for you to leave," she shot back.

"No, it wasn't."

"I just don't understand," Penrose said, sounding aggravated. "*Why* are you so intent on sabotaging yourself? On becoming this—this person I barely recognize."

"That's not what this is about."

"You were supposed to be the Keeper of the Word!" Penrose cried. "You were supposed to lead us! And you threw it away for what? Or were you just so afraid you'd never measure up that you decided you'd abandon us before you could find out?"

As much as he wanted to dismiss Penrose's words, she was partially right. The first time he'd left, he'd told himself he was chasing after Hector, but the truth was that he'd been running away from the Order, from the duty he was certain he could never live up to, the oath he was sure he couldn't fulfill.

"We all have weakness in our hearts," Penrose said. "Why did you give in to yours?"

That stung, more than Jude was prepared for. "I didn't."

Penrose's expression tightened. "You broke your oath."

"I don't see it that way," Jude said. "Not anymore. My oath was to serve the Prophet. To protect him. And loving him . . . loving him has only brought me closer to that purpose. You think that I gave up, that I lost my faith, but it wasn't that at all. I *found* it. In him. In myself."

Penrose just stared at him, her jaw clenched. Maybe she would never understand the choices he had made. But he didn't need to justify himself, to her or anyone. He wasn't the defeated shell of a person, filled with self-loathing and anger, that he'd been the last time he was in Kerameikos. He knew who he was.

"Penrose," he said. "I know you can't forgive me. I know you might never understand why I did what I did. But I didn't come here to beg for forgiveness or explain myself to you. And regardless of what you think of me and my choices, regardless of the fact that you don't believe in me anymore—" He sucked in a shaking breath, overcome suddenly with the thought that no matter what happened, his relationship with Penrose would never be what it once was. A wave of grief rose in him, as dark and overwhelming as he'd felt when Penrose had told him his father was dead.

When he found his words again, his voice was quiet, measured. "I know you still believe in our duty. Otherwise you wouldn't be here, holding the Order together."

"It shouldn't be me holding us together."

Jude smiled through a pang of sadness. "Maybe not. But it *is* you."

Penrose held his gaze for a moment and then looked away. "Your . . . friends," she said at last. "They can stay in the barracks for the night. Keric knows, we have the room."

Jude nodded, grateful. "Thank you, I'll tell them." He turned to go.

"And Jude—" Penrose said, and then stopped herself. "You're all welcome to come to dinner in the great hall."

It was not, he saw, what she had intended to say, but Jude just nodded and left the room without another word.

When he stepped back out to the veranda, Anton was hovering

a few feet from the door. The Wanderer, true to her name, seemed to have wandered off.

"What did she say?" Anton asked with an edge of nervousness.

Jude shook his head. "It doesn't matter."

"That bad, huh?"

"We should go find the others."

"Jude . . ." Anton began, making an aborted movement, as if he wanted to take Jude's hand.

Jude looked off toward the crumbled outer wall of the fort. "It was my choice to leave the Order. I'd make the same one again."

"I know you would," Anton said. "But I also know that coming back here can't be easy. And you can talk to me about this. I want—I want you to tell me how you feel. Even if you don't think I'll like it."

Jude just stared at him, momentarily speechless. "You want—Why?"

"Why?" Anton echoed. He touched a thumb to Jude's temple, fingers combing through Jude's hair soothingly. "Because I want to know everything about you. Always."

He said it like it was obvious, like Jude should take it for granted that Anton should want to know these things, every hidden truth and private shame. Jude was so used to Anton being able to see through him, further than even Jude himself saw sometimes. It had always been that way between them, right from the first night they'd met.

But it was one thing for Anton to steal past Jude's defenses and slip beyond the walls of his heart like a thief in the night. It was quite another for Jude to fling open the gates and invite him inside. To forfeit even the pretense of protection.

He wasn't sure he could bear it. Not now, still bruised from the past two and a half months and the knowledge that Anton had kept them apart. Not now that he knew exactly what pain it might bring because he had already lived through it once.

But he'd meant everything he'd just said to Penrose. The way he felt about Anton was the needle of the compass that guided him. He had tried, futilely, to resist its pull before. What was the point of pretending he could do it now? What was the sense in closing the gates when the walls themselves would just as easily crumble?

He caught Anton's hand and drew it to his lips, kissing the soft center of his palm. Anton's fingers curled, brushing Jude's cheek.

"You too," Jude said, folding their hands together. "You can tell me anything, Anton."

Perhaps it was just his imagination, but Anton's smile seemed a little dimmer.

21

ANTON

ANTON WOKE UP ALONE. HE WAS USED TO WAKING ALONE—WHAT HE WASN'T used to was the fact that he had gone to sleep curled against Jude in the tiny barracks bed. It was a tight fit, but Anton had slept in far worse places in his life. He had hoped being near Jude might mean a reprieve from his nightmares.

But instead, Anton's sleep had been plagued by dreams of Jude dying. Dreams where he drowned in the lake behind Anton's old home in Novogardia, dreams where the Witnesses gutted Jude in the Archon's villa in Pallas Athos, dreams where Jude was trapped beneath the rubble of Behezda. And the worst ones, where Jude sacrificed himself to kill the god, and no amount of pleading from Anton would make him change his mind. They left Anton raw and hollow, because he could never shake the feeling that they weren't just dreams.

He rolled off the narrow bed and managed to calm his shaking hands enough to pull on his clothes before emerging into the misty morning. He knew it was irrational, but he wouldn't feel right until he saw Jude.

He could feel Jude's *esha* like a low rolling thunderhead, and he set out to follow it, winding his way through the fort, over the many footbridges that crisscrossed the river. Finally, he climbed up the hill and through the trees until he heard the rushing sound of a waterfall joined by the ring of swords clashing.

As he rounded the bend, he was struck with the sight of the morning sun glinting off the falls, illuminating everything in fractal colors. He had been here before, he realized. Only, not really. Jude had dreamed of this place, and Anton had walked into that dream. This place meant something to Jude.

At the foot of the falls, bathed in mist, Jude and Hector fought on a rocky outcropping, swords flashing between them. Anton had seen Jude fight countless times, but always in situations where one or both of them were in grave danger. He'd never really gotten a chance to simply *watch*, to appreciate how beautiful Jude looked in motion. Every strike controlled, every feint and dodge fluid, instinctual.

Jude leapt gracefully, effortlessly, from perch to perch, until Hector had him hemmed in against the water. Jude's counterattack was so quick, Anton almost couldn't track him with his eyes, and a moment later Hector was disarmed, Jude's blade tip pointing to his heart.

"All right, I get it!" Hector said, laughing. "You're a better swordsman than me now! A fistfight, though, I'd've won."

"If you say so," Jude said, sheathing his sword.

"I say so," Hector replied. "C'mon, let's test it right now. No swords."

Jude laughed, turning away like he was going to decline. Anton abruptly realized that he'd never seen Jude laugh with anyone besides him.

Jude whirled back to Hector, waving a hand through the water behind him, splashing it onto Hector. Hector let out an undignified yelp, clearly not expecting it, and leapt at Jude. Before Anton knew what was happening, they were grappling on the rock.

"I fought in the sandpits you know," Hector was saying as he ducked under a blow from Jude. "They called me the Sandstorm. I was undefeated."

"Your opponents must not have been very good," Jude teased. He spun away from a punch and then suddenly stopped, his eyes finally landing on Anton. Hector, who hadn't yet spotted him, aimed another blow at Jude from behind, and Jude's hand shot out to catch Hector's fist without looking.

"Anton?"

Anton shifted, feeling uncomfortably like he was intruding. "I wasn't sure where you'd gone."

Jude leapt down onto the riverbank, leaving Hector on the rock. "Is everything all right?"

"Everything's fine," Anton said too quickly. "I just . . . we should probably go talk to Penrose again, right?"

"Are you sure you're all right?" Jude asked as he reached him. "I know you didn't sleep well last night. When I woke up in the middle of the night, you looked like you were having a nightmare. I tried to wake you . . ."

"Yeah," Anton agreed. The image of Jude's lifeless body flashed behind Anton's eyes, and he suppressed a shudder. "Just the usual nightmares." He smiled up at Jude. "But there were some nice dreams, too."

"Like what?" Jude asked.

"Well," Anton replied. "I seem to recall one about a handsome boy standing beside a waterfall who very dearly wanted to kiss me."

Jude's smile was slow and heated. Despite the cool mist of the morning, Anton felt warm, all the worry and dread of the night bleeding out of him. A knot of guilt remained lodged in his gut. But as long as he didn't think too hard about what he was hiding from Jude, he could ignore it.

"You know," Anton went on, "I *am* a Prophet. My dreams predict the future."

"Is that right?" Jude asked with feigned curiosity.

He seemed committed to not taking the bait, but before Anton could push the gambit any further, a heavy arm landed over his shoulders.

"Morning, Prophet," Hector said, his arm dripping water onto Anton's shirt. "I was hoping I might get a word with you."

Jude eyed them hesitantly.

"It's fine, Jude," Anton said. "You should try to find Penrose. I'll catch up with you."

Jude gave them one last inquisitive look before he made his way down the hill.

As soon as he was out of sight, Anton shrugged off Hector's arm. "Hurry up and tell me what you want. I have a lot to do today."

Hector tilted his head at Anton curiously. "You have nothing to be jealous of, you know."

Anton stared at him, incredulous. "You think I'm *jealous?*"

"I mean—aren't you?"

Anton probed the uncomfortable feeling that had been sitting in his chest. *Jealous?* He was just worried. He still didn't trust Hector, not where Jude was concerned anyway.

Hector shook his head ruefully. "I still can't quite wrap my head around it. You and him. But I guess I shouldn't be so surprised—he does tend to pick the absolute worst people to fall for."

"I'm not—" Anton stopped, taking in what Hector had said. "Wait. You knew he was in love with you?"

Hector shrugged, looking a little embarrassed now. "Jude's . . . well, you know what he's like. He's not exactly great at deceiving people. Other than himself. So, yes. We never talked about it, but I knew.

But whatever it is you're worried about, don't be. Me and Jude . . . we were never going to be anything other than what we are now. Friends. Brothers-in-arms."

"Why would I be worried?" Anton asked petulantly.

"All the dirty looks and silent treatment might've tipped me off," Hector said. "Not to mention how quickly you marched up here after us."

Anton rolled his eyes. "Has anyone ever told you that you come off a little arrogant?"

"Many people," Hector replied, as if this was a point of pride.

Anton crossed his arms over his chest. "I'm not threatened by you. I'm worried you're going to hurt him again."

"Oh." Hector looked a little stunned by this, like he hadn't considered it.

"He would have done anything for you," Anton went on, anger climbing up his throat. "Followed you to the ends of the earth. And you threw that away like it was nothing."

Hector stared at him for a moment, blank. Slowly, he asked, "You really think that, don't you?"

"I was there," Anton replied, clipped. "I saw him wager the Pinnacle Blade *and* the torc of the Keeper just to chase after you."

Hector shook his head, looking around at the trees, the hillside, everywhere except at Anton. He was almost smiling, a bitten-off, rueful thing, and Anton felt defensive, like he was being made fun of.

"What do you want me to say?" Hector asked at last. "That I regret leaving? That I shouldn't have done it? I might regret how it happened, but I *had* to leave. I never asked Jude to do any of that, and I meant what I said that day—I never should have accepted a place in the Paladin Guard. It was cruel, to both of us. He loved me, and I knew that he loved me, and I also knew that nothing would ever come of it."

"Because you didn't want it?"

"Because *Jude* didn't."

Anton stared at him, shocked. How could he even think that?

"He was never going to leave the Order for me." The certainty in Hector's voice was enough to keep Anton silent. "He would have kept me close, by his side, for as long as he could, and made us both miserable in the process. That was the only way it could end. You think Jude would have done anything for me, but you're wrong. He would have returned to the Order—maybe in a week, a month, or a year, but he would have gone back. Chasing after me was just an excuse, a way to test, once and for all, his devotion to his duty. And I'm not saying it wasn't sorely tested but—if there's one thing I know, it's that Jude could never walk away from his destiny. Not for me, not for anything."

Anton's mouth went dry as Hector's dark eyes bored into his. His thoughts returned to the secret he was keeping from Jude, the *true* destiny that Jude didn't even know of. Jude may have left the Order for Anton, but this, his destiny, well—Hector had said it, plain and simple. Jude wouldn't walk away from it. Not for Hector. Not for Anton.

"Honestly, it kind of figures that the only person who could make Jude leave the Order was the Last Prophet himself," Hector said. "You know, it scared me at first, how he feels about you. After Behezda, he would barely talk about it, but I could see it, bleeding out of him. He has so much faith in you. And I thought how dangerous that is. Here's this person Jude's been raised since birth to worship—to serve. 'Above our lives, above our hearts' and all that. But now, what? He loves you? It's all tangled up for him. You see that, right?"

"What are you trying to say?" Anton asked, swallowing down his protests, his justification. Because when Hector put it like that, it was hard to dismiss.

"I'm saying you're scared of what I might do to him, but you're the one who can really hurt him, Anton."

I would never hurt him, Anton thought fiercely, but he didn't say it aloud. It wasn't a lie, but it wasn't true, either. He *could* hurt Jude. He already had, when he'd disappeared and left Jude to think he was dead.

And keeping this secret—this huge, terrible, ruinous secret—could hurt him, too.

"I don't want to," he said at last, and this at least he knew he meant with everything in him. "I would rather die than see him hurt because of me. Before I met him, I didn't see the point in all this. In being the Prophet. In trying to stop the Age of Darkness. All I knew was just—survival. Getting by, however I could. But now . . ."

Now he had someone for whom he would save the world. And it was the exact person he was supposed to sacrifice to do it.

"I get it," Hector said. "When I met Jude, I'd just lost everything. I thought there was no way forward. But he . . . he gave me something I thought I'd never have again. Family. And when I left him behind, when I hurt him the way I did, I hated myself for it. But we found our way back to each other, and Jude, he—he has so much heart. He gave me his trust, and I'm not going to break it again."

Anton bit the inside of his cheek and nodded. He wondered, briefly, what would happen if he told Hector everything. Hector might be the only other person in the world who wanted to protect Jude as much as Anton did. The thought of it almost loosened his tongue.

"Hector," he said. But there wasn't any reason, he realized, to share this burden with him. He just didn't want to bear it alone. Instead, he said, "I'm glad he has you."

Hector smiled wryly. "I've loved him a long time. And I know he deserves better than me. I hope that's you."

———————————

When Hector and Anton returned to the fort, it was a flurry of activity. Paladin and stewards rushed past them in the courtyard, barely sparing Anton a glance. Ahead, in the shade of a slender tree, Anton spotted Jude and Penrose deep in conversation. Jude looked agitated, his brow creased as he spoke to Penrose in short, clipped bursts.

Anton hurried over, Hector at his heels.

"What's going on?" he demanded.

It was Penrose who answered. "We're evacuating all the stewards and anyone else who can't fight."

"And those who can fight?" Hector asked.

"Are preparing to do just that."

"What?" Anton asked. "*Why?* I told you, the minute we scry in the Circle of Stones—"

"You'll rain Pallas's forces down on us," Penrose said. "I know. That's why we're going to fight."

"The Witnesses have Grace now. They're not going to be defeated so easily," Hector said. "And the Paladin who've joined him know the secrets of this fort."

"I know," Penrose said. "I know all of that."

"Then why—"

"To buy us time," Jude said, before Penrose could. "That's it, isn't it? You don't even expect to defeat Pallas's forces. You just want to delay them as long as you can to give us a head start."

Penrose nodded.

"People will die," Anton said.

"Then they'll die for their cause," Penrose said. "For their Prophet."

"I don't like this," Anton said.

"You don't have to," Penrose replied. "This is what the Order of the Last Light was created for. This is why we swear our oaths."

Anton knew that better than Penrose. The Order was just the Prophets' cannon fodder if their mistakes ever came back to bite them. And the Keeper was supposed to lead the charge.

"Penrose . . ." Jude began, sounding pained. But then all he said was, "Thank you."

"Don't thank me," Penrose replied. "Just do what you came here to do. Stop the Age of Darkness. Whatever it takes."

Anton's stomach dropped. This—all of this—was only happening because Anton already knew he couldn't do whatever it took.

"We'll need to give everyone time to prepare," Penrose said. "Can you scry tonight?"

Anton nodded, the weight of his guilt clenching his gut.

"Then we'll do it at sundown," Penrose said. "And we'll get everyone who's leaving out before then."

Anton nodded.

Another Paladin approached, drawing Penrose into conversation about logistics. Her gaze flicked back to Anton and Jude, and she gave a nod, dismissing them.

"We should go tell the others," Jude said, a grim set to his mouth.

Already, Anton missed the more relaxed and lighthearted Jude from this morning. He longed to comfort him but knew the guilt weighing down his chest would make anything he had to offer ring hollow.

"I'll go with you," Hector volunteered.

"I should find the Wanderer," Anton said.

Jude nodded, but his lingering gaze told Anton he would've

preferred they stay together. He had to force himself to walk off toward the distant chime of the Wanderer's *esha*.

He found her outside the Tribunal Chambers, gazing up at the statue of Temara that guarded its entrance. Anton's heart broke a little at the far-off expression on her face.

"You know, they really couldn't capture her face quite right," she said lightly, without turning to look at him.

Anton considered the statue. It looked similar enough to the Temara he had seen when he'd scried into the Wanderer's past. A strong jaw and sharp cheekbones, framed by a sweep of cropped hair. Perhaps, then, it was the expression that the Wanderer objected to. Steadfast and sure, her face as cold as the stone it was carved from, lips pursed and eyes gazing off into the distance. This was the Temara that the Order would have known.

"I assume we were granted permission, then?" the Wanderer asked, turning to Anton at last.

He nodded. "Tonight at sundown. We'll scry for the other Prophets."

Anton could imagine the mix of emotions the Wanderer was feeling. The other Prophets had played a role in what had happened to Temara. They were the reason the Wanderer was the Wanderer, and no longer Ananke the Brave.

But Anton needed them. The *world* needed them.

"If this works," the Wanderer said. "I can't come with you to find the other Prophets."

Anton caught her eye. "*When* this works," he insisted, "I wouldn't ask that of you."

She laid a hand on his shoulder. The touch was surprisingly tender, and Anton felt himself lean into it. He still hadn't quite shrugged off the fact that she had knowingly put Jude in danger by sending him to Pallas Athos. But at the same time, she had put her faith in Anton.

INTO THE DYING LIGHT

"Thank you," he said seriously.

"For what?" she asked, sounding genuinely nonplussed.

"For not giving up on me, I guess," Anton replied. "For being there when I needed you, even if I didn't know it at the time."

She smiled. Not her usual secretive, sly smile, but one that lit up her whole face and made her look like a young woman again.

"Come," she said, gently leading Anton away. "It won't do to scry on an empty stomach."

The sun sank below the western mountain ridge of the river valley as Jude, Anton, and the Wanderer climbed up to the Circle of Stones. The low buzz of the Circle's resonance grew louder and steadier as they ascended the stone stairs and approached the heelstone that marked the entrance.

"I'll wait for you here," Jude said, coming to a halt beside the heelstone. He squeezed Anton's hand once and then let go.

He had come this far, but this part was reserved for Anton and the Wanderer. A strange wave of familiarity washed over Anton as he stepped into the circle of great monoliths with the Wanderer. Each of the Seven Prophets towered above them, the Stones burnished rose and gold in the evening sunlight. It was strange to see Pallas staring down at them, his stone face soft and benevolent. Stranger still to see the Wanderer, without a face.

"Another poor likeness." Her lips tilted into a smile as she looked up at the stone meant to represent her.

Anton squinted one eye shut, pretending to compare her face to that of the monolith. "They could have done a better job," he agreed. "For one thing, statue-you doesn't have a drink in her hand."

He smiled up at her look of mock scorn.

"All right," she said when they reached the exact center of the Circle. "Just like I taught you."

They separated, each walking toward opposite edges of the Circle. It felt like the resonance of the Stones was guiding them, rebounding off the Wanderer's *esha* and Anton's until they were each situated at the foci of the Circle.

A calm stillness settled in his chest as they turned and faced each other. Stars were beginning to glow in the dimming sky above as Anton breathed in, focusing on the resonance of the Stones. He had felt their presence once before, his first time at Kerameikos. Up here it was so much stronger, ringing in his head and through his bones. He let himself sink into their ebb and flow, until he could almost feel it lining up with his pulse, with the vibration of his own *esha*. He could feel the Wanderer doing the same thing, the clear, bell chime of her *esha* collapsing into the susurration of the Circle of Stones, reverberating, amplifying.

There was no separating the sounds now—his *esha*, the Wanderer's, the ringing of Stones all came together as one wave of sound, cresting over them and breaking outward. It felt like what he had done in the cistern of Nazirah, calling out to Jude with his Grace, and again in Behezda, using it to try to mend the Four-Petal Seal on the Red Gate of Mercy, but *more*. Like his *esha* now echoed with that of seven others—the Prophets. And he knew, somehow, that he and the Wanderer were not the only ones who could feel this sudden surge of power. Knew that even someone without Grace could feel it, as sure as if he were standing here and making a declaration.

I am the Last Prophet.

It was as if the words were echoing out from him, woven into the call of the monoliths.

He opened his eyes, his neck craning up toward the sky which was now alight with shivering color. Pinks and golds and deep purples streaked across deep blue. They swam and furled like waves across the ocean.

And then, from outside the Circle of Stones, Anton felt an echo of his and the Wanderer's *esha*. The energy they had sent out rippled back to them, changed. It was the *esha* of the other Prophets, answering their call.

The echo contracted around them, like a breath being sucked in, and then the connection broke. Anton fell to his hands and knees, overwhelmed and almost nauseated. He heard footsteps pounding across the soft earth toward him, and a moment later Jude dropped to his knees beside him.

"I'm fine," Anton said, his voice scraped raw. He held up a hand before Jude could touch him and climbed to his feet. He looked back up at the sky, where the strange light was now fading.

He glanced back at Jude and found that the swordsman had not yet risen. He remained kneeling at Anton's feet, staring up at him with a soft, awed expression.

"I saw the sky," Jude said, a tremor in his voice. "The way it looked the day you were born. It was just like this."

Anton's chest lurched. He hadn't seen that expression on Jude's face since that day he had found Anton in the cistern of Nazirah. Since he'd realized who—*what* Anton was. Hector's warning came back to him, and as much as it pained Anton to admit it, he knew Hector had been right. Jude's destiny had always been Anton. The Prophet. It wasn't the reason he loved Anton, but it was bound up in everything they'd gone through together. It was there in the way Jude followed him. It was there in the way he kissed him, the way he touched him. Faith, devotion, love, desire—there was no untangling it.

"I knew then," Jude said reverently, chest hitching. "I knew what I was meant for."

The certainty in his voice made Anton want to hide. To run.

"Anton," the Wanderer's voice sounded from behind them. "It worked. You can feel them, can't you?"

There was a note of trepidation in her voice, and it took Anton a moment to understand why. Beneath the buzzing power of their combined scrying, Anton felt the tug of *esha*, like two magnets gently pulling at him. One to the south—that must be Pallas. And the other, somewhere northwest. The other Prophets.

They were all in the same place, he realized. A place that the Wanderer knew well. A place at the edge of the world, where she had once hidden with the one she loved. He could see the question in her eyes, the same one he wanted to ask.

What were the Prophets doing there?

"We need to get back to the ship," the Wanderer said. "Pallas will know exactly where we are now, and we need to put as much distance between us as we can."

Anton nodded and let Jude pull him to his feet. He kept hold of his hand as they descended the same stone stairs. By the time they reached the fort again, it was fully dark. Soft lanterns lit the walkways, where what seemed like a hundred Paladin knelt, staring at him with expressions of awe not unlike the one Jude had worn. Some of them, Anton saw, were crying.

"Prophet," one of the Paladin murmured. "It really is you."

There was no denying it now. No hiding. No running.

I will fail these people. The thought came, unbidden and certain, like it had already happened.

They all believed in him. Anton could see it in their eyes, the way he'd seen it in Jude's.

This was what he had been running from his whole life. Not his brother, not his vision, but this moment, when he became something other than himself, when he stopped being Anton, the boy who survived, the boy who Jude loved, and became the Last Prophet. He wanted to turn and run now, and for the first time not even Jude at his side felt like enough to stop him.

These people wanted him to be a savior who could single-handedly stop the Age of Darkness and restore peace to the world. Anton knew he could do neither, but he could do what he had always done—he could play along. He could let them believe what they wanted.

It was easy, then, to melt into the role beneath the weight of the Paladins' gazes. It was just like bluffing a mediocre hand in a game of canbarra.

The others were all waiting for them back on the Wanderer's ship. The Guard had come to see them off, the four of them lined up on the dock as Anton approached.

Osei, Annuka, and Petrossian sank to their knees as they caught sight of Anton. Penrose followed suit a moment later.

The other Paladin didn't know him, but the Guard did. Even if he hadn't necessarily had many long talks with them, they still *knew* him. This might be the last time they would ever see one another. No matter what else the Guard and Anton disagreed on, they were laying down their lives for him. For their mission.

"Whatever it takes," Penrose said.

And Anton let her believe what she wanted. "Whatever it takes."

22

HASSAN

"THEY'RE IN THE UNSPOKEN MOUNTAINS."

Anton had once again gathered everyone in a sitting room on the upper deck of the Wanderer's ship as they pushed off from Kerameikos. He looked out at them from the front of the room, his back to the windows and the night sky.

After that display in the Circle of Stones, Hassan found himself viewing Anton in a slightly new light. He'd already known, of course, that Anton was the Last Prophet. But now he *believed* it—that Anton could stop the Age of Darkness. He finally understood Jude's unshakable faith in him.

"Where is that exactly?" Ephyra piped up.

"It's a chain of volcanic mountains on the western coast of this peninsula," Jude answered from Anton's side. "Across from the Gallian Mountains."

"Why would the Prophets be *there*?" Hassan asked. "It's just wilderness, isn't it?"

"As far as we know," Anton said, glancing at the Wanderer. "Maybe that was the point—they wanted to hide somewhere far away from the rest of civilization."

She looked away.

"So that's where we're going?" Hector asked.

"*We* aren't doing anything," Anton replied. "I'm going. And Beru's coming with me."

Hassan knew that meant Jude and Ephyra would both be going, too.

"But none of the rest of you need to come along," Anton went on. "The Wanderer is taking this ship to meet up with some other members of the Lost Rose. They're going to try to track down wherever Pallas hid the Relics in case—well, just in case."

In case they failed.

The Relics weren't a real solution to stopping the god, but they could be used to seal the god again, buying them time. Time for what, Hassan didn't know.

"If all goes well, the Wanderer will meet back up with us at a Lost Rose safe house on the other side of the valley, at the foot of the Unspoken Mountains," Anton continued. "The rest of you can choose to stay on the ship, and she'll take you to find shelter at another Lost Rose location."

Anton's gaze flicked to Evander. Of all of them, the merchant's son had the least amount to do with this.

Hassan avoided looking at Khepri. He didn't know what arrangements, if any, she'd made with the Wanderer to return to Nazirah. Selfishly, he wanted her with him. Even after they'd hurt each other, he still didn't want to let her go. But she had made her intentions clear on the ship. He wouldn't stand in her way, even if the thought of being separated again made him want to get on his knees and beg her to stay.

Hector cleared his throat, shooting Beru a furtive look. "Jude's obviously going with you, Anton, so I will, too."

"Me too," Hassan said firmly. "I'm part of this. I'm with you, whatever it takes. We were brought together for a reason, weren't we?"

"I'm coming, too," another voice said from the open doorway.

Hassan turned and found Anton's brother in the threshold.

"No," Anton said. "We don't have room on this quest for evil brothers who work for the Hierophant. Sorry."

Hassan still wasn't sure what to make of Illya Aliyev. He'd seen him turn on the Hierophant, and then turn back. And yet he was the reason, really, they'd all made it out of the citadel alive.

It didn't necessarily mean they could trust him. Anton certainly didn't.

"My help was certainly good enough when you needed me to rescue your swordsman," Illya replied haughtily. "I may have worked for the Hierophant *briefly*, but I turned on him. He had me executed! If that doesn't prove that we've cut ties, then—"

Anton's jaw clenched. "You're not coming."

"You need me," Illya said bluntly. "The fact that I used to work for the Hierophant is actually an *asset*. I know lots of important things—where he has Witnesses stationed, what his plans are, how his mind works."

Hassan and Hector exchanged a glance. Illya was making some valid points.

Hector wiped a hand over his face. "I hate to say it, but he's right. That kind of knowledge would be pretty useful."

"Not if we can't trust it," Anton shot back. He turned to Illya. "Why do you even *want* to come?"

Illya looked at his brother, his brows drawing up over his golden eyes. "You're never going to see me as anything besides the terrible brother who used to lock you in closets, are you?"

Anton's jaw tightened.

"He did help us, Anton," Beru spoke up quietly.

"See?" Illya said. "Beru trusts me."

Beru sighed. "I actually do. I'll vouch for him. Ephyra will, too."

Ephyra sent her sister a look of unspeakable betrayal. "Do *not* make me part of this."

Beru reached over and pinched her.

"Ow! All right, *fine*, I vouch for him, too," Ephyra said, batting Beru's hand away.

Anton glared at Illya for a long, silent moment. He was very clearly outnumbered. "Fine," he bit out at last. "But if you do anything that *anyone* finds even a little suspicious, Jude will push you into a volcano."

Jude gave a single, solemn nod of agreement.

Illya just smiled. "First off a ship, now into a volcano—your threats are getting more and more elaborate, Anton."

Anton opened his mouth to reply when Hassan made the decision that they'd all heard enough sniping from the two.

"All right, so it's the seven of us," he said, looking around at the others.

"Eight," Khepri spoke up from the corner of the room.

Hassan felt everyone else turning to stare at Khepri as his gaze found hers. She stared right back, unwavering.

"I thought you wanted to go back to Nazirah," Hassan said quietly, his heart leaping. He hadn't dared to hope that she would change her mind.

"I . . ." She looked down, bowing her head. "I *do* want to go back to Nazirah. I thought of nothing else when the Hierophant had me captive. But Hassan, you were right. Nazirah won't be safe until the god is defeated." She glanced at the others. "And, look, I'm sure you're all very capable, but if the seven of you are the *only thing* that stands between our world and complete destruction then . . . sorry, but I think you could use the help."

She flashed them a sarcastic little smile, and it stole the breath from Hassan's lungs. It was a glimpse of the Khepri that he'd met on the steps of the Temple of Pallas all those months ago. The Khepri who had challenged him to a sparring match. The Khepri who had kissed him with ferocity and fire aboard the *Cressida* on their way to Nazirah. He felt winded by how much he had missed her, as if he'd been storing it all away, every second they'd been apart.

Faintly, Hassan heard a loud guffaw from his other side, and then Hector's rueful voice. "What? She's not wrong."

"All right, then," Jude said as Khepri's gaze found Hassan's again and she dipped her head in a little nod that he wasn't sure how to interpret. "The eight of us."

The next morning, they docked in a flat part of the river and rowed two dinghies to shore. From there, they began their hike toward the Green Ridge Pass, which would lead them into the river valley. The pass was steep and treacherous, but Illya warned them that the true difficulty would begin once they hit the valley.

According to him, Pallas's forces—a mix of devout Witnesses, the Paladin who had defected to him, and hired mercenaries—were crawling all over the countryside. Any town or large growing area would be rife with them, so they would have to tread carefully and avoid civilization as much as they could.

The others were skeptical that Pallas would dedicate so much of his manpower to a relatively peaceful river valley, but Hassan saw the logic.

"There are tons of prized resources in the valley. Grain. Livestock. Wine. Lumber," he said, ticking them off on his fingers. "They supply not only Pallas Athos, but most of the other Prophetic Cities. The Hierophant is making sure he controls the valley so he can cut off supplies to the places that try to oppose him."

"Like he threatened to do to Endarrion," Beru added.

"The valley is one challenge," Jude said. "The Unspoken Mountains will be another entirely."

"Meaning?" Ephyra asked.

"They're completely uninhabited," Jude said. "Desolate. We don't actually know what's up there, because so few people have ever traveled beyond the Serpentine River. We'll be completely on our own."

Hassan felt cold thinking of it. Crossing a barren mountain range, searching for Prophets who had long since abandoned them. Maybe they were fooling themselves to think that any of this could work, let alone that they could make it out alive.

"And we have another problem," Jude said, nodding to Anton.

"The Witnesses are closer than we thought," Anton said. "The Wanderer and I were able to scry for the location of a group of them Pallas sent after us to Kerameikos. We assumed he was sending them from Pallas Athos, but they're much closer—he must have had some stationed along the river already."

"How close are they?" Hector asked.

"We think maybe a day, at most," Jude replied. "The pass is about three leagues away, so we should reach it by evening. We'll take one rest at the midpoint, but otherwise, try and keep moving."

They set off at a brisk clip, and Hassan noted what a strange group they made—a prince, a Legionnaire, two disgraced Paladins, a Prophet, a former Witness, a necromancer, and a girl with a god trapped inside her.

Hassan had kept his distance from Beru since their escape from Pallas Athos, and he saw no reason to approach her now. Khepri didn't seem to have the same qualms and spent the morning deep in conversation with Beru.

The morning mist lifted as they hiked deeper into the mountains, but the dense trees shaded them from the heat of the sun. Long before their midday break, they came to a sudden halt at the bottom of a steep slope. Ahead, Hassan could see Jude and Anton discussing something, both of them looking agitated.

Hassan approached them warily, Hector at his side. "What's going on? Why did we stop?"

The two of them jumped at the intrusion, and he saw the tension in the set of Jude's jaw and the line of Anton's shoulders.

"Anton says he senses more Witnesses," Jude replied after a beat. "More than two dozen, coming east through the pass. Some of them have stolen Graces."

"Coming through—?" Hector repeated. "You mean from the valley?"

Jude nodded. "If we keep going this way, we'll run straight into them. The pass isn't that wide—there's no way to avoid them."

"So what are we supposed to do?" Hassan asked. "Can we fight through them?"

Jude looked like he was considering the prospect. "We probably could. But more likely, they'll hem us in while their reinforcements come in from the east and we'll be cornered."

"Is there another option?" Beru asked, looking worried.

"One," Jude said hesitantly. "We can double back. There's a system of caverns and waterways beneath the mountains that will take us to the river valley."

"Underground?" Hector asked, sounding almost as nervous about the idea as Hassan felt.

"If we double back, we'll be exposing ourselves to the Witnesses already on our tail," Hassan argued. "You said they're what, a day behind us? We've already spent half a day hiking. We double back, we lose that whole lead."

"It's not ideal," Jude conceded. "But the caverns provide more cover. Even if the Witnesses on our tail catch up to us, we can lose them in the caverns."

"That sounds risky," Khepri said.

Hassan agreed. "We have to trust that you'll be able to guide us through," he said, getting frustrated. "And outpace the Witnesses. If they catch us, we'll be in the same situation."

Jude leveled his gaze at him, and Hassan glared right back. Their disagreements had been manifold in those months after Behezda, and this felt like more of the same. Hassan had thought that he himself was stubborn, but he was nothing compared to Jude Weatherbourne when he was decided on something.

"I'm with Jude," Anton said.

Of course he was.

Beru nodded. "Me too."

"I don't care what we do, let's just do it and hurry up," Ephyra said.

"I'm also with Weatherbourne on this one," Illya offered.

"No one asked you," Anton ground out.

"Fine," Hassan said. He was outnumbered, and it would take more valuable time to keep arguing about it. "We'll double back."

They packed up quickly, and headed back along the path they'd taken into the mountains. Hassan couldn't help but feel defeated with every step—all the time they'd spent on the hike was now wasted. But he held his tongue.

About half a league from the river where they'd started, Jude took them on a slanting path north, through thick trees. The path grew steep, and in some sections they had to actually climb up the rock, Hector, Jude, and Khepri helping the others. They reached the mouth of a cavern as the sun began to set.

"Those of you with lights, wait until we get inside the cavern to turn them on," Jude advised.

The air was cool and damp within the cave, the walls dripping with jagged stalactites. They pressed onward, past the time that they would have set up camp in the pass, with no signs of stopping. Hassan's feet felt heavy, like he was dragging himself through the caverns. His pack had begun to chafe on one shoulder, and it was all he could focus on.

"Jude," Hector said quietly, somewhere ahead of Hassan. "We need to rest."

"We can't," Jude replied. "If we stop, the Witnesses—"

"If we don't stop, people are going to start collapsing," Hector warned. "Even I'm getting tired, and not everyone has the Grace of Heart, all right?"

"We need to keep moving."

"Hector's right." Anton's voice joined theirs in the dark. "We can't outrun the Witnesses like this. *I* can't. The Witnesses are still hours behind us."

Jude didn't say anything for a long moment, but then Hassan heard him call out to everyone else. "All right. Three hours. Hector and I will keep watch while everyone gets some rest. No fires."

It was frigid inside the cavern, but Hassan was too exhausted to protest. He also felt mildly shocked—of all the feats he'd seen Anton perform so far, getting Jude to concede an argument might have been the most impressive yet.

Hassan sat down heavily on a rock beside Khepri. She looked

exhausted, sitting with one knee pulled up to her chest, staring off into the darkness, chewing on a roll.

He took a breath, deciding how to start this conversation. "Khepri, you didn't need to come with us just because of me."

She lowered the roll and stared at him. "What makes you think I did it for you?"

He looked away. She was right—she'd given him no reason to think that. He'd just hoped. "I guess I'm asking then."

"Hassan, neither of us has slept more than six hours, and we have probably four weeks, at minimum, before we get to wherever we're going," Khepri said. "So if it's all right with you, can we please just hold off on any deep conversations about our feelings and our—whatever, until we do what we've set out to do?"

Hassan bit down on a flash of anger. "Look, I'm trying to give you space because I know things are complicated, but I just need to know where I stand with you."

"Where you stand with me," Khepri repeated. "Right now . . . right now, we can be friends, Hassan. That's where we stand. That's all I have. All right?"

Hassan swallowed. He could tell she was annoyed—*he* was annoyed—but there was something deeper and more aching in Khepri's voice.

"Khepri," he said. "If you need someone to talk to about what you went through, about what happened to you when the Hierophant kept you captive, I—"

"I don't," she snapped. "I don't want to talk about it. I want to keep going."

He pressed his lips together. When he looked closely, he could see that Khepri was fraying at the edges. He was, too. He tugged a hand through his hair.

"So that's it?" he asked. "You're just going to shut me out because you don't want to deal with what happened?"

"That's really something, coming from you," Khepri shot back.

"I made a mistake," Hassan said. "A terrible mistake that I regret, more than anything. But don't pretend you're blameless."

"Stop," Khepri said sharply. "Just—stop."

"Yes, please, both of you stop," Ephyra groaned from somewhere in the dark. "We're trying to get some sleep so if you could go argue somewhere else that would be fantastic."

Hassan flushed.

"She's right," Khepri said abruptly. "Get some sleep."

She walked off into the dark without another word. Hassan slumped down by the rock, grabbing his pack to use as a pillow. The cold cave floor was hardly comfortable, but he didn't have time to worry about it before his eyes slipped closed and he fell deep into sleep.

Someone shook him awake a moment later.

Hassan rubbed his face blearily and sat up. "I thought we were resting for three hours?"

"We did," Hector said, sounding amused. "You slept like a rock. And you snore, by the way."

"I don't snore," Hassan grumbled, getting to his feet. "*You* snore."

Incandescent lights illuminated the others in various states of groggy exhaustion. His eyes found Khepri immediately, stretching over on the other side of the rocks. Ephyra and Beru were packing up their bedrolls.

Across from them, Jude knelt beside Anton's bedroll, stroking his fingers gently through Anton's hair. Anton stirred and then sat up. Jude stayed where he was, his hand lingering at Anton's side as Anton leaned in to say something that was too quiet for Hassan to catch. And then Jude did something Hassan had never seen him do before—he laughed.

For a moment, Hassan wondered if exhaustion was making him hallucinate. But no, Jude was still there, staring at Anton with an expression so tender Hassan almost didn't recognize him. Gone was the stubborn, surly swordsman that Hassan had lived in close quarters with for over two months. He had softened after just a handful of days with Anton, and Hassan felt his own icy regard for Jude thaw a little in response.

"Here." Hector nudged Hassan again, holding out a hunk of bread and dried meat. Hassan accepted it, digging in gratefully. He hadn't realized how hungry he was until he'd gotten some sleep.

"I would do truly awful things for some tea right now," Ephyra said, rubbing her eyes.

"Let's be honest, you would do truly awful things anyway," Hector said.

Ephyra glared at him.

"Here," Khepri said, reaching into a pocket of her bag and holding something up to Ephyra. "Made sure to grab some guaran root from the Order's storeroom. Legionnaire secret. Chew some and you'll be perky in no time."

"Unlikely," Illya said. Ephyra glared at him, too, taking the guaran root from Khepri.

"We need to get going," Jude said a little tersely.

Those three hours of sleep didn't stretch very far. Hassan still felt exhausted as they set off, his whole body aching, and now his head was fuzzy with sleep, too. The pack somehow felt heavier than it had when he'd put it down. Khepri gave him some of the guaran root, which helped but also left him buzzing with nerves and feeling somewhat nauseated.

They still had days of travel through the caverns left. And already they were flagging. But they had to push on. It was their only choice.

23

BERU

"WE CAN'T KEEP GOING LIKE THIS." HASSAN'S FACE WAS DRAWN, HIS FATIGUE obvious in the shadows beneath his eyes and the croak in his voice.

Beru couldn't even fault him for the outburst—he was only saying what they were all thinking.

They had stopped to rest only four times over the past five and half days or so, although the passing of time was hard to gauge in the dark caverns. Each stop got progressively shorter, and Beru could see the bone-deep weariness on everyone's faces. Even Jude, Hector, and Khepri were starting to look ragged.

Beru's own exhaustion made it harder to block out the god's voice in her head. Even with the Godfire collar on, she felt its presence more acutely with every passing hour.

Now, on their fifth stop, they had no sooner sat down than Jude was telling them to get up again.

"We're all exhausted," Hassan said bluntly.

"We have to go," Jude replied tersely. "The Witnesses are too close."

The Witnesses gained a little more ground each time Beru and the others stopped to rest. They must all have stolen Grace that increased their endurance, because there was no other way they could be pushing through the caverns that quickly. Beru felt a twinge of guilt at that thought.

"How close?" Hassan asked, alarmed.

Anton chewed his lip. "You remember that big rock formation we passed? The one that looked like an elephant?"

He looked terrified. Though Beru knew they were around the same age, Anton suddenly seemed so *young*. He didn't look like a Prophet at all, not like the person who had lit up the sky just a few nights ago, the one who was supposedly destined to save the world. He just looked like a scared kid.

Hector scratched at his jaw. "That was what, an hour ago?"

"They're going to catch up to us," Ephyra said. "It's not if but when."

"I *knew* coming through the caverns was a bad idea," Hassan grumbled. "I *knew* it."

"Like *you've* never had a bad idea before, Hassan," Khepri said acidly.

"What's that supposed to mean?"

She gave him a look that left him gaping in outrage.

"Something's wrong," Illya said. "We should've lost the Witnesses *days* ago."

"You're right," Anton said. "Something *is* wrong. Let's start with the fact that we invited someone who *was working for the Witnesses* on this little journey. You want to know how the Witnesses are tracking us? Let's start with *him*."

He shot Illya a venomous look.

"You really think I'm still working for them?" Illya demanded. "Why would I have helped rescue you and your friends?"

"Just because you helped us doesn't mean you won't betray us again."

"Ephyra, tell him that I'm—"

"I don't know why you'd think I'm on your side," Ephyra said.

"Her vote of support won't help your case," Hector added, shooting Ephyra a glare. "In fact, didn't anyone consider whether it was a good idea to invite *the girl who murdered me* to join us?"

"I'm here because Beru's my *sister*. And besides, I healed him, didn't I?" Ephyra gestured at Jude.

"If you think that absolves you—"

"I never said it *absolves* anything—"

"—and if Jude had just agreed to go through the pass—"

"—I know you don't want me here but don't pretend—"

Everyone was talking at once, their voices overlapping and growing in volume until all Beru could hear was sharp, acerbic cries of outrage.

YOU HUMANS ARE SUCH STRANGE CREATURES, the god sniffed. YOU CHOOSE YOUR WOUNDED PRIDE AND DAMAGED FEELINGS OVER YOUR OWN SURVIVAL.

Everyone was just tired. *Exhausted.* Conflict was inevitable under the circumstances. But the god was right—if they were already fraying this badly, they wouldn't make it through the mountains.

And if they kept arguing like this, the Witnesses were going to find them.

THEY'RE TRACKING US, the god mused idly. WE HAVEN'T LOST THEM IN THE CAVERNS BECAUSE THEY KNOW EXACTLY WHERE WE ARE.

It was the only thing that made sense. Beru would have known that even if the god hadn't suggested it. But how? Maybe something had happened when Anton had scried in the Circle of Stones? Maybe it had broken the shielding he'd devised to mask their *esha*.

GOOD GUESS, the god said laconically. BUT WRONG.

Us?

The god didn't reply, not outright, but she felt its approval.

"Guys," she hissed. No one seemed to hear her. "Hey!"

"—that has *nothing* to do with this—"

"—I don't see how you can trust him when he—"

"—it was a stupid plan and you *know* it—"

"*Shut up!*" A gale of power erupted from Beru's hands, swirling around the others and silencing them. The Godfire collar burned on Beru's neck as she stumbled back, sucking in air.

They all stared at her, wide-eyed, some terrified.

Beru pushed down her own terror at how easily the god's power had come to her, even with the Godfire collar. "All right, I'm just gonna say it. We all sort of hate each other, and we are going to die if we don't get over it, fast. You two"—she waved a finger at Illya and Anton—"have some real unresolved childhood issues that I can't even begin to get into. You—" she said to Ephyra, "*literally* murdered him." She nodded at Hector. "And I have *no* idea what's going on here." She gestured between Khepri and Hassan. "But whatever it is, you need to sort it out. Because I'm not worried about the Witnesses getting to us—I'm pretty sure we're all going to kill each other first."

Hassan, Ephyra, and Jude all had the good sense to look contrite. Khepri looked incensed, Illya amused, and Anton and Hector were both glaring.

"Now," Beru said serenely, "if everyone is done, I think I know why we haven't been able to lose the Witnesses." She hesitated. It was a huge risk, taking advice from the god. But—it was probably right. "They're tracking me."

Hector looked at her sharply. "How do you know?"

"I just do," Beru replied. If she told them the full truth they would, rightfully, object to taking ideas from the god. She could feel it pressing in on her will, drawn closer to the surface. She had to hope that the

Godfire collar's sting was enough to keep it at bay. She let her fingers hook into the edge of the collar, feeling the cool metal at her throat.

And that's when she realized.

OH, VERY CLEVER, the god said, amused. LITTLE MORTAL, SO CLEVER.

"They're tracking the Godfire collar," Beru said, regretting the words as they left her mouth. But they were *true*. It made sense. "It—it must have been artificed. That's why there are so many of them right on our tail."

She watched the realization settle over the rest of them—it was the only thing that made sense.

"I—" She swallowed. This was a terrible idea. "I think I need to take it off."

The god wanted her to take it off. *Desperately.* She was a fool to even consider it. It could easily be trying to trick her into making a desperate move that would bring it a step closer to its freedom.

"No way," Hector said when the shock of Beru's pronouncement had worn off. "It's too dangerous. If you take off the collar and the god manages to seize control from you, then that's it. We can't risk you like that."

"I agree with Hector," Jude said. "It's too big a risk. And we don't even know if it's true."

YOU DO KNOW, the god gloated. YOU KNOW THAT IT'S TRUE, LITTLE MORTAL.

"It would make sense, though," Illya said slowly. "Pallas *would* have put a safeguard in place in case Beru ever escaped. Another way to track her down."

Hassan took a hesitant step toward her. "Can I—Can I see the collar, a moment?"

Beru nodded, and he came nearer, using his incandescent light to peer at the collar in the darkness. He moved all the way around her until he was behind her, and then stopped.

"Look at this," he said. Beru wasn't sure to whom he was talking, but a moment later she felt Hector step toward her, his breath warming the back of her neck.

"That's an artificer's mark," Hassan said.

Hector touched the collar, and Beru shivered.

"Sorry," Hector murmured.

"It's fine," she said, not looking at him. Instead, she peered at Hassan. "So it's true?"

He nodded. "Yes. And I think that means we have an opportunity. We can use this to lead the Witnesses into a trap."

"No," Hector said, stepping between them. "We are *not* using Beru as *bait*. It's way too dangerous. I don't care if you think she's—"

"That's not what I was saying at all," Hassan cut in. "I agree. We can't risk the Witnesses getting anywhere near her. But we can use this to make them *think* they are."

Ephyra looked concerned. "But if she takes off the—"

"I'll do it," Beru said at once. She could feel the god's satisfaction. But she also knew that this was the only way they would make it out of the caverns alive. "I . . . I can hold off the god myself like I did on the beach. I don't need the collar."

She injected as much certainty as she could into her voice.

Hector's gaze was heavy on her, as if he knew it was a bluff.

Beru looked past him to Illya. "Do you still have the key?"

"Wait, *he* had it the whole time?" Anton asked, alarmed.

"Right here," Illya said loudly, reaching into a pocket of his jacket.

"Beru," Ephyra said tersely.

"It'll be fine," Beru said, aiming for reassuring. "I won't let the god take control. No matter what."

Ephyra fell silent, and the others waited as Illya undid the collar.

It felt like an exhale. Like the god had been pushed into a tiny, shadowed corner of Beru's mind, but was now unfurling, spilling through her like dark fog. She could feel it beginning to numb her, to fill her with its thoughts. Its relief. Its disdain.

MUCH BETTER, the god said approvingly. YOU THINK SO, TOO, DON'T YOU?

It was better in the sense that the dull, constant pain of the Godfire collar was gone. Now, instead of that pain, she felt hazy. Everything— her fear and her love, even her exhaustion—was filtered through the fog of the god's mind. She felt heavy and hollow at once.

She raised her arms, the god's power pouring through her like molten light. Delight sparked in her chest, the sudden thrill of her own limitless power filling her with glee.

NOW LET'S SHOW THEM WHAT WE CAN DO.

A hand gripped her arm. Beru turned and saw Ephyra staring at her, eyes wide and intent.

"Beru?"

Beru focused on the feeling of Ephyra's fingers wrapped around her arm, the thread of concern in her voice. These were things the god didn't understand.

I am Beru of Medea, she reminded herself. *Ephyra's sister.*

She realized the others were all staring at her, too, various expressions of discomfort and outright terror on their faces.

Beru's ears rang. Her arms were still raised, ready to bring the god's power crashing down on all of them.

She jerked them back to her sides, shaking. Leaning into Ephyra's touch, she breathed in slowly, grounding herself.

I am Beru of Medea. "I'm fine," she said aloud. "Still me."

Illya cleared his throat, holding up the Godfire collar. "Now what?"

"Give it to me," Jude said decisively. "There was a junction about half a league ago. I'll take the collar and lead the Witnesses in the wrong direction, while the rest of you continue out of the caverns."

"What—Jude, *no.*" Anton stepped toward him. "They'll catch up to you. You can't fight them all off alone!"

"I'll be fine," Jude said dismissively. "There's a cluster of waterfalls just at the exit of the caverns. When the coast is clear, I'll meet up with you there."

"Jude, he's right," Hector said. Anton gave him a sideways look. "You can't go off on your own and fight two dozen Witnesses with stolen Grace. At least let me go with you."

Jude shook his head, looking frustrated. "I need you here, to protect everyone else. If Prince Hassan is wrong about the collar—"

"I'm not," Hassan said at once. "Take Hector with you. Khepri and I can defend the others if anything happens."

"And it's not like I'm completely helpless," Ephyra added.

Jude hesitated and then gave a curt nod. "Fine. Hector, you're with me, then."

"Wait," Beru said, before she could think better of it. There was a sense of dread in her, a feeling of wrongness. Through the fog of the god's mind, it took her a moment to decipher the feeling. Worry. Fear. She didn't want Hector to put himself in danger like this. And there was a part of her that feared what would happen if the god tried to seize control while Hector wasn't there to help ground her. "Hector—"

"Four leagues until you're out, no resting until you see the sky," Jude cut in, taking the collar from Illya and shouldering off his pack, handing it to Khepri. "I'm guessing it's around sundown now, so make camp when you reach the falls and wait for us there. If we're not there by sunup tomorrow, leave without us."

Anton reached out, grabbing hold of his sleeve. "I won't let you do this."

Jude glanced at him, his expression a little cold. "It's not your decision."

"I'm the Prophet."

"And I'm here to protect you."

Their argument raged on, but Beru stopped listening as Hector's gaze fell on her. She could feel everything he wouldn't say. Longing pulled at her. Worry, twining with her own. His feelings reflecting against her own, amplifying them, helping her make sense of them even as the god's indifference pressed on her.

"Stay safe," Hector said at last, his broad hand briefly wrapping around her shoulder.

Beru's skin buzzed beneath his touch. "You too."

"Good luck," Jude said abruptly to the others. And then, in a flash of movement, he was gone, Hector after him.

Anton let out a cry of frustration and kicked a loose rock across the cavern.

"Come on, kid," Ephyra said, a hint of sympathy in her voice. "They'll be all right."

She led him back the way they'd been going, Anton cursing under his breath.

Hassan sighed, shouldering Hector's pack. "Four more leagues. We can do this."

Everyone was quiet as they made their way through the remaining caverns. Worry ate at Beru as they trudged through the dark. The farther she got from Hector, the less she could feel his emotions. Or maybe it was the god's presence blocking them out.

IT'S ONLY A MATTER OF TIME UNTIL I'M FREE OF THIS BINDING, the god said. Beru could feel it, scratching at Pallas's seal, a constant, dull pounding in her head like another heartbeat alongside her own.

YOU WANT TO GIVE IN, the god said. TO LET ME HAVE CONTROL. IT WOULD BE EASIER.

No, Beru said at once. But there was a desperate, defeated part of her that longed to sink into oblivion. *I'm not going to give you control just so you can kill all my friends.*

WHAT MAKES YOU THINK I'D KILL THEM? the god asked. MAYBE I'VE GROWN TO LIKE THEM. I COULD MAKE THEM MY PETS ONCE I'M FREE AGAIN. MY ETERNAL, OBEDIENT SERVANTS.

Beru shuddered.

"You feel that?" Khepri asked suddenly.

Beru jumped at the sound of her voice, blinking as Khepri's incandescent light wobbled a few paces ahead.

"A breeze," Khepri went on. "The exit's close."

Despite their fatigue, the idea that they might soon be out of the dark, cold caverns was enough to spur them on.

The moment Beru stepped beneath the moonlight and looked up at the sky, she released a sigh of relief. Ahead of her, Hassan whooped in joy.

They were surrounded by tall trees, stretching up toward the sky, starlight filtering through their leaves. The fresh mountain air was so different from the dank air in the caverns. For a moment, Beru let herself relax and just breathe, chasing away the oppressive fog, though Beru could still feel it curling around her.

They made camp near the foot of the falls, with the plump moon high in the sky and the sound of the river and trees in their ears. Dinner was a simple affair of dried meats and hard bread, all of them too weary to even think about starting a fire. They crawled into their tents and onto the bedrolls.

Beru was exhausted, but she couldn't sleep. Careful not to disturb Khepri and Ephyra, she clambered out of the tent and crept into the trees. She paused in the shelter of their low-hanging boughs, closing her eyes.

You are Beru of Medea, she told herself. *You can fight this. You will fight this.*

NO, LITTLE MORTAL. YOU CAN'T.

"Beru?"

Beru whirled, the god's power surging through her before she had a chance to stop it.

No! Beru pulled in a breath and tensed her whole body, clamping down on the god's power. It sparked at her fingertips, sizzling through the air.

"Ephyra!" Beru shrieked.

With a deafening crack, the bough of one of the trees splintered and crashed to the ground. Ephyra dove out of the way, clearing the branch by inches.

Beru flung herself to her sister's side. "Are you all right?"

Ephyra just stared at Beru, eyes wide and dark in the soft moonlight.

"Are you hurt?"

Ephyra slowly shook her head. "Was that you?"

"It was an accident," Beru said, breathing hard. "You surprised me."

Ephyra edged away from Beru, still staring at her with an expression akin to horror. "It was the god, wasn't it?"

Beru bowed her head. She couldn't lie to Ephyra.

"Is it taking control?" Ephyra asked, her voice so careful Beru almost didn't recognize it.

Beru looked up. "No," she said forcefully. "It was a mistake. A reflex." She could still feel its power humming through her, and the burn of the Four-Petal Seal keeping it at bay. "I'm fine."

She could see in Ephyra's eyes that she didn't believe her. It was what they always said to each other, as if by saying the words out loud they could make them true.

"Come here," Ephyra said, winding an arm around Beru and drawing her close.

Beru wanted to resist, afraid that she might hurt Ephyra again, but in the end she relented, huddling against Ephyra's side and dropping her head against her shoulder. The two of them breathed quietly in the dark, and Beru let herself pretend that this was something her big sister could protect her from.

"I'm fine," she said again. She had to be, because they still had the rest of this journey ahead of them. And if Beru lost control, if she faltered even for a moment and let the god break through, then it would all be for nothing.

24

JUDE

JUDE AND HECTOR SEARCHED FOR A PLACE TO LURE THE WITNESSES IN THEIR desperate flight through the dark tunnels. They already knew they would be woefully outnumbered—Anton had estimated at least two dozen Witnesses on their tail—so their only hope of gaining the upper hand was to use the terrain to their advantage.

At last, they found the place to launch their attack, climbing down a narrow shaft that opened out into a cavernous chamber. A fissure in the cavern wall produced a small waterfall from the subterranean river that had cut this cave system into the mountain.

They laid the Godfire collar on the floor of the cavern, just beyond a deep pool of water formed by the waterfall, and waited on a shelf of rock that overlooked the rest of the cave.

They didn't have to wait long. As Anton had warned, there were about two dozen of them, climbing one by one down the same narrow shaft Jude and Hector had descended through. What Anton had failed to predict was that it wasn't Witnesses who'd been tailing them through the caves. It was Paladin.

Jude's heart dropped into his stomach as he spotted Yarik's dark hair and thickset build crouching down to inspect the Godfire collar.

"Where is she?" Yarik growled. "Where are the rest of them?"

The others fanned out around the cave, searching and listening for signs of their quarry.

Hector gave Jude a short nod. It was time. The fact that it was Paladin instead of Witnesses meant the odds against Jude and Hector were even worse, but otherwise it changed nothing. They had to keep Anton and the others safe.

With a deep breath and a quick koah to summon his Grace, Jude sprang down from the rock shelf and unsheathed his sword, Hector at his side.

Several of the Paladin turned, unsheathing their own blades.

"Oathbreakers."

There was no hesitation as the Paladin clashed against Jude and Hector in a melee of steel. Jude stayed attuned to Hector's movements at his back, each knowing where the other would strike. They focused on penning the Paladin in between the wall of the cave and the water, cutting off the exit point. The strategy would allow the two of them to pick their opponents off a few at a time and keep themselves from being surrounded.

Jude attacked and parried, dodging through stalagmites jutting up from the cave floor like crooked teeth. Each blow he landed against his former brothers- and sisters-in-arms felt like a punch to his own gut. But there was no way to avoid the fight if he wanted to escape this place alive.

He slashed down at one Paladin's arm, his borrowed blade not sharp enough to pierce his opponent's Grace-woven armor, but the force sufficient to break the man's arm. The Paladin cried out in agony, and Jude spun away from the attack, aiming a kick at his next assailant.

With a grunt, the second Paladin went flying back into a column of rock, which buckled and crumbled on impact.

Jude spun again, his sword meeting that of yet another opponent. His eyes widened, breath punching from his lungs as he found himself blade to blade with Yarik. He was vaguely aware of the sound of ringing steel as Hector took on the remaining dozen swordsmen, but Jude's focus narrowed to the man in front of him.

"Weatherbourne," Yarik spat.

Jude might have called him a friend once. Warriors through and through, Yarik and his sister, Annuka, hadn't grown up in Kerameikos as Jude had but had joined the Order as adults. Jude still remembered sparring with them in the practice yards, the two of them always perfectly in sync, fighting as a single entity. They were the first pair of siblings Jude had ever met, and he had often felt baffled by their connection, when he wasn't aching with envy.

Now, he felt a piece of his heart break at the thought that that connection had been so irrevocably severed. All because Yarik had chosen to believe in a power-hungry charlatan over an oathbreaker.

"Yarik," Jude said, unable to keep the plea from his voice as he dodged another blow. "Please. You don't know what you're doing."

"I am upholding the ideals of the Order of the Last Light," Yarik said with a vicious slash of his sword. "Which is far more than you can say."

He struck again, his superior strength forcing Jude back as Jude met the blow.

"You're upholding a lie," Jude said desperately. "Whatever Pallas told you—whatever he said to convince you to join him, it's *wrong*. The Last Prophet is alive—he's with us, and all we are trying to do is what we pledged. Stop the Age of Darkness. Our mission hasn't changed."

He felt a shift in Yarik's next attack. A beat of hesitation that hadn't been there before. Jude's words were getting through to him. He wasn't so far gone down the Witnesses' path. He wasn't beyond saving.

Jude parried the blow, and when Yarik didn't attack again, Jude dropped his guard.

"It's not too late. You don't have to do this. You can lay down your sword now." When Yarik still made no move to strike, Jude sheathed his own sword. "See? We can both walk away. Your sister is at Kerameikos. I just saw her. If you go to her, she'll forgive you. I know she will."

A growl erupted from Yarik's throat, and he launched himself forward. He struck at Jude with abandon, swinging his sword wildly through the air. But what he lacked in finesse, he made up for in brute force. Jude dodged and ducked the onslaught, heart pounding in time with the pulse of his Grace. Yarik's blade instead met the dripping stalactites, raining rocks down.

"The Last Prophet abandoned us, as did you!" Yarik roared. "Or have you forgotten what you did? Stranded your Guard in a foreign land—the land of my ancestors' enemies—and disappeared. And who was punished for your cowardice? The people of Behezda! Pallas the Faithful was the one who tamed the god. Pallas is the *only* one who can save us now!"

In his desperation to convince Yarik, Jude had allowed himself to be separated from Hector. They were effectively surrounded, with Jude cut off from Hector, hemmed in against the water by Yarik's relentless assault.

"I will *never* follow you, Jude Weatherbourne," Yarik snarled, charging forward. Jude leapt back, sloshing into the water. "You have made a mockery of the Paladin and everything we stand for. You broke our oaths, and now you have the gall to speak to me of our mission? You should never have been Keeper of the Word. You have sullied yourself and the Last Prophet!"

Fury cracked through Jude like lightning. Lazaros's crude words in the Archon's villa flashed back to him. This was what the Paladin thought of Jude—what they all thought, even the ones who hadn't joined Pallas. That Jude had been led astray by some base instinct, that he was weak, corrupted by desire. That he had spread that corruption to the Last Prophet.

Let them. Jude knew the truth. In nineteen years of koahs, meditation, and rigorous adherence to every rule of the Order of the Last Light, Jude had never once come close to the divine harmony he felt when Anton touched him. Anton's love was sacred, his kiss a revelation, and Jude's purpose had never been clearer to him than it was when he was beside him. Even now, with Anton leagues away, the mere thought of him—his teasing smile, how his forehead crinkled in concentration when he played cards, the way his hand fit perfectly in Jude's—was enough for Jude's Grace to flood through him like a storm.

The surface of the pool shivered with Jude's power, a tremor that built until it shook the entire cavern. Jude stood perfectly still in the center, hand hovering over the pommel of his sheathed blade, the eye of the storm.

"W-what's happening?" Yarik demanded, ankle-deep in the churning water, the cavern rumbling around him. "How are you doing this?"

The other Paladin, too, had ceased their attack on Hector, pulling into a defensive formation, eyes darting nervously around the cave walls as the shaking grew more violent.

"Jude?" Hector called, apprehension trembling through his voice. "Is that you?"

"Yarik," Jude said steadily, his Grace building like a thunderhead. "Put down your sword. All of you, put down your swords! You are better than this. *Please.* Before it's too late."

No one moved, except the cave itself, quaking with the pent-up force of Jude's Grace, showering them with shards of rock and dust.

And then Yarik lunged. The silver flash of his blade cut toward Jude's chest. Jude leapt out of its path.

"Hector, now!" Jude cried, trusting that Hector would know what to do.

Gathering his Grace, Jude whipped his sword from its sheath, unleashing his Grace with it. Yarik threw himself out of the way—but Jude hadn't been aiming for him.

His Grace clapped through him like thunder, surging through his sword as it struck the rockface. The impact was a shock wave through the cave.

For the length of a heartbeat, the cavern was still and silent. And then the rock began to crack, and a moment later, it exploded inward.

Jude flung himself up toward the rock shelf as water burst through the cave wall. It blasted toward the other Paladin, flooding the cavern and sweeping them from their feet. Jude grabbed hold of the first handhold he could find, scrambling for purchase on the rock shelf. But using his Grace for that single blow had sapped him, and he lacked the strength to pull himself to safety. He dangled from his precarious handhold, arms aching, as the water rapidly rose beneath him.

A warm hand gripped his arm and started to haul him up. Jude looked up, his gaze connecting with Hector's, and he felt a deep relief gust through him. With Hector's help, he climbed onto the rock shelf.

"Are you out of your *mind?*" Hector raged as soon as Jude was safely on his feet. "You could have killed us both! How did you even—how is that—Behezda's mercy, Jude, what *was* that?"

Jude sucked in a gasping breath, his eyes not on Hector, but on the rapidly flooding cavern below. Water continued to surge out of the gaping hole Jude had punched into the cavern wall. The more the water blasted against the wall, the bigger the hole became and the faster the cavern filled up. The Paladin thrashed and struggled as the deluge dragged them down and dashed them against the walls of the cave. Flashes of dark blue cloaks, gasping faces, and kicking feet appeared and disappeared in the rush of water. Jude caught a glimpse of what might have been Yarik's dark hair.

He had to look away.

"We have to get out of here, now," he said to Hector. The cave rumbled as more water forced its way through the wall. "I think this entire cavern is going to collapse. We need to get to higher ground before that happens."

Hector gaped at him for a long moment and then shook his head. "Fine. But you're going to teach me that trick later."

Hector led the way to the narrow shaft, back the way they'd come, as the cavern below began to collapse.

"Jude, hurry!"

They ran through the dark caves until Jude's energy left him completely and he collapsed against the rock wall.

"We're close," Hector said. "I can feel it."

Jude slid down onto the ground, his face in his hands. "I . . . I killed them."

"No," Hector said, crouching beside him. "No, come on, that wasn't—"

"They're dead because of me." He felt like someone had seized hold of his heart and squeezed. He couldn't breathe.

"They would have killed us. They would have come for the others. For Anton," Hector said firmly. "You did what you had to do."

"Yarik—"

"Made his choices," Hector said. "And you aren't responsible for them. You never were."

Jude looked up, meeting Hector's somber gaze, and knew he didn't just mean Yarik. There was a time when Jude had insisted he was responsible for Hector's choices, too. It hadn't been true then. And it wasn't now.

"Come on," Hector said, hauling Jude to his feet. "Let's go find your Prophet."

As if invoked by Hector, Anton's Grace gave a small tug on Jude's. He was safe, then. And close. Jude felt something lighten in his chest, even as the rest of him remained impossibly heavy.

"This way," he said, setting off into the darkness, trusting his true north to guide them.

Dawn had just broken when they reached the mouth of the caverns. Mist blanketed the mountainside, drifting between the trees and shrouding the rising sun, turning the whole sky a rosy pink.

Anton's *esha* led them up a rocky slope, toward the sound of waterfalls. And then, layered over the sound of the falls, they heard voices and the snap of a crackling fire. Jude almost didn't realize he'd broken into a run until he reached a clearing between the trees and had to skid to a stop to avoid being sliced in half by Khepri's blade.

"Whoa!" Hector cried, yanking Jude back.

Khepri looked rattled, and she sheathed her sword at once. "You could have called out a warning. I thought you were Witnesses!"

"Glad to see you're on alert, I guess," Hector replied.

"Jude and Hector are back!" Hassan called out as he jogged toward them. He patted Hector's shoulder approvingly. "Glad you're all right." He turned to Jude. "Both of you."

Jude nodded, accepting what felt like a peace offering from Hassan. His gaze moved past the prince and found Anton staring at him from across the clearing, one hand clenched around a waterskin. He looked shaken, paralyzed, his dark eyes wide.

Jude was moving toward him before he'd consciously made the decision. All he knew was that he was desperate to touch him, to take him into his arms, to feel grounded and solid.

But steps away from Anton, Jude faltered. There was something remote about Anton's expression, like Anton was a block of solid stone that Jude was hurtling toward at top speed. Without a word, Anton took his wrist and turned sharply on his heel.

"Jude and I are getting water," he called over his shoulder, dragging Jude with him through the trees.

He didn't look back at Jude once as they tramped through the trees and down the muddy slope of the riverbank. Finally, at the edge of the river, Anton turned. He opened his mouth to speak, but before the words could pass his lips Jude stepped forward and kissed him.

It was a kiss unlike any they'd shared before, frantic and crackling with something more than need. Part of Jude was still back inside that dark cavern, the rush of water roaring in his ears, watching Yarik disappear below the surface. He dragged Anton closer, clinging to him like he would drown if he let go.

A low whimper escaped from the back of Anton's throat. He broke away, breathing heavily. His hair was a mess where Jude's hands had raked through it, his eyes wide and dark and glinting dangerously.

Jude wanted to fall into him, to lose himself entirely. He leaned in again, but Anton pushed him back, hands braced on his shoulders.

"You can't do that anymore," he said fiercely. "You can't risk your life like that."

His voice was icy with anger. Suddenly Jude was hurtled back several months, to another day in the Gallian Mountains, another close call with the Witnesses. He stared at Anton, a fog of confusion, desire, and desperation rendering him speechless.

"Do you hear me?" Anton demanded. "You can't just run off like you were *waiting* for the opportunity, like you weren't just—" He let out a harsh breath and rocked back on his heels.

Jude grasped for words, trying to make sense of Anton's anger. He'd known Anton was upset when they split up in the caverns, but this felt like something more. "Anton, I'm—"

"*Don't* say it," Anton warned. "Don't tell me it's your duty to protect me. That's not—I don't want you bound to some oath, I don't want that."

Jude recoiled, bewildered by the bitter edge in Anton's voice. Something hot and prickling crawled up his throat. Just when it had felt like the two of them were on equal footing again, Anton changed the rules.

"Well, that's too bad," Jude snapped. "Do you have any idea what I just had to do?"

Anton met his gaze, jaw set and eyes blazing. "You almost got yourself killed trying to take on two dozen Witnesses by your—"

"Paladin," Jude broke in sharply. "They were *Paladin*, not Witnesses, and I killed them. I killed Yarik. And I would do it again, without hesitation, if it meant keeping you safe. Because even before I knew who you were, I swore I would, and that is an oath I will never break. The very least you can do is not throw it in my face."

"You want me to be *grateful?*" Anton bit out, shoving Jude back a step. "Grateful that you throw yourself into danger the first chance you get like you don't care what it would do to me if—" He cut himself off, shaking. "I want to keep *you* safe, Jude. How do you not get that?"

Jude's jaw clenched. "That's not your job."

"Then whose job is it?"

Jude had no answer because the question had never crossed his mind before. He searched Anton's face, his heart thudding. Beneath Anton's fury, there was a dark shadow of something else. He wasn't just worried—he was haunted. Jude had seen flashes of it before, in the nightmares that plagued Anton as he slept. Jude had been so desperate to make things right between them, he had let himself believe it was just the same fear they were all shouldered with—the god, Pallas, the Witnesses. The Age of Darkness.

But the truth was staring him in the face, and Jude couldn't look away anymore. Anton was hiding something.

Jude raised a trembling hand to cup Anton's face, anger bleeding out of him. "What is this about?"

Anton bit his lip, shaking his head. With a fierce gleam in his eyes, he grabbed a handful of Jude's shirt and yanked him into another furious kiss.

Unbalanced by Anton's sudden move, Jude stumbled. His foot slid on the slick mud and he went splashing down into the shallows of the river. Anton followed him down, climbing dangerously closer and pushing Jude back against the rocks to seal their lips together again.

It felt like a challenge, one Jude didn't know how to back down from. River water soaked through his pants but he didn't care, dragging

Anton closer, one hand curled around Anton's wrist, the other sliding to his waist. Like if he could just hold on to Anton, keep him close enough, then he'd be safe.

It was only later, after they'd picked themselves off the ground and dried off as best as they could, that Jude even realized Anton had never answered him.

———————————

A cloud of grim hopelessness seemed to follow them down the mountain. They reached the valley the next morning, the mountainous terrain giving way to the hilly lowlands. Every evening, Jude watched the sun sink behind the ridge of the Unspoken Mountains, the silver ribbon of the Serpentine gleaming on the other side of the valley. The distance between them and those jagged peaks only reminded Jude of how far they had to go.

Witnesses lurked in nearly every town. Each morning, Anton scried to see if there were Witnesses close by, and they did their best to avoid the farms and villages dotting the prairie.

At night, they switched off keeping watch. When Jude wasn't on duty, he slept beside Anton in their tent. It reminded him of the days they'd spent in the Gallian Mountains, fleeing to Endarrion after the Witnesses's attack on Kerameikos. The distance between them had felt so impassable then. Now they slept curled together, knees slotted against knees, but a distance still remained.

He sensed it in the gaps and silences. The questions that Anton left unanswered. Even in the way that Anton reached for Jude sometimes, desperately, as if to confirm that he was still there. But the closer Anton tried to keep him, the further away he seemed.

On the third morning in the valley, as they camped in a wooded area outside the nearest hamlet, Jude woke alone. He crawled out of his tent and found everyone already awake.

Khepri and Hassan were tending to a fire, and Beru had roped Illya into helping her reorganize their packs more efficiently while Ephyra looked on, sipping something out of a clay cup.

"Where are Hector and Anton?" Jude asked.

Ephyra shrugged. "Haven't seen them all morning."

A faint shout echoed toward him, followed by the unmistakable sound of a body hitting the ground. Before Jude knew what he was doing, he was sprinting through the trees, sliding over the damp detritus until he caught sight of Hector and Anton.

Anton was picking himself off the ground, glaring at Hector, who just laughed.

"Was that really necessary?" Anton grumbled.

Jude watched as Hector set himself into an offensive position, his shoulders squared toward Anton, who immediately mimicked the stance.

"Try to block this time," Hector said patiently, before lunging forward with an obvious strike.

Anton successfully turned against the attack and blocked with his arm.

"That's it!" Hector said, sounding delighted. A moment later, he caught sight of Jude. "Morning."

Jude blinked as Anton spun around, his expression still lit up with success.

"What are you . . ." Jude gestured weakly at the two of them. "What's happening here?"

"Hector's teaching me how to fight," Anton replied cheerfully, pushing a tuft of blond hair out of his face. He looked unbearably pleased with himself, like he'd just won another hand of canbarra.

"Oh. That's . . ." Jude didn't know how to make sense of the feelings churning in his gut. "Good."

"I just figured he might as well be able to defend himself," Hector said, rubbing a hand over the side of his neck. "Make your job a little easier."

"Right," Jude replied.

Anton avoided his gaze.

"Well, anyway," Hector said with false cheer, "great job, Anton. I'll just . . . go help Hassan with the fire."

He backed away through the trees, leaving Jude and Anton alone.

"Stop looking at me like that," Anton chided.

Jude schooled his features. "I'm not looking at you in any particular way."

Anton's nose scrunched. "It's the look you get whenever I do something you disapprove of. I'm deeply familiar with it."

"I don't disapprove," Jude said. "Hector's right. You should know how to protect yourself."

The thought of Hector and Anton bonding made him feel a little strange, but he didn't *disapprove*.

Anton appraised him. "*You* could always teach me some moves, you know."

"Of course," Jude said, thinking back to his most basic training, the stances and forms he'd learned before his Grace manifested. "Whatever you want to know."

Anton huffed out a laugh.

"Oh." Jude flushed, catching on. "You meant—"

"Yeah," Anton replied, winding an arm around Jude's waist and reeling him in. "I meant."

It was a feint, and Jude knew it. And he didn't care. Because Anton was here, smiling at Jude in the morning light, freckles sprinkled like stars across his cheeks. It was more than anything Jude ever thought he'd have.

It didn't matter if Anton was keeping something from him. It didn't matter if Jude was still carrying around this hurt and this longing. It didn't matter, he told himself.

And almost believed it.

25

EPHYRA

AFTER NEARLY A WEEK IN THE VALLEY, THEIR SUPPLIES WERE RUNNING LOW. They would have to risk venturing into civilization.

It was too dangerous to simply walk into a town and buy supplies. But they were coming up on a cluster of farms, and as the fall harvest was currently underway, there was an opportunity for someone to sneak into one of the farms and take what they needed.

Not everyone was entirely on board with this plan.

"It's *stealing*," Hassan protested for the fifth time. "It's wrong. These farmers are just trying to make a living—we can't just threaten their livelihoods!"

"And what exactly do you know about making a living, *Prince* Hassan?" Ephyra asked pointedly.

"Jude," Hassan said beseechingly, "you agree with me, right? We should at least leave them some money."

Anton rolled his eyes. "Jude barely knows what money is. It's not like Kerameikos has a thriving trade economy."

The swordsman looked mildly affronted. "There's no honor in thievery—"

"But there's plenty of honor in saving the world," Ephyra cut in. "Which we can't exactly do if we all starve."

"She makes a very good point," Illya chimed in, looking amused by the argument unfolding.

Ephyra glared. "Do *not* back me up."

"Ephyra *is* right, though," Hector said, looking pained to be on the same side as her. "Sorry, Hassan. It's for the greater good."

"All right, well it sounds like Prince Hassan is outvoted, and we are definitely going to rob a farm," Anton summarized. "So, who wants to commit some crimes?"

"I'll go," Ephyra volunteered. Hector and Khepri looked at her skeptically. She rolled her eyes. "We need stealth, right? I'm the one you want."

"You shouldn't go alone," Khepri said, and Ephyra was oddly touched by her concern. "I'll go with you."

Ephyra knew very little about the Herati girl. Like her, Khepri had been a captive of Pallas. If her captivity had been even half as awful as Ephyra's, then Khepri must be strong because she hadn't been broken by the experience. Ephyra thought she might like her.

They set off at dusk, climbing over the hill to the farmland below.

"So," Ephyra said into the silence. "You and the prince. You're what—his consort? Is that what they call them?"

Khepri shot her an unamused look. "I don't know. We were . . . something. But that's in the past."

"You came here for him, though," Ephyra said. It wasn't a question. Despite the obvious tension between the two, there was really no other explanation for Khepri's sudden agreement to come with them.

"No," Khepri replied flatly.

"My mistake."

Khepri sighed. "I don't know anymore. I love him. But all we seem to do is hurt each other."

Ephyra thought of Beru, and how many times things had fractured between them. How many times they'd repaired their relationship. "Well, it's always the people you love the most that can hurt you the worst, isn't it? At least, in my experience."

Khepri nodded. "You and the traitor, right? It's pretty obvious he's in love with you."

"What?" Ephyra choked, blindsided. "You mean *Illya?*"

Khepri's expression was somewhat abashed. "Apparently not that obvious, then."

"Illya's not really a love kind of person."

"Well, my mistake," Khepri said, smirking a little.

Ephyra quickened her pace, heat rising to her cheeks as Khepri's words rattled around in her head. "Looks like there's a farm ahead. Let's try there."

They climbed easily over the low fence hemming in the row of crops. Ephyra spotted turnips, carrots, and something that might have been some form of grain. As a rule, vegetables were not an efficient resource, as they tended to be heavy and yet not filling. They still grabbed some of them, but the real trove would be in the barn. With her far superior night vision and hearing, Khepri stayed outside to keep watch while Ephyra stole inside.

She crept through the darkened barn, her eyes adjusting slowly. She heard hens rustling in their nests. Jackpot.

She slunk toward them, her cloth sack in one hand, ready to pounce. The chicken squawked belligerently as Ephyra seized hold of it, shoving it into the bag. It put up a vicious fight, clucking and flapping as Ephyra attempted to close the bag. Just when she had the chicken under control, she turned toward the back of the barn and found a pair of eyes staring at her.

Human eyes.

With a muffled squawk, the chicken emerged from the bag and flapped away. Ephyra stumbled back.

"Who's there?" a voice whispered through the dark.

Ephyra held still, peering toward the back of the barn where she could see a silhouette.

"If you've come to take me to the Witnesses—" the tremulous voice said.

"Be quiet," Ephyra hissed, stalking toward them. "No one's taking anyone to the Witnesses."

The silhouette shrank back, and as Ephyra neared, she saw it was a slight, dark-haired girl about Beru's age.

"Then what are you doing here?" the girl asked.

"What are *you* doing here?"

The girl stared at Ephyra, suspicion shining in her eyes.

"Fine, I'll go first," Ephyra said. "I was trying to steal a chicken."

"Yeah, I heard," the girl said, irritated. "I could go inside and turn you in, you know. The family that owns this farm doesn't take well to thieves."

"Then do it," Ephyra challenged.

The girl glared at her, unmoving.

"That's what I thought."

She was reasonably certain that this girl didn't pose an actual threat to her, but she didn't seem convinced of the same about Ephyra.

"So," Ephyra said, "why don't you just pretend like you never saw me, I'll pretend I never saw you, and we'll all have a good night?"

Before the girl could reply, the door of the barn wrenched open, and

Ephyra dove behind the hay bales, grabbing the girl and dragging her into the shadows on instinct.

"Ephyra?" Khepri's voice called out quietly.

Ephyra sighed in relief, slumping back against the hay and letting the girl's arm go. She crawled back from behind the hay. "Over here. But I should warn you—"

Khepri stopped, staring down at the girl behind Ephyra. She froze. "Who is that?"

"I think she's living in the barn?" Ephyra offered.

The girl crossed her arms.

"Well, we have a problem," Khepri said, coming toward them. "A . . ." She glanced at the girl. "Robed sort of problem."

Witnesses. The girl seemed to clock Khepri's reference, too, because she immediately jerked back from them.

"Wait," she said. "You're hiding from the Witnesses, too?"

Ephyra exchanged a glance with Khepri. "Something like that. Do you want to explain why they're here?"

There was silence for a long moment.

Finally, the girl spoke up. "They're looking for me, obviously."

"You're . . . Graced?" Khepri guessed.

The girl didn't answer, which Ephyra took to mean yes.

"We are, too," Ephyra said quickly. She could feel the worried gaze Khepri shot her. Dangerous to out herself like this, but this girl was clearly scared, and if they put her at ease maybe she'd just let them take the chicken and go. "We heard the Witnesses' presence had been growing around these parts."

"Yeah, well, it's not like they have much opposition," the girl said darkly.

"What do you mean by that?" Khepri asked.

"This land was originally owned by the Galanis family," the girl said. "My family is one of many that works the land, tends to the crops. I was hired by Lady Galanis as an attendant in her home. And a few years ago, Lady Galanis turned over the deed to our land to us, so it would be our own. But a few months ago, she got sick, and her grandson, Dracon, took over. He refused to make good on the deal, told all the families that the land belonged to him and always would. There were rumblings of revolt across the farms, but then Pallas returned, and the valley was flooded with Witnesses. Dracon saw it as an opportunity to get all of us serfs in line."

"Let me guess," Khepri said. "He's giving the Witnesses the names of the families that oppose him?"

The girl nodded, and Ephyra glanced at Khepri in surprise. She seemed to be speaking from experience.

"He's threatened to turn over anyone who doesn't comply with his demands," the girl said. "His demands are . . . We have no money to give, and he's been taking so much of our crop that we can barely feed ourselves. And my sister . . . she's . . . I've seen him looking at her. He wants her to—" She broke off. "She'll do it. She'd do anything to protect me."

Anger coiled in Ephyra's gut as she took in the fear in the girl's voice, how skinny she looked. How weary.

But when she spoke again, her voice was hard, her spine straight with steel. "I decided to run away, so that my family doesn't have to protect me. I was planning on stealing a boat and heading downriver, but I saw a Witness patrol and hid in here instead."

"What's your name, kid?" Ephyra asked.

The girl eyed her, and for a moment Ephyra thought she might not answer. But finally she said, "Nephele."

Khepri took Ephyra's arm. "Can I talk to you for a moment?"

Ephyra followed her out from the hay bales and toward the other end of the barn.

"We have to do something," Ephyra said, before Khepri could speak. "This girl—"

"I agree with you," Khepri replied. "But we can't do anything to draw attention to ourselves. It sounds like this Galanis person has contacts with the Witnesses, maybe even with the Hierophant. If he sees us, they'll know exactly where we are."

"What then?" Ephyra asked. "Sneak her out of here? Take her with us?"

Khepri didn't argue, just frowned a little, like she was thinking. "We take her back to camp with us for the night. And then we figure out what to do in the morning."

"Fine," Ephyra agreed. "But first let's grab a chicken."

They returned to camp, the chicken, two bags of food, and Nephele in tow. Ephyra half expected someone to put up a fuss about the fact that they'd brought someone back with them, but once the others understood what had happened, no one said a word.

Khepri got the fire started, and they cooked dinner with their freshly replenished supplies, voices mingling with the crackling fire as Illya regaled them with tales of his exploits in Endarrion, wooing lords and ladies to give him their patronage.

Nephele was listening with rapt attention, Hassan with more interest than he was trying to let on, while Khepri and Hector interjected every so often to ask intentionally ridiculous questions. It had taken him a lot longer this time, but it seemed Illya had successfully won them over, the same way he'd done to Shara and her treasure hunters. If nothing else, he knew how to spin a good story.

It reminded Ephyra of what she'd asked him, once. *What story do you tell about yourself?*

And his answer, *One you don't want to hear.*

She studied his face in the firelight as he spoke, his fine-boned hands gesturing gracefully. She could now admit to herself that she still wanted to hear that story. She still wanted to know why he was here, why he had turned on Pallas and risked himself. No matter how she looked at it, it didn't make sense, didn't fit with the version of Illya she thought she knew.

People can change, Beru had said, that hopeful note in her voice.

Khepri's words from earlier that evening came back to her. *It's pretty obvious he's in love with you.*

Ephyra snorted. The only thing Illya loved was power. Ephyra turned away from him, from the warmth of the fire and the comforting rise and fall of the others' voices, and retreated into the tent. She curled up on her side and pushed away all thoughts of Illya's elegant, firelit face and silken voice. She turned her mind instead back to Nephele, to the man called Dracon Galanis, who loved his power so much he would crush anyone to keep it.

She was still thinking about him later that night, after the voices had died down and the fire burned out, when Khepri, Nephele, and Beru were all sleeping silently around her.

"Hey," Ephyra whispered, turning over and nudging Nephele.

The girl evidently hadn't fallen asleep yet because she rolled over immediately, her eyes blinking open in the dark.

"This Galanis guy," Ephyra said. "Where does he live, exactly?"

Nephele's eyes narrowed in the darkness of the tent. "Why?"

"Your sister's not safe, even if you leave. If Dracon Galanis doesn't have you to hold over your family's head, it'll just be something else. Men like him . . . they always find ways to hurt people."

Nephele stared at Ephyra in the dark, and then she said, "About a league past the farm where you found me. Up on a hill. You can't mistake it."

Ephyra nodded, getting up quietly.

"I want to go with you," Nephele said, that same steel in her voice that Ephyra had heard back in the barn.

"No, you don't."

"What are you going to do?" she asked, her voice shaking.

"What I do best," Ephyra replied, and then she was gone.

The Galanis guards were easy enough to slip past. The wind had picked up over the course of the night and by the time Ephyra reached the manor, it was raining. The water made the climb up to Dracon's window slippery and slow. She had to fight to keep her teeth from chattering.

Clutching the side of the window with one hand, she banged the rock against the glass. It splintered and Ephyra struck again, as hard as she could. The window shattered inward.

"Who's there?"

A bolt of lightning cracked through the sky, and Ephyra used the opportunity to make a dramatic entrance. Silently, she vaulted up onto the windowsill. The room flashed with more lightning, illuminating her in the window.

Dracon leapt from the bed, his broad torso bare, his hair and beard a wild tangle. "How did you get past my guards?"

Rain slammed against the walls outside, blowing into the room.

"The guards?" Ephyra repeated. "You should really be worrying about yourself."

"Get out of my house," he demanded. "Or I'll call the Witnesses here."

"You'll be dead before you can," Ephyra replied, slinking closer. "Actually, you'll be dead either way."

"What are you talking about?"

"I know what you've been doing," Ephyra said. "Threatening people's lives, their livelihoods. Threatening to throw the Graced to the Witnesses. It ends now."

"You're going to stop me?" he asked, laughing. "You're just a girl."

"And you're just an oversized child who's never been told that people aren't toys for you to play with," Ephyra shot back, advancing. "And you should know, I'm not just a girl. I'm the Pale Hand of Death."

Whatever fame the Pale Hand had possessed before, Pallas had multiplied it tenfold when he'd tried to use her as an executioner. Dracon's eyes widened, and he snatched up a candlestick from the table beside the bed.

"I'll kill you," he growled, brandishing the makeshift weapon.

"That's my line," Ephyra replied with a flash of teeth.

Three steps and she was across the room. He swung the candlestick clumsily. Ephyra caught it, taking advantage of his unbalanced stance to jab a knee into his groin.

With a pitiful groan, he crumpled to the ground. Ephyra tossed the candlestick aside and pinned him there, hand at his throat.

Beru's bracelet rolled down her wrist and Ephyra froze, staring at the seashells she'd collected from the beach of Pallas Athos, the fine thread Beru had picked out of the drapes in her room.

It was always so easy for Ephyra, the killing.

When she'd been the Pale Hand, killing so Beru could live. And after, in Behezda, writing her own rules in blood.

She stared into Dracon's eyes, and she had no remorse for him. His cruelty, his utter disregard for the desperation of others. He didn't deserve the life he had. He had no right to it.

But then, what right did she have to take it from him? Just because she *could*? Because she'd seen the fear in Nephele's eyes, the impossible decision she'd made to protect the sister she loved?

Was this what she was meant for or was it just the story she'd told herself, until she began to believe it was the truth?

You don't have to be what they say, Illya had said to her, once.

"On second thought," Ephyra said, shoving herself to her feet as Dracon stared up with wide, terrified eyes. "You're not worth my time."

––––––––––

Ephyra had to work quickly. Dracon would've summoned the guards by now, and they were probably sweeping the grounds, searching for her. It turned out, however, that worked in her favor, because when she arrived at Lady Galanis's quarters, there were no guards in sight.

Ephyra slipped into the room. The last embers were smoking in the fireplace across from a grand bed where a tiny figure was curled beneath thick blankets.

"Lady Galanis?" Ephyra called. There was no answer, except a slight whistling snore.

She crept closer. Nephele had said Lady Galanis had gotten sick months ago, and when Ephyra looked down at the woman she saw that was clearly the truth. The woman was so frail she looked almost skeletal, her white hair matted to her head. Her skin was an ashen brown, except beneath her eyes where it looked almost blue.

Ephyra closed her eyes and curled one hand on Lady Galanis's bony wrist, the other pressed against her heart. She took a breath and thought back to the ship, when she'd healed Jude. Focusing on Lady Galanis's pulse, Ephyra poured some of her own *esha* into the woman. She could feel her growing stronger, more substantial, and when Ephyra opened her eyes, she saw the color returning to Lady Galanis's face.

The woman coughed, and then suddenly bolted up in bed. Ephyra reeled back, startled, as Lady Galanis's eyes opened.

Ephyra took a breath and hoped that what Nephele had said about this woman was true.

"Lady Galanis?" Ephyra asked gently.

The woman turned to her, blinking owlishly in the dim light. "Who are you? What are you doing in my bedchambers?"

"It doesn't matter who I am," Ephyra said. "We don't have much time. Your grandson—"

"What has he done?" Lady Galanis asked sharply.

"You've been sick," Ephyra said.

"Sick?" Lady Galanis replied. "No, I . . ." She trailed off, touching her fingers to her mouth. "That's right, isn't it? I haven't been out of bed in weeks."

"In the meantime, Dracon took control of your estate, and he's been threatening the villagers if they don't comply with his demands," Ephyra said in a rush. "One of your servants here, Nephele, told me everything. I thought if you knew, you'd want to put a stop to it."

Lady Galanis sighed, putting her face in her hands. "I told my people that under no circumstances was he to inherit a cent of this estate. That boy . . ." She shook her head, looking up at Ephyra. "Sometimes there's no fixing evil."

Ephyra shivered under the woman's piercing gaze.

Guards burst into the room before Ephyra could reply. They surrounded the perimeter, swords pointed at Ephyra.

"Step away from the bed!" one of them barked. "Hands up where we can see them!"

Ephyra stumbled away from the bed, but before she'd gone too far Lady Galanis rose to her feet, gathering a long, sheer robe around her.

"What is all this commotion?" she demanded. "Startling your poor old lady like this!"

The guards faltered, staring in awe at Lady Galanis as she moved smoothly and easily across the room.

One of them finally spoke up. "Lady Galanis, that girl is—"

"She is a healer," Lady Galanis said, with a quick glance at Ephyra. "She healed me of my ailments and has informed me what's been going on here."

"Grandmother, thank the Prophets you're all right!" Dracon cried, storming into the room from behind the guards. "Guards, seize that girl and make sure she—"

"Guards," Lady Galanis countered, eyes blazing. "Seize my grandson."

The guards didn't move for a very tense moment. Then one of them lunged toward Dracon. The others followed suit a second later.

"This very kind and helpful young woman told me all about what you've been doing to these poor villagers while you've had me shut away here," Lady Galanis said as the guards trussed Dracon up. "I am ashamed to call you my blood. See to it that you never set foot at this estate or on these lands ever again."

"She's lying!" Dracon said at once. "Grandmother, I would never—"

But the guards were already dragging him from the room.

"I'm going to have to fire half my staff," Lady Galanis said wearily. "Whoever let Dracon take over." She turned to Ephyra, who was still frozen by the bed. "I must thank you for your assistance. You said Nephele sent you?"

"Well, she didn't exactly send me," Ephyra replied. "I found her hiding in a barn."

"That Nephele's a smart girl," Lady Galanis said. "What were *you* doing in the barn?"

Ephyra did not think it wise to admit she was stealing. "Waiting out the storm."

"Well, please, let me offer you a dry place to stay the rest of the night," Lady Galanis said. "It's the least I can do."

Ephyra shook her head. "Thanks, but I have people to get back to. Friends." The word felt strange on her tongue.

"Are you sure?" Lady Galanis asked. "There's nothing I can do to thank you for healing me?"

Ephyra opened her mouth to refuse again, and then thought better of it. "Actually, there is something."

———————

Beru was outside the tent when Ephyra arrived back at camp carrying a pack full of food, clothing, and blankets gifted by Lady Galanis.

It wasn't yet dawn, so Ephyra was fairly certain Beru hadn't simply woken early. And from her tightly crossed arms and the set of her shoulders, it was clear she was waiting for Ephyra.

She opened her mouth as she spotted Ephyra, but before she could speak, Nephele rushed out of the tent, Khepri at her heels.

"What happened?" Nephele asked.

"Dracon Galanis will never bother you or your family again."

Beru's gaze whipped toward her. "You killed him?"

Her voice was sharp, accusatory. Ephyra supposed she deserved that, but it still stung. There was some part of Beru that was all too ready to believe the worst of Ephyra.

"He's alive," Ephyra said, looking at Nephele instead of Beru. "But you have my word. You and your sister are safe and so is the rest of your village. From him, at least. Lady Galanis will do everything she can to protect you all from the Witnesses, too."

"Lady Galanis?" Nephele asked, her forehead creased with confusion. "You mean—"

"She's back in charge," Ephyra replied. "All healed up."

Nephele stared at her. "You did this?"

Ephyra nodded. "It's safe to go home. I promise. Go back to your family."

"I'll take her," Khepri volunteered.

Nephele was still looking at Ephyra. "I can't . . . I can never repay you."

Ephyra smiled weakly. "It's not your debt, kid. It's mine. Just . . . keep yourself safe. Your sister, too. I know you thought you were doing the right thing by leaving, but . . . you gotta stick together, all right?"

"Right."

Nephele gave a little wave and then followed Khepri back toward the farms, the sky lightening ahead of them.

Beru didn't move for a long moment, staring at Ephyra with her arms crossed.

"I did go there planning to kill him," Ephyra admitted, breaking the silence. "I got close." Maybe it would never sit right, this power inside her. Maybe she'd always be drawn to the darker parts of it. "I think . . . I've believed this whole time, since we were young, that killing is just what I'm meant for. What I *am*. I pretended like I didn't have a choice in it because that was easier than admitting I did. Though I don't know if I can be sorry for it, even now, because I still think your life is worth a thousand Dracon Galanises."

"So why didn't you kill him?" Beru asked, her voice strangely toneless, like she was merely curious.

"When we escaped from Pallas Athos, Jude was hurt pretty bad by the Witnesses. Hector asked me to heal him. Trusted me to do it. It felt . . . different. Like waking up. I've hurt a lot of people, Beru. And I don't just mean the people I've killed or the people I've left behind."

"You mean me," Beru surmised. "I can remember . . . the fights we used to have. How upset I was when you didn't listen. That day in Medea . . ."

Ephyra flinched at the reminder. One of the worst days of her life—second, perhaps, only to the day in the tomb of the Sacrificed Queen, when the Daughters of Mercy had told her Beru was dead.

"I don't blame you for leaving," Ephyra said. "Not anymore."

Beru shook her head. "It's not that. It's just . . . I don't remember why I did. Or—I *do* remember, but it doesn't feel like it was *me*."

A dark feeling settled over Ephyra as she looked at Beru, the girl she'd known for almost seventeen years. The girl she thought she knew better than anyone. But right now, it was like she was looking at a stranger.

When they'd been Pallas's captives, every day was a struggle, but now that they were free, Ephyra realized the struggle had never ended for Beru. Hour after hour, she was fighting a losing battle against the god inside her.

"I'm not making sense," Beru mumbled, wiping a hand over her face. "Don't listen to me. I'm just tired."

Ephyra's chest tightened. Beru was lying to her.

Suddenly, Ephyra felt like she understood what Beru had endured all those years when Ephyra was the Pale Hand. They'd fought then, often, but worse were the fights they refused to have. Because at the center of every argument was a truth that Beru couldn't have faced until it was staring her in the eyes—Ephyra's bloody palm and Hector's lifeless body. Only then had Beru let herself see the darkness that had taken hold of her sister.

And it had broken them.

But Ephyra had meant what she'd said back in Pallas Athos—she wouldn't give up on Beru. Even if she didn't know what was happening to her.

Beru turned away, but before Ephyra could figure out what to say, her attention was drawn to the others, who were gathered in a tight knot near Jude and Anton's tent, deep in discussion. Anton was running a hand through his hair, Jude close at his elbow. On his other side, Hector's arms were crossed over his chest, face pulled into a deep frown. Hassan was speaking rapidly, his expression strained with worry.

Beru moved toward them, Ephyra at her heels.

"What's going on?" Ephyra asked.

Jude glanced at them as they approached.

But it was Anton who answered. "I've been feeling the same *esha* for a few days now. Following us. Maybe tracking us."

"Witnesses?" Ephyra asked.

"I think so," Anton replied. "One of them felt familiar. I think it's the Witness with the Godfire scars."

Lazaros. Ephyra felt a chill. He had been Beru's constant shadow for over two months, always staring at her with those oddly clear gray eyes.

"How far away are they?" Ephyra asked.

"Maybe a day?" Anton replied.

"Well, great," Hector said to Ephyra. "If anyone saw you at the

Galanis manor, the Witnesses are going to quickly make the connection. And since it sounds like Dracon Galanis was pretty friendly with the Witnesses in his town . . ."

"I was careful," Ephyra protested.

"You were reckless."

"Enough, both of you," Beru said, with uncharacteristic rancor. "I can't stand you two arguing all the time."

Hector gave Beru a bewildered look, and then caught Ephyra's eye. For once, he wasn't glaring. He looked worried.

"It doesn't matter how the Witnesses tracked us down again," Jude broke in. "We'll just have to take precautions. We'll move out as soon as possible and double up on watches tonight."

The others started moving at Jude's command, but Ephyra held Hector's gaze. She knew exactly what he was worried about because she was thinking the same thing. The others might not have noticed—at least not yet. But Ephyra and Hector understood Beru well enough to know when something was wrong.

And something was definitely wrong.

26

BERU

"*NO*, THAT WAS *MY* CARD!" EPHYRA LAMENTED AS HASSAN PICKED UP THE SIX of crowns.

Beru tried to muster a smile. Their nightly game of canbarra had become a ritual, although tonight Beru sensed that everyone was more on edge than usual. After three days, they still hadn't shaken the Witnesses on their tail. Every morning, Anton returned from scrying pale-faced and worried. Lazaros and the other Witnesses were only getting closer.

But the Witnesses weren't Beru's biggest worry. Since she'd taken off the Godfire collar, the dark fog of the god's mind had taken up residence in her. She hardly ate anymore. She didn't sleep. Even when the god was silent, even when she didn't hear its voice, she *felt* it. Felt it struggling against Pallas's seal. Felt its impatience. Its disdain.

"You really shouldn't give your hand away like that," Illya commented from behind them.

Beru had seen him watching their card games, like he wanted to join them, but he usually didn't dare approach.

"Why don't *you* play if you're so good?" Ephyra challenged.

Illya opened his mouth to reply, but before he could say anything Anton set down his cards and got to his feet.

"I'm going to find Jude," Anton said, and then walked away.

Hurt flashed across Illya's face.

"I had a bad hand anyway," Ephyra said, tossing hers into the center.

"I was finally going to beat him," Hassan muttered, putting down his as well.

They both wandered off, leaving Beru to clean up the cards.

Illya flopped to the ground beside her. "He really hates me, huh?" he said after a moment. "Even after I—It's like he doesn't notice, or care, that I'm trying to . . ." He trailed off, staring at Beru almost beseechingly. ". . . do better."

The words conjured a memory for Beru. When she'd been desperate to gain Hector's forgiveness, to sacrifice herself so that he would live, like a debt owed for everything she'd taken from him. Looking back at that time, she barely recognized herself. Where had that desperation come from? Why had she wanted to save Hector so badly? She couldn't make sense of it.

"He's my brother," Illya went on. "I have to—I have to try to make amends, right?"

He was genuinely asking her, and Beru had no idea what to say. Illya seemed to want her to say yes.

He let out a wry laugh. "I never used to think about it before. Never used to worry if I was a good person or not. I couldn't afford it. But now I know I'm not and I—Why should I care? Why should it matter?"

IT DOESN'T.

"It doesn't," Beru said automatically.

Illya raised his eyebrows at her. "That's not what I expected you to say."

She snapped her mouth shut, horrified. "I . . . I don't know why I said that. Of course it matters."

THERE IS NO SUCH THING AS GOOD AND BAD, LITTLE ONE, the god said. THESE ARE HUMAN INVENTIONS. LIKE LOVE. THINGS THAT HUMANS TELL THEMSELVES ARE REAL. I DID NOT MAKE HUMANS TO BE "GOOD" OR "BAD." I MADE THEM TO CARRY OUT MY WILL.

"Shut up," Beru hissed. Only after she'd said the words did she realize she'd spoken them aloud.

"I didn't say anything," Illya said, baffled. He looked at her more closely. "Are you . . . all right?"

Beru put her head in her hands. "Yes. Sorry. Just a headache."

Illya didn't say anything for a long moment. Then, quietly: "The god's talking to you right now, isn't it?"

Beru glanced up at him sharply. She hadn't told anyone the extent to which the god's influence on her had worsened. Not even Ephyra, though she knew that her sister suspected something was wrong. But if there was anyone she could talk to about what it felt like to have a monster lurking inside her, it was Illya.

Illya watched her, firelight flickering across his face. "You know, supposedly my ancestor Vasili spoke to the god."

"The Raving King?"

"The myth goes that he scried into the past and talked to the god in the time before the Prophets killed it."

"What did the god say to him?" Beru asked.

Illya poked at the dying fire with a stick, sending a spray of sparks winking through the air. "Oh you know, just that it was his destiny to defy the Prophets and rule the Novogardian Empire. Something to that effect. But whatever it was, it supposedly drove him mad."

Beru peered into the fire. "You think I'm going mad?"

He shrugged, looking for a moment so much like Anton. "Do you?"

She was too exhausted to do anything except laugh. "I don't know. Probably." After a stretch of silence, she said, "It's getting louder. Harder to block out its voice. And now that the collar's off, it's like I'm seeing everything through this dense fog. I can make out the shapes, people and feelings I recognize, but they're ... warped."

Illya shook his head, his lips curled into a half smile.

"Is that funny to you somehow?" Beru asked.

"It just sounds like how I used to feel," Illya replied. "About everything, really. Like I knew there were all these things I was *supposed* to feel—love and care and affection—but instead I just felt this anger. This ... *hate* that never went away. No matter how much I tried to bury it beneath charm and good manners, it was always there, warping everything."

Beru pulled her knees to her chest and set her chin there. When she'd first met Illya, she'd thought she would never understand him, even as she had relied on him for help.

Now, she saw herself in him, and it scared her.

"So what happened to all that anger?" she asked at last.

He glanced at her from the corner of his eye. "It's still there." He let out a breath, which fogged in the chilly evening air. "All the time."

"But you're helping us."

Illya shrugged. "What can I say? I might be a terrible person, but I'm a terrible person who wants to live. And ancient, vengeful gods tend to put a damper on survival plans." He swallowed, looking down. "What ... what does it want?"

She stared into the dying flames. "It wants to make the world its own again. A world where its will is obeyed. Where there's no defiance, no love. A world that's ..."

AT PEACE, the god said.

Beru looked at Illya. "Hollow."

———————

The Witnesses were close. Anton had sensed them only a league away, and that meant their group needed to get moving. The others hurried about packing up camp as Beru looked on.

"We're only half a league from the Serpentine," Khepri said to Jude. "We should head toward it and find boats to paddle upriver."

"What if we don't find boats?" Jude asked, shaking his head. "We'll be hemmed in against the banks, and the Witnesses will have an easy time surrounding us. We need to keep going north."

"And just keep trying to outpace the Witnesses?" Hassan cut in. "It will be like the caverns all over again. We're all exhausted. We won't survive."

The conversation grated at Beru. Someone needed to make a decision around here.

"We should go after the Witnesses," she spoke up. "Why keep running when we can find the Witnesses ourselves and kill them? Problem solved. I could do it right now."

A stunned silence followed. Beru looked around at the others. None of them met her gaze, save for Ephyra. She looked *horrified*.

"We're not doing that," Jude said calmly. "We stick together, and we keep moving."

The others finished packing up. Ephyra stepped toward Beru.

"What's going on with you?" she asked in a low voice.

Beru looked at Ephyra's face, grasping for some feeling of compassion, of concern. She felt nothing.

"I'm fine," she answered.

"No, you're not," Ephyra said softly. "I know you haven't been sleeping. And what you just said about killing the Witnesses . . . the Beru I know would never have even suggested it."

"I said, I'm fine," Beru said through gritted teeth. "And since when are you so worried about killing?"

"I'm worried about *you*."

"Well, don't be," Beru said, spinning on her heel and marching through the trees. She didn't know where she was going, she just had to get away from Ephyra before she did something she would regret.

The trees in this part of the valley were strange, with slender trunks and pale bark notched with dark scores. This late in the year, the ground was blanketed with their golden leaves, and when the morning sun peeked out from the mist, it gilded the whole forest.

Beru crossed the damp ground until she reached a small stream that rambled off from the river. The god had been quiet all morning, she realized. In fact, she heard its voice less and less now. But it wasn't because she was getting better at blocking it out. It was because the god's thoughts were seeping into her own. It didn't need to speak to communicate with her anymore. She could *feel* it.

A sudden chill spiked through her. She knelt beside the stream, cupping her hands and splashing cold water over her face. The stream was so still that when Beru looked down, she could see her own face staring back at her.

She touched her cheek. The Beru in the water did the same. Her reflection looked exactly as it always did—her eyes a little more tired, perhaps, her face a little thinner. But somehow, she didn't recognize the girl that stared back at her. She felt almost nauseated when she looked at her own face, like there was something wrong with it. Like there was someone—or some*thing*—else she was expecting to see.

She took a breath, and as she exhaled, she realized that she wasn't alone. She didn't know how exactly the awareness came to her, except that when a familiar figure emerged between the birch trees, she wasn't surprised.

"Lazaros," she said calmly. "You found me."

"Did you doubt that I would?" he asked. "The Holy Creator lives inside you. Nothing would stop me from searching for you. I will do whatever it takes to keep you from those who would harm you."

"You mean like Pallas?" Beru asked, spinning around to face him. "You know the god hates him, don't you?"

Lazaros didn't answer.

"But go ahead," Beru said, holding out her wrists. "Drag me back there in chains."

"Pallas is putting right the sins of the Prophets," Lazaros said, drawing closer. "Cleansing the world of their mistakes."

"Pallas *is* a Prophet," Beru said. "He killed the god. He led the charge."

"None of us are born pure," Lazaros said. "We must make ourselves so. As I did."

He touched one of the ragged Godfire scars at his jaw.

"Pallas doesn't want purity—he wants *power*," Beru replied. "At any cost. And you? You're just a convenient tool to help him get it."

He stared at her, his gray eyes cold and indifferent.

"So are you going to call your friends, or what?" Beru challenged.

And she saw it. Hesitation. It was just the space between one breath and the next, but there Beru saw a flicker of doubt.

"Beru!"

She turned to find Hector barreling through the trees toward her.

"Get away from her!" Hector yelled.

Lazaros unsheathed his Godfire blade and charged at him.

Beru didn't think. She just reacted, thrusting out her hand and sending a gust of power toward Lazaros, knocking him forty paces into the trees, out of sight.

The god reached for control.

No! she pleaded, shutting her eyes tight, grasping for the protection of Pallas's seal, trying to wrestle the god's power back.

The god roared at her, fury like she'd never felt before consuming her.

She was frozen, paralyzed as the god's fury stormed through her.

"Beru, we have to go," Hector was saying frantically. "There are more of them. We have to move, *now*."

"Get away," Beru gasped. It was all the warning she could manage. "Get away from me."

She wanted to kill him. She wanted to *end* him.

She squeezed her eyes shut.

Hands on her face, fingers tugging through her hair.

Lips on hers.

Fear and love and desire crashed against the god's fury. Beru swayed in Hector's arms. His lips captured hers, and the pounding of Beru's heart drowned out the roar of the god. The soft warmth of Hector's mouth drove all other feeling away.

She remembered the night in the desert, when the Daughters of Mercy had left them in the desolate nothingness to die. She remembered the sandstorm that had raged around them, and the way Hector had wrapped her in his arms, shielding her.

Now, the god was a storm, threatening to bury her. But Hector's love and his longing was something to cling to while the storm raged mercilessly on.

She felt his emotions pour into her like honeyed light seeping through her veins. It shone brilliantly, breaking up the dark clouds that had consumed her. Quieting the storm. Hector was the sun and she was the moon, absorbing his light and reflecting it back.

But that wasn't right. *She* was the one who had forced her feelings onto him. Whatever longing she felt was her own, mirrored back to her through the connection in their *esha*.

Her eyes flew open and she shoved herself backward, out of Hector's arms, putting a few precious inches of space between them. Horror and desire thundered through her in equal measure. He had just *kissed* her.

Why had he just kissed her?

He pulled in a labored breath, staring at her. "Did it work?"

At first she had no idea what he was asking, but as she felt the thump of her heart in her ribs, she realized the constant disdain and irritation was gone. The murky fog that had clouded her mind for days, while not gone completely, had dissipated. For the first time in days, she felt like she could see clearly again.

"Oh," she said, touching the pad of her finger to her lip.

Hector looked relieved. Then his expression crumbled a little. "Sorry that I—I just panicked. I shouldn't have—"

"Hector, it's all right," Beru said.

"I just mean—I know you didn't want that."

Beru's stomach gave a little lurch. *Didn't want that.* Is that what he thought?

"Hector, I—"

He turned his head over his shoulder and then grabbed Beru's wrist again. "Come on. We need to get to the river."

They sprinted through the trees, skidding over the leaves, and emerged at the bank of the Serpentine. A few hundred paces down the river, Beru caught sight of the others. A dozen or so boats lined the shore beside a narrow dock. Khepri, Illya, and Hassan were crouched beside two of them, unhooking them and pushing them into the water. It seemed Hassan had warmed to the concept of stealing.

Ephyra looked up, spotting Beru and Hector racing toward them, and bolted over to meet them.

They crashed together, Ephyra's arms wrapping around Beru tightly. "I thought they had you," Ephyra said. "I was so scared."

"I'm fine," Beru replied, squeezing back. "We need to move."

"Where's Jude?" Anton asked Hector worriedly.

"Right here!" Jude yelled, emerging from the trees. "Get in the boats! Go!"

Khepri, Illya, and Hassan pushed the boats into the water as the others piled in. Beru hit the deck, her heart racing as she helped Ephyra climb in behind her, wielding an oar.

Six Witnesses raced after Jude, closing in on him. Jude dove into the river, wading toward the boats. The Witnesses dove after him.

"Jude!" Anton cried, balancing precariously on the edge of the boat as he knelt over the side. Hector joined him, and together they pulled Jude from the river and into their boat.

Khepri tossed Hector another oar, and they began to paddle furiously. Beru sat back, heart pounding, as they heaved themselves upriver, leaving the Witnesses behind in the shallows.

The mountains loomed above as the river snaked up toward them. These were not the gently sloped forested mountains of the Gallian mountain range, but instead jagged and starkly bare.

Around dusk, they reached a patch of coast at the base of the mountains, where they decided to pull the boat over to the far side of the river and make camp for the evening. They drew up on shore and hid the boat in the rush.

"Hector and I can go get firewood," Beru said, and before anyone could object, she grabbed Hector's arm and dragged him off through the trees.

"Look," Hector said, the moment they were out of earshot of the others. "I need to apologize."

"I don't want you to apologize," Beru blurted.

Hector just stared at her.

Beru took a steadying breath. "Hector, do you really think I didn't want you to kiss me?"

His brow furrowed. "I know you're dealing with a lot right now. I wasn't trying to add to your problems. But I do care about you. That's . . . that's all it has to be, for now."

Beru sighed, pacing away from him. "It's not that." She had to do this before she lost her nerve. "I don't even know how to say this." She stared down at her hands. "Hector, your feelings for me aren't real."

He stared at her, dumbfounded for a moment. Then he let out a snort of laughter.

Beru took a step back, stung.

"What—You're serious?" he said, the mirth draining from his face. "What . . . explain what you mean."

"The connection between our *esha*," Beru said with a wave. "It sort of . . . transferred my feelings to you. That is, my feelings *for* you spilled over to you, the same way fear and anger and everything else does. The feelings you think you have for me? Those are *my* feelings. How I feel when I'm with you. I *made* you fall in love with me. I mean, it wasn't on purpose but still—I'm the one who put those thoughts in your head."

His expression grew increasingly more troubled, his lips pressed tightly together, his eyes narrowing. Finally, he said, "Beru. That is . . . the most ridiculous thing I've ever heard."

"Think about it," she said tersely. "Why would you *ever* have cared about me if it wasn't for that? What reason would you have? I—I'm the reason your family is dead, and I'm the reason Ephyra *killed* you. I'm—"

"Hey," he said, cupping a broad hand over the side of her neck where it met her shoulder. "You think I haven't thought about this? You think I just started feeling this way one day and didn't question it?"

"So you *did* question it," Beru said. "You thought that it was wrong somehow, that you would never—"

"That's not what I'm saying," Hector broke in. "It wasn't . . . I didn't wake up one day with feelings I couldn't explain. They were *always* there. On the train to Tel Amot, when we were in Medea. They were already there." He let go of her abruptly, dragging a hand through his hair. "I couldn't accept it, at first. That day when I found you on the train you were so—different from what I thought you'd be. It made me *furious*. At myself, mostly. That I could feel anything for the person responsible for my family's death."

"Hector—"

"But that doesn't mean that I didn't know *why* I felt that way," Hector went on. "It wasn't because of our *esha* or because your sister killed me to save your life. It was because you looked me in the eye on that train car and held your ground. It was because I could see your fear and your pain and I knew that you had lived with it all your life, and you had never let it consume you. It was because every moment I've spent with you since then proved to me that you are the bravest, strongest person I've ever known."

He was looking at her so earnestly. "No," she whispered. "No, I'm not. You don't know what I—what I'm—"

"Beru," he said, taking her hand. "You have suffered more than most people ever will in their whole lives. And somehow, you haven't let those things twist you. Even now, with the rage of a god locked inside you, you're still fighting for *us*, all of us. Even *Illya*. So the question isn't why I care about you, after everything. The question is, why *wouldn't* I?"

She swallowed, staring at his dark eyes and the intense, almost challenging look on his face. There was nothing, she realized, she wanted more than to kiss him again.

His gaze flicked to her lips and she knew that, impossibly, he was thinking the same thing. His eyes closed, those long, dark lashes fanning against his cheekbones as he leaned into her.

"I'm losing," Beru whispered in the disappearing space between them. He stopped, breath hitching. "Hector, I'm fighting, but I'm losing. You think I'm so strong, that I haven't let any of this twist me, but you're *wrong*. The god . . . I can feel it eating away at me. Turning me into something else. I can't . . . I don't know how much longer I can fight it."

Tears bit at the corners of her eyes, her voice shaking with the effort of holding them back.

Hector's warm, broad hand cupped her face, his thumb wiping gently at the unshed tears. She couldn't stand the way he was looking at her, tender and open and like he wanted nothing more than to take care of her.

"I believe in you," he murmured. "If there's anyone who can do this, Beru, it's you."

I can't, she wanted to say. She wanted to scream it in his face. *I can't do it. I'm not strong enough.*

Then suddenly Hector's expression changed, his eyes flicking over Beru's shoulder and his whole body going still and tense.

"Beru," he said in a low voice. "Get behind me."

She did it without question, following his gaze toward the tree line.

A dozen people emerged from the woods, crossbows aloft. The others—Ephyra, Jude, Illya, Anton, Khepri, Hassan—were being slowly marched ahead of the crossbows, hands held up.

The woman in front of them trained her crossbow on Hector. She wore an elkskin cape and had a bandana tied around her head and slipped over one eye.

"There are a dozen more of us hidden," she said. "So come with us peacefully, or all of you will be dead before you can land a blow."

27

ANTON

THEIR CAPTORS BOUND THEIR HANDS AND LED THEM ON A STEEP, ROCKY CLIMB up the mountains. Without the full use of their hands, it was slow going, but the length of the journey gave Anton some hope. If these people intended to kill them, they would have done it already and saved the trouble.

They walked in tense silence, until at last they reached a town sheltered by a great spur of rock and bracketed by trickling waterfalls that flowed into a small tributary of the Serpentine River. The only entrance, it seemed, was a single bridge that crossed beneath the falls.

Their captors led them over the bridge and into a stout, stone building situated right on the river.

"Wait here," the one-eyed woman said, and then left, locking the door behind her.

The room was dark and smelled pungently of sulfur. Iron tools lay neatly on worktables, and a kiln, now cold, sat in one corner of the room. This room was a forge.

"So," Hector said, breaking the silence. "We're going to die, right?"

"You think she's going to get the Witnesses?" Khepri asked.

Illya shook his head. "There aren't any Witnesses in the mountains."

"That you know of," Ephyra muttered.

"Let's just think for a second," Hassan said. "Maybe there's a way we can escape."

Anton glanced around the forge. Narrow windows, thick stone walls, a heavy iron door—it didn't seem likely.

"Maybe we can bargain with them?" he suggested, fidgeting with his bindings.

Jude opened his mouth to answer when the door banged open again and in walked a girl who could not have been older than twelve, flanked by four of the crossbow-wielding captors, including the woman with one eye.

"You found them on the river?" the girl asked. Her short, auburn hair was pulled severely from her face in two neat braids. A smattering of light freckles dotted her sharp, pointed face, and there was a surprising amount of authority in her clear gray eyes.

"Yes, Lady Iskara," the one-eyed woman replied. "They had a boat that looked to be stolen."

"We didn't steal it," Ephyra said immediately. "It was more of an emergency borrowing."

"You will speak when spoken to, or I will cut out your tongues," Lady Iskara said sharply.

Anton had never been threatened by a twelve-year-old girl. He had also never been genuinely afraid of a twelve-year-old girl, but there was a first time for everything.

"You should already know what it is we do to Pallas's followers here."

"Wait," Anton said. "Do you think we're Witnesses?"

Lady Iskara leveled her gaze at him, and Anton had never seen so much ferocity on a face so young. "Don't be coy with me."

"I'm not!" Anton said indignantly. "We're fighting *against* the Witnesses."

Lady Iskara's eyes narrowed. "So you claim."

"We can prove it," Hector spoke up. "We're Graced. Well, not all of us, but—"

"Do you take me for a simpleton?" she asked. "Or is it my age that makes you think you can fool me so easily?"

"What?" Hassan said. "No, we—"

"We are well aware of Pallas's new tricks," Lady Iskara said. "Removing Grace and transferring it to his followers. If you do have Grace, it must have been gained through these monstrous means, and we will have you strung up outside our city walls as a warning to Pallas."

"We're not—"

"That's enough," the girl barked, her voice so effortlessly commanding that Hassan fell silent at once. "We will speak to you one at a time and find out the truth."

Her cool gray eyes swept over the group of them. "You first," she said, nodding at Illya. Two of the crossbow wielders pulled him toward the door, and Anton's heart sank.

Of the eight of them, she just *had* to choose the one who actually was connected with the Witnesses. On the one hand, Illya *was* good at lying. On the other, if he was caught lying that would be it for all of them. From what Anton had seen of this girl, she was not going to offer them much in the way of leniency.

And a third thought occurred to him—that somehow Illya would find a way to save his own skin by tossing the rest of them to the wolves.

The door clanged shut behind them, Illya on the other side.

"I think I know where we are," Beru said after a moment. "On a few occasions, Pallas mentioned a mining town in the Unspoken Mountains called Anvari. A stronghold against the Witnesses, one of the few left.

He spoke of it as little more than a nuisance, but I could tell it bothered him. Just the idea of these people resisting his claim of power."

"Well, that's great, but it doesn't help us if they think we're on Pallas's side," Anton said wearily. "And honestly, I don't see a good way to convince them."

"I do," Hassan said. Anton looked up as Hassan pushed himself to his feet. "We tell them the truth."

Anton blinked at him. Hector barked out a laugh, and when Hassan turned his steady gaze on him, he cut himself off.

"Oh. You're serious?"

Hassan nodded.

"There's no way they'll believe us," Ephyra said.

Hassan shook his head. "I mean, maybe they won't. But you'd be surprised at the faith people have when you offer them a little hope."

"We can't," Jude said at once. "I won't risk Anton like that."

Anton sighed. He'd expected as much.

Hassan's jaw clenched. "But you'll risk letting these people lock us up or execute us because they think we're working for Pallas?"

"We'll find another way to convince them," Jude said. "Something that doesn't put Anton in—"

"Actually," Anton cut in. "I kind of think Prince Hassan has a point."

Jude stared at him, his green eyes burning.

"Anton," Hassan said. "This is your choice. If you tell them you're the Last Prophet, I think they'll believe you. Jude isn't wrong—it is dangerous. But it might be our only option."

He was right—Anton knew it. And so did Jude, as much as he was pretending otherwise.

But before he could reply, the door clanged open once again and a dozen more people poured into the forge, seizing them by the arms and dragging them all outside.

"Hey, hey!" Hassan protested as they shoved him out toward the river.

"What did Illya tell you?" Anton demanded, struggling against his own captors. "What did he say?"

No one answered him as their captors silently marched them down a stone path, heading into the town. They passed homes and shops, people spilling out into the street to watch the sorry parade.

They wound up a narrow stone path toward the apex of the surging waterfalls. There, a stone platform jutted out over the water, looking down at a plaza hewn into the rockface.

Lady Iskara waited on the platform, along with more of her guards and Illya.

"What did you do?" Anton bit out, glaring at Illya.

Illya looked genuinely bewildered and a little frightened. "Nothing, I swear."

A crowd of curious onlookers was forming in the plaza below them. Anton heard people hollering to their neighbors and saw others climbing up on their roofs.

"What are they going to do?" Beru asked worriedly.

"People of Anvari!" Lady Iskara cried, her voice enhanced by some trick of artificery. "Earlier tonight, your brave and valorous rangers found a group of Witnesses plotting to attack our city."

Hushed mumblings of unease and worry broke out over the crowd.

"These Witnesses were quickly caught, and they stand before you now," Lady Iskara said. "As your ruler, it is my duty to carry out the will of the people."

The rangers pushed Anton and the others toward the edge of the platform. Anton stared over the edge, where the powerful surge of the falls crashed down into the river below, and suppressed a shiver. It reminded him too much of all his nightmares of being submerged, of seeing the vision of the end of the world flash before his eyes.

"You're up first," one of the rangers said, grabbing Hector and attempting to force him over the edge of the platform.

"Let go of him!" Hassan yelled, struggling against his own captors.

The cold knot of fear in Anton's stomach hardened to resolve.

"Wait," he said. "Lady Iskara, please. Listen."

Lady Iskara held up a tiny hand to still her rangers.

"We're not Witnesses," Anton said, his voice trembling. "We were afraid to tell you the truth. Who we really are. Who I really am."

He could see it on her face—she was curious.

"The truth is—" Anton swallowed hard. He glanced at Jude, and while there was a storm in his eyes, he didn't try to stop Anton. "The truth is, I am the Last Prophet."

"The Last Prophet?" she repeated, skepticism dripping from each word. "That's just a rumor. There's no truth to it."

"There is," Anton said. "It's all true, my lady. The last prophecy. The Age of Darkness. And me—the person who can stop all of it."

Lady Iskara paused. Anton could see her hesitation. The flicker of doubt coming up against her need to appear strong before her people.

"You're lying," she said at last, her voice low and poisonous. "You expect me to believe that?"

Anton shut his eyes, letting his Grace spool out of him like he did each morning when he scried for the Witnesses. He reached out, letting the echoes of his Grace disturb the patterns of *esha* around him. Calling out with his Grace, the way he'd done in the Circle of Stones.

"What are you doing?" Lady Iskara demanded. "What is he doing?"

A sound like thunder rolled over the mountains, starting low and then building, a surge of power resonating around them.

He felt something pull at him. His vision. It was like it had been lurking there, since he'd seen it for the third time on the lake near his childhood home.

The vision swallowed him again. He saw Behezda, breaking apart. The sky above Tarsepolis exploding with bright fire, the twin statues at its harbor looking on. Pallas Athos, its white streets running red with blood. The familiar, glittering river city Endarrion, its citizens stumbling through cobbled streets, afflicted with sores and sickness. The mountains around Charis, bellowing black smoke into the sky. And finally, Nazirah, battered by a storm of lightning and hail.

Anton opened his eyes, stumbling back as flashes of destruction overtook him. His gaze climbed to the sky, where ribbons of gold, green, and blue light cracked open the night.

"What's happening?" Lady Iskara asked, a thread of fear in her voice that made her sound, for the first time, like a child. "What *is* he?"

"He's a Prophet," Hassan replied, raising his voice over the reverberation of Anton's Grace. "Just as he said."

Anton fell to his knees and released his Grace, gasping. The air went quiet. The sky dark. Jude was instantly at Anton's side, bracing him with an arm around his waist. Anton let him support some of his weight, raising his eyes to meet Lady Iskara's awed face.

"We all have reasons to want to hide from Pallas and his Witnesses," Anton said. "But now we've laid all our cards on the table. I . . . hope you can find it in yourself to extend that trust back to us."

Lady Iskara just stared at him for a moment and then looked away. "All right," she said at last. "But you will tell me everything."

———

Lady Iskara brought them all to her citadel, a stone castle set into the bare rock of the mountain. As they climbed down the stone stairs, Jude hovered at Anton's side, as if afraid he might collapse again, but he said nothing to him. When Anton tried to catch his gaze, he looked away.

Down in the great hall, they all sat at a long table, with six of Lady Iskara's rangers rounding out their group. Servants brought trays of warm bread and a thick venison stew with turnips and cabbage. The food was plain, but hardy, and Anton hadn't realized just how hungry he was until he was shoveling some into his mouth.

"Radka will see to it that there's space in the barracks for you all to stay the night," Lady Iskara told them.

"As guests or prisoners?" Hector asked through a mouthful of stew.

"I'm still deciding," Lady Iskara replied archly. "You still haven't told me why it is you're in my city."

"Well, your rangers captured us by the river," Anton answered.

Lady Iskara did not look impressed by his wit.

"We're trying to find the other Prophets," Anton said. "The remaining Prophets, aside from Pallas. They . . . we think they'll know how to stop him."

"The other Prophets," Lady Iskara repeated. "And you mean to tell me they're what—somewhere in my backyard?"

"They're in the Unspoken Mountains," Anton replied, ignoring Jude's warning glance.

Lady Iskara's expression darkened. "Is this a joke?"

"No, my lady," Anton said, with a quick glance of confusion at the rest of them. "Why would it be a joke?"

"Because no one goes into the Unspoken Mountains," the one-eyed ranger said from Lady Iskara's other side. "And if they do, they don't come back."

"No one?" Hector echoed. "Surely over the years *someone* has."

The ranger shook her head. "There are stories that say when you venture too far into the mountains, voices call to you from afar. The ridges are blanketed in steam from underground thermal springs, and the steam hides deep chasms and caverns where travelers can fall, and if they don't dash their heads against the sharp rocks then they get trapped and die."

"Sounds promising," Illya said drily.

"Or," Hassan said, "it sounds like a convenient rumor to make sure no one ventured far enough into the mountains to find whatever—or whoever—didn't want to be found."

"Come on, Radka," a younger ranger on the one-eyed woman's other side said. "Stop scaring the guests. If they want to go offer themselves to the mountains, that's their business!"

Anton's stomach lurched at the thought of the danger he was dragging everyone into. This quest to find the other Prophets had started as a desperate gambit, and now they'd come so far, but Anton realized how much further there was to go. And seeing the destruction in his vision again only reminded him of how much they had to lose if they failed.

He looked across the table at Jude, who was talking to another of the rangers, and felt the weight of the secret he was keeping from him. From all of them.

Abruptly, he stood from the table, making a flimsy excuse to Lady Iskara, and left the hall through a different set of doors. They led him out into a stone courtyard, dotted with crooked trees that drew jagged shadows in the moonlight.

A moment later, he heard footsteps behind him and felt the familiar storm of Jude's *esha* brush up against his own. He closed his eyes, steadying himself with a breath before he turned around.

"Is it your turn to lecture me about risking my life?" Anton asked, venturing a smile.

Jude shook his head mutely.

"Telling them who I am was the right thing to do," Anton said. "You know it was."

"I'm not arguing with you about this," Jude said flatly.

"Because you know I'm right."

"Because you're trying to pick a fight instead of telling me what's really wrong," Jude shot back.

Anton's retort died on his tongue. He hadn't even realized he was doing it, but Jude was right.

"Something happened when we were separated after Behezda," Jude said haltingly. "Something you've been keeping from me."

Anton's stomach dropped.

"You said that I could talk to you," Jude pushed on. "That you wanted me to tell you what I was feeling, even if you wouldn't like it. So why don't you trust me with the same?"

"I trust you," Anton said, reaching to touch his face. "I always trust you."

He drew Jude toward him, but Jude stopped him with a hand on his chest.

"You keep doing this," he said, breath hitching. "Every time we get close to talking about—whatever it is you don't want to talk about— you look at me like that and kiss me and I—I just let you do it. It's not fair and it's not—It's *cruel*, Anton."

He knew Jude was right. He felt sick. It was something Illya would have done. It was something Anton *had* done, back when his only thought was survival. Allowing people to have what they wanted from him, what he thought they wanted, so they wouldn't ask for something he couldn't give.

But that was before Jude. Before he understood how hands and lips and touch could transform you. How you could want more and more of something and have it never be enough. How for a few short moments you could be the center of someone's whole world, and how powerful that was. How dangerous.

Jude curled his fingers in Anton's shirt. "Don't shut me out. *Please.*"

This was what he'd been trying to avoid since leaving the Wandering City. Jude's earnest face, his careful touch, his wide-open heart. This was the warning Hector had tried to give him.

Anton brushed a thumb along the ridge of Jude's cheek. "I don't want to hurt you."

"Then tell me," Jude pleaded. "Whatever it is. You have to tell me, Anton."

Anton swallowed down the panic and fear rising in his throat. "It's nothing, Jude. It's—"

Anything, he thought desperately. *You can have anything you want. Just not that.*

He looked into Jude's eyes. "You have to just trust me."

Jude drew back an inch, squaring his shoulders like he was preparing for a blow.

And then he was pulling Anton in, his lips crashing against Anton's in a kiss that swelled between them like a storm. Anton held on to him like he was drowning, tasting his desperation, his fear, taking it all and pouring it back into him.

Jude broke away, breathing hard, his gaze crackling like a tempest.

Anton swayed back, putting a few scant inches of space between them. Having all of Jude's considerable focus on him was always overwhelming, whether he was arguing with Anton or kissing him breathless. It brought Anton back to that first day in the harbor of Pallas Athos, feeling the echo of Jude's Grace reflected against his own— leaving Anton trapped, exposed, unbalanced. The intensity of his gaze had once made Anton almost lose a game of cards. It could make him do a lot of things.

He opened his mouth and then realized there was nothing he could say. Silence hung in the air like a thick shroud. Guilt roiled in Anton's gut. He wanted to give Jude everything he wanted. He wanted to keep Jude for himself. He couldn't do both.

Jude waited another heartbeat, and then he let go of Anton completely, backing away and stalking off into the night. Anton watched him go, only his own labored breath filling the silence Jude left behind.

28

HASSAN

HASSAN FOUND HIMSELF ENJOYING THE COMPANY OF LADY ISKARA'S RANGERS as evening turned into night.

"Tell us more about Anvari," Hassan said, ripping off a chunk of bread to dip in his stew. "How is it your city has resisted the Witnesses for this long?"

"Well, it hasn't been easy," the younger ranger said, pushing her raven hair over her shoulder. "The moment we heard the reports about Witnesses in the river valley, Lady Iskara made it known that anyone seeking refuge from them would be welcomed into Anvari. I was one of them—a lot of us joined up with the rangers. We knew that our own regional lords would do little to protect us, but Lady Iskara showed us that she meant what she'd said."

An unexpected surge of defiance and reverence washed through Hassan. These people weren't so different from his and Khepri's little group of Herati refugees or the Scarab's Wing. Just people standing up to the Hierophant, fighting for themselves as best as they could. He felt renewed respect for this Lady Iskara. Young as she was, she was clearly strong enough to stand against the Witnesses. Smart enough to know that in a fight like this one, hope was the most powerful weapon.

"Though it might all be for nothing, in the end," the one-eyed ranger said. "With the Witnesses controlling most of the river valley, our food stores are limited beyond what we can smuggle in and what we can hunt. Come winter, we'll starve unless something changes."

"There's always hope," the younger ranger said gently.

Hassan thought of the Scarab's Wing, holed up inside the Great Library and fighting to stay alive. Of Zareen, and Khepri's brothers, Sefu and Chike, left there without Khepri or Hassan or Arash to guide them. The guilt of his decision not to return to Nazirah weighed on him more heavily than it had since those first days after Behezda.

They finished their meal and one of the rangers showed them to the barracks. It would be nice to sleep somewhere other than the ground for the first time since they'd entered the river valley, even though the barracks themselves were drafty and smelled vaguely like mildew.

The barracks sat at the edge of the shelf of rock that had been carved out from the mountain, adjoining a courtyard that overlooked the rest of the citadel. Hassan drifted into the courtyard as the others prepared for bed.

"You should really get some rest, Hassan," Khepri said gently.

Hassan turned from where he'd been peering over the low wall that bracketed the courtyard. Khepri leaned in the doorway of the barracks, arms crossed loosely over her chest. He felt the sudden urge to reach out and touch her, a pang of longing he'd managed to keep at bay since the caverns.

"Are you all right?" Khepri asked, uncrossing her arms and approaching him.

Hassan shook his head. He wasn't all right—hadn't been since Behezda. Since before then. Maybe not since that fateful night when he'd woken to a palace under attack, when he'd been forced to flee on a ship without his parents or anyone he trusted.

"These people are all going to die," he said. "This city is basically under siege by the Witnesses. We should do something, shouldn't we? We should help."

Khepri leaned her elbows against the wall beside him. "How?"

"I don't know. But Lady Iskara has held this town against the Witnesses for months. *Alone.* Don't she and her people deserve some respite from that? Some aid?"

"You admire her."

"I relate to her," Hassan replied.

"This place isn't Nazirah," Khepri said. "Our city . . . our people are a world away. Fighting against Lethia and the Witnesses alone. You can't think that helping these people is going to change that. You can't just assuage your guilt—"

"Who says I have guilt?" Hassan demanded.

Khepri gave him a look. "Hassan, I know you."

"It was the right decision not to go back," he said firmly.

"We won't know that until this is all over," Khepri replied, looking down at her fidgeting hands.

She was probably right. And maybe this was why Hassan's ancestors had had it so easy. They'd had the Prophets to tell them how things would turn out, for better or worse. They'd had warnings to guide their choices.

It made him think of what the Wanderer had told them, about fate and destiny and bringing them together. It made him think of the moment he'd realized he wasn't the Prophet and had decided to keep pretending he was anyway. The moment he'd realized Lethia had turned on him. The moment he'd gone to the Hierophant, offering him the secrets of the Relics in exchange for Nazirah. Those were all things that weighed heavily on Hassan, that stirred up his gut with guilt. But maybe they weren't mistakes—maybe he wouldn't know until it was all over. Or maybe not even then.

———————————

"Have you seen Anton?" Jude asked Hassan the next morning as they made their way to the great hall.

"He's not here?" Hassan peered at the group filing out the door and saw that, in fact, Anton was not among them. "Maybe he's already in the great hall."

They followed the others to breakfast and found Lady Iskara waiting for them. But no Anton.

"Captain Weatherbourne," Lady Iskara said, catching sight of him and waving him over to where she was huddled with a group of rangers, deep in conversation.

Hassan and Hector followed at his heels.

"What's going on?" Hassan asked warily.

"My rangers have sighted a small band of people in the foothills," Lady Iskara replied. "We tried to capture them, but they evaded us. They appeared to be led by a man with Godfire burns."

Hassan's blood went cold. The Witnesses had found them again.

Lady Iskara flicked her gaze to him. "You know these people."

Hassan nodded. "They're after us. A group of Pallas's Witnesses have been tracking us through the valley."

Lady Iskara nodded. "Radka, call all your rangers back to Anvari and take up position at the bridge. If these Witnesses come to our doorstep, I want us to be ready."

"The Witnesses won't risk entering the city," Hector said. "They must know it's protected. They're most likely waiting for us to depart so they can ambush us."

Jude had been strangely silent throughout this exchange, and when Hassan turned to look at him, he saw that he looked pale and shaken.

"Jude?" Hector asked.

"Anton," Jude replied, swinging his gaze to Hector. "We need to find him. If the Witnesses are here—if he left the city—"

"I'll go with you," Ephyra called from the table, unfolding herself from her seat.

Jude looked a little bewildered at her volunteering.

"What?" Ephyra asked. "Is it that weird that I'm worried about the kid, too?"

"I'll go, too," Hector said.

Illya cleared his throat. "I can help."

Hassan nodded. "Me too. Khepri and Beru can stay here and work with the rangers on finding a safe way out of the city once we're back."

They split up, Jude and Ephyra heading toward the falls, leaving Hector to search the citadel, and Illya to venture toward the river. Hassan went east, into the city's old quarter, its stone buildings crumbling and its labyrinthine streets pocked with holes.

He wandered farther into the city, stopping passersby, asking if they'd seen Anton. The fifth person he stopped, a harried-looking young woman who appeared to be delivering sacks of grain, pointed off toward a narrow alley, where Hassan could see a group of children huddled in a tight circle.

It took Hassan a moment to realize that Anton was among them, his fair hair starkly visible. A discarded basket sat behind him.

Just as Hassan began to approach, the whole circle erupted into hoots and howls.

"Aww, you're all going to bleed me dry," Anton protested, tossing a button into the center of the circle, where several chipped dice sat beside a bowl. He glanced up, his dark eyes locking on Hassan. "Prince Hassan!"

He waved him over, and, somewhat bemused, Hassan joined him.

"You're a *prince?*" one of the kids exclaimed loudly, sounding amazed and aghast.

"Oops," Anton said guiltily. "Sorry."

"It's fine," Hassan said with a wave. "Did you know everyone's looking for you?"

Anton blinked, surprised. "They are? I must have lost track of time."

"Jude was worried," Hassan added pointedly.

Just as pointedly, Anton didn't answer.

"Dice!" several of the kids hollered.

"I'm pretty sure they're just conspiring to take all my buttons," Anton lamented, fingering a loose thread where he'd clearly ripped a button from his jacket.

"Are *not!*" insisted a small boy with a gap tooth.

"Play with us, mister Prince Hassan!" another kid said, tugging on Hassan's sleeve.

Hassan sighed. He really should get Anton back to the citadel so they could leave. Instead, he plopped himself down in the circle. "All right. One round. How do we play?"

They explained the rules to him, growing more and more excitable, correcting and talking over one another.

"All right," Anton said, rubbing his hands together. "Roll 'em again. I've got a good feeling about this one."

The gap-toothed boy giggled. "That's what you said last time!"

"Oh, did I?" Anton asked, pretending to think. "Well, this time I *mean* it. Roll again!"

They played a few rounds, the kids shouting with delight or dismay, their dramatics getting more and more elaborate with every roll. Hassan recalled the Herati refugee children he had played with in those first few weeks in Pallas Athos. Their joy and wonder had been a balm to him.

Now, the cheerful innocence of these children twisted Hassan's heart. They probably understood, on some level, what was happening in the world around them, but here on the steps in the city they knew so well, they felt safe.

But when winter came, and the Witnesses's siege persisted, that safety would crumble, and this moment when they'd played dice on the steps would seem endlessly far away and impossible to reach.

"Pieter! Mila!" a voice barked from down the block.

Hassan turned to see what looked like the father of two of the children Anton was currently entertaining.

Spotting the cluster of children, the father marched down the street toward them. "What have I told you about playing in the street?" He grabbed the tiny gap-toothed child and his sister, pulling them to his side. "You know you—" He cut off with a gasp as his gaze fell on Anton.

Anton's smile froze in place.

"That's the Last Prophet," the boy's father whispered to him. "He's the one who's going to save us all."

He was staring at Anton with watery, awed eyes.

Anton's face wilted a little. "Time for me to go, I think."

The children's whines and moans of disappointment followed Anton as he walked away.

The father's gaze fell on Hassan. "I didn't mean to—"

"It's all right," Hassan assured him. "It wasn't you." He turned to the other kids. "Good game, everyone. Don't go spending your winnings all in one place."

The kids gathered up their buttons and scrambled to their feet. He noticed that their clothes were patched, that the few of them with jackets had mismatched buttons. It hadn't occurred to him to wonder why they were betting buttons on dice—they would need them to stay warm in the winter.

Hassan's gaze returned to Anton's retreating form. He would bet all the buttons on his coat that Anton could have easily won if he'd wanted to.

Hassan jogged after him, trailing him until Anton stopped beside the wooden fence that blocked off the sharp drop down into the river.

"This is just a guess," Hassan said, "but you didn't have a lot of happiness in your childhood, did you?"

Anton blew out a breath, an edge of humor in his eyes. "That's one way to put it."

Hassan remembered the strange mix of kinship and alienation he'd felt playing with the Herati refugee children. He had felt a responsibility to them. He thought of little Azizi, trying to steal meat to bring to his mother. The deep care and protectiveness he had felt for those kids was the same obligation he had as king of all Herati people, young and old.

But when he watched Anton play with these children, it was different. Anton wasn't a guardian of these children—he was *one* of them. He knew exactly what it felt like to play in a dirty street because you had nowhere else to go, to wonder where your next meal would come from, if it would come at all.

"It was good, what you did for those kids," Hassan said hesitantly.

"Letting them have a handful of buttons?" Anton asked bitterly. "How generous of me."

"Not that," Hassan said. "Just . . . being with them. Seeing them."

Anton turned his gaze on Hassan. "We should help them."

The deep cavern of grief that Hassan had learned to ignore in his chest seemed to open a little wider. He wanted to tell Anton that he had said the exact same thing the night before, that he agreed with him, that they should find a way.

Instead he said, "The best thing we can do for these people is to do what we came here to do. Find the Prophets, stop the Age of Darkness, take away the Hierophant's power."

Anton looked back toward the river. "Find the Prophets," he repeated quietly.

"This was *your* plan," Hassan reminded him, frustration bleeding through his voice. "Now isn't the time to lose faith. And these people—you *have* helped them, Anton. You told them who you are."

Anton scratched at the wooden post. "How does that help them?"

"Because now they have hope," Hassan said. "That's a powerful thing, more powerful than you think."

"And what if it's false hope?" Anton asked. "What if . . ."

Hassan looked at his pale, freckled face, the bruised-looking bags beneath his eyes that only seemed to grow more pronounced, and knew that he, Hassan, was probably the only person in the world who understood the weight that had been laid on Anton's shoulders. Even if Hassan hadn't turned out to be the Prophet, those few days where he'd thought he was had been some of the hardest of his life.

Even after he'd learned the truth, he hadn't been able to put down that burden. It would always be part of him.

"That's what happens," he said to Anton, "when people put their faith in you. You become responsible for them."

"This is why . . ." Anton shook his head. "I never wanted this, never wanted to *be* this."

"You should have gotten a choice," Hassan agreed. "But few people do."

They were quiet for a moment.

"I'm not strong enough," Anton said suddenly. "I know I'm not. Jude could do it, Beru could do it, *you* could do it, but I'm . . ."

"Thank you for that," Hassan said. "But you're wrong. I don't think a single one of us is strong enough to do this."

"Then we're doomed, aren't we?"

"No," Hassan said, his heart swelling for a moment. "No, we're not, because none of us is doing it alone. *That's* why we were brought together."

Anton peered up at him, his gaze oddly calculating, like there was something he was holding himself back from saying.

"Come on," Hassan said, when it was clear Anton was going to remain silent. "We shouldn't keep the others waiting."

Anton nodded, and they set off toward the citadel, turning their backs to the rest of the city.

29

JUDE

"WHERE DO YOU THINK HE WENT?" EPHYRA ASKED AS SHE AND JUDE WALKED the stone streets of Anvari.

Jude shook his head, trying to think. "I don't know. Are there gambling halls in Anvari?"

Ephyra snorted. "Remind me to tell you about the time I found him in one in Pallas Athos, about to get ground into a pulp."

Jude swung his gaze toward her, alarmed. "What?"

"Don't worry, I rescued him," she said. "So, you two had an argument?"

He didn't answer, jaw clenching as he recalled the impasse they'd come to the night before.

"Not trying to get involved," Ephyra said, holding up her hands. "It's just . . . you know. We're kind of all counting on both of you."

He let out a weary sigh. "He can be so infuriating. He just does whatever he wants, and he doesn't care about how it affects anyone else."

"I thought you two were . . ." Ephyra waved a hand vaguely.

It was just as well that she didn't try to put words to what Jude and Anton were to each other. Jude certainly couldn't. "I would do anything for him. And he won't even tell me the truth."

Ephyra narrowed her eyes. "Did you ever think maybe that's the problem?"

The *problem* was that after everything they'd been through together, Anton still had to keep Jude at arm's length and pretend that wasn't what he was doing.

"Look, I know you didn't ask for my advice," Ephyra began haltingly. "And it's not like I'm a bastion of healthy relationships. But I've sort of been where you are. Desperate to keep someone I love safe. Willing to sacrifice anything. And in the end, that was what . . ." She swallowed, seeming to struggle with the words. "That was what drove her away."

"Your sister," Jude said, understanding.

Ephyra wiped a tear with the back of her hand. "When Hector—when I killed Hector . . ."

Jude's heart clenched with the reminder.

"Beru gave up on me," Ephyra said, choking out the words. "She left, decided she'd rather die than . . ." She paused. "But before that, I knew the role I had forced her into was driving a wedge between us. I knew, and I ignored it because I thought if I just held on tightly enough . . ."

Jude tugged a hand through his hair. He understood. Too well.

"I guess what I'm saying is that whatever Anton's hiding, whatever he won't tell you, it's probably because he's scared," she said. "Scared of what you would do if you knew."

He thought about all the times Anton had told Jude, in words and deeds, that he didn't need his protection, didn't want it. When it came down to it, that was what had hurt Jude most. The idea that Anton was rejecting the only real thing he had to offer.

He hadn't considered, until now, that the truth was something much worse. That Anton refused to allow Jude to protect him because he knew that he *couldn't*. That whatever waited for them at the end of this journey, whatever answers the Prophets gave them, might require a sacrifice that Jude could not bear.

"After Behezda, he was gone," he said, staring off into the horizon. It was still hard to recall those dark months, when he'd dreamed of Anton every night, not knowing if he was even still alive. "I thought I'd lost him for good, but then I got him back and I just thought . . ."

"You thought the rest of your problems wouldn't matter anymore."

He met her soft, wry smile with one of his own and in that moment he felt less alone than he had in days. *Months.*

She nudged her shoulder against his. "You're not so bad, you know. For a stodgy swordsman."

"You're not so bad, either," he replied. "Aside from the murder."

"Hey, look," she said, brightening and pointing ahead. Jude followed her gaze to the bank of the river, where Hassan and Anton appeared to be deep in conversation. Jude's heart stuttered in his chest as Anton's dark eyes met his. Some indecipherable expression crossed his face, and Jude was torn between relief that he was safe and anger that he'd disappeared after their fight.

He ran toward Anton anyway.

"I'm sorry," Anton said, the moment Jude reached him. "For disappearing. I just needed some time."

It was Ephyra who answered, not Jude. "We're just glad you're all right, kid."

She eyed Jude, and Jude felt his anger shift, cast in a new light by

Ephyra's words. But he didn't quite know what to say. He just stared at Anton, trying to divine the answers that Anton refused to give him.

"We should get back to the citadel," Hassan said.

They bid farewell to the rangers and Lady Iskara before the sun was high in the sky, and set off along a path that took them back to the waterfall and then cut around and climbed higher into the mountains. They passed the quarries around lunchtime and kept moving.

By nightfall, exhaustion struck. Just before dark, Anton scried for the scarred Witness, Lazaros, and deemed it safe enough to make camp without fear that he would happen upon them.

Over the next few days, as they hiked deeper into the mountains, Jude thought about what Lady Iskara had said about Anvari being the edge of civilization. It certainly felt like they'd left the settled world behind. The landscape grew barren as they traversed it, starkly alien and somehow breathtaking. Dramatic cliffs plunged down from jagged black ridges. The Unspoken mountain range had been formed eons ago by volcanic eruptions, and they somehow seemed to carry that legacy with them.

It truly did feel like they were on the edge of the world, without another living soul for hundreds and hundreds of miles.

As they journeyed, the question persisted in Jude's mind. Why had the Prophets come here? And, perhaps more pressingly, why had they stayed?

The landscape changed yet again as they descended down the other side of the mountain. A strange, uneven field of volcanic rock spread out below them, like there were thousands of creatures moving beneath the earth, blanketed with golden moss and pocketed with rainwater.

As they crossed the strange plateau, chasing the sun as it sank into the western sky, the air began to thicken with warm steam.

"You guys smell that?" Illya asked, stopping to sniff whatever the steam had brought with it.

Now that he mentioned it, the air did have a sort of sulfurous stench to it.

"What are you—"

A smile cracked Illya's face. "What's the one thing you wish we could have right now?"

"Food," Khepri and Hector answered at once.

"A real bed," Hassan groaned.

"Wine," Anton offered.

"Some quiet," Beru said.

Ephyra rolled her eyes at Illya. "You shutting up would be pretty nice."

"Fine, the *second* thing you wish you could have?" Illya asked.

"Illya, just tell us what you're—"

But Illya didn't need to tell them because at that moment they reached the edge of the lava field, where it dropped off into a short cliff, below which a patchwork of pale pools of milky blue water exhaled clouds of warm, sulfurous steam. Formations of the same black rock that made up the mountain separated the pools from one another, forming little caverns and jutting towers, and waterfalls that cascaded from one pool to the next.

"The one thing we could *all* use right now," Illya said with a grin. "A bath."

Hassan looked elated, Khepri cautiously excited. Even Ephyra looked less annoyed than usual. Jude was concerned about everyone dropping their guard when they knew the Witnesses were still tracking them, but even he had to admit a bath sounded nice. They'd been traveling for almost three weeks, and they'd had little opportunity to wash themselves in anything aside from freezing cold water.

They ate dinner and Jude set up camp as the others dispersed into the pools and the sun set over the jagged peaks ahead, turning the milky blue water a blushing pink.

Jude took the first watch, which he'd been doing the last few nights to avoid the awkwardness of laying inside the tent with Anton, stewing in silence. Tonight, as the others stumbled off to sleep, he stripped out of his clothes and waded into the springs, making sure to keep his sword nearby.

The water felt nothing like the river in Kerameikos. Not just the temperature, but the texture, too, was different. It felt denser, heavy with minerals and salt as Jude moved through it, steam rising off his skin and spiraling into the night sky.

He breathed it in, turning his face to the stars and letting his mind drift to the thought that wouldn't leave him alone, the secret Anton was holding back.

Ephyra's words lingered in his mind. *Whatever Anton's hiding, it's probably because he's scared of what you would do if you knew.*

Or, the voice in the back of Jude's head posited, what it would do *to* him. He saw now that Anton wasn't hiding something to protect himself. He was doing it to protect Jude.

He heard a faint splash behind him and turned. For a moment, he wondered if he'd imagined it and then Anton emerged through a curtain of steam. It kissed his shoulders and made his collarbone flush the color of the dawn sky over the Gallian Mountains.

"I was hoping I would find you in here," he said.

The warmth of the pool made Jude feel light-headed. He braced a hand on the rocky edge as Anton drew closer.

"Can we call a truce?" Anton asked, gazing up at Jude with those dark eyes. "Please?"

A bead of water rolled down the back of Jude's neck as he groped for words. But all he seemed to be able to do was stare at Anton, and *want.*

"I know you're mad," Anton said. "I've been trying to give you space, but . . . the truth is, all of this is so much harder without you."

"Anton," Jude said, squeezing his eyes shut. He couldn't just come to Jude like this, in the middle of the night, and expect Jude to be able to refuse him.

"Can't we just . . . move past this?" Anton asked, drifting dangerously closer. "Can't you just trust me?"

Jude swallowed, breath labored, as Anton backed him against the edge of the pool but didn't touch him.

"Can't this be enough?" Anton asked, his lips skating just barely against Jude's.

And Jude was lost. He closed the space between them with a soft inhalation, crushing their lips together and pulling him in by the waist.

Let me have this, Jude thought fervently, sending the prayer into the night. To the Prophets they were on their way to find. To anyone who would listen. *Please just let me have this.*

"Jude," Anton murmured, laying his palm flat against Jude's heart. "Jude, wait."

"I don't want to talk," Jude said, pulling him in again. "Not anymore. Please, let's just—"

Anton gently squeezed the back of Jude's neck, and Jude let his head fall to Anton's shoulder. They just stayed like that a moment, curved around each other, breathing in the steamy air.

"I know," Jude said quietly against Anton's shoulder. "Anton, I know what you've been hiding."

Anton pulled back sharply, his eyes wide and shocked. His hair was a little wet, matted down where Jude's fingers had run through it.

"I mean, I don't *know*, not really," Jude amended. "But I just . . . I have this feeling. That this journey, finding the Prophets . . . there's more to it, isn't there? There's something you left out."

Anton trembled in Jude's hands.

"I think it's why you stayed away all that time," Jude said. "You were trying to protect me."

"Jude," Anton said, sounding so miserable and lost Jude could hardly bear to go on.

But he had to.

"You were trying to spare me the pain of losing you all over again."

Anton's expression flickered with confusion and then crumbled.

"But I want you to know," Jude went on, his voice shaking. "That whatever it is you think you have to do to win this, whatever reason you have for trying to sacrifice your life—we'll find a different way."

Anton buried his face in his hands, his shoulders hitching on a silent sob.

"It's all right," Jude soothed, stroking a hand through his hair. "You don't have to bear this alone, now. I'm here and I—I won't let anything happen to you."

"It's not that," Anton choked out, his voice muffled in his hands.

Jude took Anton's hands gently, pulling them away from his face.

"It's not me, Jude." Anton looked up at Jude through his tears. "I'm not the sacrifice. *You* are."

———————

In fits and starts, the story came out. Some parts Jude already knew, like how Anton had scried into the past with the Wanderer and seen what the Prophets had done to defeat the god.

But other parts, Anton had kept hidden. How the Wanderer had refused to sacrifice the one she loved. How, after they had all turned on the god and killed it, the other Prophets had taken the one the Wanderer loved and made her the Keeper of this Sacred Word, hiding it away in her very *esha* until they needed it again, passing down the power of the Sacred Word over the generations, to every Keeper of the Word.

To Jude.

Jude, who had the power of this Sacred Word hidden away somewhere inside him. Waiting for a Prophet to unlock its immense power. Waiting to let it consume him. Destroy him, so that the god could be destroyed again, too.

"How . . . how does it work?" he asked, his voice breaking. "What do I have to do?"

Anton looked at him, his eyes red-rimmed and bleak. "You don't have to do anything, Jude—"

"Anton," he said, squeezing his eyes shut. "I just . . . I'm just trying to understand. Please."

When Anton spoke again, his voice was flat, toneless, and so quiet it was almost a whisper. "I would—I would have to use my Grace to unlock it from your *esha*. But it would kill you. And then I would touch the god with the Sacred Word and it—it would destroy it."

Jude trembled as they sat beside each other quietly, bare from the waist up, their feet submerged in the spring.

"Why didn't you tell me?" Jude asked into the quiet.

Anton hung his head, his hands clenched in his lap. "Because if you found out, then you would have to make a choice."

Jude stared at him, anger and disbelief climbing up his throat. "So you made one for me?"

"I—"

"You shouldn't have kept this from me. I deserved to know. I deserved to—It's *my* choice, Anton. Not yours."

"I know it's selfish," Anton said. "I know it is, but I can't lose you, Jude."

Jude opened his mouth, but no words would come. So instead he stood up swiftly, even as his legs felt like they might collapse from under him. "I need—I need a minute."

Anton didn't try to follow him as Jude stumbled away from the springs, out toward the stark, alien land that lay beyond.

The Order, the Prophets, his destiny—all of it, *all of it*, was a lie. The Keeper of the Word wasn't destined to protect the Prophet.

He was destined to die.

The Prophets had *made him* for this. This sacrifice, this destiny, was the only reason Jude Weatherbourne existed to begin with.

This was it. The way to stop the god, to stop the Age of Darkness. It had been in him the whole time, and Jude hadn't even *known*.

But he did now, and there was only one thing he could do with this knowledge. Anton had realized it, too—that the moment Jude discovered the truth would be the moment he lost him. Because how could Jude let the world continue to crumble around him when he had the power to stop it? When all it would cost was his life? He couldn't.

And yet.

He had told Anton, hadn't he? *We'll find a different way.*

That's why they were here, searching for the Prophets. Anton had dragged them on this quest knowing full well they could fail, that the Witnesses could find them and return Beru to Pallas, that the god could break free, that they could never find the Prophets and spend the end of the world wandering in this bleak, beautiful landscape.

What is one life, Jude thought to himself, weighed against all those who suffered under Pallas's regime? Against all those who might yet be spared?

The balance could never be in his favor.

And yet.

It was the same scale he had weighed when he'd thought Anton was the one who would have to sacrifice himself. And there, he had found a different answer. Anton's life was worth more to him than every chance that they might fail.

But when it was his own life in the balance, Jude's first instinct was to do what he had been brought up to do—sacrifice in order to serve.

He had done away with that instinct, he thought. He had done away with it in that taverna in Tanais, taking Anton into his arms and kissing him like he'd wanted to for weeks. He had done away with it in Behezda, facing Lazaros with the Pinnacle Blade singing in his hands.

Lazaros had claimed that the Godfire flames had remade him, transformed him into something new. Maybe they had done the same to Jude after all. Maybe he had become something new the moment he had reached for Anton on the parapet of the lighthouse.

And maybe what he was, what he was still becoming, was more than what the Prophets had planned.

30

ANTON

THE SKY WAS GROWING LIGHT BY THE TIME ANTON FELT JUDE'S *ESHA* approaching camp.

Anton had barely moved since Jude had stalked off into the night hours ago. He felt numb, paralyzed by grief and guilt as he sat perched at the edge of the rock overlooking the springs, knees pulled to his chest.

He didn't even turn around when he felt Jude stop at his side, only inches away.

"Just tell me," he said without looking up. "Tell me what you're going to do."

Jude sat down beside him and asked softly, "What do you want me to say?"

Anton turned to him. "I want you to say you believe in me enough to save you."

Jude met his gaze, his expression one of grief rather than anger. "I do believe in you. I always believe in you, Anton. I just don't understand why you don't believe in me."

Anton blinked back the tears that threatened to fall. "What?" How could Jude think that?

"You just thought I would do it," Jude said. "You kept this from me for *months* because you thought I'd make up my mind the moment you told me."

Anton felt gutted and raw beneath the tempest of Jude's gaze. He didn't want to hear what Jude would say next.

"You didn't want to let me make a choice because you thought you knew what it would be," Jude said. "But you're wrong."

Anton lifted his head, the faintest spark of hope flaring in him.

"We still have a chance. Find the other Prophets and kill the god. I don't think it will be easy, but I think we can do it." He reached for Anton's hand, folding it in his own. "If, that is, we do it together."

Anton sucked in a shaking breath that turned into a sob. He sagged against Jude, aching with relief as tears spilled down his cheeks. He hadn't let himself hope for this, not once. It was too painful.

Jude held him, his hands carefully cradling Anton's face, wiping at his tears. "That means no more keeping things from me," he warned, lips brushing Anton's temple.

Anton leaned into the kiss. "No more," he vowed.

He would have been content to stay there, leaning against Jude, basking in the relief of this secret *finally* being shared between them, of his worst fears disappearing in the face of Jude's faith in the both of them.

But the sound of voices yelling behind them startled them from their moment of peace.

Jude was on his feet and sprinting back toward camp in a flash, Anton scrambling after him. Ahead, he could see Beru crouched in front of the ashes of last night's fire, smoke rising from the ground around her. Ephyra was in front of her, yelling something at Hassan, who was several paces away, one arm wrapped around Khepri. Hector was on Beru's other side, his hands up as he edged slowly toward her like one would approach a spooked animal.

"What's going on?" Jude demanded.

Hassan turned toward him and Anton. "She almost killed Khepri," he said, a bite of anger in his tone.

"Hassan, I'm fine," Khepri said placatingly.

"I'm sorry," Beru said. There was something strangely hollow about her voice. "She startled me."

"So you almost set her on fire?" Hassan demanded.

"It was an accident," Ephyra protested.

Hassan glared at her. "She's losing control of the god. That thing is dangerous! We can't keep pretending—"

"She's not a *thing*. She's my sister," Ephyra said fiercely.

"That's not your sister, and you know it," Hassan replied. His gaze locked on Hector. "You both do. You've been keeping it from us."

"Is that true?" Jude asked. Ephyra and Hector exchanged a glance.

"We weren't—" Ephyra began.

"We all know Beru is fighting to keep the god contained," Illya spoke as he emerged from his tent. "Don't pretend like that's news to you, Prince Hassan."

Beru covered her face with her hands. "I don't—It's so much worse now. The god is changing me. I can feel it. And I don't know if . . ." She sucked in a breath and curled in on herself, squeezing her eyes shut like she was tensing for an invisible blow.

Hector drew closer to her, gently curling a hand around her shoulder.

Beru flinched beneath his touch. "Don't."

She was still covering her face, but Anton saw the wounded look on Hector's.

"It will be days before we reach the Prophets," Illya said. "Beru might not last that long. We need to be prepared if the god takes over."

"How?" Hassan asked, incredulous. "That thing ripped apart an entire city like it was nothing. It can crush us just as easily."

Illya didn't have an answer for that.

Anton's gaze found Jude's. He knew what the swordsman was thinking—they were taking an even bigger gamble than they'd thought. They weren't just trusting that the Prophets could help them—they were trusting that they'd even make it there at all.

Jude slipped Anton's hand in his, reassuring. Then he looked at the others.

"We'll keep an eye on her at all times," he said decisively. "Trade off watch shifts, just like we do for the Witnesses."

"We should bind her hands, too," Illya added.

"And what exactly is rope going to do against a god?" Hassan asked.

"Illya's right," Beru spoke suddenly. She uncurled her body, drawing herself back to her feet. "It might hinder the god for only a second, but that's better than nothing."

"I don't like the idea of you tied up again," Ephyra said.

Beru shook her head. "It's the only way. I don't . . ." She looked around at all of them, and Anton could almost see the struggle in her dark eyes. She looked exhausted, thin and pallid. "I don't know if I'll be able to fight it off again. I don't want to hurt any of you. Please."

She thrust out her hands. They were shaking.

Illya approached cautiously with some of the extra rope from their tent rigging. He wrapped it around Beru's wrists, tying it tightly.

"You all realize that none of this is going to matter, right?" Hassan asked. "If the god really does take control, what are we supposed to do?"

It was Beru who answered. "Run."

They trekked west. The barren mountains gave way to verdant, steep, sweeping cliffs cut away by great tongues of the sea.

The echoing pulse of the Prophets that Anton had found scrying in the Circle of Stones grew louder and more pronounced the closer they drew to them. But so too did the *esha* of Lazaros and the other Witnesses, following on their heels. Anton dutifully scried for them every night, and every night they were nearer than the night before.

They each took turns watching Beru a few hours of the day at a time. For the most part, she kept to herself, quiet. When it was Anton's turn, he couldn't help thinking of the promise he'd made to her after they escaped the citadel. To kill the god, no matter what it took.

On the sixth day, they finally saw it.

"Is that . . ." Hassan began.

"A temple?" Illya said, completing the thought.

It looked like one, or the ruins of one in any case. Perched high on a thin spine of rock that jutted out over a vast caldera, a hundred crumbling arches led to a circular rotunda surrounded by the remains of five monoliths.

"Is that where they are?" Khepri asked.

Anton nodded. They proceeded up a narrow and steep stone staircase. It was dusk by the time they passed beneath the first arch. The setting sun seemed to hover just above the temple, soaking the ruins in red light.

The Prophets' *esha* called to Anton, a beacon that had drawn him here, over hundreds of miles. Anton let himself be pulled, leading the others through the arches, until at last they reached a crescent of stone with broad steps climbing up to the temple itself. The ruins looked so strangely out of place in this remote wilderness. They didn't look anything like the temples of the Prophets in the Six Cities. Who had built this place? And for what?

"Hello?" Anton called as he mounted the steps to the crescent gate. "Is anyone there?"

Wind rustled through the crumbling walls, but Anton heard no other sound.

"Hello?" he called, louder. "Behezda? Tarseis? Nazirah?" He cupped his hands around his mouth. "Is anyone there?"

Maybe he needed to call with his *esha*, not his voice. He hesitated a moment and then closed his eyes, summoning his Grace. It was easy now to send out an echo of it through the temple. He felt the call come back to him and stumbled into the ruins, following it, until he reached a circular platform, surrounded by the five stone monoliths.

The Prophets' *esha* rang out around him, rebounding through the stones.

It was a moment before he realized. The Prophets' *esha* wasn't bouncing off the monoliths. It was *inside* them.

When Anton and the Wanderer had scried for them in the Circle of Stones, he had assumed that the answer he'd felt had been the Prophets themselves. That it meant they were alive. But the answer he'd felt hadn't been the Prophets.

It had been their tomb.

"No . . . no, this can't be," Anton said weakly, falling to his knees.

Jude reached him a moment later, kneeling beside him. "What is it? Are you all right?"

The Prophets were dead, and somehow, their *esha* had been trapped in these stone monoliths.

His heart slammed against his ribs as Jude's arms went around his shoulders.

Jude.

The Prophets were dead, and with them, any hope of stopping the god without Jude sacrificing himself. Grief and anger crashed over Anton, so acute he felt like howling with it.

This couldn't be how the journey ended. This couldn't be the answer.

"They're gone," he said in a ruined voice. "Jude . . . the Prophets are dead."

He could feel the others behind him, heard their soft gasps and quiet horror. All of this—their journey, the weeks it had taken to get here—had been for nothing.

"Jude," Hector said in a low, urgent voice. "I think the Witnesses have found us."

Anton turned, following Hector's gaze to a few figures in the distance, standing at the crumbling gate of the temple. He spotted Lazaros, with his gruesome scars, who seemed to be staring directly back at Anton. He shivered.

"We should go," Jude said in a hard voice. And then, to Anton, softer, "We need to go."

But what was the point of running?

"Why not stay a little while longer?" a familiar voice drifted over them. And there, from behind one of the Prophets' tombstones, Pallas emerged, his white and gold robes flapping in the wind. "After all, you only just arrived."

31

BERU

BERU WATCHED AS PALLAS STEPPED OUT INTO THE RUINS, FLANKED BY SIX Witnesses. The god's power lit up like a fire inside her, its voice booming out in fury.

LET ME KILL HIM, it begged. LET ME—

Beru wanted to obey and strike Pallas down in a storm of lightning.

But the tiny scrap of her that she still recognized held firm. If she gave in, if Pallas died, then it was all over. The seal would break. The god would be free.

She squeezed her eyes shut, breathing in and focusing on Hector, standing somewhere near the entrance of the tomb behind her. She felt his horror and fear ripple through her, grounding her.

"Pallas," Anton said, staring across the stone platform at the other Prophet. "How did you find us?"

"You think I didn't know where you were heading the moment I felt you scrying at the Circle of Stones?" Pallas asked, in that soft voice that sent chills down Beru's spine. "I'm sorry to say you're too late. Much, much too late."

"What happened to the other Prophets?" Anton demanded.

Pallas paced a wide circle before turning back to Anton. "I killed them, of course."

Anton flinched. "But why?"

BECAUSE, the god snarled in Beru's mind. HE NEVER WANTED TO SHARE HIS GLORY. HE WAS THE FIRST PROPHET TO RECEIVE THE POWER OF SIGHT, AND WHEN I GAVE IT TO THE OTHERS HE COULDN'T ABIDE BY IT. HE WANTED TO BE THE ONLY CHOSEN MESSENGER OF GOD.

The god's fury clouded Beru's mind, shrouding her own feelings in its dark fog.

"Because they were nothing but frightened children," Pallas spat. "They wanted to stop me from doing what needed to be done to finally purge the world of our mistakes and return it to order. When we made the prophecy of King Vasili, we had no idea what we would unleash. Vasili wanted to best us, to prove our prophecy wrong. He pushed the Grace of Sight to its limit, a limit only we Seven had ever breached before. And while it did not give him the gift of foresight, it did allow him to speak to the god we had vanquished two millennia ago. And in doing so, he released a little bit of the god's *esha.*"

"He broke the Four-Petal Seal," Anton said.

"Yes," Pallas said. "And while Vasili's endeavors drove him mad, they also succeeded in doing what he had planned—they brought an end to our power as Prophets. The return of the god meant the end of our foresight. The last prophecy came to us the moment Vasili cracked the Four-Petal Seal."

Beside Beru, Illya tensed at the mention of his ancestor. He slid his gaze to her, his expression grim.

"The other Prophets saw it as a disaster," Pallas continued. "They hid themselves away, plotting to undo what Vasili had done. But I saw it for what it truly was—an opportunity. I had never wanted the

Wanderer and her followers to seal up the god's *esha*. I wanted to wield it. With the Four-Petal Seal finally cracked, I sought to open the floodgates and take the god's *esha* to restore us to our power. So that we might guide the world again."

HE WANTED TO TWIST MY POWER TO HIS PURPOSES, the god said. I SEE NOW THAT HE WAS NEVER WORTHY OF DELIVERING MY MESSAGE—NO HUMAN CAN BE, FOR YOU ARE ALL SELFISH AND HUNGRY CREATURES. HE THOUGHT HE COULD BECOME LIKE ME, A TRULY DIVINE BEING, BUT HE WILL ALWAYS BE CORRUPTED BY THE WEAKNESSES OF YOUR KIND.

"The other Prophets feared my plan, but theirs was destined to fail," Pallas went on. "So I killed them. It broke my heart, but it had to be done. I could not let them stop me from saving the world from the Age of Darkness. And now, I'm afraid I cannot let you stop me, either."

HE IS LYING, the god boomed in Beru's mind. I CAN SEE INTO HIS HEART AND I KNOW THAT HE IS LYING. HE KILLED THE OTHERS BECAUSE THEY THREATENED HIS POWER AND NOTHING MORE.

"So," Pallas said, his gaze zeroing in on Beru. "Beru of Medea. Return to my service and I will let the rest of your friends live."

Beru froze under Pallas's bright blue gaze. Paladin emerged from behind the other monoliths, closing in.

Hector, Khepri, Jude, and Hassan shifted their positions, surrounding the others against the advancing Paladin. Beru stood at the epicenter with Anton, Ephyra, and Illya.

They were outnumbered by Witnesses and Paladin four to one.

"Very well," Pallas said to Beru's silence.

Before Beru could react, the Witnesses attacked, rushing forward with inhuman speed.

Jude unsheathed his sword. Wind and leaves whipped around him, swept up by the force of his Grace. To their left and right, Paladin closed in on Khepri and Hassan. And behind Beru, Hector fought off even more of them. The ringing of clashing swords and cries of pain filled the air, and in the chaos Beru could only hope that none of her friends were the ones being wounded.

"We need to get her out of here," Illya said to Ephyra.

To do so they would have to double back and avoid the Paladin and Witnesses Hector was currently fighting. Or jump off the edge of the platform, over two hundred feet into the caldera below.

Or Beru could just disappear, use the god's power to take her far away from here. And take everyone with her.

And possibly free the god, with no way to chain it again.

As Beru grappled with an impossible decision, some of the Paladin broke through Hassan's defenses, despite his best efforts, and Ephyra launched herself in front of Beru.

"Ephyra, no!" Beru cried.

Anton darted past her. A disarmed Witness rushed forward to seize him, but Anton used his forearms to block the Witness and sent a fist flying into the Witness's throat.

"Ha!" Anton cried. "Hector, did you see that?"

In front of Anton, Ephyra ducked under a Paladin's sword and kicked his legs from under him. She launched herself into the fray, battling at Hassan's side.

Beru's gaze swung around, trying to make sense of the chaos, and her eyes caught on a figure standing above it all, perched on the top of one of the crumbling stone pillars that surrounded the tomb. Lazaros. She could see his Godfire sword blazing against the gray sky, but he did not leap down to join the fight. His gaze was locked on Beru.

What was he waiting for?

"NO!" Ephyra's voice roared, and Beru jerked her gaze away from

Lazaros to see Ephyra dive toward Hassan, who was crumpled on his knees, blood spilling between his hands where he clutched his stomach. On instinct, Beru lunged toward them, but Illya yanked her back.

Beru's fearful gaze found Hector, barely holding his own against the Paladin, his movements labored like he had been injured. Khepri fought her way toward Hassan and Ephyra, bloodied and bruised herself. Jude had returned to Anton's side, fighting off Paladin with desperate strokes of his blade.

They were losing.

Pallas would win this battle, and the only question was how many of Beru's friends would be hurt—or killed—in the cross fire.

She had to do something.

USE MY POWER, the god offered. USE MY POWER AND YOU CAN PROTECT THEM. YOU CAN SAVE THEM.

Beru closed her eyes. She was out of options.

"Illya," she said softly.

"Don't," he said, his grip tightening on her arm. "Beru, *don't*."

A roar of pain sounded from somewhere. Beru could not keep track anymore. Her eyes found Pallas, standing calmly across the platform. A slight smile curled his lips as he surveyed the battle before him.

This was all because of *him*. Her friends were going to die, and it was because of this man, who sought to seize power that wasn't his to wield. She ripped herself away from Illya as fury burned through her veins. It was an anger she'd felt before—she'd felt it in Hector, those first days after finding him in the desert. In the god, every day in Pallas's control. But she had never claimed this anger for herself.

She did now. She seized hold of this lethal rage that had lived somewhere deep in her bones for years and years, growing in the darkness and now finally given light.

She didn't need to think, didn't need to control it, just let her fury blaze as she raised her arms. She didn't hear the god's thoughts, nor did she feel its conspicuous silence, only its presence, its anger that joined with her own and sent power flooding out from her palms.

It was like Beru had released a breath, the exhale booming out across the battlefield. It might have gone for miles, felling trees and shaking the earth, but Beru could only see what happened in front of her as every one of Pallas's soldiers froze in place.

Silence echoed over the tomb.

Beru took in the sight of her friends—injured but alive. *Alive.* They were all staring at her, shock and fear etched onto their faces.

Her gaze locked on Pallas, and suddenly she didn't know whether it was her or the god who started striding across the stone platform to reach him.

She saw movement from the corner of her eye. Lazaros had finally come down from his perch, rushing to Pallas's side as Beru stalked toward him.

It didn't matter.

"The sword," Pallas gasped out, backing toward one of the monoliths. "Use the sword to stop her!"

The Godfire sword would incapacitate the god. It couldn't burn out her power like it burned out Grace—but it could temporarily cut Beru off from the god's powers, like the Godfire collar had.

Beru's rage carried her to Pallas. She clenched her fist and Pallas collapsed to his knees, choking as Beru crushed the air from his lungs.

His fearful blue eyes darted up to hers, their whites overtaken by thin red lattice. He gasped for breath.

Beru contemplated how helpless he was, at her mercy now. It was only Beru's human heart that had given him power over her for so long. Her love for her sister, her fear of what it meant to wield true power. She considered how easily she could snuff out his life.

No.

The thought surfaced in her mind, clear as the sun breaking through the clouds.

She couldn't kill Pallas. His death would unleash the will of the god. And more than that, she could not kill him because Beru knew who she was, and all the pain and rage in her heart could not turn her into a killer.

She released her hold, and Pallas doubled over, heaving.

Beru stood frozen, stunned at what she had almost done to Pallas. Had the god taken control? Or had it been her?

She didn't know anymore. The difference seemed insignificant.

But the part of her that was good, the part of her that had walked away from Ephyra in Medea, that had pushed her to Behezda to save Hector, that had come to care about every single person who had joined her on this journey, had proven to be stronger than every poisonous feeling that lurked in her heart.

She was stronger.

She gazed down at Pallas. The god struggled against its seal, against the iron strength of Beru's will.

Pallas's gaze met hers again, and she knew that he saw it, too—her power; her strength; the vast, bottomless ocean of faith that he could never understand.

Pallas the Faithful knelt before her, defeated.

And then his eyes widened as the Godfire sword pierced through his chest and set him aflame.

Shock rooted Beru to the ground as Lazaros pulled his sword from Pallas's chest.

"You have betrayed the mission of the Witnesses," Lazaros spat as a ragged scream tore from Pallas's throat, the white flames climbing up his robes. "You are a charlatan who has desecrated the holy will of the

Creator. You call yourself the Immaculate One, but you are no better than the heretics you have sought to purify, and now I see that the world can never truly be cleansed until you are gone."

He ran the sword through Pallas again, and the screams abruptly stopped. The flames overtook him and the light in his bright blue eyes extinguished.

Lazaros sheathed the Godfire sword and knelt at Beru's feet.

"Holy One," he breathed, his scarred face shining with adoration. "Blessed Lord of All. I humbly pledge myself to you."

The seal that Pallas had created, the binding that had caged the god all this time, dissolved. The god's will stormed through Beru's body, a roaring tide so powerful Beru could not even begin to fight back.

She was drowning beneath it, buried in a darkness so complete that no light could touch her. A prisoner in her own body.

The god was in control.

32

EPHYRA

EPHYRA'S HEART CATAPULTED INTO HER THROAT AS SHE WATCHED PALLAS'S body burn, Godfire smoke spiraling up into the sky.

Beru stood over him, but even from this distance Ephyra could see that it was no longer Beru. There was an eerie stillness to her, an unnatural, chilling rage on her face.

"*No!*" Ephyra shrieked, her voice echoing across the stone platform. Tears sprang to her eyes as she fell to her knees.

The god raised Beru's arms, and the five great monoliths exploded. Chunks of rock flung out, and Ephyra felt someone pull her down to the ground.

"Pallas is dead!" Lazaros called out across the platform as the dust cleared. "You so-called Witnesses, tell me—to whom do you devote yourselves? To the betrayer who deemed himself a Prophet? Or to your all-powerful creator and god?"

The Witnesses stumbled forward.

"Our god will bring a glorious new era to the world!" Lazaros cried.

One by one, the Witnesses knelt, trembling, at Beru's feet.

"YOU HAVE DONE ME A GREAT SERVICE," the god said to Lazaros in a terrible voice that both was and wasn't Beru's. "YOU HAVE FREED ME FROM THE TYRANT PALLAS." It turned and surveyed the others. "BUT THE REST OF YOU WHO NOW SWEAR YOURSELVES TO ME . . . YOU HAVE DEVOTED YOURSELF TO PALLAS AND FOR THAT, YOU MUST END."

The god snapped Beru's arms out. In a spray of blood, the Witnesses and Paladin collapsed, their throats slashed cleanly.

A sob shook Ephyra. "Beru," she whispered. "Beru, *fight it.*"

The god turned and looked directly at Ephyra.

"AND THE REST OF YOU," it said with contempt. "THOSE OF YOU WHO HAVE PLOTTED TO DESTROY ME . . ."

The god raised a hand and pain suddenly erupted from Ephyra's chest. She felt like she was being crushed by some unseen force. She heard the cries of the others—Hassan nearby, and Jude and Anton just ahead of her. Pain wracked her body, so acute Ephyra thought she might pass out.

And then it stopped. The god blinked, like it wasn't sure what had happened, one hand still raised in the air. For the length of a heartbeat, nothing happened, and then the ground began to shake. The god's gaze burned into Ephyra, and she was sure they were all about to die.

And then suddenly the god disappeared in a flash of bright light, along with Lazaros.

Ephyra just stared ahead, numb.

"Get up!" Illya pulled Ephyra to her feet, and it was like they were back in Behezda, beneath the falling ruins of the Red Gate, when Ephyra had first resurrected the god.

"We need to go, now," Jude said tersely. "The caldera is going to cave in!"

"Help me with him!" shouted Khepri, hauling a bleeding Hassan against her side. Hector ducked to support Hassan's other side.

Ephyra barely registered the others through the raining debris. She let herself be pulled back over the platform, through the gate, and underneath the arches as they crumbled behind them.

Ephyra's feet carried her away. She glanced over her shoulder to see Khepri and Hector moving as fast as they could, Prince Hassan swaying between them, barely conscious.

In front of her, Jude pulled to a stop, and Ephyra saw that dead ahead of him the narrow stone pathway had dropped away completely, leaving a gap of several feet, below which was a sheer drop into the caldera.

Khepri and Hector, supporting Hassan, leapt across first, followed by Illya. Jude nudged Anton forward next.

The Prophet jumped over the gap, reaching for Khepri's waiting hands. The stones crumbled beneath his feet as he landed and he slipped down, out of Khepri's grip.

"Anton!" Jude cried.

Ephyra's chest loosened in relief as Illya caught Anton's arm, stopping his fall. With Khepri's help, he pulled Anton back onto the path.

"Your turn," Jude said to Ephyra, his face still white with panic.

With the deftness she had learned as the Pale Hand, Ephyra launched herself over the gap and let Khepri pull her forward on the other side. Jude soared after her, just as the path they'd been standing on crashed down into the caldera.

"Keep moving!" Jude cried, and the others obeyed, sprinting across the stone bridge as it collapsed behind them.

They reached the stone stairs that had led them into the caldera. At the top of the stairs, Ephyra stopped as the others rushed past her down the other side of the slope. She turned back toward the sight of the Prophets' tomb crashing down into the water.

"Ephyra, we need you over here!" Khepri's panicked voice called to her, and when Ephyra turned she saw Khepri sitting with Hassan sprawled in her lap.

He was shaking, gasping wetly, and Ephyra knew that he was moments from death. Her heart seized in her chest as she knelt beside them.

The numb pain of losing Beru had hollowed Ephyra, but for a moment her worry for Hassan blotted it out.

"I need the cuttings," Ephyra heard herself say. Someone—it might have been Hector—dug through their packs to find them.

Ephyra focused on Hassan's bloodless face and the wound in his side that had bled over his entire shirt.

"Take off his shirt," Ephyra said, and Khepri complied just as Hector appeared with the plant cuttings.

Ephyra's hands shook as she assembled everything. She could feel their eyes on her, but she stayed focused on the uneven sound of Hassan's breath. He was in shock, shivering violently under Ephyra's hands.

Somewhere beneath her ruthless calm Ephyra knew a storm of fear raged inside her. And it was not just Beru who she was afraid for. Prince Hassan's life was in her hands, and Ephyra was taken aback by the desperation she felt to save him. Somehow over the past few weeks, Hassan had joined the fold of people for whom Ephyra would do almost anything to save. It was a category that had previously included only one person, but which now, she realized, included every single person around her.

But it wouldn't help any of them if Ephyra fell to pieces now. She locked up her grief, her fear, her anguish and set them aside as she ground up the cuttings, drew the *esha* from the plants into Hassan's body, one hand pressing against his pulse, the other hovering over his wounds. One by one, the wounds closed, his body taking the *esha* and using it to repair itself.

And when it was done, and Hassan was breathing evenly, sitting up with Khepri's help, Ephyra sat back, exhaustion filling her bones. She closed her eyes, letting darkness take her.

———————

Ephyra woke to murmuring voices and the faint smell of woodsmoke. She opened her eyes to peer up at a gray sky. It gave her no indication of what time it was or how much time had passed since they'd escaped from the tomb.

She sat up. As she blinked around at the others, they suddenly went silent. Their somber gazes prickled at her skin.

Finally, Anton spoke from beside the dying fire. "You should eat something."

"How's the prince?" Ephyra asked, instead of replying.

Jude nodded toward the tent. "Resting."

"You should eat something," Anton said again.

Ephyra turned away. "I'm not hungry."

Without another word, she stalked into an empty tent and lay back down. She'd shared the tent with Khepri and Beru, but Khepri was off tending to Hassan, and Beru was—

She cut the thought off at the knees and rolled over on the bedroll, slipping back into sleep.

———————

When Ephyra woke again, someone was in her tent.

Illya sat at the edge of Ephyra's bedroll, his face shadowed in the darkness.

Ephyra wiped at her face, fuzzy with sleep. "What are you doing here?"

"I didn't think you should be alone," Illya replied. He had his hands in his lap, palms pushed into his thighs, like he was trying to calm his nerves.

"I'm fine," Ephyra said. She turned to gesture him out. "You can leave."

Illya didn't move. "You're not fine. I was there at the Sacrificed Queen's tomb, remember? When the Daughters of Mercy told you that Beru was dead."

She did remember, though she wanted to forget. She remembered the anger, the emptiness. The heat of Illya's lips on hers.

"I want to help," he said, softer.

"You want to help?" she repeated, sitting up and leaning toward him.

He swallowed, nodding, as she crawled to the end of the bedroll where he sat.

"What did you think?" she whispered, twining her arms around his neck. "That I would just fall into your arms? That I'd be so lost in grief I'd let you into my bed again?"

"No," he answered, looking up at her. He didn't touch her. His hands clenched into the blankets.

"Are you sure?" she asked, leaning down to brush her lips against his. She felt his breath quicken and she tightened her arms around him. "It doesn't seem like that to me."

"Ephyra," he said, sounding pained. "I just wanted to see if you were all right."

"Since when does that matter to you?" she asked. "Since when are you this caring and concerned for my welfare? That's not the Illya that I know."

"You don't know everything about me," he muttered, reaching to unhook her arms from the back of his neck.

He held her wrists, gentle but firm, between them. A bolt of frustration struck through Ephyra, and she leaned forward, capturing his lips the way she had in the tomb all those months ago, wanting the fire, wanting to burn again.

He didn't push her away this time. He cupped her face with one hand, the other still gripping her wrist as she surged against him.

But it was like he wouldn't play along. He still kissed her back, but he was gentle, tender in a way that made Ephyra feel like she would shatter.

She pulled away abruptly. "What are you doing?"

He stared at her, his golden eyes reflecting what little light there was.

"What do you think this is?" she demanded, her voice going brittle to hide how close she was to tears. "That's—that's not what I want from you."

"Then tell me what you do want," he said, frustration bubbling beneath the surface of his voice. "Because I have no idea."

She sat back, putting distance between them. "You can't just kiss me like that. You can't just act like you *care* about me and expect me to believe it."

He swallowed, looking away.

"That's not what this is," she said forcefully.

"I should go." He stood.

"Wait." Her hands clenched at her sides. She could feel a numb hollowness rising within her, and she knew it would consume her if she was left alone.

He paused, turning back to her. Waiting.

"In Pallas Athos," she began, "Beru told me that you were the one who approached her and said you wanted to help get me out. Why?"

He shrugged. "I guess I owed you. For Behezda."

"No," she said, scraping herself off the bedroll. "Illya Aliyev doesn't *owe* people. Why would you risk betraying Pallas? What did you have to gain?"

"Not everything is about gaining something."

She barked out a laugh. "For you, it is."

"If that was the case, I wouldn't have joined back up with Pallas in the first place."

"What do you mean?" Ephyra asked, somehow fearing the answer.

"Pallas knew exactly why I joined him again," Illya said. "Beru figured it out, too. It was obvious to everyone except you."

"*What* was obvious?"

"That I only pledged myself to Pallas once he took you captive!" Illya said, raising his voice. "I threw myself at his feet because I couldn't watch him take you away, not when there was a chance I could save you."

Ephyra let out a high trill of laughter. "That is such horseshit. You can't rewrite the past, Illya, no matter how many times you change allegiances. I can't believe you think I would fall for—"

"I love you."

Ephyra stopped cold. He couldn't have just said that. He couldn't be staring at her now, with that vulnerable expression on his face.

"What do you mean," she asked, voice shaking, "you *love* me?"

"I mean, I love you," he replied, defiant. "I have since Behezda. Maybe before then. Maybe I fell for you when you pinned me to the ground in a taverna in Pallas Athos and threatened to kill me. I don't really know."

"You don't love me," she bit out. "You don't even know *how* to love someone. Look at Anton! He's your brother, and you messed him up so bad when you were kids he's *still* afraid of you. You hide behind your charm and your nice clothes because you're terrified that if anyone saw what was underneath they'd walk away from you and never look back."

Ephyra didn't realize she'd started to cry until she'd stopped yelling. She choked back a sob as Illya's gaze dropped to the ground. She was suddenly *furious*, all too aware that everything she'd just said had been more about herself than him.

Wasn't that what Beru had done? Walked away once she'd seen who Ephyra had become? And the others, her *friends*—none of them would want to stick around, either. Not when they saw how broken she really was.

Illya looked back up at her, the vulnerability in his face vanishing beneath a familiar mask of amiable charm.

"You're right," he said, nodding with that practiced smile. "Thank you for . . . making that all so clear."

Ephyra watched him leave and said nothing to stop him.

She fell back against the bedroll, winded, fury still coursing through her blood. She had driven away the last person who had any reason to care about her. She had made her worst fears about herself come true. It was like the Wanderer had said, back on the ship—sometimes prophecies became true *because* you believed in them.

She had to leave. She had to go somewhere—anywhere that wasn't here. She had to find Beru.

It was this last thought that got her to her feet. She packed her bag quietly and then waited for the rest of the camp to go silent for the night before slipping out the front of the tent.

"Wondered when you'd come out," a low voice drawled from outside.

Ephyra froze. In the dim moonlight, she made out a figure leaning against a tree beside her tent.

"Hector," she said. "What are you doing out here?"

"What are *you* doing sneaking off in the middle of the night?" Hector countered. "Or actually, why don't I guess—you're going after her."

Ephyra shifted the weight of the pack on her shoulder. "I know it's dangerous. I know this is all my fault. I'm the one who brought the god back. But Beru's still in there somewhere, and if there's a chance to free her, I'm taking it. And I don't care what you or any of the others have to say about it."

Hector just eyed her for a moment, considering. "Good."

"Wait, what?" Ephyra asked. "You're . . . letting me go?"

"No." Hector leaned down and picked up his own pack. "I'm coming with you."

She stared at him for a long moment. Briefly she considered that this might be a dream.

"You," she said dubiously. "You want to come with me. The person who killed you to save her." She shook her head. "You hate me."

"That may be so," he said. "But I love your sister. And if there *is* a way to get through to her and free her of the god, well—you two have defied death for each other. So I'm betting if anyone can do it, it's you."

"It's probably impossible," Ephyra said, staring him down. "I'm a fool for trying to find her. The god will likely just kill me. And Beru will have to watch."

Hector shrugged. "Yeah. Maybe. But you're going anyway, aren't you?"

She remembered what she'd told Beru in Pallas Athos. *I will never give up on you.* Never.

"Fine," she said at last, striding past Hector. "Just as long as you don't slow me down."

He didn't reply, but a moment later Ephyra heard his footsteps following behind her.

III

THE GOD OF RUIN

33

HASSAN

THE LOST ROSE SAFE HOUSE SAT IN A POCKET OF LAND BETWEEN THE SLOPING base of the mountains and the banks of the Serpentine, in what was known as Crow's Bend. It was little more than a collection of small cottages, some stables, and a barn, but it was their first taste of civilization in almost three weeks, and Hassan was grateful.

After Hector and Ephyra had disappeared, Hassan and the others had waited a day to see if they would return, before deciding to press on. Wherever Ephyra and Hector had gone, Hassan didn't think they were coming back.

Hassan and the rest of the group had traveled down the coast for three days and four nights, trudging through the rain as a storm swept over the mountains. Then they'd crossed through a lower pass that took them back into the valley. It was the most miserable week Hassan had ever endured—and he had endured some pretty miserable weeks.

They barely said a word to one another throughout the journey. There wasn't much to say. They had failed. They had *lost*. The

Hierophant was dead, but Hassan didn't feel any measure of triumph. He just felt hollow.

He was half a world away from Nazirah. And for what?

When they'd arrived at the safe house three days ago, waterlogged and exhausted from the journey, a diminutive old man had greeted them at the door. The moment Anton had said that the Wanderer had sent them, the old man, Tuva, ushered them inside. He hadn't asked any questions, just let them bathe in warm tubs, fed them their first hot meal in over a week, and told them they could stay as long as they needed.

Tuva put them to work on the farm, which turned out to be a much-needed distraction. Hassan passed two days milking goats and helping with the late fall harvest of cabbage and turnips. It felt nice to do the simple but hard work of putting food on the table, and not think about anything else. But Hassan knew that this pause, this breath, would have to end, and soon. They didn't know what kind of destruction the god was wreaking on the world, and they needed a plan.

On the third day, Khepri found him in a copse of pomegranate trees, gathering fruit into baskets and letting the sun warm his back.

There was a certain glint in Khepri's eyes that Hassan recognized. It was the look she got when she set out to do something and had decided that nothing would stop her. Hassan loved and feared that look in equal measure.

"There's news," she said without preamble.

Hassan set his basket down at his feet, wiping his face on his sleeve. There was only one topic that would make Khepri this apprehensive. "Nazirah?"

She nodded. "Tuva says there are a few members of the Lost Rose still in the city. He reached out to them to see what's happening there. And Hassan, things are . . . they're bad. Now that the Hierophant is dead, Lethia is cracking down even harder. There have been uprisings in other towns along the river, and she's used them as an excuse to imprison anyone suspected of dissent."

"She knows her grip on the city is weak now that the Hierophant is gone," Hassan said. "She'll do anything to hold on to control."

"Yes," Khepri said gravely. "But there's more. There are rumors that some of the regional lords from upriver have joined forces to contest Lethia's right to rule Herat."

"So why haven't they taken action yet?" Hassan asked.

"I don't know," Khepri replied. "Fear, probably. With no one else to sit on the throne if Lethia is deposed, Herat could fall into a bloody civil war. They don't want Lethia, but . . . they don't want that, either."

Hassan nodded. "And Lethia knows that. She'll use that fear to hold on to the throne. Khepri—"

She cut him off. "I'm going back to Nazirah. Tuva's arranged everything for me—a boat to take down into the delta, and then a ship that will set sail from there."

Hassan tried not to flinch. "All right."

"I want you to come with me."

She looked at him the same way she had the day she'd snuck inside Lethia's villa and demanded an audience with Hassan. When she'd kissed him on the *Cressida* the night before their return to Nazirah. They'd both lost their way, more than once, since then. They'd made terrible choices. Done things they couldn't take back.

But at the end of it, they were both still here.

Khepri's expression softened. "Hassan, when you . . . when you got hurt, I was so terrified. All I could think about was that I never told you that I . . . I forgive you for what happened in Nazirah. I forgive you for trying to find another way to defeat Lethia. I know you, I know your heart, and like the compass your father gave you, I know where it points. And I know I've hurt you as well, lying to you about what Arash was planning at Lethia's coronation, but—"

Hassan didn't think. He just strode forward, took Khepri in his arms, and kissed her like he'd wanted to do for weeks. She let out a startled gasp and just as Hassan started to pull away, she melted against him, deepening the kiss. He had missed her, missed that earth and citrus scent she carried with her, missed her strong arms wrapped around him, the feeling of her hair in his hands.

Khepri slowed the kiss, the urgency fading, and then pulled back, just far enough to rest her forehead against his. "I'm not leaving without you. I don't know if we can ever make things right between us, but I don't care. I won't go unless you're there with me."

"We'll fix it," Hassan promised, kissing the top of her head.

She pulled back slightly, looking him in the eye. "You'll come with me, then?"

She was right. They couldn't stay here, in this limbo, forever. Anton's plan had failed. The other Prophets were dead, and Beru was somewhere out there, a prisoner to the god. There was nothing for Hassan to do here anymore. And though he'd failed to protect his people from this threat, he could still protect them from Lethia.

"Yes," he said, holding her gaze.

It was time to go back. If the god rained destruction down on the Six Prophetic Cities, at least Hassan would die where he belonged.

To Hassan's surprise, it wasn't Jude who argued when he and Khepri gathered everyone in Tuva's dining room and told them they were planning to leave.

"What happened to us doing this together?" Anton demanded. "What happened to 'we were brought together for a reason'?"

"We tried that, and it didn't work," Khepri said bluntly. "We think that with the Hierophant dead, there might be a chance at regaining control of Nazirah from Lethia."

"And what good will that do if the god destroys the city?" Anton demanded.

"Anton—" Jude began placatingly.

"No," Anton replied, leaping to his feet. "If you want to go, then go."

He stalked out of the room without another word, and Hassan felt a swoop of guilt in his gut.

Jude glanced at Hassan and Khepri apologetically. "He's just—he's upset. Not really at you, it's just . . ."

Hassan understood all too well. Hassan and Khepri's decision to leave confirmed what they all knew in their hearts to be true—they had failed.

"Khepri, it was an honor to fight alongside you," Jude said. "And Prince Hassan, thank you for everything. I know it hasn't always been easy putting up with me these past few months."

Hassan cracked a smile, pulling the baffled swordsman into a brief, one-armed hug. Despite himself, he was going to miss Jude. It might have been that they were far too similar to ever get along well. In Jude, Hassan saw his own flaws reflected back at him, magnified and inescapable. But he also found himself admiring the swordsman. Jude always did what he thought to be right, no matter how difficult the choice was.

With a firm clap on Jude's shoulder, Hassan released him. "You take care of yourself. And Anton."

Jude nodded solemnly.

"Well," Illya spoke up. "For what it's worth, I'll miss you two. And if you do succeed in dethroning your aunt, please send her my regards."

Hassan glanced at him sharply. "You know Lethia?"

"Unfortunately," Illya said with a grimace.

Hassan laughed for the first time in days. "Maybe you're not all bad."

Illya smiled. "A certain brother of mine might disagree."

———

In the morning, Hassan and Khepri woke at dawn to meet a member of the Lost Rose who spent her time ferrying people up and down the Serpentine River.

As they traveled farther and farther from the safe house, Hassan couldn't shake the feeling that this—leaving the others behind—was wrong, somehow. His heart was in Nazirah. He knew that. And while he missed Zareen and the Scarab's Wing rebels, he felt an aching sense of loss at leaving his friends behind. That's what they were—his friends. Perhaps the first real friends he'd had in his life, not bound to him by duty or ambition. Just friends.

As they reached the harbor and boarded the ship that would take them home, Hassan sent a prayer up into the sky. In hopes that they would be safe, and that they'd see one another again.

"You ready?" Khepri asked, looking over her shoulder at him as they boarded.

Hassan nodded, taking her hand. "Let's go home."

34

JUDE

JUDE'S DAYS WERE FILLED WITH SILENCE. THE THREE OF THEM THAT REMAINED—he, Anton, and Illya—moved about the safe house like it was a tomb. With Hector and Ephyra gone, and now Hassan and Khepri, their group, united in their quest to find the Prophets and kill the god, had dissolved.

Anton spent most of his time in the herb garden, tending to the lavender and sage. Jude wasn't sure what Illya did with his days—nor why he had stuck around—and Jude passed the time by practicing koahs.

The days stretched out before them as they waited for the Wanderer to arrive. They all avoided the topic of what they were going to do next, but each morning felt like another slow step toward the inevitable. There was only one option left to him. The moment that Lazaros had killed Pallas, the moment the god had broken free, Jude had known.

He was their only hope. His sacrifice—*his death*—was the only thing that could stop the god now.

Two days after Hassan and Khepri left for Nazirah, Jude returned from practicing koahs and found the Wanderer in Tuva's sitting room, sipping a glass of wine. Anton sat across from her on a cushioned bench, looking wary.

"Good of you to join us," the Wanderer said when Jude stopped in the doorway.

"I—I didn't know you were here already." Jude felt like he'd been caught wrong-footed. Silently, he went to sit beside Anton.

"I just arrived," she replied.

"You know what happened, then?" Jude asked. "The Prophets and . . . Pallas?"

"Yes," she replied with a sigh. "I . . . should have guessed that Pallas might have killed the others. He always saw them as threats to his power. I was wrong to imagine that had changed."

"You said there was news," Anton prompted.

The Wanderer nodded. "I managed to track down the Relics while you were away. Pallas hid them in Pallas Athos. Somewhere only he could reach them while the city was under his rule."

"Where?"

"The Temple of Pallas," she replied. "Back when Pallas dwelt in the City of Faith, the temple was where he received pilgrims and made his prophecies. There was a special hidden chamber in the temple, accessible only to him. That's where I think he hid them."

"Wait," Jude said. "Why do we need the Relics?"

The Wanderer merely looked at Anton, who remained stubbornly silent, his lips pressed into a grim line.

Swiftly, Jude understood his plan. "You mean to trap the god again."

"Yes."

"No," Jude said. "Beru told us that the seal was going to break, sooner or later, even if Pallas hadn't died. That's not a solution, and I'm not going to pretend it is."

"Well, neither is what you want to do," Anton replied, eyes burning.

"It's not about what I *want*—"

"It *is*," Anton replied, leaping to his feet. "You said it, Jude. It's *your* choice."

They stared at each other for a moment, fury and despair crackling in the silence. Then with one last blazing look, Anton stalked out of the room. Jude watched him go, speechless.

"I think you've upset him," the Wanderer said mildly, pouring herself more wine.

He could not fathom what Anton was thinking. Using the Relics, trapping the god again—it was all just a way to delay the inevitable. Jude had the power to stop the god for good, and he had to do it now, before it tore the world apart. Anton had to understand that.

Jude would make him understand.

———————

He found Anton where he usually was these days—in the garden. The sky was dark and swollen with storm clouds, a gentle rain already beginning to fall. As he watched Anton from the veranda, Jude let himself believe that they really could stay here as long as they wanted. That they could grow old here, tucked away on the river bend, spending their days out in the dirt, safe. It wasn't a future Jude had ever allowed himself to want before. His own happiness was something he had scarcely considered until the night in Endarrion when Anton had kissed him.

Now, he wanted to seize happiness and hold on to it as hard as he could for as long as he could.

Jude stepped out into the rain, making his way toward Anton. He knew that Anton could sense him there, but he didn't look up from his task just yet.

"I don't want to fight with you," Jude began. "I don't want to keep fighting."

Anton paused, shoulders tensing. "We fight all the time, Jude. We fought three different times the day we met."

A smile twisted Jude's lips as he sat down in the dirt beside him. "That's only because you're very good at riling me and I'm very good at being riled."

Anton snorted. "And at being obstinate."

"Whereas everyone knows how yielding and agreeable you are," Jude said drily.

"That's right," Anton replied, smiling for the first time in days. But it quickly faded as he dropped his gaze. "I'm guessing you didn't come out here to say you've changed your mind."

"You know we have to do this."

Anton didn't answer for a long moment, running a soft sage leaf between two fingers. Finally, he looked up at Jude. "When your Grace was damaged by Godfire, you thought that the only way to get it back, the only way to fulfill your destiny, was to cut out your heart."

Jude didn't deny it. He knew they were both recalling the first time Anton had kissed him, and how Jude had begged him to keep his distance, convinced that giving in would be his downfall.

"But you couldn't do it," Anton went on. "Even when you thought it was your only choice, you wouldn't do it."

"This isn't the same thing," Jude said. "There are other lives at stake. The *world* is at stake. You've seen what will happen."

"I know," Anton said, guilt creeping into his voice. He sighed. "I'm not going to make you promise anything. I can't choose for you. But it *is* a choice Jude. You don't have to do it just because that's what the Prophets decided."

Jude looked away.

Anton drew Jude's hand to his lips, brushing a kiss to his knuckles. "You wanted me to believe in you, right?"

Jude pulled him close, kissing him as the rain came down harder. He just wanted to feel Anton in his arms, Anton's gentle breath and his warm hands. One last moment of closeness. One last moment of promises unbroken.

"All right." He eased away, eyes still closed so he wouldn't have to see the expression on Anton's face. "Let's go to Pallas Athos. Let's get the Relics. Let's keep trying."

They spent the evening making plans with the Wanderer. On the surface, it was fairly simple—all they needed to do was get all four Relics in the same room with Anton and Beru. Anton could then use the Relic of Sight to draw on the power of the other Relics and create a new seal that would once again trap the god and give Beru control of her body. Just like Pallas had done in Behezda.

Jude wasn't sure exactly how they were going to lure the god to them, but the first step was finding the Relics.

"Pallas may be dead, but the city is still filled with those who are loyal to him," the Wanderer said. "It may be difficult to get to the temple. And I can guarantee the Relics will be under heavy guard."

"Now, I know you're not planning to storm the Temple of Pallas without me."

Jude flicked his gaze to the arched threshold of the sitting room, where Illya stood.

Anton stiffened. "Actually, we were."

"Come on, I'm part of the team now, right?" Illya said. "I helped you cross the valley. And I can help you get into the Temple of Pallas. Or . . . whatever the plan is now."

Anton narrowed his eyes at his brother. "Which would give you the perfect opportunity to turn us over to the Witnesses the second we set foot in Pallas Athos."

"You really think I'd do that, after everything?"

Anton gave him a challenging look. "Do I think you'd turn on us, the second it becomes convenient? Yes."

"Well, once again, Anton, you seem to be in a position where you can either trust me or you can go it alone," Illya replied. "Need I remind you that *you* were the one who came to me to help save your beloved swordsman?"

Jude stared at Anton, whose thunderous gaze was fixed on his brother. Illya had once before referenced the fact that he'd helped Anton rescue Jude from the citadel in Pallas Athos, but Jude hadn't realized that Anton had sought him out. How desperate must he have been to have willingly gone to Illya for help? What else would he be willing to do, Jude wondered, his chest tight, to keep Jude safe?

"Whether you believe me or not, brother, I *have* changed," Illya said quietly. "I want to help."

"Fine," Anton snapped. "You can come. But you're at Jude's command. If he tells you to do something, you do it, no questions asked."

Illya glanced at Jude, the flash of fear in his eyes quickly buried beneath cool disaffect. He crossed his arms in front of his chest. "Fine."

They resumed their planning, talking through each contingency, now with Illya's admittedly helpful inside information on the city. By the late hours of the night, Anton was nodding off against Jude's shoulder, each of his comments punctuated by a yawn until finally Jude had to shuffle him off to bed.

By the time he was tucked in, he was already asleep, warm and relaxed, his hair a tousled mess against the pillows. Everything in Jude wanted to curl up beside him in the soft blankets. He allowed himself one moment to perch at the edge of the bed, taking in Anton's peaceful face, listening to his soft breath, before he forced himself to his feet. His heart felt like it would tear in two as he pushed through the door and back down the hall.

When he reached the sitting room, it appeared Illya had also retired, leaving Jude and the Wanderer alone for the first time since she'd arrived.

She looked up at him, almost expectant.

"Whatever it is," she said after a long silence, "just say it."

Her gaze always unsettled him, since the first time he'd met her at that party in Endarrion. She always seemed to know what he was thinking. She was not unlike Anton in that way. Maybe that was just the nature of Prophets.

"You know the truth about me," Jude said at last.

The Wanderer looked at him thoughtfully. "There are many truths about you, Jude Weatherbourne. To which do you refer?"

"About what the Keeper of the Word really is." He looked down. "What *I* am. What I have to do to kill the god."

She inclined her head.

"So why didn't you stop him?" Jude asked.

Pain flashed across her face, so brief Jude almost missed it. "If I could have stopped Pallas from doing what he did to Temara—"

"No," he cut in, realizing that she thought he blamed her for that. "I want to know why you didn't stop *Anton*. All of this would be over if he'd just accepted what we needed to do. If he hadn't tried to go looking for the other Prophets."

"Have you ever successfully stopped Anton from doing anything?" she asked.

He couldn't say that he had. From the moment he'd met Anton, it had been one acquiescence after another—letting him gamble the Pinnacle Blade; letting him walk into the Order's Tribunal like he owned the place; letting him drag Jude to a party, of all things; letting Anton kiss him. Letting him make Jude believe that they could have a future together.

He didn't answer the Wanderer's question, but he didn't need to. He could see her dark eyes reading it all from his face.

"I had my doubts about the other Prophets," she admitted. "I thought that they had given up and hidden themselves in the farthest corner of the earth to escape the fate they had thrust upon the world. I didn't think that they were—" She cut herself off, and Jude realized she was emotional. He'd never seen her anything less than perfectly composed, yet here she was, at a loss for words, her dark eyes misting over. "We had our differences. Enough of them that kept us apart for centuries. But what Pallas did . . . I would despise him for what he did to the others, if I hadn't already reason enough to hate him."

Her voice was far away, her gaze distant like she had left the room entirely.

"Tell me about her," Jude said softly. "Temara. The first Keeper of the Word."

She uncrossed and recrossed her legs, the sweep of her dark blue skirt rustling. "She was, and still is, the most beautiful, the most ferocious girl I ever laid eyes on. This was forbidden by the other Prophets—we had vowed that in our roles as chosen Prophets, having attachments such as this would cloud our faith. I'm sure you can appreciate how difficult this was for me to accept."

Jude was stunned that he and the Wanderer had something so fundamental in common.

"And then the girl I loved became a servant to Pallas. A sacrifice.

And her children, and their children, were all born into this life of servitude. A life without love and family and all the things I had hoped for us to one day have."

Jude felt his throat grow thick with tears. All his life he'd been told that his legacy as Keeper of the Word was born of duty, solitude, and service. But in truth, the legacy of his ancestor—the legacy of the first Keeper of the Word, was one of love.

Her gaze settled heavily on Jude's face. "And now you. The last of the line of Weatherbourne. The last living descendant of my Temara. Knowing who she was, what she meant to me, what was done to us . . . can you understand why I let Anton go on this quest that I knew would almost certainly end in failure? Can you understand why I held out hope for him? For the both of you?"

Jude closed his eyes, wiping at his cheeks. "Thank you for telling me."

"Even now, at the end, I can't help but still hope," she said, leaning forward and taking Jude's hand. "You have her strength. I saw it the moment I met you in Endarrion."

Jude gripped her cold hand tighter, steeling himself to do the unthinkable. To make the choice that he would give anything not to make.

"Anton's plan won't work," he said, meeting her gaze. "I know it. You do, too. But I can't wait around for him to accept it. The god is out there, and it's going to bring this world crashing down if I don't do something about it. If *we* don't do something."

He kept his eyes trained on her, so she would know what he meant by *we*.

She gave him a look that felt like a warning.

"Only a Prophet can unlock the Sacred Word," he said slowly. "You're a Prophet."

He watched understanding settle on her face. "You want me to betray him. Lie to him."

"You've lied to him before," Jude replied, refusing to look away from the accusation in her eyes. "You've kept things from him."

It was not lost on Jude that in carrying out this plan, he would do to Anton almost exactly what Anton had done to him. Keeping a secret like this, just to protect Anton.

But this was different.

"We'll go to Pallas Athos, as we've said," Jude said. "Find the Relics. And when we go to confront the god, instead of binding it with the Relics, we'll kill it. You'll unleash the Sacred Word inside me and use it to kill the god."

She was silent for a long moment, but Jude could see the resolve in her eyes. "He won't forgive me for this. Either of us. This will destroy him."

"I know," Jude said. He couldn't bear to think of what this would do to Anton. Jude had sworn to protect him, and now, at last, he would break that oath. "I know it's too much to ask of you."

The Wanderer laughed hollowly. "Too much to ask of me? You are the one giving up your life, Jude. You are cursed to make this choice because I dared to defy Pallas and the god. The other Prophets, they could have found another way to preserve the Sacred Word, but they *chose* to make you its Keeper because they wanted to punish me. Maybe it's fitting, then, that I should be the one to have to do this. Perhaps that was the punishment they intended all along."

"So you'll do it," Jude said, focusing on her words rather than the bitterness that suffused them. "You'll help me slay the god."

She sighed. She looked suddenly much older. Wearier. "I will. But Jude, do you really think keeping it from Anton will make this any easier on him? It might be better for him to have time to come to terms with it."

"We can't tell him," Jude said. He had managed to keep the desperation from his voice this long, but suddenly his voice cracked with it. "We just—We can't."

The Wanderer searched his face in that familiar, assessing way, until she found the answer she was looking for.

"Ah. You don't want to keep this a secret to protect him. You're doing it because you're afraid that if he begs you not to do this, you just might obey."

Jude dropped his gaze to the floor, ashamed.

"You want to live," the Wanderer said quietly.

"I want . . . time," Jude admitted. "Even just a little of it."

A ghost of a smile flickered across the Wanderer's face. "I've had a lot of time in my life. And I can tell you that how much or how little you have doesn't matter. What matters is what you do with it."

35

BERU

THE COLOSSAL STONE GUARDIANS OF JUSTICE TOWERED OVER THE ENTRANCE to Tarsepolis's harbor.

The god stood on the outstretched hand of the torch-bearing statue, gazing down at the city. Beru felt its will wrapped around her body, dark tendrils of power that pulled at her like the strings of a puppet.

At her side, Lazaros knelt. "Holy One, it is time that you visit your wrath upon this city. Show them what happens when they turn away from your light."

You don't have to do this, Beru said. *You could help these people. Ease their suffering.*

HUMANS NEED SUFFERING. IT'S HOW THEY LEARN TO OBEY. YOU TAUGHT ME THAT, LITTLE ONE.

No, Beru said forcefully. *That's not—*

"SERVANT," the god said to Lazaros. "TELL ME—DO HUMANS REQUIRE SUFFERING?"

Lazaros bowed his head. "O Holy One, it is not for me to question the world as you made it. But I can tell you that the greatest suffering I endured, the pain and agony of cleansing my body of your stolen power . . . that made me who I am, your devoted servant. My suffering freed me."

SO THEN PERHAPS SUFFERING IS WHY HUMANS LOVE ME, the god said to Beru. PERHAPS THEIR SUFFERING GIVES THEM THEIR FAITH. THEIR SENSE OF MEANING. SO I WILL HELP THEM, AS YOU HAVE ASKED.

He is wrong, Beru said. *He needs to believe that suffering has a purpose because he cannot bear the alternative.*

The god raised Beru's arms, and the sky flashed red and white. Fire and light howled through the sky. The clouds themselves seemed to burst into flame—flames that rained down upon the city of Tarsepolis.

Don't do this, Beru pleaded. Her arms were outstretched in front of her, her palms open to the sky. She felt a sick strangeness wash over her at seeing her own hands bring about this destruction. Hands that had strung beads together into jewelry, poked her sister in jest, touched Hector's face with tenderness.

She reached for those memories. Ephyra's black handprint still stood out against her arm. Beru focused on it. Focused on trying to touch it, to lay her own hand there, and remember.

But it was futile.

The fiery rain struck the Hall of Justice at the heart of the city first. It bloomed with bright, rippling fire. Another flame hit the Temple of Tarseis, setting it alight.

Beside her, Lazaros watched the sky in awe and rapturous delight.

Beru watched the city with horror.

People in the burning buildings poured into the streets, pushing past one another, some of them alight with flames. Screams of terror and anguish rose in a thick wave of sound as they scrambled and ducked and cowered, searching fruitlessly for cover as fire hemmed them in.

Please, Beru thought again. *Don't do this. Don't punish them.*

The god's thoughts, its vindication, pressed in on her. These people had forgotten who their god was. They had worshipped its murderers, the Prophets. The god wanted to punish them. *Had* to punish them.

This is revenge, Beru said. *You want revenge for what the Prophets did to you. But these people are not responsible. These people didn't betray you.*

STOP.

They have lives and families and homes.

I SAID STOP!

The flames ceased falling. The fires went out in puffs of smoke. The Hall of Justice smoldered gently.

"Holy One," Lazaros said, turning to the god. "What has happened? Are we not here to show these people that you are their god?"

The god did not answer him. Instead, it spoke to Beru.

WHAT HAVE YOU DONE?

It was angry at her. But she did not know why.

YOU HAVE DONE SOMETHING TO ME. YOU HAVE MADE ME . . .

Disdain, disgust, and helplessness swam through Beru like nausea.

WHY DO I FEEL THIS WAY?

The god's confusion rose above the churning tide of its scorn. It turned to Lazaros. "WE ARE LEAVING."

Sunlight blazed against the red rock as the god walked through the rubble of Behezda to where the Red Gate had once stood.

Lazaros waited a long time to speak, but when they reached the remains of the Red Gate, he finally asked, "Holy One, why have you taken us here? I ask not to question you, but because I am flawed and stupid as all humans are, and I want only to deepen my understanding of your greatness."

The god did not answer for a long moment, one that stretched out as the sun sank beyond the red cliffs and the ruins cast long, jagged shadows across the earth.

Finally, it said, "THIS IS WHERE I BEGAN AGAIN."

"It is a holy place," Lazaros agreed.

"SOMETHING HAPPENED TO ME HERE. I WAS RESURRECTED. AND I WAS JOINED TO ANOTHER."

"The girl?"

The god finally turned back to him. "YES. THE GIRL. WHEN THE NECROMANCER RESURRECTED ME, SHE PUT ME IN THIS BODY. BUT IT IS NOT JUST THIS BODY I AM BOUND TO."

Beru understood before Lazaros did. The god had been in her body, in her mind, for so long. *You have seen the world through mortal eyes. My eyes. You know pain and suffering now. You have felt them for yourself.*

"I HAVE FELT HER HUMANITY. HER HEART."

Hope flickered inside her, a light that Beru had thought long extinguished. She sheltered it from the dark weight of the god's horror and anger and waited for what the god would say next.

"I WANT IT GONE."

Her hope sputtered out, leaving her cold with certain dread. Her love, her heart, hadn't changed the god. It had only made it despise her.

Lazaros bowed his head. "Yes, Holy One. I freed you from Pallas's binding, and I will free you from the chains of humanity, too. Tell me what I must do."

"THERE IS NOTHING YOU CAN DO!" the god snapped.

Lazaros swallowed and slowly met Beru's gaze. Something sparked in his cold gray eyes. "Perhaps not. But I may know of someone who can help."

36

EPHYRA

EPHYRA SIGHED, LEANING HER HEAD AGAINST THE CAVE WALL AS SHE AND Hector waited out the storm. Hours earlier, they'd tried and failed to start a fire, and now they sat huddled against the rock, watching the deluge outside.

"That's the sixth time you've sighed in the past five minutes," Hector informed her.

She turned to glare at him. "Like you're not annoyed that we're stuck here."

It had been a slow trek through the Unspoken Mountains, their progress hindered by frequent rainstorms. At least twice a day Ephyra regretted parting ways with the others.

"It's not like it makes a difference," Hector grumbled, shifting beside her.

"What's that supposed to mean?"

"It means we don't have a plan, Ephyra," Hector replied, turning to her. "And the god—it can go *anywhere*. Even if we manage to track it down, it could be gone the moment we get there."

Ephyra leaned her head back against the rock. Hector was right—and that was exactly why she didn't want to hear it. "You could feel it before, right? When it first . . . woke up, in Behezda. You're still connected to Beru, so you're still connected to the god, too. Can't you use that to figure out where it's going?"

"It's not really that simple," he replied, fidgeting and not meeting her eyes. "The connection is weaker over a distance. When she was here with us, sure, maybe I could figure it out. But she could be on the other side of the world, while we're stuck here, getting more waterlogged by the day."

She curled her arms around her knees, drawing them tight to her chest. "I would've been fine alone."

"Really?" Hector asked. "Because the last time you went chasing after Beru by yourself, you killed me."

Ephyra winced. Hector hadn't shied away from bringing up the topic during their journey to the Unspoken Mountains, but once they'd split off from the others he hadn't mentioned it. Until now.

In a softer voice, he said, "You know, I don't remember that day. I don't remember dying."

"You don't?" Ephyra could remember every second of it. How Hector had struggled and struggled and finally went limp.

He shook his head, his gaze catching on her face and tracing the long scar that split her cheek. "I gave you that, didn't I?"

"Yes." They'd both left marks on each other that day.

"I probably would have killed you, if you hadn't . . ."

The silence hung between them for a long moment, and then finally Ephyra said, "No. You wouldn't have."

He looked at her in surprise.

"You might not remember it, but I do," she said. "You had me pinned. You could have killed me. You lowered your sword. You were going to let me go. Even after what I did to your family, even with—You would've let me go." She couldn't bear to look at him anymore. "In that moment, I knew there was no going back. It wasn't an accident. I didn't lose control. It was a choice."

She wanted to say that if she had to do it again, she'd choose differently. But she wasn't sure it was the truth.

"I just—" She stopped. Didn't know if she could get the words out. "I just want to say that I'm sorry. For your family . . . for you . . . I'm sorry."

He didn't say anything for a long moment, just watched her with coal-dark eyes.

"We can't go back," he said at last.

"I know."

"I mean," he said, kicking his legs out in front of him. "I can't go back, either. I might've chosen differently—with the Guard, with Jude. That day in the crypt in Pallas Athos. If I had, I never even would have been in Medea. But it doesn't matter. We made the choices we made, and now we're here."

She didn't say anything.

"I know why you did it."

She looked up at him in surprise. He didn't sound angry.

"I don't remember it, but I know why you did it," he said. "Why you became the Pale Hand, too. As soon as Beru took me to Medea, I understood you in a way I never had before."

Ephyra kept her gaze trained on him, certain that she didn't want to hear what he had understood about her. Yet she had to know.

"I walked through the village of the dead," he said. "I saw what you had to do to bring her back. My parents deaths' . . . Marinos's . . . all the people you killed as the Pale Hand. Every death just made it more and more impossible to stop. You couldn't let her go, because if you did, all the sacrifice and pain you caused would've been for nothing."

She didn't move her gaze from his, even as she felt a warm, wet tear slip down her cheek.

"I used to think the same thing, in my own way," Hector said roughly. "That because my family had died and I had lived, I had to make it worth it. I had to have a purpose. It was the only way I knew how to mourn them. And I guess I just realized that . . . even though Beru's still alive, even though you kept her alive for seven years, you've been mourning her the whole time. Ever since she died the first time."

His gaze went distant, his expression soft in a way Ephyra had never seen before. "When the Daughters of Mercy took me and Beru into the desert and left us to die, I knew, then, that we had it wrong. You and me and her. She was trying to make it right, to give back what you'd taken from me." He ran a hand over his face. "But as we were standing in the middle of the desert, waiting for this storm to hit us, I had this realization. We can't go back. We can only move forward. But just because we can't change what we've done doesn't mean we can't choose different the next time. Doesn't mean we can't heal. Ourselves. Each other."

Ephyra remembered Hector standing in her cell in Pallas Athos the morning that everything started to fall apart. *Fate has decided my purpose for me*, he'd said.

Looking at Hector then, as she was backed in a corner in her cell, his heart howling with loss and a grief too huge to endure, part of her had believed it. Had believed it was his destiny to put an end to the Pale Hand and avenge the deaths of the innocent lives she had taken. Part of her had believed it up until she'd taken *his* life.

And then he'd saved hers.

He'd made a different a choice, in Behezda. He'd chosen to be more than the loss he'd endured. More than his broken oaths.

"After I resurrected her, after what I did to your family, it was just the two of us," Ephyra said, her voice shaking. "I told myself that the life we'd carved out together was enough. I had to *believe* it. But—the past month, with Jude and Khepri and Anton and Hassan. Even Illya. I saw how different things could have been."

He was watching her carefully.

"You gave her that, too, you know," she said haltingly.

"What?" he asked warily.

"I'm saying she loves you," Ephyra replied. "Anyone can see that."

"Right," he replied gruffly. He cleared his throat.

But he never got the chance to awkwardly navigate a reply because at that moment there was a flash of bright light illuminating the darkness of the cave and a crack that seemed to split the air.

When the light dimmed, Beru was standing right in front of them.

Neither Hector nor Ephyra moved.

Lazaros hovered beside Beru, but Ephyra didn't dare take her eyes off her sister.

"Is that . . . really you?" Ephyra lunged toward her, but Hector held her back.

She knew, on some level, that he was protecting her. It was most likely the god in control and not Beru. But there was a large part of her that didn't care. Her sister had appeared in front of her like she'd heard Ephyra calling for her.

"Ephyra?" Beru said.

And then nothing could stop Ephyra from flinging herself across the space between them. "Beru, we went after you, we were searching for you—"

"Ephyra, please," Beru was saying. "Please, you have to—"

She cut off abruptly, her expression blank, her posture stiffening.

"YOUR SISTER IS VERY PERSISTENT," the god said.

Ephyra froze, the god's voice ringing through the cave like a discordant note.

"SHE DESPERATELY WANTS TO SPEAK TO YOU. BOTH OF YOU."

Its gaze found Hector again, who was staring at Beru in horror.

"PERHAPS I WILL LET HER," the god said. "IF, OF COURSE, YOU HELP ME."

Ephyra stared at her, swallowing roughly. "What do you want us to do?"

"I BELIEVE IT IS THE SAME THING YOU WANT," the god replied. "TO EXTRICATE MYSELF FROM YOUR SISTER'S BODY."

Ephyra didn't know how to respond, so it was Hector who spoke.

"You want to let her go? Why?"

The god tilted Beru's head. "SUFFICE IT TO SAY, I WILL BE BETTER OFF WHEN I DON'T HAVE TO TAKE THIS FORM. AND AS YOU WERE THE ONE WHO PUT ME INTO THIS BODY . . ."

"You figured she could get you out," Hector finished.

"I'll do it," Ephyra said at once.

Hector snapped his gaze to her sharply.

"I THOUGHT YOU MIGHT AGREE," the god said, contorting Beru's features into something like satisfaction.

It made Ephyra almost dizzy, staring into the face that she knew so well and having it look so little like her sister. Her vibrant expressions were flattened, the light in her eyes extinguished.

"When I brought you back," Ephyra said. "I had something. A Chalice. It made me stronger."

"YOU NEED THIS CHALICE TO SET ME FREE."

"I think so," Ephyra replied.

The god cocked Beru's head, the gesture strangely alien. "VERY WELL. WE WILL GET THIS CHALICE."

"I don't know where it is."

"Holy One, I know the location of the Chalice," Lazaros said. "Pallas kept it, along with three other desecrations of your original holy form."

"IN PALLAS ATHOS?"

"Yes," Lazaros replied. "And may I humbly suggest that we leave this one behind?"

He gestured to Hector.

Hector's eyes burned with fury, and Ephyra felt like she was glimpsing that murderous boy she'd met in Pallas Athos. "Don't think I didn't see your creepy little obsession with her when we saw you in the valley. If you think—"

"Hector," Ephyra said warningly. She straightened her shoulders and looked at the god. "I have to disagree with your friend. Hector stays with us."

Hector shot her a grateful look, doused in surprise.

"WHY?"

"Because they're connected," Ephyra replied, thinking quickly. "Their *esha*. It might help me to . . . separate out your *esha* from hers."

The god appeared to contemplate this, although it was hard to tell.

"IF IT WILL HELP YOU," the god replied at last. "WE WILL ALL GO, THEN."

Before Ephyra could think about what they had just agreed to, the god transported them in a flash of bright light.

37

ANTON

"DEAL ME A HAND."

Anton didn't look up as he collected the cards on the table before him. He and the Wanderer had just finished their last round of canbarra, their nightly ritual since setting sail for Pallas Athos.

But this was the first night Illya had caught him at it. The Wanderer had already departed for bed, and Anton wondered whether Illya had just been lying in wait for this opportunity.

"I'm not playing cards with you," Anton said in a clipped tone.

"But we always have such fun," Illya replied, sidling into the room. "Don't you remember how we used to stay up at night, playing cards until nearly dawn? Every time you won you'd get so excited. You were so proud of beating me. Of course, I was letting you win most of the time."

"I remember the last time we played cards," Anton retorted. "You were holding me prisoner in Nazirah."

"Are you still upset about that?" Illya asked.

Fury ignited in Anton's gut, fast and hot. "Am I still upset that you *tortured* me and almost got Jude killed?"

Illya looked contrite, which only made Anton angrier. "After everything we've been through these past few weeks, everything I've done to help you . . . I thought perhaps you'd see that I've changed."

"Please," Anton said with a humorless laugh, "please don't tell me that's why you're helping us."

Illya shrugged, bracing his hands on the back of the chair the Wanderer had vacated.

"You told me you changed once before, remember?" Anton said. "When Ephyra and I went to meet you in Pallas Athos. You said you were there to *apologize*." He didn't need to remind his brother that it had been a lie.

Illya's golden gaze was steady, sincere. "Maybe deep down, I meant it."

"Whatever you felt *deep down* counts for nothing," Anton said. "Do you know what it was like for me? To have the only person who *ever* cared about me treat me the way you treated me? You made my life a *nightmare*."

"I know," Illya said quietly. "But if there was any way I could ever earn your forgiveness for what I did . . . for who I was back then—"

"You don't earn forgiveness, Illya," Anton spat. "You either get it, or you don't. It's not up to you. You can't just do good thinking it cancels out the bad." He swiped at his tears furiously. "You want to help us, then fine. But I don't owe you my forgiveness."

Illya's jaw clenched. "So none of it matters, then? Nothing I do has any effect on how you see me? I'll always be the monstrous older brother who tormented you, is that it?"

"Why does it matter what I think?"

"Because you're my brother," Illya said. "You know me better than anyone else ever will. And if you look into my heart and only see evil there then that's all there is. I can't change it. I can't—" He made an aborted movement, like he wanted to throw the chair across the room. But instead he just gripped it tight, his knuckles turning white.

"It's not my job," Anton said in a low voice, "to tell you what you are. You want to be better? Then *be better*, Illya."

Illya just stared at him for a moment, his golden eyes wide. For the first time in what was probably years, he didn't have any slick words or careful deflections.

"It's late," Anton said abruptly. "We need to focus tomorrow. I'm going to sleep."

He left Illya by the dying fireplace and strode down the hall into the room he and Jude had chosen.

Jude was making up the bed as Anton entered. He looked over his shoulder as Anton pressed the door shut behind him.

"Is everything all right?"

In a few short strides, Anton crossed the room and wrapped his arms around Jude.

"Maybe a foolish question," Jude said, and Anton could hear the smile in his voice. "Are *you* all right?"

"Probably not," Anton admitted, pulling back to look at Jude's face, half smiling and a little concerned. "But I'm a lot better now. Illya . . ."

Jude's expression darkened. "I'm sorry that we need his help."

Anton shook his head. "I thought after all this time, and everything he did to me, I wouldn't *care* so much."

"He hurt you," Jude said. "That doesn't just go away."

"No," Anton agreed, looking away. "But it's also that . . . I told him he couldn't earn my forgiveness, but I still wanted him to ask. It's not that I want him to suffer like I did. I never wanted that. I only ever wanted him to . . ."

Jude guided Anton's face back toward him. "To what?"

It was something Anton had buried so deep, he'd thought it was gone. But staring at Jude's bright green eyes, resting his cheek against his careful palm, he knew that it had always been there, growing in the spaces of his starving heart. "To love me. Still. Even now. And I *hate* that I want that from him. It's pathetic."

"It's not pathetic," Jude said, cupping Anton's face with both hands. "It doesn't make you weak, wanting to be loved. You taught me that."

Anton pulled him close again, tucking his face into Jude's neck.

"You don't have to forgive him," Jude murmured. "But you need to forgive yourself for still loving him."

Anton closed his eyes, breathing Jude in. "I didn't even know what I wanted. All that time, I didn't know what it was to be loved. Not until you. And now . . . I don't know what I'd do without it."

Jude didn't answer, but his grip on Anton tightened, as if he was afraid Anton might slip away from him.

Their ship docked in the marina of Pallas Athos just before twilight.

By the time they reached the agora, the sky was blanketed in darkness. Jude paused before the Sacred Gate.

"What is it?" Anton asked.

"I—I don't . . ." He looked unsure. "This is a holy place. Or—I thought it was. The Temple of Pallas, the place the Order of the Last Light served until the Prophets disappeared. The first time that I came here, I thought that this place was my destiny. I guess I was right, after all."

Anton felt heavy with the reminder. He slotted Jude's fingers between his own, and they crossed the gate together, the Wanderer and Illya following after them.

And then they all stopped short. Anton choked out a gasp.

Spread out across the agora were bodies. There must have been hundreds of them, collapsed along walkways, slumped over the stairs that led up to the Temple of Pallas. Each of them wore the familiar gold and black robes of the Witnesses.

Anton tightened his grip on Jude's hand, feeling suddenly dizzy.

"Behezda's mercy," Illya muttered. "It killed all of them."

"Their punishment at the god's hands for following Pallas," the Wanderer said. "And there's almost nothing the god hates more than Pallas. In fact, I may be the only thing above Pallas on that list."

Anton suppressed a shudder. If this was what the god did to the people who followed Pallas, what would it do to them?

They mounted the steps up to the temple, avoiding the fallen Witnesses. The blackened threshold welcomed them inside the sanctum. As Anton moved to enter, Jude squeezed his hand, stilling him.

"What if it's still here?" Jude asked, pitching his voice lower.

It was as he asked the question that Anton felt it. *Esha*, reverberating within the temple walls. Familiar *esha*.

But it was impossible.

Anton stepped into the threshold. "Ephyra?" he called hesitantly. "Hector?"

Illya and Jude both stared at him in disbelief.

But Jude didn't hold him back as Anton stepped into the sanctum. The entryway opened up to a set of stairs that led up a long, narrow platform that cut across the sanctum. It was lined by Godfire torches, and at the end of it was a circular dais upon which the altar sat, reaching up toward an open sky. And there, below the altar, stood Ephyra and Hector.

"What are you doing here?" Ephyra asked, panic lacing her tone.

Anton mounted the stairs two at a time, climbing onto the narrow platform, Jude at his heels.

"Jude," Hector said. "Get out of here. Now."

"What's going on?" Jude asked carefully.

It was Ephyra who answered. "We're here for the Chalice."

"Why?" Anton asked.

Ephyra swallowed. "Because I'm going to use it to release the god from Beru."

Anton gaped at her, stunned. She couldn't be serious.

"It's too dangerous," Illya said. "If the god is completely free from Beru, then we have no hope of sealing it again."

"Sealing it again?" Hector asked. "Is that what you're here to do? Because that's worked out so well before."

"Illya's right," the Wanderer said. "If we release the god's *esha* from its vessel, we'll create a creature even more dangerous because it won't be connected with humanity. I've faced the god before, unshackled by a human body. Killing it almost ended us."

"I don't care," Ephyra said.

"You will if it decides to kill Beru," Anton replied. "Think about it. The minute it no longer needs her, it will turn on her."

"You don't know that," Ephyra replied.

"Are you really willing to risk it?" Anton asked. "You have *no* idea what you're about to unleash. Once the god's free, what's to stop it from killing *all* of us?"

"They have a point, Ephyra," Hector said in a low voice.

Ephyra stared at him. "You *agreed* to this."

"I did," Hector said. "I'll do whatever it takes to save Beru. But we can't let the god go free."

Ephyra looked like she was considering killing Hector again.

But before she could unleash her anger, Hector continued, "So when you release it from Beru, put it inside me."

"*What?*" Ephyra demanded.

Jude started toward them. "Hector, *no*."

"I'm a revenant, too," Hector said steadily. "I'm the only other person who can hold the god without dying. Anton can bind it again, in me, with the other Relics. It's far from a perfect solution, but until we come up with another plan—"

"No," Jude said, his tone ringing with finality. "Hector, you're not sacrificing yourself."

"Beru is already sacrificing herself," Hector replied evenly. "And she didn't get a choice."

"We have a plan," Jude said. "You don't need to do this."

"What plan?" Ephyra asked.

Jude looked past Illya to the Wanderer. Something seemed to pass between them, a communication so subtle it was just a blink of the eyes. Anton might have imagined it.

But before Jude could explain, the god materialized at the altar in a flash of bright light, Lazaros at its side. Between them sat a silver chest.

"I SEE THAT YOUR FRIENDS ARE HERE." It would never cease being strange, hearing that ancient and terrible voice coming out of Beru's mouth. Its gaze landed on the Wanderer. "YOU AGAIN."

It curled a hand, and the Wanderer's body jerked violently.

"No!" Ephyra cried out. "If you want my help, you'll let them go."

The god cocked its head at Ephyra. "YOU SEEK TO BARGAIN WITH ME?"

"Not bargaining," Ephyra said, a faint tremor in her voice. "Threatening."

"YOU DO NOT THREATEN A GOD, LITTLE MORTAL," the god boomed as it rounded on Ephyra. "I CAN SKIN YOU ALIVE."

It tossed the Wanderer to the ground. She fell off the side of the platform, landing on the floor of the sanctum below. Anton scrambled to the edge of the platform, gripping the railing and looking down. It was at least a twelve-foot drop.

"I'm all right," the Wanderer said, bracing a hand against her side as she stumbled to her feet. A cracked rib, most likely. Her eyes moved back to the god, and Anton followed her gaze.

"You need me," Ephyra said. "Beru's still fighting you in there, isn't she? You thought she'd give up by now, but she hasn't. And she won't. I know my sister, and I know what she's capable of. So let me free you from her, and in exchange, leave my friends alone."

When the god spoke next, it was to Lazaros. "GIVE HER THE CHALICE."

Lazaros obeyed at once, reaching inside the silver chest and pulling out the familiar, jewel-studded Chalice and holding it out to Ephyra.

Ephyra curled her fingers around its stem, darting a glance at Hector before she closed her eyes. After a moment, the Chalice began to glow. She reached her other hand out and, trembling, cupped Beru's face. Thin tendrils of black smoke seemed to seep out of Beru.

Now was Anton's chance to get the Relics.

Anton started forward, his gaze zeroed in on the silver chest beside Lazaros. But a sharp tug on his hand reeled him back. Before he could make sense of what was happening, Jude stepped into Anton's space, taking his face in his hands and kissing him. Anton was too stunned to kiss back. He was too stunned to move, his mind whirring madly, blood thrumming through his veins.

He broke away from Jude, holding tightly on to his shoulders and searching his face.

The answers were all there, laid bare for Anton to see. In Jude's eyes, dark with desperation. In his brow, pulled taut with anguish. In his mouth, soft and trembling with guilt.

"I love you," Jude said, and it sounded like an apology.

It sounded like a betrayal.

Jude turned on his heel and launched himself over the platform to the sanctum below. To where the Wanderer stood. She reached for Jude's hand and that's when Anton knew.

"What is he doing?" Hector asked.

But Anton couldn't answer. A rage like he had never known thundered through his blood.

"Ananke!" Anton yelled, gripping the platform railing, his voice scraped raw. "You *liar*! You *coward*! You're just like Pallas!"

He threw himself back along the platform, toward the stairs as the temple shook around him. He could feel the Sacred Word. A faint echo at first, and then building like a thunderhead. He felt like he was drowning again, his lungs straining against ice-cold water. He couldn't breathe.

Jude was dying, and Anton couldn't get to him in time to stop it.

And then the temple went still. The storm of Jude's *esha*, of the Sacred Word within it, quieted.

Anton looked down, afraid of what he would find. His gaze sought Jude first. He was on his knees, one hand braced against the cold marble ground, the other clutching his chest as it rose and fell on a panicked breath.

He was alive. The Sacred Word still locked within him. The Wanderer had not finished unleashing it.

Because, Anton realized, his blood going cold, the god had stopped her.

The god, still in Beru's body, was right beside the Wanderer and Jude, one hand outstretched. Tendrils of dark smoke trailed from Beru's arms and legs, curling around her waist and up to her neck. They furled out, wrapping around the Wanderer, holding her in place as the god contemplated her.

"ANANKE," the god said. "YOU WERE MY GREATEST DISAPPOINTMENT."

"Greater than Pallas?" the Wanderer choked out. "Isn't that why you made us, after all? The other Prophets? It was because you knew, even then, that Pallas was not the stalwart servant you thought he was. You sensed the weakness in him."

"I WANTED YOU TO BE BETTER THAN HIM," the god agreed. "BUT ALL HUMANS ARE WEAK. I HAVE ALWAYS KNOWN THIS."

"And yet," the Wanderer said, "there is something in us that was strong enough to overcome the will of a god. You didn't understand it then, and it cost you your life."

The Wanderer's eyes met Beru's, something fierce and unrelenting in her gaze. Anton recognized the expression—the same one she had worn over two thousand years ago, standing in front of Temara and facing down the other Prophets.

"YOU ARE WRONG," the god spat. "THERE IS NOTHING IN YOU THAT IS STRONGER THAN MY WILL."

The god raised its arms to the sky, light pouring from them, enveloping the Wanderer. The Wanderer choked back a scream. Anton felt the delicate, silver bell sound of her *esha* ring out and then stop abruptly, cutting into awful silence as she collapsed to the floor.

Anton cried out, his knees hitting the cold marble floor as he watched the Wanderer die.

38

BERU

BERU FELT THE WANDERER'S LIFE FLICKER OUT LIKE A FLAME. THE GOD'S RAGE thundered inside her.

The Wanderer's death did not satisfy it.

Beru's own anguish, her fear and despair, lashed at the god's hold on her. She could feel its resistance, its disgust for Beru's human feelings.

It whirled away from the Wanderer's body, back toward Ephyra, who was staring in shock, the Chalice still clutched in her hand.

"KEEP GOING," the god urged. "FREE ME."

Ephyra stared in horror, hesitation written all over her face.

"DO IT."

Ephyra's eyes snapped closed, and she trembled. The Chalice began to glow, and once again Beru felt her sister's power tugging at the god.

It felt like being torn in two.

Light poured from Beru's hands and eyes, spilling out of her. Searing through her.

They were too entwined, had spent too much time trapped together. Wrenching the god from her body would kill her.

And the god would kill everyone else in the sanctum.

Stop! She wanted to scream. She struggled, frantic, against the tendrils of the god's control.

Hector, she thought. His feelings had centered her before. She sought them, beneath the god's rage, beneath her own hopelessness.

And felt . . . resolve.

"Ephyra," Hector said from beside her. "You have to do what I asked. Now, before it's too late."

Their eyes met as he stepped toward Ephyra. Beru's confusion slotted into understanding.

Ephyra wasn't going to let the god go free. She was going to put it in Hector.

No.

She could feel the god being ripped from her.

No, she said again. *They're trying to trick you. They're trying to trap you again.*

SHE IS FREEING ME FROM YOU.

You are a fool, Beru said scornfully. *This was all a trick. They will trap you in the other revenant.*

She felt the god hesitate.

Why would I lie? Beru asked. *I don't want you here. You know that.*

YOU WOULD RATHER BE CAGED BY ME THAN LET ME BE FREE.

Yes. Stay here. Stay with me.

Ephyra clutched the Chalice tighter, the glow of its power washing her in light. Beru reached for the bright coils of the god's power and tried to hold on.

She gasped in a deep, desperate breath, as if breaching the surface of water. Her lungs heaved. She could feel it, the barest gap in the god's control as it left her body.

She opened her mouth and screamed as loudly as she could. *"Ephyra, stop!"*

Ephyra froze, her eyes widening and her mouth going slack. In a second, she was at Beru's side, touching her face.

"Beru, is that you?"

Streaks of light cascaded from Beru, spooling out like ribbons. The god, still trying to break free.

"It's me," Beru confirmed, clutching Ephyra's shoulder. "You have to listen to me. You have to stop. Don't—don't do this."

"But—"

"You want to save me," Beru said, shaking her head. "You've always wanted to save me. But I never asked you to. So for once in your life, stop trying and do as I say."

Ephyra lifted her tearstained face. Beru saw all the remorse and pain that Ephyra had kept bottled up for so long.

The hand that was holding the Chalice went slack, and the Chalice clattered across the marble floor. Beru closed her eyes as she felt the god flood back into her, its scorching light filling her from head to chest to feet. She gritted her teeth against the onslaught and focused on Ephyra, on her own pride and heartbreak. Beru had to maintain control, just a moment longer.

"Anton!" Illya's voice cried. "The Relics!"

Anton hesitated a split second before sprinting back up the platform, toward the chest that held the other Relics. Lazaros whirled after him, but Anton reached them first. He seized the Oracle Stone and dove out of the path of Lazaros's Godfire sword.

"No!"

As Lazaros took another swing at Anton, Jude leapt back onto the platform to parry the blow.

Anton clutched the Oracle Stone and staggered toward Beru as Jude held off Lazaros.

The Relics. Of *course*. They were trying to reseal the god and give Beru control again.

Only Beru knew it wouldn't work. The god was much too strong now.

But maybe it would buy them time.

NO! the god roared, fighting for control. I WILL NOT BE BOUND AGAIN.

"Do it," she said to Anton.

The Oracle Stone glowed in his right hand as his left touched Beru's forehead. She felt the god's *esha* jolt violently. The more power Anton poured into binding it, the more the god struggled. White-hot stars burst behind Beru's eyes.

"In the name of the Holy Creator!" Lazaros's voice rang out through the sanctum.

Beru turned. Lazaros stood at the base of the altar, a font of chrism oil overturned at his feet. The oil had spilled out into a glistening river across the marble floor, pooling around the chest of Relics. Lazaros's gaze was locked on Beru, his Godfire sword raised high above him.

It took Beru a split second to understand what he was about to do. And another split second to act.

Summoning every last tattered scrap of control, Beru threw out her arms. Ephyra, Anton, Illya, Jude, and Hector vanished from the sanctum just as Lazaros brought the Godfire blade down, igniting the chrism oil.

The temple exploded into flame.

A shower of rubble and fire crashed down around her.

The god's power surged through Beru, overtaking her. The Relics were destroyed. The blackened, charred corpse of Lazaros lay crumpled beside them in the ruins.

Flames licked at her back as the god stepped out onto the temple's portico, hundreds of dead Witnesses spread out around it in the agora.

It wasn't enough. The god's rage only burned brighter.

It wanted this city to bleed.

It flicked Beru's hand and blood rose from the Witnesses' bodies in a fine mist. The god thrust out her arms and the mist coalesced into a towering wave of dark blood.

"PEOPLE OF PALLAS ATHOS," the god's voice boomed out. "YOU HAVE LOST YOUR FAITH. YOU HAVE FALLEN BENEATH THE SPELL OF A MAN WHO CALLED HIMSELF A PROPHET. BUT HEAR ME—HE WAS NO PROPHET. HE CLAIMED TO SPEAK THE WORDS OF THE DIVINE, BUT HE SPOKE ONLY LIES. I AM YOUR CREATOR. I AM YOUR GOD."

Beru could hear the screams echoing up from the city below as the wave of blood crashed over it, flooding down from the temple and into the pristine, white streets. It swept over the limestone buildings, cascading over the walls of the first tier, into the second, and down into the Low City.

It still wasn't enough. With a wave of Beru's hands, the god turned all the water in the city into blood. It spewed from the fountain in Elea Square. It ran through the sewers. It spilled into the sea.

She had turned the city itself into a wound, staining everything red.

"IT IS TIME YOU FIND YOUR FAITH AGAIN."

39

HASSAN

HASSAN'S NERVES RATTLED AS THE BOAT EASED TOWARD THE SHORE. TO AVOID being sighted by Lethia's people, they had dropped anchor in a cove far from Nazirah's harbor. As an extra precaution, they'd disembarked in the dead of night, just Hassan, Khepri, and two crew members rowing themselves across the waves, their path illuminated by the moon.

"You seem anxious," Khepri commented. "Remember the last time we arrived back in Nazirah?"

"You mean when Lethia betrayed me and captured our army?" Hassan asked. "That's not really helping."

"I'm just saying, this could be a lot worse."

"Well, we don't really know yet," Hassan reminded her gruffly. "It's been months since either of us heard from the Scarab's Wing."

They reached the rocky shore and disembarked. With a wave of farewell and good luck, the two crew members rowed back to the ship.

Now that Khepri had brought up their last return to Nazirah, Hassan couldn't stop thinking about it. Then, he'd been surrounded by an army, full of righteous fury. Now, it was just the two of them, no less motivated, but significantly underequipped for battle.

They set off up the beach, winding toward the low, craggy cliffs. The sun had nearly risen by the time they reached the cypress grove that overlooked the cove. From here, they could see the outskirts of the city, sandstone buildings blushing pink with the dawn light.

"The King of Herat returns," Khepri said, leaning against his shoulder.

He turned to her. "Khepri, I'm not . . . I was never the king Nazirah needed me to be. You know that better than anyone. That's not why I came back."

Her amber-brown eyes searched his face. For a moment, Hassan thought she would argue. Instead, she just took his hand, pulling him down the hill. "Come on."

Khepri might have seen him as a king, yet he was stealing into this city like a thief. But then, he'd learned from Anton and Ephyra what a thief could do. Maybe it wasn't the worst thing to be.

When they neared the Artificers' and Alchemists' Quarters, he and Khepri kept their gaits quick and even, like they had somewhere innocuous to get to. Hassan wore a cowl to obscure his face—the last thing they needed was for someone to recognize him.

He was sweating by the time they reached a familiar wine cellar, his heart pounding. It occurred to him, as Khepri twisted the wine barrel revealing the secret passage underneath, that they had no idea what awaited them in the Great Library. What losses the rebels may have suffered since Hassan and Khepri had been captured. Whether Zareen and Chike and Sefu were even still there.

For all they knew, the Witnesses had discovered this place. Were they walking into a trap?

He reached for Khepri in the darkened passage. His anxiety only grew as they crept down the long tunnel and finally reached the door that led inside.

"You still remember the password?" Khepri asked. Hassan nodded, and together they twisted the dials on the door so they lined up.

As they turned the final dial, Khepri's gaze caught his.

"Are you ready?" he asked.

She nodded. Whatever waited behind the door, friend or foe, they were about to find out.

The door creaked open, and they found themselves face-to-face with the point of a sword.

"Identify yourselves." The woman holding the sword was not someone Hassan had ever seen before—an older woman, her dark hair streaked with gray and pulled back the way the Legionnaires wore it.

"Uh," Hassan said helpfully.

Over her shoulder, he could see the Library atrium, bustling with people beneath the gleaming armillary spheres. It looked like over half the rebels were here, although when Hassan looked closer at the people milling about, he recognized few of them.

"Could you possibly put the sword down?" Hassan asked.

"Would you prefer to have this conversation in the dungeons?"

Dungeons? Since when did the Library have dungeons?

"No," Khepri said quickly. "I'm Khepri Fakhoury, and this is Hassan Seif."

The woman did a double take. Then her expression darkened, her grip on her sword tightening. "Tell me who you *really* are and who gave you the password to enter."

Hassan and Khepri exchanged a glance. "That was the truth. My brothers, Sefu and Chike, can vouch for us. Are they . . . here?"

She peered over the woman's head like she might catch a glimpse of them.

"The prince is dead," the woman said with finality. "And Khepri Fakhoury has been missing for some time, so whatever it is you're trying to accomplish here, I would give it up."

Over the woman's shoulder, Hassan spotted a familiar face—Faran, one of the original Herati refugee soldiers who had come over from Pallas Athos with them.

"Faran!" Khepri called out to him as he trotted briskly across the atrium, carrying a stack of maps under one arm. She waved her hand. "Faran!"

He looked up distractedly. "Oh, hi, Khepri, I just need to get these to the war room, but I'll see you there!"

The woman turned to Faran, bewildered, as Hassan and Khepri both stared, equally perplexed as he walked right past them.

And then he froze, and the entire stack of maps went fluttering to the floor in front of him.

"*Khepri?*" He wheeled back to them. "Prince Hassan? What are you—what—*how*—?"

"It's a rather long story," Khepri said. "So we'd prefer to tell it only once. Are my brothers here?"

Faran nodded. "They're probably already waiting in the war room. Zareen, too."

The woman who had stopped Hassan and Khepri looked thoroughly embarrassed as she fumbled to resheathe her sword. "I—My apologies, Your Grace."

Hassan waved a hand. "Not the first time someone thought I was dead, probably won't be the last. Faran?"

"Follow me," Faran said, setting off across the atrium.

"Don't you need these?" Hassan asked, stooping down to collect the maps.

"Right," Faran said, spinning right back around and crouching beside Hassan. But instead of helping pick up the maps, he just stared. "I never thought I'd see you again. None of us did."

He sounded relieved and a little awed. Hassan offered him a tight smile and straightened. Once the maps were safely tucked under Faran's arm, he led Hassan and Khepri through the atrium.

As they strode down the wide, vaulted corridor, Hassan took in the scores of people rushing between rooms. A few months ago, when they'd resided here, there had been maybe three hundred people total in the rebel base. Now, Hassan had already seen almost twice as many. The Library was huge—who knew how many more were sheltered in its halls. This wasn't a ragtag group of rebels anymore, he realized.

This was an *army*.

His stomach squirmed. He was relieved—overjoyed, really—that the rebels were still here and seemed to be doing better than ever. But he knew they would have questions for him. Questions he'd told himself he was prepared to answer, though the closer they drew to that moment of reckoning, the less sure he felt.

Khepri slipped her hand into his, squeezing gently. They approached the north reading room, which Hassan assumed must have been converted into what Faran had called the war room. As they crossed over its threshold, he heard voices within.

After all this time, Hassan still recognized Zareen's voice—and her annoyed tone. "I told you, it's not ready yet. You can't rush *genius*, Chike."

"What about mediocre intelligence, can we rush that?"

A guffaw from Sefu.

"You are *not* as funny as you think you are," Zareen replied haughtily. "Where is the general? She should be here by now."

General? It really *was* an army.

"Zareen!" Faran called as he, Hassan, and Khepri emerged into the main chamber. There were roughly two dozen people in the room, all talking in small clusters, only some of whom Hassan recognized. But his gaze zeroed in on Zareen, sitting on the edge of a table with her legs dangling off the side. The alchemist was diminutive next to the towering forms of Chike and Sefu, who both turned toward the sound of Faran's voice.

Hassan watched as they caught sight of him and Khepri and froze.

"Faran," Zareen said sedately. "You've brought guests."

Everyone else in the chamber had gone silent, staring. There were a few low murmured whispers, and Hassan thought he caught his name on more than one person's lips. He could not read the expression on Zareen's face, and his stomach churned with trepidation.

"Khepri!" Sefu thundered, breaking the silence. "Prince Hassan! You're alive!"

He strode toward them, Chike at his heels, and when he reached Khepri he stopped for a moment, looking at her, before he curled his hand into a fist and punched her arm.

"*Ow!*" Khepri gasped, and immediately punched him back. "Sweet Endarra, that *hurt!*"

"Four months," Zareen said to Hassan as Khepri and her brothers bickered loudly behind them, the rest of the room filling up again with chatter. "*Four months.* You've been gone, and we had no idea what had happened to you. Is Arash—"

"Arash is . . ." Hassan began, and then hesitated. The animosity between him and Arash had been no secret, and Hassan feared what Zareen would think. "He's dead. I'm sorry, Zareen. I know you were close with him."

She straightened her shoulders, swallowing hard, and nodded. "What happened?"

"We were captured by the Hierophant. Taken to Behezda."

Zareen's eyes widened in understanding. Hassan didn't need to go on.

"There's much we need to catch you up on," Hassan said.

Zareen nodded. "A full debrief would be wise. But there's something I should probably tell you first."

She looked nervous, uncertain, and Hassan steeled himself for the worst. But before she went on, her eyes widened as she caught sight of something over Hassan's shoulder.

"General!" Zareen exclaimed.

Hassan turned, heart thudding with desperate curiosity.

At first his mind could not process what he saw. The general strode into the room with a confident if slightly uneven gait, owing to the fact that one of her legs was missing below the knee. In its place was an artificed prosthetic. Her hair was cropped much shorter than usual, perfectly framing her high cheekbones and a face that, while more lined than Hassan remembered, was as familiar to him as his own, right down to the light brown eyes they both shared, which at the moment were widened with shock.

"Right," Zareen said faintly behind him. "So, that's what I was going to tell you."

Hassan stared at the general, his heart beating double time in his chest until at last he cracked open his mouth and let his disbelief spill from it.

"Mother?"

Even after an hour, Hassan still couldn't believe it. His mother was *here*. Alive. Safe from Lethia's and the Witnesses' clutches.

And apparently leading an army.

They sat beside each other at the war room table. Everyone else had cleared the room. Hassan's mother held his hand, stroking her thumb idly over his knuckles. She could not seem to stop touching him. He could not seem to stop staring at her.

"And that's when we decided to return," Hassan said. He'd told her everything—from the day he'd fled the palace during the coup to the moment he boarded a ship to come home.

"I thought you were dead," she said tearfully, cupping his face. "Lethia said you were *dead*. If I'd known—Hassan, if I'd known, there would have been nothing that would have stopped me from finding you."

"I know," he said. He felt tears gather in the corners of his eyes. He could not keep them from falling. "I missed you so much. When I learned of Father's execution, I just . . . I had to hold on to hope that you hadn't met the same fate."

She shook her head, her face crumpling. A vulnerability she showed to few people. "Your father is the one who got me out. We were both imprisoned in the palace during those weeks after the coup. We could only hope that you had escaped. We had no way of knowing. And your father—he had allies. Ones even I knew nothing about. They were able to infiltrate the palace and smuggle me out. I couldn't bear to leave him behind, but I knew if you were alive that I had to find you. But as we fled the city, we were attacked again. Many of the people who protected me lost their lives. I lost my leg."

Hassan had wondered about the wound.

"They put me on a boat on the Herat River. I don't know for how long we sailed upriver, but eventually we came to a safe house, where they patched me up. By the time I recovered my strength, we received reports that the lighthouse had fallen and that you were—" She sucked in a shaky breath instead of saying it. "I lost myself in grief for days.

Weeks. I couldn't bear to live in a world that would be cruel enough to take my sweet boy away from me."

Hassan held his mother's hand tighter, not knowing what to say.

"By this time," she said, "your aunt's soldiers had poured downriver. Securing key resources and towns. And I knew what I needed to do. So one morning I just woke up and decided—my time on this earth would not be finished until I had taken Herat back from Lethia and made every single one of her soldiers pay for what they had done."

Hassan had forgotten how formidable his mother could be, how downright ruthless. She was not one to shy away from emotion—in contrast to Hassan's more reserved father, his mother felt everything strongly and expressed herself vividly. That included her temper—once her anger was incurred, one simply had to let it run its course. It was something that she and Hassan shared, something his father had never truly understood.

"And so that is what I have been doing," she said. "I have traveled all over the highlands, trying to win the support of the regional lords. Mustering an army to take back Nazirah. One month ago, we received information that there was a group of rebels operating within Nazirah. I, and a select group of my commanders and their fighters, snuck into the city. They told me that you had been with them, after the lighthouse. And I began to hope, once again, that you were still alive. That our paths might cross."

"We'd heard that the regional lords had united," Hassan said. "But I had no idea that *you* had done it. We had no idea that you had an *army*."

"We plan to work with the rebels on a coordinated attack," she said. "The lords will march on Nazirah while the rebels strike from within."

"When?" Hassan asked.

"Soon," she replied. "But we need something before we can launch the attack. I was able to persuade the lords to unite and back my claim to the throne, though it is far more tenuous than Lethia's. But without a strong claim, there will be more bloodshed, and in the end, Lethia will keep her power or Herat will descend into chaos. We need a true heir to unite us. We need a king."

Her gaze settled on his face.

He pulled his hand away. "Mother, I tried. I tried to be the leader Nazirah needed me to be, but it . . . it went wrong. I failed, in so many ways. I didn't come here to repeat my mistakes."

"My sweet son," she said, holding him by the shoulders and appraising him with a tenderness that made him ache. "You are not a boy any longer. A true leader is not a man who never makes mistakes. He's a man who learns from them."

He shook his head. "You're the one who won the support of the regions. You're the one in command of the army. You're the one they'll rally behind."

"You are their king," she said fiercely, gripping his shoulders. "If there is anyone who can unite our country, Graced and Graceless alike, it is you."

"But I'm—" He wanted to say he couldn't do it. That he'd tried and failed, twice before. That Herat did not need him. That it never had. "I—Shouldn't you discuss this with the others?"

"They will agree with me," she said dismissively. "I can win you this battle, but I have not the head for politics and ruling. That was your father's domain."

Actually, his father hadn't much cared for it, either. He was, perhaps, too honest. Too good-hearted. Too forgiving and not ruthless enough. He liked things he could pull apart and put back together with his hands. Politics was slippery, ever shifting.

It was Lethia who excelled at statecraft. How else could she have not only staged a coup against Hassan's family but also held the city of

Nazirah together when all the forces of chaos were descending upon it? She had been ruthless enough to strike a deal with the Hierophant. Cunning enough to use him and the Witnesses to secure her power. And deceptive enough to lie to Hassan to get him and his fledgling army out of the way.

He remembered what he'd told Zareen, the night he'd left the Scarab's Wing following Arash's brutal attack on the city.

I want to bring them justice. But I can't do it like this.

Maybe that was why he had gone to Lethia. Why he'd made a deal with the Hierophant. He wanted a bloodless solution. He wanted, above all, peace in the country he loved so much. But such a peace was not possible, could not be possible, without ripping out the poison that the Hierophant and Lethia had spread.

He'd failed to do what was required to restore order to Herat.

His mother believed that he could do it now. Hassan didn't know if that was true, but he knew if he wanted to save his country, if he wanted to protect his people, he had to become that person.

If he was to beat Lethia—not just win the battle, but truly beat her, and begin to heal the fractures she had exposed—he would have to accept the parts of himself that were like her.

"All right," he said at last. "I'll do it."

40

JUDE

WAVES CRASHED AGAINST THE PIER AS JUDE LANDED ON HIS KNEES BENEATH it. The sharp cry of a gull pierced the air.

Around Jude, the others staggered to their feet, leaning on the pier pilings as the tide washed in at their toes. Jude took stock of them—Illya, Hector, Ephyra. Anton. They didn't appear to be harmed—the god must have transported them here from the temple. Or rather, Beru had, in her few short seconds of control.

He watched as Ephyra climbed to her feet and then froze, a gasp of horror escaping her throat. Jude followed her gaze, looking up at the City of Faith. The city Jude had once believed held his destiny.

Now, like his destiny, Pallas Athos was stained with blood. It was drowning in it, its white streets overflowing with thick, red rivers. Jude, watching from the barren beach, drowned with it.

He turned away from the sight, fury and hopelessness tangling in his chest. He had failed. The Wanderer was dead, and he had failed. The anger built and built until finally he turned and slammed his fist into the piling behind him.

It wasn't enough, so he did it again. And again. And again.

"Hey! Easy!" Hector yelled, wrapping an arm around Jude's shoulder, holding him back.

Blind with rage, Jude summoned his Grace to throw Hector off him.

Nothing happened. Where Jude should have felt the swirling storm of his Grace, he felt emptiness. It was like those awful days after the lighthouse, when all Jude could feel was the ache of the Godfire scars.

He sucked in a shaking breath and slumped back against Hector, all the fight leaving him at once.

"Hey, you're all right," Hector said soothingly.

"My Grace," Jude said, pushing out of Hector's arms to look him in the eye. "It's gone."

"What?" Hector asked. His eyes widened, and he looked suddenly stricken. "I—I can't feel mine, either."

"It's happening to me, too," Ephyra said.

Jude turned and saw her standing a few feet behind them, the blood-red tide lapping at her feet.

Hector shook his head. "Did the god do this somehow?"

"No," Ephyra replied. "What Lazaros did with the Godfire—he must have destroyed the Relics. And if the Relics are destroyed . . . that destroys the source of our Graces."

"How do you know that?" Jude demanded.

"It's something a lorist once told me," Ephyra said. "It's why the Daughters of Mercy didn't just destroy the Chalice when the Necromancer King reigned. She said it was the source of their power—that destroying it would destroy the Grace of Blood entirely."

"So our Graces are just gone?" Hector asked, panic edging his tone.

"Anton?" Ephyra asked, tilting her head to peer around Jude's other side. "What about you?"

Anton was on his knees in the sand, not looking at any of them. His hand, down at his side, was wrapped around the Oracle Stone.

So one Relic had made it out. And Anton still had his Grace. But the other Relics were destroyed, and with them, any way to bind the god again.

Anton's head bowed toward the sand. He still didn't look at them, but Jude knew what he was thinking. The world was on a precipice. They were out of options.

"Anton?" Ephyra asked again.

Anton slowly picked himself off the ground. His movements seemed measured, almost calm. But when he turned and locked his gaze on Jude, Jude saw the cold, fathomless anger on his face.

He stalked up to Jude without a word, grabbing a handful of his shirt and shoving him back against the piling. Seawater splashed up at their ankles.

"What were you *thinking?*" he demanded. "How could you do that to me?"

Jude met the blaze of Anton's eyes evenly, his own anger sparking back to life.

"It was the right choice, and you know it," he ground out. "You can run from that like you've run from everything else in your life, but you know it's true."

Hurt flashed across Anton's face before his features hardened into icy anger. "You *lied* to me. You and the Wanderer. And now she's *dead.*"

Tears glimmered at the corners of Anton's eyes, and Jude could see the wave of grief he was holding at bay. He knew that Anton and the Wanderer had a complicated relationship, but he also knew that she was one of the few people who *knew* Anton, really knew him. Perhaps the only other person aside from the ones with Anton now.

"The Wanderer died doing what she knew she had to," Jude replied.

"Doing what was *right*. That was our one chance. I knew we might not get another, so I took it. And I knew you wouldn't accept that so, yes, I lied."

Anton's hand slackened on Jude's shirt, hurt crumpling his face. "How can you look at me and be so calm? How can you just accept this?"

"What do you want me to say, Anton?" Jude snapped. "That I'm angry? Of course I'm angry. But it doesn't change the fact that this is the only way to stop the god. To protect our world. To protect *you*. All of you. And if you'd accepted that sooner, none of this would have happened. We spent *weeks* wandering through the mountains, looking for saviors who weren't there. *We* are the saviors. And we weren't strong enough to do what needed to be done."

He was more furious than he'd ever been in his life. At Anton, at the Prophets, at himself.

He should have known. The moment Anton had told him about the Prophets and the Sacred Word and the Keeper, he should have known what he would have to do.

He wanted to live. He wanted to keep loving Anton. He wanted a world where what he wanted mattered.

"What are you two yelling about?" Ephyra asked.

Jude stiffened. He'd forgotten the others were there. Anton was still glaring at Jude, pinning him against the piling.

"Anton lied to you," Jude said at last, looking over Anton's shoulder at Ephyra. "There is a way to stop the god. Without the Prophets."

Silence descended like a storm cloud.

Finally, Hector croaked, "How long have you known about this?"

The quiet stretched until Anton finally turned to face the others. "Since before I found you all in Pallas Athos."

"And you didn't—"

"I didn't tell you," Anton said, "because I wasn't willing to do it. Because what it would cost is—"

He stopped abruptly, seemed to fight against the words.

"Me," Jude said quietly. "My life."

He watched horror flicker over Hector's face.

"What do you mean, your life?" Hector demanded. "Jude—"

"It's a long story," Jude said. "I don't even know all of it. I just know that when the Prophets slew the god the first time, they created this . . . weapon. Something called the Sacred Word. And after the god was dead, they hid the Sacred Word inside the *esha* of the first Keeper of the Word. And that secret has existed in the Weatherbourne line for over two thousand years. But to unleash it, to use the Sacred Word, I would have to give up my life."

Hector opened his mouth for what looked like another angry reply, but Jude cut him off.

"It's no different from what you were offering to do back there," Jude said steadily. "Taking Beru's place as the god's vessel."

Hector fell silent.

"So that's it?" Illya asked. "That's the plan?"

"No," Anton said at once.

"Yes," Jude answered. "I planned to do it in the temple. I tried. But the Wanderer . . ." He trailed off into uneasy silence. They'd all seen what had happened to her.

"Well, none of this matters if we can't get to the god again," Illya said firmly. "We need to figure out where it's going next."

They all looked at Anton.

"You saw all this in your vision, didn't you?" Hector asked.

Anton's jaw clenched. "Yes. I saw Behezda. And then Tarsepolis. And now Pallas Athos."

"So what comes after Pallas Athos?"

"Endarrion," Anton replied, closing his eyes briefly. "A . . . plague in Endarrion. But we won't get there in time."

"We need to at least try," Hector said angrily.

"No, Anton's right," Illya said. "The god can go anywhere at any moment. In order to get to it, we have to stay ahead of it."

"If we don't go to Endarrion, we're dooming thousands of lives," Hector replied. "Maybe *hundreds* of thousands."

Guilt rose in Jude's throat. He looked at Anton, and he could see the same horror in his eyes. His resolve cracking.

"Nazirah is the last city in my vision," Anton said.

The weight of Anton's words hung heavily between them. The last city. Their last chance to stop the Age of Darkness.

"Then that's where we make our stand," Illya said grimly.

"And how, exactly, are we getting there?" Ephyra asked.

"The Wanderer's ship is docked right over there," Illya replied, pointing down the pier. "I'm pretty sure they'll take us wherever we need to go, under the circumstances."

"Then let's go," Jude said shortly, stalking back up the beach. "We don't have any time to lose."

He could feel Anton's furious, wounded gaze on him, but he didn't look back.

It was a silent walk down the pier and onto the deck of the Wanderer's ship. Illya seemed content to take up the task of talking to the captain. Jude was content to let him.

His gaze found Anton at the prow of the ship, facing the distant horizon as they sailed toward it, the sun sinking in the western sky.

Jude approached, recalling another night on another ship, sailing away from Nazirah, when he'd stood beside Anton and touched his hand in the dark. That night felt far away, like another life they'd lived.

I saw the breaking of the world, Anton had said. *But I have no idea how to stop it.*

It was happening. Anton's vision unfolding, just as he had seen it that day. But now, he knew how to stop it.

Anton turned to Jude as he approached. He looked exhausted, deep purple bruises beneath red-rimmed eyes, his hair a mess, and his cheeks colored from the harsh wind.

The sight of him, the weary slump of his shoulders and the aching sadness in his eyes, subdued Jude's anger. In its place he felt only a tender desire to do what he had always done—protect Anton.

"You lied to me," Anton said, but there was no heat to it.

"You lied to me first," Jude countered. "And for longer."

"So what, we're even?" Anton asked.

Jude gave him a little shrug. "We tried it another way. We did everything we could."

"I know," Anton said, voice cracking. "And it wasn't enough. I can't save you. I failed at the one thing—the *only* thing—that matters."

"I don't see it like that."

Anton looked up at him, his eyes dark and wet with unshed tears.

"I don't," Jude said. "Everyone dies eventually. Everything comes to an end. But if I have to die, then I'd rather die knowing that I gave my life everything I could. That I wanted. That I loved and was loved. That I was afraid, and I didn't let fear hold me back. That I leapt from the top of a lighthouse without knowing what lay below. That I walked down a path darker and stranger than the one set out before me, with only the faith of the boy I love to guide me."

He covered Anton's hand with his own.

"You gave that to me," he said. "All the things I wanted for myself, things I didn't even know I could want. Whatever happens when we get to Nazirah, whatever happens to me, you can't forget that."

Anton turned his hand palm up below Jude's and laced their fingers together, knuckle to knuckle.

"All right," he said into the wind. "I won't."

41

BERU

MOST OF THE ACOLYTES OF THE TEMPLE OF ENDARRA FLED WHEN THE GOD arrived.

Beru stood on the steps of the temple, looking out at the river where the acolytes had piled into boats to row themselves into the city.

But some of them remained, lowering themselves to shaking knees in supplication.

The god didn't try to stop the ones that fled. It had no need to.

It would show these people that they had been worshipping false idols these last two millennia. Building monuments like this temple to the god's murderers. Letting their beliefs corrupt them, spreading lies like invisible poison.

It was then that the god knew what it would do.

"THIS WAS THE CITY NAMED FOR ENDARRA THE FAIR. ITS BEAUTY DISGUISES THE SICKNESS THAT FESTERS INSIDE IT. BUT NO LONGER—NOW THAT SICKNESS WILL BE EXPOSED FOR ALL TO SEE."

It closed Beru's eyes and summoned a plague. An invisible cloud of infection rose above the temple, and the god let its poison waft toward the fleeing acolytes until it filled the very air they breathed. It would be hours before the sickness took hold, and by that time they would have spread it across the city. And when the people called out to their Prophets, there would be no answer.

From within her shackles deep in the god's mind, Beru fought against the god's will.

I am Beru of Medea, she told herself. *Sister of Ephyra. A revenant.*

WHY ARE YOU SAYING THIS?

Because I don't want to forget, Beru replied. *I can't forget.*

IT WOULD BE BETTER IF YOU FORGOT. IT WOULD BE EASIER.

Part of her agreed with the god. She saw how pleasant it would be to slip into nothingness rather than bear witness to this destruction. But another part of her, a part deeper than the god could touch, rebelled. Even if she could not so much as lift her own pinkie finger, it mattered that she still knew who she was. She could not explain why, but she knew it mattered.

YOU WOULD CHOOSE STRUGGLE. YOU WOULD CHOOSE SUFFERING. I SUPPOSE THAT IS VERY HUMAN OF YOU. BUT IT WON'T MATTER IN THE END.

Behezda had been crushed by the very earth. Pallas Athos had been overtaken by a river of blood. Endarrion would fall to plague. And still it was not enough.

The Prophets are all dead, Beru thought. *They are gone. You've gotten your revenge.*

NOT ALL OF THEM, the god responded. NOT THE LAST OF THEM.

And will that be enough? Beru asked, already knowing the answer. *Will taking his life satisfy your wrath?*

YOU HAVE TAUGHT ME MUCH ABOUT HUMANS, the god said. HUMANS HAVE SQUANDERED THEIR FREE WILL. THEY USE IT TO START WARS AND CREATE SUFFERING. I WAS RIGHT—HUMANS NEED

SUFFERING. WHY ELSE WOULD THEY CAUSE SO MUCH OF IT? BUT YOU WERE ALSO RIGHT TO SAY THAT SUFFERING IS BAD.

Then why? Beru pleaded. *Why do this? Why cause more of it?*

BECAUSE THERE IS ONE WAY TO ERADICATE SUFFERING.

And Beru saw what the god would do. Saw that she could not stop it.

The god would fix the world the only way it knew how.

By breaking it.

IV

THE LAST PROPHET

42

ANTON

THEY'D BEEN STAKED OUT INSIDE AN ABANDONED ARTIFICER'S WORKSHOP across from the Great Library for almost the entire afternoon, and not a single person had entered or exited.

"This is where Hassan said the rebels were based, right?" Ephyra asked for the second time in as many hours.

"There must be another entrance," Illya insisted.

"Or they moved," Jude said.

"If they moved, the Library entrance wouldn't be protected," Hector pointed out. When they'd tried to simply walk up the steps, they'd all been forcefully, violently thrown back by some sort of invisible shield.

"We need to come up with another plan," Jude said. "We're too exposed here, and it's getting dark."

Before the Relic of Heart had been destroyed, the darkness wouldn't have made much of a difference to Jude. Anton could see how much it bothered him, to once again be without his Grace.

"I think we should—"

The sound of swords scraping free of their sheaths cut off whatever Jude had been about to say next.

Anton whirled. Six swordsmen surrounded them, hemming them in against the windows. Two of them had drawn their blades.

"Who sent you?" the one in front asked, his blade aimed at Anton.

"You'll regret pointing your sword at him," Jude said in a dangerous voice.

Anton glanced at the swordsmen, assessing. They weren't wearing any sort of uniforms. Nor did they look like Witnesses.

Taking a risk, he said, "We're friends of Prince Hassan."

The swordsman's eyes flashed with surprise. "What makes you think Prince Hassan is here?"

"Lower your weapons," an authoritative voice commanded from behind the six swordsmen.

"Yes, General," the swordsman replied, sheathing his sword immediately and standing at attention as a woman strode into the room. Her right leg, Anton noticed, was missing below the knee. She wore what looked like an artificed prosthetic of wood and lightweight copper, fastened to her knee with leather straps.

"My patrol spotted you on this roof hours ago," the general said. "Who are you, and how do you know my son?"

"Your *son?*" Hector repeated.

"That's a very long story," Anton replied. "How much time do you have?"

The general's gaze lingered over him. "Ah," she said. "I think I know who you are after all." She turned to her swordsmen. "Continue on your evening patrols. I will personally escort these five to the king."

The soldiers saluted, and the general led Anton and the others out of the artificer's workshop and across the road. Where the five of them had been forced back from the steps, the general simply waved a hand. A ring on her right hand glowed slightly, and she walked through freely.

"Quickly now, it won't stay disabled for long," she said over her shoulder.

They hurried after her, trailing her up the steps and through the doors of the Great Library.

Even this close to nightfall, the halls of the Library were bustling with activity. The general led them down several long corridors, and though almost a dozen people tried to get her attention, casting curious glances at Anton and the others, she didn't stop once. Finally, the general turned a corner and threw open the doors to what looked like a meeting room.

Hassan stood at a long table with Khepri and a few other soldiers, deep in conversation. They looked up as the doors banged open, and Hassan's eyes widened.

"What are you doing here?" he blurted, striding over to them, Khepri at his heels. "I mean—not that I'm not glad to see you all!"

"You might not be," Anton said, "when we tell you why we're here."

───────────────────

"So the god is coming," Hassan said slowly, after Anton and the others had recounted what had happened in Pallas Athos.

"Anton's vision was pretty clear," Jude said gently. "Nazirah is the final city the god will attack."

Anton's gaze found Hassan's. "We don't know when exactly. But soon. It's already wrought destruction on Tarsepolis, Pallas Athos, and Endarrion. Only Charis and Nazirah remain."

"We . . . we were going to take the city back from Lethia," Hassan said. "We were going to launch the attack tomorrow. But if what you say is true . . . we should be evacuating as many people as we can."

"It won't matter," Jude replied. "You won't be able to flee fast enough or far enough to escape it. Which is why we're here to stop it before it destroys Nazirah."

"How?" Hassan asked.

Anton looked out at the night sky through the broad windows instead of facing any of them. He couldn't look at Jude while he explained in that calm, measured tone what they were here to do. Couldn't watch Hassan's face as he realized the sacrifice Jude was about to make.

He felt like he was drowning all over again, being pulled beneath the ice by a grip so strong it felt like a vise.

Before he knew what he was doing, Anton was tearing from the room, out the door, down the hall. Vaguely, he heard the others call after him, but he didn't stop.

As he banked around a corner in the hallway, he spotted two doors that led to what looked like a courtyard—not that he could see much of it in the darkness. Anton pushed them open, flinging himself into the night air. His whole body was shaking, wracked with uncontrollable tremors. He crumpled down onto the steps, his back against a pillar, and just counted his breaths for a few moments.

He heard footsteps behind him and turned.

Ephyra stared at him from the threshold. A jug dangled from one hand, the other held the door open. There was something raw about her expression, something that tugged at Anton and clenched his chest.

Without a word, Ephyra ambled forward and sprawled down beside Anton on the steps. She took a long sip from the jug, wiped her mouth, and then offered it to Anton.

Anton took it hesitantly, tilting it to his lips. Tart, sweet wine rolled over his tongue.

"Herati pomegranate wine," Ephyra said. "Not bad, right?"

Anton took another sip and then handed the jug back to Ephyra.

And suddenly he was crying—big, gulping sobs that had him collapsing against Ephyra, burying his face in her shoulder.

"I can't do this," he said, clinging to her.

"I know," she replied, slinging her arm around him. "I know."

"I need him too much."

Ephyra's fingers tightened over Anton's shoulder, and he knew that she understood the awful grief he felt. It was the same grief that had driven Ephyra to bring her sister back from the dead, to kill over and over to keep her alive.

Ephyra just sat there, arm around him, as he wept against her shoulder, and when his sobs subsided she passed the wine back to him.

"Hey," Hector's voice said from behind them. "Mind if I join you?"

Anton glanced at Ephyra, knowing that her and Hector's relationship was still a delicate balance. But her expression softened when she saw Hector in the doorway.

Anton nodded, and Hector sat on his other side, accepting the wine when Anton passed it to him.

"I know it feels like you won't survive this," Hector said quietly. "Losing him. But you will."

If their plan tomorrow succeeded, then Hector stood to lose the only two people he truly loved. If anyone knew how Anton and Ephyra felt, it was him.

"How do you know that?" Anton asked, his voice wracked with tears.

"Because we've got you," Hector said. "Me and Ephyra and Hassan and Khepri. Even Illya. You're not alone." He looked at Ephyra. "Not anymore."

They stayed out there on the steps, passing around the jug of wine until it was empty.

"All right, come on," Ephyra said, rising and punting the jug out into the courtyard. It landed somewhere in the dark with a clatter. Hector snorted.

"Where are we going?" Anton asked, letting Hector pull him to his feet.

"Can't go to sleep on wine and an empty stomach," Ephyra replied, pushing back through the doors. Anton didn't think he'd be doing much sleeping anyway, but he followed her nonetheless.

The others found them, close to an hour later, sitting on the floor between bookshelves, slowly demolishing the tray of sugar-dusted pastries they'd stolen from the kitchen while Ephyra recounted the time Beru had accidentally adopted a dozen street cats in Tarsepolis.

"We wondered where'd you gotten off to," Hassan said from the doorway, where he was flanked by Khepri, Jude, and Illya.

Khepri made a beeline for the tray of pastries, reaching between Hector and Anton.

Anton met Jude's gaze from where he hung back by the doorway. He didn't look angry that Anton had run off. He just looked—relieved, almost. Understanding.

"Hector, Jude, come with me a moment," Hassan said, and swept back through the door.

Jude cast another glance at Anton, but followed Hassan without protest. Hector glanced around curiously and disappeared after them.

Ephyra resumed her story, and Hassan, Hector, and Jude reappeared as she was finishing it, toting several baskets of pillowy flatbreads, a platter of still-smoking skewers of meat, and several large jugs of wine.

"Now this," Khepri said, rising to help them, "is exactly what you should be using your kingly powers for, Hassan."

"I have to agree," Ephyra said, reaching for the bread.

Hassan shrugged. "I figured—tomorrow the world might end, right? Might as well have as much fun as we can tonight."

Everyone fell silent. Of course, they all knew what might happen tomorrow, if Anton and Jude failed.

The silence was broken by Ephyra as she grabbed a jug of wine and sloshed some of it into a cup.

"What?" she asked, handing the jug back to a surprised Hector. "He's not wrong."

Hector barked out a laugh and poured himself a cup before handing it off to Khepri.

When they each had a cup, Hassan held his up.

"A toast, then," he said. "To the end of the world."

They raised their cups.

"To Beru," Ephyra murmured.

"To Ananke, the Wanderer," Anton added.

"To us," Khepri said simply as they touched their cups together.

Soon the seven of them were sprawled out across the floor, propped against bookshelves and soft sitting cushions, teasing one another and telling stories. Anton shook out a deck of cards from his pocket. It was the deck the Wanderer had gifted him, the gold backs glinting in the low light. He dealt them out to Ephyra, Hassan, and Hector, like this was any other night they'd spent camped beneath the stars, passing time and buoying one another on the long journey.

Anton won the first hand easily, and the second.

"Come on," Hassan said. "Last night before the world ends. You can't go a little easy on us?"

"What would be the fun in that?" Anton replied, gathering up the cards to deal again.

In the corner, Jude and Khepri spoke in low voices, although Jude glanced up every so often, his eyes drawn unerringly to Anton. They were soon joined by Illya, who gazed longingly at the card game.

Without really thinking it through, Anton shifted over, clearing a space between him and Hassan, and when he dealt the cards again he dealt five hands. He caught Illya's eye and gave him one, brief nod.

Wordlessly, Illya came to sit beside him, taking up the cards. No one else commented, just resumed the game, lightheartedly goading one another as Illya and Anton traded victories.

"Ah, so *that's* why you wouldn't let him play with us," Hassan said knowingly as Illya narrowly won another hand. "He's the only one who can beat you."

Anton peered over his cards at Illya, who met his gaze with a tentative smile. Anton's answering smile was a little brittle at the edges, but genuine.

It still felt a little raw, sitting next to Illya, playing cards and joking, like all was forgiven. It wasn't—it might never be—but it counted for something that he was here. For this night, the one that stood at the cusp of the end of everything, it was enough.

43

EPHYRA

THE NIGHT WORE ON AND STILL THEY LINGERED, EATING AND DRINKING AS THE candles burned down to stubs, their stories turning from funny and bizarre to melancholy and wistful.

Ephyra felt comforted that they were all together again, somehow, against all odds. She had friends. Anton, Jude, Khepri, Prince Hassan. Even Hector, she supposed. People she could trust and who trusted her. Surrounded by these people, she felt a part of her mend that she hadn't even known was broken.

Unbidden, her gaze found Illya across the untidy circle. He was sitting in a loose sprawl, one knee pulled up with an arm wrapped around it, the other supporting his weight as he leaned back. The firelight cast shadows over his face and the sharp angle of his jaw. Ephyra let herself look. It was the most relaxed she'd ever seen him before, miles and miles away from the prim, buttoned-up boy she'd met for the first time in Pallas Athos. He wasn't looking at her, focused instead on Hector, who was gesticulating about something—Ephyra had lost the thread of the conversation.

She knew she owed Illya an apology of some sort. In her grief and anger, she'd treated him with cruelty.

But apologies were not exactly something Ephyra was adept at. Her gaze fell on Hector. It had taken her years to say she was sorry for taking his family from him. For taking his life.

But she didn't have years. Tonight could very well be all any of them had left.

As Hassan laughed loudly at something Hector had said, Ephyra spotted Anton pulling Jude to his feet and the two of them slipped out of the room without a word. Jude turned over his shoulder and caught Ephyra looking. He gave her a small smile.

She smiled back, and didn't say anything to the others as Jude and Anton disappeared through the doors.

With Hector, Khepri, and Hassan entertaining one another on one side of the room, Ephyra picked herself up and made her way toward Illya. He looked up at her approach but didn't say anything as she settled beside him, leaning against the bookcase.

"You're worried about tomorrow, too," Ephyra said after a moment. It wasn't a question.

Illya nodded.

"About Anton?"

"Of course."

"There's something I've been wondering," she said. "A long time ago, when you were trying to manipulate Shara's treasure thieves to get the Chalice, you said that Pallas made you torture your own brother. Is that true?"

He bowed his head. "Yes."

"Why did you do it?"

"The Hierophant wanted—"

"No," she said. "I mean *why*."

He stared at her for a moment and then with a ragged sigh raked a hand through his hair. "I think there was a part of me that wanted to punish him."

"For what?"

"There were times when we were young," he said haltingly. "When I'd see a glimpse of—of what this power would do to him. What it would take from him. In those moments, I would lash out at him even harder. I would hurt him. And after, at night, when he was asleep, I would just—sit there, looking at him. Crying."

He wiped at his face, a breath shuddering through him. Ephyra's heart clenched in her chest, and she didn't try to stop herself from reaching to touch him, her hand resting gently on his shoulder.

"I—I've never told anyone that before," he croaked.

Ephyra was silent for a long moment. "You felt guilty? For what you did to him?"

Illya hunched his shoulders. "I hated myself. I knew it was wrong. But I still did it. When his Grace manifested I just—I knew. That our lives as we knew them were over. We didn't have much, but we had each other. And I just . . . I knew he was going to leave me. In some ways, it felt like he already had. I guess I wanted to punish him for it. I think I just wanted to make myself hate him, to make him hate me, so when he left me alone it wouldn't hurt as much."

Ephyra shivered. She understood all too well what Illya meant. She'd lived with the same fear her whole life—that Beru would leave her and she'd be alone. While she had never let that fear twist her against her sister, she had seen how that fear had corrupted her in other ways. How she had turned it on anyone else in her life that had dared to get close.

"Pretty awful, right?" he said ruefully, one hand twisting in his hair. "And it didn't work. Well—he does hate me, that part worked. But the rest? It still gutted me when he ran away. Nearly killed me."

"It is awful," Ephyra said, and when Illya looked over at her she just shrugged. "But—have you ever told him any of this?"

Illya's fingers pulled at his hair until it stuck up and Ephyra ignored the urge to smooth it. "Sort of. That night in Pallas Athos, remember?"

"Kind of ruined by the fact that you had us arrested by the Sentry five minutes later," Ephyra reminded him. "So I don't know if that counts."

Illya laughed humorlessly. "You're right. But what would it matter, anyway? I didn't love him enough. I should've, and I didn't. Maybe I didn't know how."

Ephyra looked away, the reminder of what she'd accused him of sharp in her mind. "Illya," she said quietly. "About . . . what you said to me."

He shook his head. "We don't need to do this. Not tonight."

She turned to face him head-on, tucking her knees to her chest. "Maybe I do."

He waited.

"You were there for me when I had no one else," she said, her voice shaking.

"I get it," he said. "I was the option when there were no others. You were grieving, and I probably took advantage of that—"

"You didn't." Her gaze caught on his face, half turned to her. He'd always been handsome, that much she could admit even if it had irritated her. "I'm not . . . saying that I was in a good place. Or that I would've done it in other circumstances, but it was my choice."

He looked at her for a long moment. "You liked me because you didn't need to try to be good while you were with me. Because you didn't have to worry about hurting me or disappointing me."

He was right, of course. "I did hurt you, though," she said, gazing up at the bookshelf instead of at him. "I tried to convince myself I couldn't, but the truth is I knew exactly how to hurt you, and I did it. When I said that . . . about you not knowing how to love someone . . . I was really talking about myself."

When she looked back at him, his expression was mystified. "You love more fiercely than anyone I've ever known."

"No," she said. "It isn't love. Or—if it is, it's a selfish love. Look at what it's brought. Look at everything I've done."

She thought of Anton, sobbing into her shoulder. Of the tense line of Jude's shoulders when he'd told them about the Sacred Word and what it would cost him to release it.

Ephyra was responsible for all of it. She'd raised the god from the dead in Behezda. She'd started all this. She'd done terrible, unthinkable things to keep her heart from breaking. And it was going to break anyway. It had been breaking for seven years.

"I tore the world apart for my sister," she said. "But I wouldn't do the one thing she wanted. The only thing she ever asked me to do."

"What?" Illya asked softly.

"Let her go."

She thought of Beru, using her last scrap of strength to ask Ephyra—no, to *beg* her—to stop.

"But I'm going to," Ephyra said, wiping a tear as it slipped down her cheek. "It might kill me, but I'm going to."

"Well, I'll be here," he said. "If you'll let me."

"You don't owe me anything."

He smiled wryly. "The funny thing is, while you had yourself convinced that you could only ever make things worse, you made me want to be better. You made me believe I could be. That I could open myself to someone again, that it might even be worth the pain."

"And is it?" she asked, afraid of the answer.

"I'm still hoping I get to find out."

She sucked in a sharp breath. "Illya—"

"I'm not asking for anything," he said. "It's late. And the world might very well end tomorrow. So if you want, I will sit here with you until it does or until the sun rises. Whichever comes first."

"All right," she said, softly, and laid her head against his shoulder as the voices of the others washed over her.

44

JUDE

JUDE DIDN'T ASK WHERE THEY WERE GOING. HE DIDN'T HESITATE AS ANTON LED him through the darkened halls of the Library. It was so simple in that moment—where Anton went, Jude followed.

They climbed up the stairs and out into a broad courtyard garden crisscrossed with streams of water, over a small footbridge to an enclosed pavilion.

Jude slowed as Anton nudged open the door of the pavilion. The interior was canopied with gauzy fabric, billowing inward and giving the impression that they were standing in a tent rather than a room. A bed was nestled in one corner, piled high with pillows and draped with soft sheets.

But what drew Jude's gaze was the low table on the other side of the room, where one candle burned and another sat untouched. A goblet of wine sat between the candles, along with a wide, damascened silver bowl filled with chrism oil, and two crowns of laurel. Laid out before the table was a small rose-colored rug.

"Anton," Jude started, and then didn't know how to continue. He looked carefully at Anton and then back at the table, a sudden joy quickening his heart, elusive as light moving through water.

"You did this?" he asked at last.

"I arranged for it," Anton replied.

"I don't—" He didn't know how to ask. He knew what this was. What it must be. But he needed to be sure. "Is this—?"

Anton nodded quickly, looking suddenly a little shy.

"And these?" Jude asked unsurely, touching one of the laurel wreaths.

"Well," Anton said, "the Novogardians do marriage a little differently."

"The Order doesn't do marriage at all," Jude reminded him gently. "Anton—"

"It's just . . ." Anton began haltingly, his eyes trained on the table instead of Jude. "We've been bound together from the start. From—from the day I saw your ship arrive in Pallas Athos. Before then, even. And neither of us had a choice, to begin with, and then we did and we—we kept choosing each other. Right?"

Only now did he lift his gaze. Jude nodded slowly, silent, sensing that Anton wasn't done.

"So I thought . . . what if we could be bound together in a different way." He stepped toward Jude. "A way we get to choose."

Jude looked at him, limned in soft candlelight, so like the first night he'd met him. He had knocked the breath out of him then, too, with his easy smiles and dirty jokes. And Jude hadn't even known yet, everything that was contained in this infuriating, sweet, impossible boy.

He took a breath and steeled himself. He needed to be sure.

"And if . . . what we have to do tomorrow," he said. "If we weren't doing it. If tonight was just a night like any other. Would you still want this?"

It was painful to consider a world in which they could have

years—decades—together. A future in which tonight was the first night of many and not the last.

Anton took his hand. "If you're asking me if I only want to do this out of guilt or some stupid attempt to comfort you or—or because I'm scared I'll never have it otherwise, the answer is no. I want to do this because I love you. I want you with me, now and always, and if I cannot have always then I will take now."

Jude stopped breathing. There was nothing on earth that he wanted more than to kiss Anton. A heartbeat later he realized there was no reason not to. He surged toward him, cradling him close, kissing him almost frantically.

When he broke away, he could hear both of them breathing in the silence of the pavilion.

"Is that—yes?" Anton asked after a moment.

"Yes," Jude said, punctuating it with another kiss. "Yes."

They knelt on the rug, side by side. Anton took the burning candle, Jude the other. Anton offered the flame, and after a moment Jude let it light his wick.

"I don't actually know what we're supposed to do," Jude confessed. It wasn't as if there'd been any marriage ceremonies in Kerameikos to observe. He'd only heard about them secondhand from other Paladin who hadn't grown up there, and those conversations had been brief, Jude too ashamed of his own curiosity to dig any deeper.

Anton smiled. "We'll just have to make it up, then."

He took the laurel crown and laid it on Jude's head. Jude crowned Anton with the other and let his hands trail down his neck to his shoulders, resting them gently there.

Anton reached for the goblet of wine next, taking a long sip, dark eyes peering at Jude over the rim. He then offered the wine to Jude, who cupped his hands around Anton's and lifted the goblet to his lips. When

Anton placed the goblet back on the table, his eyes looked darker, his gaze piercing.

A new intensity built between them. Anton's hands shook as he dipped his fingers into the silver bowl and brushed the perfumed oil across Jude's brow before touching his own forehead.

"If I could give you forever," Jude whispered, "I would."

Anton kissed his palm. "You are. You will. This is forever, Jude. Right here. Tonight."

Somehow, the twisted path of Jude's life had led him here, to this boy, and whether by fate, chance, choice, or all three he knew he had to hold on to him, to love him, as much as he could for long as he could. Anton was a part of him now, like his hands, like his lungs, like his heart.

Jude closed his eyes as Anton's thumb stroked his temple and then his lower lip.

"Anton," Jude said again, dipping his fingers into the anointing oil and touching it ever so gently against Anton's mouth.

Anton's lips parted, and Jude leaned into him. It was not a kiss so much as the suggestion of one, but it made something deep within him ache as Anton chased another, his lips bitter from the oil.

They separated, and Anton rose to his feet, crossing the pavilion in a few steps before turning back to Jude to offer him his hand.

Jude didn't move for a moment, gazing at Anton. He almost said, *Stop.* Almost said, *One more day. One more night like this. Just one, and that will be enough for me. Let's stay here until the stars burn out and the sky goes dark and this one moment, this one night, will stretch into forever.*

Instead, he took Anton's hand, slotting their fingers together.

One night. Forever.

At the end of the world, what was the difference?

45

BERU

THE PEOPLE OF CHARIS FELL TO THEIR KNEES, BOWING TO THEIR GOD. BEHIND them, the volcanos that ringed the island bellowed out thick black smoke.

The god surveyed them from the top of the Great Steps.

Flames rained from the sky in Tarsepolis. Pallas Athos had been drowned by a river of blood. Endarrion had fallen to plague. And now Charis would be destroyed, crushed beneath a blanket of tar-filled smoke and rivers of molten rock.

THESE VOLCANOES CREATED THIS ISLAND, the god said. JUST AS I CREATED THIS WORLD. BUT NOW THE CREATOR BECOMES THE DESTROYER. IT IS NATURAL, YOU SEE.

Lava cascaded down the side of the mountain, flowing in thick, rippling waves. Beru watched, helpless, as the city disappeared beneath plumes of smoke, obscuring the desperate people as they fled toward the sea, pleading with a god that did not care.

If you don't stop, Beru thought desperately. *There will be nothing left.*

THERE WILL BE ME.

46

HASSAN

THE MORNING DAWNED WITH RAIN.

It beat against the roof of the Great Library as Hassan surveyed his squadron of soldiers in the observatory. Khepri had hand-selected them from the remaining rebel forces, including both Sefu and Chike. To Hassan's surprise, Hector had volunteered to join them.

"I can't sit here doing nothing," he'd said. "And I can't watch Jude sacrifice himself. I need to be useful."

Hassan could understand all too well the frustration of sitting idle. He was grateful that Hector wanted to fight for him—he felt better having his friend at his side.

His mother and the rest of the army had already taken their positions throughout the city. Reclaiming Nazirah would require several coordinated attacks, but the main thrust of their assault would be on the palace itself. They would surround it and force Lethia to draw her soldiers in while the rest of Hassan's mother's army marched on the city. Once they secured Ozmandith Road, Hassan and his squadron would lead the charge into the palace.

The wait was excruciating. Hassan had nothing to do but consider everything that could go wrong. The loss of their Graces was a blow to the rebels. Without the enhanced strength of the Legionnaires, they had lost most of their advantage. Luckily, the explosives and smoke bombs Zareen and her alchemists had created before they lost their Graces would still work. Hassan hoped it would be enough.

As if she could sense his thoughts, Khepri took Hassan's hand.

It was then that they saw it. Red smoke, bright against the gray sky, billowing up from Ozmandith Road.

"It's time," Khepri said to the others.

"Good luck," Ephyra said from the corner of the room. She and Illya would remain in the Library, away from the fighting.

Hassan and his squadron moved swiftly, bracing themselves against the downpour. Khepri led them up the road, where a mile out from the palace gates he could see his mother's soldiers defending the road from Herati footmen.

"We need to get closer," Khepri said, her gaze focused on the far end of Ozmandith Road.

She and the others formed a tight knot around Hassan as they pushed through to the road.

Just a few hundred feet from the gates, a loud boom cracked through the air. Someone shoved Hassan to the ground. Panic flared in his chest as the world spun around him. Dust and debris pelted down.

Hassan's mind went white, his ears ringing. He lay there, pinned and motionless, until he felt Khepri sit up, seizing Hassan by the elbow.

"Are you all right?" she asked, her voice sounding strangely muffled, though she was only inches away.

Hassan sat up in the mud, head swimming. "What happened?"

On his other side, Hector looked up toward the gates. "It looks like your aunt's soldiers have some kind of explosive. Bright white flames."

"Godfire," Hassan said. And, if he had to guess, chrism oil. A trick that Lethia must have learned from him, when he'd toppled the lighthouse.

"Well, whatever it is, it worked," Hector said. "Your mother's soldiers are falling back."

"Lethia knows she's beaten," Hassan said. "This is nothing but a desperate gambit."

"Prince Hassan!" Faran emerged through the fray, mud-splattered and limping.

Hassan leapt to his feet. "Faran!"

"The usurper has barricaded herself in the throne room," he said, stumbling toward them. "But we'll be blown to bits if we try to go through the gate."

"Then we wait her out," Khepri said. "A siege."

And meanwhile their soldiers would go on killing one another until the god arrived and destroyed them all.

"No," Hassan said. "I know Lethia. She'll let every single one of her soldiers die before she surrenders. The only way to end this is to get to her ourselves."

"You mean break into the palace?" Faran asked. "There's no way. We checked all the points of entry. They're all too well defended."

"I might have an idea," Hassan said. "The night that the Witnesses took the palace, there was a guard who snuck me out. We went through the east garden, over the wall. I can get us inside that way."

Faran looked uneasy. "With an entire squadron? It will draw too much attention."

Hassan shook his head. "Not a squadron. Just me."

"No way," Khepri said at once. "You're not going alone. You don't know how many soldiers are inside."

"Lethia won't waste forces within the palace—they'll all be guarding the walls," Hassan said. "Besides, I know my way around the palace better than anyone. I can get to the throne room without being seen."

"And once you're in there?" Khepri asked. "What about the guards who are with Lethia?"

"There won't be any," Hassan replied. "Lethia knows she's lost by now. She wouldn't let anyone see her at her moment of defeat."

"You're still not going alone," Hector said. "Take us, at least. In case you're wrong."

"All right," Hassan agreed. "Hector, Khepri, Sefu, and Chike, you're with me. Faran, find my mother and get word to her. Tell no one else what we're planning."

Faran hesitated a moment and then nodded. "Yes, Your Grace."

A second later, he slipped back through the ranks toward the front lines.

"Let's go," Hassan said, and they sped off in the opposite direction.

Hector, Khepri, and Hassan crouched behind a cypress tree at the edge of the palace walls as Sefu and Chike created a diversion.

They waited several long minutes before they heard shouting from the rampart and the sound of crossbows firing as Chike and Sefu drew the guards away from their posts.

"Now," Khepri barked, and the three of them sprinted across the grass to the towering sandstone ramparts.

The large, rough-hewn bricks made for fairly good handholds as they started to climb. Khepri went first and then Hassan, with Hector bringing up the rear. But the rain had made the wall slippery under their feet.

They were about halfway up when the first crossbow bolt whizzed past Hassan's ear.

"Get down!" he cried, flattening himself against the wall.

He glanced up and saw a lone guardsman with a crossbow, taking aim. Hassan cursed under his breath. They should have made sure the rampart was clear before trying to traverse it.

Above him, Khepri continued to climb, propelling herself up the sandstone bricks with quick, sure movements. The guardsman leaned over the parapet to aim his crossbow down at her.

Khepri cursed, then flung herself wide as the guardsman took aim. She dangled by one hand as the bolt flew past her.

"Khepri!" Hassan yelled, but there was nothing he could do from his position below her.

She swung like a pendulum and caught another toehold, using it to launch herself up to the edge of the rampart. The guardsman fumbled to reload, but Khepri was already there, seizing him by the ankle and hauling herself up and over the parapet. His feet slid out from under him, the crossbow flying out of his hand as he scrabbled for purchase.

Khepri pushed to her feet, kicking the crossbow off the wall and turned to jab her knee into the man's face. With a wheeze, he flopped back onto the wet sandstone. Khepri leapt onto him, pinning him down with a foot at his throat.

"Please," he whimpered. "Don't kill me."

Heart pounding in his throat, Hassan hauled himself up after her. At the top of the rampart, he reached for Hector's hand, helping him up.

"I'm not going to kill you," Khepri told the guard pinned under her foot. "Your side has lost. So you can stay loyal to your defeated usurper or you can cut your losses now. What do you say?"

The man looked terrified. "I won't raise the alarm. Just let me go."

"Good answer," Khepri said, satisfied. She let him up and he scrambled across the rampart.

Hector stared at Khepri in wonder. "I think I might be a little in love with you now?"

Hassan narrowed his eyes at him, but Khepri just laughed.

"How did you even do that without your Grace?" Hector asked as they lowered a rope over the other side of the wall.

"It's called trusting yourself," Khepri replied, knotting the rope. With a glance at Hassan, she added, "And I learned it from the best."

Hassan caught her tender look just before she disappeared down the other side of the rampart. He and Hector followed her down, the rope easing their way.

"Stay on guard," Khepri said as they regrouped at the edge of the garden.

With a sharp nod, she led the way, darting down the walkway, toward an open window that overlooked the garden. Hassan knew exactly where that window led, recalling his escape the night the Hierophant had taken the palace. It was a memory that had often filled him with shame, a reminder that he had fled rather than stood his ground.

"Through here," he said, grabbing hold of the windowsill and hoisting himself up. He toppled through to the other side, knees banging against the hard wood of the library's floor. Khepri and Hector followed much more gracefully.

"Hear anyone?" Hector whispered.

Hassan shook his head. They crept out of the library and into the adjoining corridor. It was ominously empty.

"Which way to the throne room?" Hector asked.

Hassan led the way through the halls and up the stairs. As they approached the interior entrance to the throne room, they saw the first sign of a guard presence inside the palace. Six of them, posted along the hallway.

"Hassan," Khepri said warningly as her hand went to the sword at her belt.

Just beyond the guards, Hassan could see the doors to the throne room.

He turned to Khepri. "Can you two hold them off?"

She briefly hesitated and then nodded.

"I'm going in alone," he said. "Just keep the guards from entering."

Khepri stared at him, a fierce look in her eyes, and then moved forward, kissing him briefly. "Fix this, Hassan," she said against his lips. "I believe in you."

Without another word, she spun away and mounted the stairs with Hector, bolting toward the guards.

Hassan waited until he heard the sound of clashing swords and then followed. Khepri had half the guards engaged in a melee, Hector the other half. As Hassan sprinted up the stairs, he heard the guards calling attention to him, but he just tucked his head low and kept running, trusting that Hector and Khepri could keep them at bay.

They had cleared a path to the door, and Hassan charged at it with all his strength.

The moment he reached it, though, he hesitated. He knew what lay on the other side. Lethia, the throne. The chance, at last, to seize his rightful place as king.

This time, he would not fail.

47

ANTON

THE SEA BATTERED THE BARREN ROCK WHERE THE LIGHTHOUSE HAD ONCE stood. The wind was ferocious today, the surf swollen with rain.

Anton hadn't slept at all the night before. He'd barely closed his eyes. Jude had drifted off for an hour or so, tucked beside Anton, his body warm, his heartbeat steady under Anton's palm. Anton had thought about the first night they'd spent together like this, Jude's sweet, awkward inexperience yielding to eager confidence with every encouragement.

I found you. That means I get to keep you, Jude had said.

It isn't fair, Anton thought. *I should get to keep you, too.*

He had held Jude's hand all the way from the palace, and he didn't let go as they stood at the perimeter of the lighthouse ruins, facing the sea. It was strange to recall that he and Jude had been on the tower itself when it fell. That they had crashed down with it, together.

Jude pulled Anton into his arms, shielding him from the wind. He kissed him as the gale howled over them.

When he drew back, Anton didn't let him go far, kissing him again, cheeks wet with tears.

"We have to do it now," Jude murmured. "Or I don't think I'll have the strength to do it at all."

He pressed another kiss to Anton's cheek and closed his eyes.

Anton breathed in and felt the echoes of Jude's *esha* crash over him. It overwhelmed him for a moment, pulling at some deep, central part of him. Jude's pulse thumped against Anton's thumb with vital, precious life.

Anton cradled Jude's face with one hand and bowed their foreheads together, a sob rising in his chest. He choked it back.

He breathed in and sent his Grace rippling out, latching onto Jude's *esha*, delving into each vibration. Searching for the power he'd sensed from the very beginning, though he hadn't recognized what it was, then.

The Sacred Word. He could feel it, pulsing inside the cocoon of Jude's *esha*. To unleash it, Anton had to use his Grace to unravel Jude's *esha*, release it back into the world.

I love you, he thought helplessly. *I'm sorry. I love you.*

It was a plea. A promise. It was the raging drum of his heart against a merciless god. It was every fear and hope, every wound and tender touch, crying out at once. It was the very core of him, stripped down and laid bare. It was truth and dream and the delicate place where one became the other. It was Jude's hands on him, his sweet, cherished smile, every beloved line of his body pressed to his.

Anton's Grace touched the tight spool of Jude's *esha* and was met with resistance. Jude's *esha* pulled taut around the Sacred Word. It did not want to let go. *Jude* did not want to let go.

And Anton didn't want to let *him* go.

But he had to. Had to tear apart the sacred energy of the boy he loved, piece by agonizing piece. This was what they had decided. This was what they had chosen. Even if some deeply rooted part of Jude fought against it.

Sobs wrenched from Anton's chest as his Grace pulled on a thread of Jude's *esha*. It raged back at him like a storm. And in the tempest, Anton saw him. Saw *them*. Kneeling in a garden, Anton threw a handful of dirt onto Jude before Jude fought back, tackling him to the ground. Standing in a crowd, Jude's arm wrapped around his shoulders, their faces craned toward the night sky as colorful lights exploded and the crowd cheered around them. Jude, older than he was now, his face lean and lined, pressing a kiss to Anton's forehead as he slept.

None of these things had happened before, not even in the dreams Anton had walked into.

What is this? he wanted to scream. His mind's last attempt to torture him. A dream of a life he'd never have. Another vision that would haunt him until the end of his days.

48

HASSAN

THE DOOR SLAMMED SHUT BEHIND HASSAN.

He hovered at the edge of the silent throne room, a hushed stillness coming over him in the wake of the chaos of the battle that raged on outside.

"I was hoping you'd get here soon." His aunt's voice echoed off the cavernous walls.

She sat with her light green kaftan pulled up to her knees, feet resting in the tiled pool below the throne and the pyramid on which it perched. Her hair was loose, unbound. One hand was wrapped loosely around a jug of wine.

"Drink, nephew?" she said, offering it to him.

Hassan crossed the room toward her. "It's over, Lethia. We both know it. My mother's army is outside your gates, and your forces are no match for them."

"Hmm," she replied.

"Do you have anything you want to say?"

"Are you going to kill me, Hassan?" she asked, overenunciating the words in a way that made it clear she had drunk most of the wine.

"Will I have to?" he asked. "Or will you surrender and bring an end to this?"

He already knew the answer. He had come here hoping for a different one.

"I thought your father would accept his defeat," Lethia mused. "Go quietly and give up the throne. I was wrong about that. Do you know what he said, before they cut his head off?"

Hassan's hand twitched at his side. He did want to know—he wanted to know so badly his heart seized with it. But he didn't know if he could stand to hear his father's last words from the mouth of his murderer.

"He said, 'you may take the throne from me, but Hassan is Herat's destiny,'" Lethia said. "*Destiny*. I always hated that word. There are no great destinies for people like me, so I made my own. Who of your beloved kings and emperors can say the same? Everything they had was given to them—I had to take it."

"And you didn't care who you had to hurt to do it," Hassan said. "As long as you had the power you longed for. It's no wonder you and Pallas worked so well together."

"Pallas," Lethia spat. "Well, I knew not to trust him. After what he did to the other Prophets."

"You knew about that?" Hassan asked sharply.

Lethia turned to him, raising an eyebrow. "You think I didn't learn everything there was to know about the man who called himself the Hierophant before I agreed to help him? I sought out his darkest secrets, so that if I ever needed to, I could use them against him. Of course, it seems that was taken care of for me."

"Lucky you."

"It didn't surprise me to learn he had killed the other Prophets," Lethia said. "I only had to speak to him once before I knew that he was a man who didn't like to share power. I was careful never to seem like I was undermining him the way the Prophets tried to."

"You mean because they wanted to stop him from taking the god's *esha*," Hassan said.

"He certainly didn't like that," Lethia said. "But that isn't why he killed them."

"Then why?" Hassan asked, and immediately regretted it. Lethia looked almost amused. She had drawn him in. Teased information that he wanted to have. Was she stalling? Bargaining? Or simply toying with him, as she was so fond of doing?

She lifted her feet from the water and let her kaftan fall back to her ankles, stepping toward Hassan, leaving a wet puddle in her wake.

"Do you really want to know?"

He hesitated.

"I'll tell you," she said. "The other Prophets had figured out something that Pallas didn't want them to know. A plan that Pallas found so detestable, he killed them before they could succeed."

Her words scratched at Hassan's memory. Of Pallas, right before his death, saying, *The other Prophets feared my plan, but theirs was destined to fail.*

"They were trying to create more Prophets," Lethia said, watching Hassan's face carefully as the impact of her words landed.

"What?" Hassan asked, his voice barely a whisper. "You're lying."

"Why would I?" she asked. "It makes sense, doesn't it? Nothing would threaten Pallas's power more than the possibility that there would be others to take his place. It was the ultimate betrayal to him. So they had to die."

Hassan's mind reeled. "Why are you telling me this?"

"Consider it my parting gift."

And before Hassan knew what was happening, she drew the sword from his belt.

Hassan took a wavering step back, arms up. "What are you doing?"

"I won't let them make me a prisoner," she said.

Hassan stood frozen.

"Goodbye, Hassan."

She plunged the sword through her chest. Hassan watched in horror as her kaftan turned dark with blood and she swayed back one, two steps before she collapsed into the pool of water.

"No!" Hassan cried, diving toward her.

But it was too late. Blood dribbled from her mouth and poured from her chest, clouding the water pink. She gasped, choking on blood as Hassan took hold of her bony body, trying futilely to staunch the wound.

"No, no, no," Hassan pleaded, a sob rising in his throat.

Her body convulsed in his arms. Her eyes went vacant. And then she was still.

Hassan didn't know how long he sat there, half submerged in the water, before the doors of the throne room burst opened and Hector and Khepri rushed inside.

"Hassan!" Khepri screamed. She froze as she spotted him, and then sprinted over to him, pulling him out of the water, away from Lethia's body.

"I'm all right," Hassan said.

Hector looked skeptical. "You're covered in blood."

"It's not mine," he assured them. "Lethia, she . . ."

Khepri hugged him tight against her and only then did Hassan realize he was sobbing.

"It's all right," she soothed. "It's over. It's over. Herat is free."

Lethia's words came rushing back to him, shoving past the horror and shock of her death. Hassan gripped Khepri's shoulders.

"We have to go," he said. "Right now."

"Sefu and Chike have already gone to signal that the throne has been captured," Khepri said. "The fighting will end soon."

"No," Hassan said. "Not that. Lethia told me something before she died. We need to get to Jude and Anton before—"

A great roar drowned out Hassan's words as the entire throne room shook violently.

"What's happening?" Khepri yelled.

A crack as loud as thunder boomed as the roof of the throne room tore clean off the walls. Khepri shoved Hassan to the ground as chunks of rock crashed down around them.

"I think," Hector said, shouting above the howl of wind and falling debris, "the god is here."

Dazed, Hassan stared up at the sky. It was no longer gray and heavy with clouds—it was blood red.

Another deafening crack split the air. The sky flickered, and rain pelted down on Hassan's face.

"We have to move," Khepri shouted, hauling Hassan to his feet and bolting toward the great double doors that opened out into the palace's front steps, Hector at their heels.

They slammed through the doors and onto the portico that over-looked the central courtyard. Beyond it lay the destroyed gates and Ozmandith Road, flooded with rain and littered with bodies and debris.

Hassan couldn't see the god, but there were signs of its arrival everywhere he looked. Smoke rising from the Artificers' Quarter. Whole blocks completely leveled by the god's power, market squares and stadiums reduced to piles of sandstone.

It was like Behezda all over again. Except this time, it was *Hassan's* city the god was destroying.

A slash of silver light forked through the sky, startling Hassan from his horror and spurring him back to action.

"Come on!" he yelled to Khepri and Hector, sprinting down the steps. They could cut through the central courtyard and exit through the south gates, which would put them in striking distance from the lighthouse ruins. They could get to Jude and Anton.

He just hoped they wouldn't be too late.

A bolt of lightning whipped down from the sky, cracking one of the pillars that lined the steps.

"*Hassan!*" Khepri's terrified voice shrieked.

It was the last sound he heard as the pillar came crashing toward him.

49

EPHYRA

EPHYRA WASN'T USED TO WAITING. THAT HAD ALWAYS BEEN BERU'S JOB—countless nights waiting for Ephyra to return from a kill, not knowing whether she'd come back hurt. Whether she'd come back at all.

Ephyra had never realized how excruciating those nights must have been for Beru. Not until she found herself in the same position—except now, Ephyra couldn't hope that Beru would return to her. Because if Jude and Anton succeeded, then Beru would die. And Ephyra would have to figure out how to go on.

Illya had kept the promise he'd made the night before. He'd stayed at her side all through the morning, as the storm outside the Great Library raged harder with every passing minute. Occasionally, soldiers arrived carting their wounded and fallen comrades. Ephyra watched them hurrying through the corridors, but without her Grace there was little she could do to help any of them.

The storm outside reached a crescendo some two hours after Hassan and the others had left. Thunder boomed through the sky, so loud and persistent that at first Ephyra thought it was the sound of

Zareen's explosives, echoing all the way from the palace. But a glance out the atrium window showed a blood-red sky and blinding, silver bolts of lightning crackling through it.

The doors of the atrium burst open, and a cascade of hail and wind followed two figures inside.

It was Sefu and Chike, Khepri's brothers.

"What's going on out there?" Illya asked, hurrying toward them.

"The fighting's over," Sefu said. "But the storm—"

"She's here," Ephyra said. The god had arrived in Nazirah. The end was coming.

"It attacked the palace," Chike said. "Ripped the roof clean off. Khepri, Hassan, and Hector were inside. We don't know what happened to them."

Ephyra was halfway to the door before she even registered she'd started moving.

"Where are you going?" Illya called after her, jogging to keep up.

"We can't just stay here," she said. "We have to help find them."

Illya reached for her wrist, pulling her back to him. He didn't say anything, just studied her face, his golden eyes dark with concern. She knew what he was thinking—that if the god was at the palace, Ephyra wouldn't be able to handle seeing it. Seeing *her*.

Then he blinked, steeling himself, and nodded. "All right. Let's go."

The storm outside was worse than any Ephyra had ever seen. The streets were more like rivers, almost knee-deep with water and crowded with debris. Lightning sizzled through the sky, flickering and flashing around them, the thunder so loud it sounded like planets colliding. The rain that had been falling steadily since morning had frozen into hailstones the size of fists, striking hard enough to break roof tiles and bruise skin.

Wind buffeted them as they waded toward the palace, moving slowly beneath the arcaded walkway alongside Ozmandith Road. The closer they got to the palace gates, the more signs of battle and destruction they saw. Soldiers from both sides of the battle scrambled to find cover from the hail and wind.

When the palace gates finally came into view, Ephyra bit back a gasp of horror. The walls had been completely ripped apart, sandstone and twisted metal forming a dam against the water rushing toward the palace.

"What do we do?" Illya called over the wind.

Ephyra pushed ahead of the others, scanning the ruins of the gate. It would be tricky, but she could climb up, and hopefully spot Hassan and the others from a higher vantage point.

"I'm going up there," she told Sefu, and before any of them could object, she stepped out from beneath the arcade and swung herself up to the first stable foothold she could find. One wrong move could potentially collapse the entire wall, so Ephyra was focused, methodical as she made her way up. She felt a ruthless calm come over her, the same mindset she'd sunk into night after night as the Pale Hand.

Her hands were past numb by the time she reached the top of the wall—or what was left of it—and gazed out across a courtyard, now scattered with broken pillars and crumbled arches. And there, on the far side of the courtyard at the bottom of a grand set of stairs, Ephyra saw them. Two figures, crouched beside an overturned pillar.

"I see them!" Ephyra called down to Illya, Sefu, and Chike.

There was a gap in the rubble about a hundred paces down from where Ephyra perched. The water flowed twice as fast through it, making any potential crossing a risk. Sefu led the way, clinging tightly to the uneven sandstone as he fought against being swept up by the current. Chike followed, with Illya unsteadily bringing up the rear.

Halfway through the gap, Illya lost his grip and the current swiftly caught hold of him, dragging him below the surface.

"*Illya!*" Ephyra cried, her heart leaping into her throat. She scaled down the craggy wall toward him.

Chike was faster, grabbing Illya's arm before the water ripped him away. Ephyra skidded down the side of the wall, plunging her hand into the cold water to help Chike pull Illya back to the surface.

He emerged, spluttering like a drowned cat, and Ephyra didn't let go of his arm even after he'd regained his hold.

"You're shaking," he said.

They were both soaked from the rain and the freezing river of water, but that wasn't why she was trembling.

Ephyra released his arm and climbed down the other side of the wall and into the flooded courtyard. The water was nearly up to Ephyra's waist here, forcing her to half wade and half swim to the palace steps.

"Khepri!" Ephyra hollered when they were near enough.

Khepri emerged from behind the collapsed pillar, Hector beside her.

"Ephyra? Sefu? What are you—?"

"Is she here?" Ephyra asked, climbing out of the water and onto the steps. "Beru—the god. Is she here?"

"She was," Hector replied. "We didn't see her, but she ripped apart half the palace and then must've moved on to another part of the city."

"You have to help," Khepri said frantically. "Please—It's Hassan. He's trapped underneath the pillar. We don't know if he's—" She cut herself off with a ragged breath.

"What do you need us to do?" Chike asked.

"I can almost reach him," Khepri replied. "I need your help to shift this."

The pillar she pointed to was wedged against the plinth at the bottom of the steps. With enough force, they could use the plinth as a sort of fulcrum to lift the pillar away and let Khepri crawl beneath.

The five of them lined up, pressing their backs against the pillar and bracing their feet against the steps for more leverage.

On Khepri's count of three, they pushed as hard they could against the pillar. Slowly, it started to shift.

"Almost there!" Khepri called from below.

Ephyra's muscles strained. Her legs trembled. If she let go now, the pillar would crash back down on not only Hassan, but Khepri, too. She sucked in a breath, gritting her teeth.

"We're clear!" Khepri's voice cried, just as Ephyra thought her strength would give out.

Ephyra relaxed, collapsing against the pillar as it teetered back to its original position. Khepri stooped over Hassan's crumpled form, cradling his face in her hands.

Ephyra crawled toward them, choked by panic as she took in Hassan's still face, and the sound of Khepri's broken voice as she repeated his name over and over.

Ephyra remembered healing Hassan after the god had taken over Beru. She wished there was something, anything, she could do now.

"Khepri," Hector said quietly, stilling her with a touch to the arm.

Khepri's eyes found his, her desperation clear and so familiar to Ephyra. "No," she said. "No, he's not . . ."

Hector put an arm around her, tucking her close to his side. Ephyra's chest seized. Silence hung thick in the air despite the storm that raged around them.

Ephyra bowed her head. She couldn't stand to look at Hassan's still face. He didn't deserve this. And Khepri—she didn't deserve the grief she would now have to live with.

Illya's hand fell to her shoulder, and unthinkingly, Ephyra took it, holding tight.

"Wait," Illya said softly. Ephyra looked up at him and saw his gaze was pinned on Hassan. He crouched at the prince's side, fingers finding his pulse. "Khepri—"

She whipped back around.

Hassan coughed, wheezed. His eyes flew open.

"Hassan!" Khepri cried, tears springing to her eyes as she threw herself toward him, shoving Illya out of the way.

Ephyra sagged with relief, balling her hands into fists.

"What . . ." Hassan seemed to struggle for a moment, his eyes darting around to take in the scene. Then he bolted upright, nearly ramming his head into Khepri.

"Whoa, easy," Hector advised, approaching from his other side. "Take a moment and just—"

"What happened?" Hassan demanded. "Is the god dead? Did they kill it already?"

As though in response to his question, the sky roared with thunder.

"Good," Hassan said.

"Good?" Illya echoed. "How is the god still being alive *good?*"

"We need to go, right now," Hassan said, trying to struggle to his feet despite Khepri's and Hector's protests. "There's no time. Sefu, Chike, go find my mother and Zareen. Make sure they're safe."

With a nod of understanding, they waded back toward Ozmandith Road.

"The rest of you, come with me," Hassan said. "I'll explain on the way, but we need to find Anton and Jude, *now.*"

Thunder boomed across the sky, so loud it rattled Ephyra's bones.

"All right," she said, before any of the others could speak. "Then let's go."

With the howl of the wind in their ears and the destruction of Nazirah at their backs, they ran.

50

JUDE

ANTON'S GRACE THRUMMED ALL AROUND JUDE. HE HADN'T FELT IT THIS strongly since that day in the lighthouse—in the place they stood now—when Anton's Grace had first called out to him.

But it wasn't Jude that Anton was calling to now. It was this power, this ancient thing inside of him. The Sacred Word. Coaxing it, little by little, from where it hid within Jude's *esha*.

The storm raged around them, as merciless and unyielding as the power that cleaved from Jude's *esha*.

It *hurt*. It was not the scorching pain of Godfire, but something deeper, more visceral. Every part of Jude, his bones and his skin and his blood, vibrated at a different frequency. He feared he would eventually come apart, his body trembling into dust, into nothing.

And through it all, Jude felt Anton's hands clenched in his own, like if he could hold on tight enough, Jude would stay.

It's all I want, Jude thought desperately.

It would kill Anton to do this. Jude had tried to spare him that pain, at least. He'd failed at that, too.

And now, here, this was the end. The path had run out. And Jude couldn't let go.

In spite of his decision, in spite of everything, he wanted to live. Some deep, central part of himself resisted the call of Anton's Grace. It fought against the Sacred Word. It fought to keep living.

"*Stop!*"

At first, Jude thought he imagined the voice calling out. That it was just a manifestation of his own heart, crying out for deliverance.

But then he heard it again.

"Stop!"

Instinctively, Jude stumbled back, his eyes blinking open to find Anton's face staring at him, shock lighting his dark eyes, his cheeks wet with tears and rain. The silver-forked sky lit up around them.

"Jude! Anton!"

Jude startled at the sound of more than one voice calling out to them. And there, over Anton's shoulder, through the sheets of falling rain, Jude caught sight of them. Hassan, Khepri, Hector, Ephyra, and Illya all sprinted toward them, waving their arms and shouting across the barren rock.

But before Jude could make sense of their presence, Anton let out a choked sob and collapsed to his knees.

"Anton!" Jude crouched beside him, hands hovering over his shoulders.

Anton just shook his head, trembling. "I'm sorry. I'm sorry, Jude, I'm so sorry."

Hassan skidded to a stop, doubling over in front of them with his hands on his knees as Khepri slowed beside him.

Jude reached for Hassan instinctively. "Prince Hassan, what—"

"You don't have to do this," Hassan huffed. "You don't have to sacrifice yourself. There's another way."

Everything seemed to freeze for a moment. Jude could only hear the wind, howling around them, echoing the rush of blood in his ears.

And then Anton launched to his feet, seizing Hassan with both hands.

"Tell me," he said, his voice full of steel.

"Lethia," Hassan said at once. "She knew that Pallas killed the Prophets. And she knew why. Pallas wanted to stop the Prophets from creating more of them. More Prophets."

"You mean . . ." Anton trailed off, his grip going slack. "You mean *I* could make more Prophets?"

Hassan nodded. "It took Seven Prophets to defeat the god." He spread his arms as thunder shook the sky. "*We* can defeat the god."

Jude swept his gaze over the seven of them, understanding, at once, what Hassan wanted them all to do. His chest felt tight.

"How do you know Lethia wasn't lying?" he asked. "And even if it is the truth, how do we know that it's possible to create more Prophets? Maybe they failed. Or maybe—"

"If there's a chance," Hassan said fervently. "If there's a hope. We *have* to try."

Hassan didn't understand. They *had* tried. They had held fast to hope. And every time, they'd watched as it was trampled underfoot. Every time, Jude's fate became more painful to accept.

Now they stood at the brink of the end of the world, and no matter how hard they tried, no matter how much they hoped, they couldn't deny destiny.

"It's too late," Jude heard himself say in a hollow voice.

Hector's expression flashed with anger. Ephyra and Illya hesitated a few feet behind him.

Lightning struck down into the sea in a violent burst.

"The god is already here," Jude said in a stronger voice. "And the longer we delay, the more people will suffer. We don't even know how to do what you're suggesting."

"But I can find out," Anton said quietly. His eyes were on Jude, dark and full of challenge. "The Wanderer showed me how to scry into the past. Maybe I can see what they tried to do. And maybe I can finish what they started. *We* can finish what they started. But only if—only if you're all willing."

He looked around at the others.

"No one ever asked me," Anton said. "No one gave me a choice. So I'm asking you. All of you. You get to choose."

Everyone was silent for a long moment.

Hector was the first to speak. "Of course my answer is yes."

"So's mine," Khepri said.

Hassan nodded. "Me too."

"None of this would be happening if it wasn't for me," Ephyra said. "So if I can save one person—if I can help save Jude, then I'm in."

Anton looked at Illya.

"You told me to stop trying to redeem myself in your eyes," Illya said. "So don't take this as an attempt to earn your forgiveness. But yes, sure, why not? Let's save the world."

"Thank you," Anton said. He looked at Jude. "It's your choice, too, Jude. I won't do this if you don't agree."

Jude couldn't speak for a moment. He wanted, more than anything, to say yes. But he didn't want the others to put themselves in danger for him. Didn't want Anton to risk himself more than he already was.

"We can't," he said, his voice breaking. He sounded desperate. He sounded like he was *asking*. "We—"

"I had a vision," Anton said abruptly. "Or . . . I think it was vision. I saw . . . I saw *you*. And me. Under the stars, in a garden . . . together. I saw the life we could've had."

It felt like Anton had reached inside Jude's chest and tore out his heart. He could only stare at Anton. He wanted to know everything he'd seen.

And he knew that if he did, it would destroy him.

Anton was trembling, his lips pale blue from the cold rain that fell around them. "What if it was real? What if it was our future?"

"It wasn't," Jude said, too sharply. "You know that. You know we don't have a—a future."

Jude's heart pounded, that same innermost part of himself warring against his words. It was a part of him that was deeper than thought, deeper than emotion. It was pure will.

Anton reached for him, laying a cold palm against Jude's cheek. "But what if we could?"

His gaze held on Jude's, and Jude felt it reach behind his ribs and brush against the tender thing that beat within his chest. Jude stared back, transfixed by those eyes, that face, the sprinkle of freckles across the bridge of his nose, so dear to Jude, his heart's true north.

Bet on me, Anton had said once.

He remembered standing on the parapet of the lighthouse as it fell. Remembered leaping after Anton. Remembered kissing him above the river in Endarrion. Remembered taking his hand and slipping away from the Paladin Guard.

He took Anton's hand once again, moving it from his face and drawing the soft underside of Anton's wrist to his lips. Anton's answering smile was like the rising sun.

It was simple. It always had been.

There was no place Anton could go that Jude would not follow.

51

ANTON

ANTON STOOD ON THE RUINS OF THE LIGHTHOUSE, THE ORACLE STONE CLUTCHED between his hands. The last time he had scried into the past, he'd been guided by the Wanderer.

Now, he had only himself.

He reached for his Grace, closing his eyes. He breathed in and as he exhaled, he sent his Grace rippling out, spooling through the complex array of *esha* that flowed through the world. Searching. Following. He held the memory of the other Prophets' *esha*, how it had rung through the Circle of Stones, and let it carry him.

He held their names in his mind. Tarseis. Behezda. Nazirah. Endarra. Keric.

His Grace called out.

And something answered.

Anton opened his eyes in the center of a familiar circular stone platform. Five figures surrounded him. Anton recognized them instantly from the first time he had scried into the past. When he'd watched them slay the god.

The Prophets.

But unlike that time, they were all looking directly at him.

"Good," Behezda said, tossing her thick mane of dark curls. "We were wondering when exactly you'd show up."

Anton was so startled that he almost fell over. He glanced around, just to be sure Behezda wasn't speaking to someone else. But there was no one there. She was talking to *him*. *Looking* at him.

At her left, Keric beamed. The scruff on his chin aged him, but his eyes were young and bright. Something about them made Anton want to trust him. "Welcome!"

"What . . ." Anton didn't know where to begin. Finally he said, "Is this a vision?"

"Not exactly," Nazirah said. "You're scrying into the past right now."

"I know that," Anton said. "But how are you *talking* to me? I've scried into your past before, and it wasn't like this."

"Well," Tarseis said, his face stern as he primly adjusted the sleeves of his dark robes. "As you are scrying into the past, we are scrying into our future. We have been trying to do so for some time."

Nazirah stepped toward them, towering over tiny Behezda, her long, dark hair streaked with gray. "We have reason to believe we might be killed before we can speak to you in person. We have a message for you, and now that Pallas has turned on us, the Order can't be trusted with it."

"Then why can't you tell the Wanderer?" Anton asked. The others looked confused. "She's still alive, in your time. She—she tried to help me."

"If we could find the Wanderer, then we would," Endarra said. She looked rueful, her ethereally beautiful face lined with regret. "But we lost her trust years ago. I doubt she would help us now, even if we could find her."

"Why . . ." Anton trailed off. "Why *now*? If you've been trying to scry into the future for some time, then why did it work now?"

The Prophets exchanged looks.

"We don't know exactly," Behezda said gently. "You were the one who called out to us. You asked for *our* help."

"So tell us, young Prophet, how can we aid you?" Keric asked.

Anton swallowed. "The god is back. It's here to unmake the world. The only way to stop it is to do what you did last time—use the Sacred Word to kill it."

"If you know all that, then surely you must know we hid the Sacred Word in the Keeper," Nazirah said gently.

"Yes," Anton said. "And unleashing it will kill him. But there's another way. *You* found another way. Show me how to create more Prophets, and we can make a new Sacred Word."

"You were meant to be the Last Prophet," Tarseis said, his voice cold. "That is what was written in the final prophecy."

Anton blinked away tears. From the moment he'd had the vision of the end of the world, he'd understood how lonely it would make his life. The Last Prophet. The only Prophet. But just because his fate had been written that way didn't mean he had to accept it.

It had started with Jude, beside him on the lighthouse. But it hadn't ended there. Then there had been Hector, helping to pull him from the wreckage of the Red Gate even before he knew who Anton was. Hassan, who'd had good reason to resent Anton, but had joined him instead. Khepri, who had gone with them to the edge of the world when there were countless reasons for her to stay behind. Ephyra, who like

Anton had learned not to trust anything that came without a price, and yet who time and again had risked herself for Anton and those he cared about. Even Illya, whom Anton hadn't forgiven and might never forgive, yet who had handed his fate over to Anton anyway.

And Beru, who among everyone Anton had ever met always seemed to know how to do the right thing, and never hesitated to do it. Who had fought harder than any of them for a world that she would never get to fully live in.

"I don't care what the prophecy says," Anton said fiercely. "I don't care about destiny, about fate, or any of it. I care about stopping the god. I care about saving Jude."

Tarseis clucked his tongue. "This is why we hold ourselves apart. Why we don't take lovers or have children. When your fate is tangled with the fates of others, when you have the power that we do, you will always be tempted to change destiny."

Nazirah looked at Anton thoughtfully. "You were meant to have two choices. You could watch the world fall. Or you could sacrifice that which you love to save it."

"I don't understand," Anton said. "This was what you were trying to do, wasn't it? Make more Prophets to replace you after your powers stopped working? So why won't you help me?"

"What we did followed the lines of fate," Tarseis replied sharply. "We fulfilled our final prophecy."

"What—you mean *me?*"

"You were meant to be the Last Prophet," Tarseis said again. "And so we made you the Last Prophet."

"You . . ." Anton's voice faltered. "You made me into a Prophet?"

Nazirah nodded.

"Then you can do it," Anton realized, brushing past the rest of this strange realization. "You can make more Prophets."

"Not without defying fate."

"Then defy it!" Anton demanded. "What's stopping you?"

"For two thousand years, we were careful never to step outside the bounds of our prophecies," Nazirah said. "Never to change their outcomes."

"What Nazirah means to say," Keric cut in, "is that if you do this, you will shatter the pathways of fate and destiny for good. There will be no more prophecies. No more visions of the future. Your new Prophets will have all the power that we have now—that is to say, the powers of the Grace of Sight. The power to create the Sacred Word. But not the power to see the shape of fate. You will be blind to the future."

"Good," Anton said firmly. "We'll find our own way. We'll make our own choices. If that is the price of saving the world and the boy I love, I will gladly pay it."

"We spent two thousand years denying our humanity," Tarseis said brusquely. "And you refuse to follow in our footsteps. At the end of the world you come to us and you ask for what? Love?"

Anton didn't hesitate. "Yes."

Endarra considered him carefully. "You have never asked for it before."

"I didn't know how."

"But it is what you want?"

"Yes," Anton said again.

"That was what Ananke wanted, too," Behezda said quietly. There was grief on her round face. "I have always regretted that we took it from her."

"Perhaps . . ." Nazirah said thoughtfully. "We've been wrong all along. Perhaps keeping ourselves apart from the world was a mistake, if it has led the world here. Perhaps you have the right of it." She turned to the others. "I say we do as the young Prophet asks."

Anton's heart lifted.

He stared at Tarseis. The Prophet of Justice seemed by far the most reticent.

"We gave you this power," Tarseis said at last. "I suppose that means it's up to you to decide how to wield it."

Relief swelled inside Anton. "What do we do?"

"The first Graced people were not born, but made," Keric said. "We bestowed it on them with the Relics."

"The Sacrificed Queen," Behezda said. "The Keeper of the Word."

"The first King of Herat," Nazirah said.

"But of course, our powers didn't originate with the Relics," Tarseis said. "We got them from the god. It chose us. And so we can choose others."

"You mean you can give your own Graces to someone else?" Anton asked. "But . . . you're all already dead. At least, in my time you are."

Nazirah gave him a rueful smile. She spread her arms. "This place, like the Circle of Stones in Kerameikos, is a particular conduit of *esha*. We built these monoliths such that when we died, our *esha* would remain locked here. Preserved, so it could be accessed by another Prophet. By you."

"That's why I felt it," Anton realized. "When the Wanderer and I scried for you in the Circle of Stones. It led me here. To your *esha*."

"So it worked," Nazirah said with satisfaction. "I assume you have the Relic of Sight?"

Anton lifted the Stone, warm in his palm, and held it out to her. She touched it reverently, closing her eyes.

The Stone began to glow, and Anton felt a surge of power, like the ringing of the Circle of Stones, wash over him. Nazirah stepped away, her arm dropping to her side, but the ringing didn't cease. Endarra was next, smiling at Anton and cupping her hand over the Stone to add her own power. The ringing grew louder, brighter, more layered. Keric followed, giving Anton a conspiratorial wink before he added his. Tarseis gave Keric a vaguely disapproving look before following.

Behezda was last, adding her own power to the harmony. When she was done, and the thread of her Grace had joined the others, she leaned toward Anton and placed a kiss on his forehead.

"Go," she said. "Go and see it done."

52

JUDE

LIGHTNING SPLIT THE SKY AS ANTON COLLAPSED. JUDE DOVE TOWARD HIM, bracing his fall.

Anton's eyes fluttered open. His grip tightened around the glowing Oracle Stone.

"What happened?" Jude asked.

Anton reached up to touch his face, his expression dazed.

"Did you see them?" Hector asked from behind them.

"I spoke to them," Anton said softly as Jude helped him sit up.

"To the *Prophets*?" Hassan asked.

Anton held up the glowing Oracle Stone. "They gave me their power. They gave *us* their power."

Jude opened his mouth to ask one of the thousand questions running through his mind. Questions like *How?* And *What did they say?* But what came out was, "So it's really possible? You can make us into Prophets?"

Anton nodded.

"Well," Hassan said grimly. "Let's not waste any more time. What do we need to do?"

"Just stay where you are," Anton replied. "I can—"

"Wait," Jude said sharply, grabbing Anton's wrist. "Let me go first. It should be me taking the risk. If something goes wrong, you can still unleash the Sacred Word."

Anton looked like he wanted to argue, but instead he met Jude's gaze and nodded. His eyes closed again and Jude let go of his wrist. He watched as Anton breathed in deeply and then, on the exhale, the Oracle Stone glowed brighter. Anton held the Stone in one hand, and with the other seemed to pull out a thread of light. Not light—Grace. Jude heard a faint ringing sound, and as Anton touched his palm to Jude's chest, it grew louder, until it blocked out all other sound except the beating of Jude's own heart.

Light shattered the air around Jude like an explosion. Jude fell to his knees as it enveloped him. The first brush of it against his *esha* left Jude gasping. The Grace burned through him. It felt almost like Godfire flames, except it was the opposite. Where Godfire had hollowed him out, this Grace filled him, like water bursting from a dam.

"*Jude!*"

Anton clutched at him, but it was too late. The Prophets' Grace was inside him, pulsing like a star, and Jude could only hold on and hope it didn't consume him. For a moment, it overwhelmed him—he couldn't see, couldn't hear, couldn't feel anything except the Grace as it reverberated through him.

And then just when Jude thought it would break him apart, the world bloomed into focus. Suddenly he could feel *everything*—the soft waves of Anton's *esha* near him, like wind blowing through grass, the distinct *esha* of each of the others, and an awareness of how they all fit, the connections and intricate patterns that bound the world together.

Jude opened his eyes to find Anton staring at him with an expression of utter terror.

"I'm all right," Jude said at once, laying his hand on Anton's cheek. The pure, physical sensation of it shocked him. Everything felt sharper, louder, and more harmonious at the same time. "Is this what it's like for you all the time?"

The terror bled away from Anton's face as he let out a breath and leaned into Jude's touch.

"Did it work?" he heard Hector ask from behind him.

Jude turned to face him. "I can feel your *esha*. It's like . . . steel and stone."

Hector gave him a confused look.

"That looked . . . painful," Illya said hesitantly.

"It was . . ." Jude trailed off. It was like nothing he'd ever felt. It was transcendent.

"If anyone's planning to back out, now is the time," Anton warned.

None of the others moved to leave.

"All right," Anton said, closing his eyes. "Stand still. And try not to panic."

This time, Jude was able to watch as Anton pulled five more threads of power from the Relic of Sight and sent them spiraling toward the others. Grace swirled around them, and now Jude could feel exactly what it was doing—weaving through the others' *esha* until Grace and *esha* coalesced as one.

In Anton's hands, the Relic of Sight broke apart as light poured out.

The others all fell to their knees, just as Jude had. Ephyra let out a sharp cry, Hector a pained groan. Illya seemed on the brink of tears.

But then, the pain seemed to subside. They opened their eyes and climbed to their feet, looking amazed and perplexed by their new sense of the world. As the others recovered themselves, Jude realized that Anton was shaking, breathing hard.

On instinct, he tucked himself against Anton's side. "Are you all right?"

"Fine," Anton replied. But he was trembling. "Just—give me a second."

"So this is what it feels like to be a Prophet?" Hassan asked, looking down at his hands like he was expecting flames to come shooting out of them.

Jude watched the five of them, a strange feeling welling up inside him. He had devoted his whole life to the Seven Prophets. People he thought holier and more worthy than himself. Whose legacy he'd felt he'd never be able to uphold.

And now here he was. Here *they* were. The Seven Prophets. The *new* Prophets.

"We need to work quickly," Anton said. "I don't have time to give scrying lessons right now, so just do as I say. We all need to scry together—each of our Graces will emanate at a slightly different frequency. But when they're combined, they'll create the Sacred Word. Once it's formed, one of us has to touch the god, and the Word will burn through the god's *esha*, destroying it."

"Meaning someone needs to get close to Beru," Illya said. "That won't be easy."

Jude, Anton, and Illya all looked over at Ephyra and Hector.

"I can—" Hector began.

But Ephyra cut him off with a shake of her head. "It should be me. I'm the reason any of this is happening."

"No," Hector said forcefully. "Listen, I know what it's like to lose your family. I can't let you do this. I can't let you be the one to end her life."

Ephyra stared at him, her eyes filling with tears. She blinked them away, nodding. "Thank you."

Jude's stomach lurched at the thought of Hector putting himself in more danger—but they were all putting themselves in danger at this point.

"The rest of us will protect you as best we can until you can get close enough," Jude said.

"How do we do this?" Hassan asked Anton.

"Close your eyes," Anton said. "Focus on your Grace."

Jude closed his eyes and let his Grace flow through him like he had once done with his koahs. His Grace echoed through the air around him, nudging up against that of the others. He could feel them all, bright and dark, low and high, swirling and crashing together.

"Let go!" Anton's voice called above the cacophony.

Jude obeyed, trying to mimic the sensation of using his Grace to power a strike of his blade. At first it felt like too much, the wall of sound crashing over him, but slowly, it began to resolve, to strengthen.

It was working. He could feel the others' Graces echoing off his own, suffusing him with a power he'd only ever glimpsed before, when he'd felt Anton scry in the Circle of Stones, when he'd unsheathed the Pinnacle Blade, when he'd felt the birth of the Last Prophet.

But this was the same feeling multiplied ten times over. His body tingled with it, and the very air rang with the call of their Graces.

He opened his eyes. His friends—the Prophets—glowed from the inside out.

A gasp hitched in Jude's throat. He could feel the Sacred Word forming, a tangible power like lightning shooting through his veins.

Then a roar of thunder drowned out the call, and a flash of light burst over the barren rock. Jude dove to the side on instinct, and for a moment he was blinded.

When his vision slowly returned, he saw a smoldering crater. In its center was the god.

Beru stood unnaturally still, a strangely flat, alien expression on her face as she surveyed the seven of them sprawled on the rock.

"WHAT HAVE YOU DONE?" the god demanded, swinging its gaze to Anton. "WHY HAVE YOU CREATED THESE ABOMINATIONS?"

Jude suppressed a shiver, unable to stop the visceral reaction his body had to that ancient, terrible voice. He struggled to his feet, slipping on the rock, and clambered toward Anton.

"Who are you calling an abomination?" Khepri hollered from the god's other side.

It swiveled to her. Jude, grateful for her distraction, rushed to Anton's side.

"I'm all right," Anton said quietly as Jude helped him to his feet. "Jude, the Sacred Word—"

Jude cut him off with a nod. He could feel the combined power of their Graces, but the Sacred Word was still only half formed. They needed to buy time.

He stepped toward the god, putting himself between it and Anton. "Why are you doing this? Why not just let us live in peace?"

The god whirled toward him. "THERE IS NO PEACE WHILE HUMANITY EXISTS!"

The god's power seized Jude, raising him into the air. Jude choked off a scream. He had to stay focused. As long as the god was distracted, they could still finish this.

"Maybe you're right," he replied. He pulled in a breath, then another. He felt the Graces of the others begin to coalesce again, strengthening the seed of power they'd created.

The god tightened its invisible grip on him.

"THERE IS NO RIGHT OR WRONG," it said. "THERE IS ONLY ME."

The god's grip grew painful, squeezing Jude so hard his lungs could no longer draw breath.

But it didn't matter. Jude could suddenly feel the Sacred Word all around him, the threads of Grace pulling taut into a glowing knot inside each of them. A tiny star.

Triumph burst through Jude's chest. They had done it. They'd made a new Sacred Word.

"WHAT IS THAT?" The god cocked its head, as if listening.

Jude's elation shattered. *No,* he thought helplessly.

But of course, the god could feel the power reverberating all around them. After all, the Sacred Word was a piece of its own power.

"YOU THINK YOU CAN KILL ME AS THE FIRST PROPHETS DID?" the god asked. "YOU ARE WEAKER THAN THEY EVER WERE."

Jude gasped desperately for breath. Darkness crept at the edges of his vision. The god was going to squeeze the life from him.

"Jude, no!" Anton's terrified scream pierced the air.

Jude fought to stay conscious, pressure building in his chest and inside his head. His vision went black. After everything, after the others had all risked their lives for him, Jude was still going to die.

From somewhere nearby, he heard Hector's voice. "Beru, I know you can hear me."

Suddenly, Jude was plummeting to the ground. He crashed against the rock.

"THE MORTAL HEART INSIDE ME WILL NOT STOP ME FROM KILLING YOU," the god said. "MAYBE ONCE, BUT NO LONGER."

Jude sucked in a deep lungful of precious air.

"Jude," Anton's soft, urgent voice murmured.

He felt Anton's hands cup his face. Jude blinked open his eyes with a groan. Pushing himself up on shaking arms, his gaze found Hector.

"I know you're still in there, fighting," Hector called to Beru, stepping toward her.

In a swirl of wind and light, the god raised Hector off the ground.

"THIS ONE. SHE LOVES THIS ONE. RIGHT NOW, SHE IS PLEADING WITH ME NOT TO KILL HIM."

Terror distorted Hector's features. Jude watched as he kicked his legs, like he was trying to swim through the air as the god lifted him higher.

"SHE WOULD DO ANYTHING TO SAVE HIM."

"*Hector!*" Jude bellowed.

"BUT THERE IS NOTHING SHE CAN DO," the god said. "NOTHING YOU CAN DO. I AM GOD. AND YOU CANNOT DESTROY ME."

Jude couldn't look away. Not as the god held up Beru's hand. Not as Hector's expression turned panicked and a scream tore from his throat. Not as a beam of bright white light pierced through Hector, and the scream abruptly cut off.

A dull roar filled Jude's ears, and it was a moment before he realized it was the sound of his own voice, a wail that seemed to break around him.

Hector was dead.

Impassive, the god turned to him. "YOUR WORLD IS COMING TO AN END. AND THERE IS NOTHING YOU CAN DO TO SAVE IT."

Jude closed his eyes and braced his hands against the stone ground. He could still feel the Sacred Word thrumming through him, but it felt muted, dissonant as the god's voice surrounded them.

"IN ITS PLACE I WILL BUILD A BETTER ONE. A MORE BEAUTIFUL ONE, FILLED WITH CREATIONS THAT WILL NOT BETRAY ME. CREATIONS THAT WILL HEED ME AND LIVE IN HARMONY AS YOU HAVE FAILED, TIME AND AGAIN, TO DO."

Grief crashed over Jude, drowning his last spark of hope. They had been here before, facing a vengeful god as it rained destruction down on them. But this, he knew, was the very last time. Their very last failure.

"THIS IS YOUR END."

The end of the world was here and just like Anton had predicted, they could do nothing to stop it.

53

EPHYRA

EPHYRA WATCHED, HORROR TURNING HER BODY TO STONE, AS HECTOR FELL TO
the ground.

The god's words boomed over her, but Ephyra barely heard them.
Hassan and Khepri rushed to Hector's side. But they already knew it
was too late—they all did. They had felt the moment Hector's *esha* had
gone quiet.

The Sacred Word surged through Ephyra like a storm.

You can do this, she thought to herself. *For her. For her, you can. For
the rest of them.*

It was up to her. It had always been up to her. She was the Pale
Hand of Death, a reaper of monsters, slayer of humans and gods alike.

And this was the last life she would take.

She stepped toward the god.

It reacted instantly, zeroing in on her.

"DO YOU THINK I WON'T KILL YOU, TOO?"

Ephyra didn't stop. She walked toward the god, toward its snarling
face, a mockery of her kind and loving sister.

"JUST BECAUSE YOU ARE HER SISTER, JUST BECAUSE YOU BROUGHT ME BACK . . . THESE THINGS WON'T PROTECT YOU ANYMORE, EPHYRA."

When Ephyra spoke, she spoke to Beru and not the god. "Beru," she said, her voice threatening to break. "Remember what I told you."

The god raised its arms. Bolts of lightning crashed down on the barren rock.

Ephyra did not waver. "I will never, ever give up on you."

"ENOUGH. WE BOTH KNOW YOU WON'T DO THIS. YOU WON'T KILL HER."

But Ephyra didn't stop. She drew closer to the god, close enough to touch it.

"I'm sorry, Beru," she said. "I love you."

She closed her eyes. She wrapped her fingers around Beru's wrist, around the black handprint.

The Sacred Word burned through them both.

54

BERU

BERU DID NOT REMEMBER THE FIRST TIME SHE'D DIED. SHE REMEMBERED ONLY after, her sister's viselike grip on her arm and the quiet that surrounded them.

But now she felt every second, stretched out as if each lasted a lifetime.

The Sacred Word blazed over the god. Beru felt it pour through her veins, its heat scorching her bones.

The god bellowed in her mind. It could remember the cold light of creation. The torment of those first few eons. The agony of becoming.

Beru remembered it, too. How the world began as chaos, darkness, and light.

Dying felt much the same.

The throes of the god quaked through her. It flared like a star, bright and hot, swallowing the cold, dark space around it.

She waited for the moment it would burn out to nothing, but it did not come.

Instead, she felt more than she ever had before. Threads of vibrating *esha* weaving their way around her.

This was what the god had once been, she realized. It had been *everything*.

And when the Prophets had slain it, it had been cut off, severed from the *esha* that flowed throughout the rest of the world.

The voice in her head, the creature that had seized control of her body, was not the god. Or, it was not *all* that the god was.

She saw now.

She saw the parts that had been forgotten to it.

I know you, she thought as she felt the *esha* of the world stretch out from her. Just as the god had once been everything, it was also *her*.

The god screamed inside her. Beru called back.

You loved them. You loved them, these creatures you created who became so much more and so much less than you wanted. You loved them, even in their wickedness and selfishness. You loved them in their grief and their joy, in their broken parts and in all the things you could not understand.

NO.

You loved them even as they betrayed you.

She remembered. The creatures that had been of it, the mortals it had created. How they made the god more than it ever had been before. How they made it too much. How they created their own wills as the god had once created its own.

And you love them now.

YOU ARE WRONG.

I can see into your heart.

LOVE IS HUMAN.

And it is divine.

Beru reached for the god, every thread of her *esha* straining as the god burned and burned.

I know your heart. It is my heart. I know your mind. It is my mind. I know your love. It is my love.

With a voice that shook the sky, Beru spoke the name of the god. The name that lived at the core of it, that bound it together, that unraveled it. It wasn't a name like mortals gave themselves, but a name that existed in the language of all things, the language that made up the universe—vibration and resonance, thunder and light.

She spoke the name of the god, and it was her name, too.

The name of the girl in the shade of the acacia tree, saying goodbye to her sister. The girl stringing beads and glass together, searching for beautiful things in an ugly, brutal world. The girl standing beside Hector in a hidden grotto, unable to hide the love that filled her heart, like a cup brimming full of water.

The girl who lived and died and lived again.

The name was burden and grief and atonement. It was love and joy and kindness. It was anger. It was fury quelled by love. It was hope. Resurrection and rebirth.

And the god answered her, calling back until their voices were one, and then Beru could no longer hear it, could no longer feel its will as separate from her own.

She sang out the name of the god, and the universe answered.

Light tore through the darkness.

Beru could feel breath as it moved through her lungs. She rose to her feet. When she looked down, she could see the rock below her had been scorched a bright white in the pattern of a many-pointed star, with her at the center.

And at her feet, Ephyra lay crouched on the ground, her arms over her head, shielding herself.

Beru reached out and touched her shoulder. Ephyra flinched, but then her arms came away from her head and she gazed up at Beru, eyes filling with tears.

"Beru?"

"It's me," Beru confirmed. "And also . . . not me."

"The god, is it—is it gone?" Ephyra asked.

Beru shook her head. "It's . . . part of me, now."

"What does that mean?"

"It means that it won't hurt you. I won't hurt you." She swept her gaze over the others, who were frozen, staring at her with expressions of horror and wonder. "Any of you."

Her gaze found the place where Hector's body lay. Hassan and Khepri knelt over him. She walked toward him, noting how Hassan flinched as she neared.

She felt the tug of her mortal heart in her chest, felt the pain of this loss acutely, even knowing that she—or at least a part of her—had killed him. But the pain felt different than it had when she was just human. She could feel his *esha*, that sacred energy that had been, uniquely, Hector, as it dispersed into the air, returning to the earth. Returning to *her*. And for a moment, she glimpsed what would become of it—re-forming itself, reshaping into new life.

She turned back to face everyone. Anton stared at her, exhaustion written plainly on his pale face. Beside him was Jude, grief and hope on his. Illya, assessing Beru carefully. Khepri, awed and a little fearful, but not without the spark of courage that always lingered in her eyes, like she was ready to face down the world if she had to. And Hassan, suspicious and thoughtful.

And last, Ephyra, who looked at Beru with love. Always with love.

"I am not the girl you wanted to save," she said to Ephyra. And then, to the others, "Nor am I the ancient god you wanted to slay. The god is dead. So is the girl."

"Then what are you?" Anton asked.

She told them the truth. "I don't know." She wasn't mortal anymore. Yet her mortal heart still beat. "But you can trust that I will not harm you. Or any human."

"How can we trust that?" Hassan asked.

"I suppose you must have faith."

And she would prove that their faith was deserved.

55

ANTON

ANTON WATCHED AS A BRIGHT LIGHT ENVELOPED BERU—OR WHAT HAD ONCE been Beru. He raised an arm to shield his eyes, and when the light faded, she was gone.

For a long moment, no one spoke. The only sound was the sea crashing against the rocks and the wind whistling through the crumbled ruins of the lighthouse.

"Do we trust it?" Hassan asked, breaking the silence. "Her? What if she's just going to finish what the god started?"

Anton's gaze flickered to the sea. It was Beru's voice that had spoken. Not the god's. And if what she'd said was true, then the god was dead.

"I trust her," Anton said firmly.

Ephyra was strangely quiet, staring at the place where Beru had disappeared. Khepri, who was closest to her, stepped forward, laying a hand on her shoulder gently. Ephyra startled under the touch.

Jude, too, was quiet. He knelt several paces away from where Hector's body lay, staring at him, unmoving. Anton let the others' voices wash over him and went to Jude's side. Wordlessly, he wrapped his arms around him, letting Jude's head fall against his shoulder as Jude wept.

"It should have been me," Jude whispered. "If I'd just gone through with it—" He cut himself off with a wet sob.

Anton didn't say anything. He had no doubt that they had done the right thing. That Hector had believed it, too. And later, when the dust had settled and they'd laid Hector to rest, Anton would tell him so. He would sear the words into Jude's skin with his lips and his hands.

But for now, he just held him and didn't let go.

Jude and Hassan prepared Hector's body. They cut a lock of his hair and put it inside a reliquary of chrism oil. Jude said the blessing, and Hassan, Khepri, and Anton lit the pyre. The smoke spiraled against the blaze of the dying sun.

As the fire dwindled down to embers and the sky grew dark, they departed. Hassan and Khepri first, with an invitation to return to the palace to rest. Then Illya and Ephyra. And finally, only Jude and Anton remained.

"You should go," Jude said to Anton. "You look exhausted."

"I can stay with you," Anton said at once. "I don't mind."

Jude smiled at him faintly, and then cupped a hand around his face and kissed his forehead. "Go. I . . . I want to be alone. For a little while."

Anton bit his lip and then nodded shakily. His heart ached. But instead of turning away, he stepped toward the pyre and laid a hand on a charred piece of wood, still warm from the fire.

"I'll take care of him. I promise," Anton said.

Only then did he turn and walk away, following the path back to the palace.

Evidence of the god's destruction greeted him at every turn. Buildings had been ripped apart, their debris blocking the streets. Small fires smoldered in various pockets of the city, with neighbors working together to put them out. People huddled in broken doorways, wounded and confused as strangers tried to lead them to safety.

But in the wake of the destruction, Anton also saw evidence of quiet joy and resilience. People spilled into the streets, talking and even laughing with one another, sharing cups of wine and food. Voices joined in song echoed out from rooftops.

The sounds of merrymaking carried Anton through the decimated palace gates. Crowds of people spilled out of the front courtyards. Someone perched on a crumbling wall launched bright, alchemical lights into the dark sky. Music filtered out from a banquet hall, and Anton could see people dancing and drinking within. The darkness had lifted. The world turned on.

He bypassed the banquet hall and entered through a different corridor, climbing the stairs and wandering through unfamiliar hallways until he found an open bedroom.

It wasn't until he was inside that it hit him how exhausted he truly was. He hadn't slept at all the night before, not wanting to miss a single second of what he thought would be his last few hours with Jude. And the process of scrying into the past, of turning the others into Prophets, of facing the god, had taken almost everything out of him.

He curled up on the rumpled sheets, and, perhaps for the first time in his life, fell instantly into dreamless sleep.

———————————————

Fingers stroked Anton's hair. A soft sigh eased its way from his chest.

The hand pulled away, and Anton let out a noise of displeasure.

"Ah, so you are awake," Jude said teasingly.

Anton opened his eyes to find the swordsman perched at the edge of the bed.

"Good morning," Jude said, his voice soaked in fondness.

"It's morning?" Anton asked. Somehow he thought he would've woken up when Jude returned. He rubbed his face. "I slept the whole night."

"You slept *three* whole nights," Jude corrected. "And two days."

"What?" Anton demanded, sitting up.

"Well, you woke up halfway through and ate almost your weight in bread," Jude amended. "And then went back to sleep again. Then you woke up again in the middle of the night and tried to persuade me to marry you."

"No, I didn't," Anton said, fighting back a smile even as embarrassment made him flush with heat.

"Yes, you did," Jude assured him. "You were quite upset when I said I was already married."

Anton reeled him in by the front of his shirt. "Quit teasing me."

"I would never tease you," Jude said solemnly, letting Anton maneuver him into a slow, sleepy kiss.

"What about you?" Anton asked when they parted, pushing Jude's hair off his forehead gently. "Did you sleep at all?"

"Some," Jude said, which of course meant he had not.

"So what happened while I was asleep?" Anton asked. "I mean . . . Beru. The god. Whatever she is now."

"There's been some news," Jude replied. "Rumors of the god appearing in Endarrion. In Tarsepolis. They say she's rebuilt Behezda. There have been no more plagues. No more storms of fire or volcanic eruptions. Things seem to be . . . at peace."

"Have you talked to Ephyra?" Anton asked.

"A little," Jude answered. "She's . . . all right."

Anton nodded. He knew there was a lot more to it than that, but he would trust Jude's judgment for now. "I guess people must be wondering, though. What happens if they incur the god's wrath again?"

Jude shook his head. "They may wonder that. But I think you and I know the truth." He curled a hand around Anton's and lifted it to his lips. "She won't harm us again. She's . . . still Beru, in a way. And she'll protect that part of her. The mortal part. The part that loves us."

"So you believe," Anton said.

"So I choose to believe, yes," Jude replied. "There's something else."

There was a quiet, glowing smile on Jude's face that pulled at Anton's heart. "What is it?"

"You remember how the god destroyed the Relics and all the Graces?"

"Sounds familiar," Anton said drily, narrowing his eyes.

"Something happened when the goddess was . . . reborn," Jude said. "I don't know how to explain it. But I felt . . ."

"You got your Grace back?" Anton asked.

Jude paused. "In a way. It's . . . different than it was."

"What do you mean?"

"It isn't *mine*," Jude said. "It just *is*. I can call to it, I can use it, but it doesn't belong to me anymore. And it's not just me. It's everyone."

"All the Graced?" Anton asked.

Jude shook his head. "*Everyone.*"

Anton blinked at him. "You mean anyone can summon Grace?"

"It seems that way," Jude replied. "Some are more adept than others. And some are more attuned to certain Graces than others. My theory is that when we used the Sacred Word on the god, it didn't just become part of Beru. It became a part of *everything*. And its *esha* is now connected, in some way, to everyone in the world. Enough that we can access it, draw on its power."

"That's . . ." Anton trailed off. He didn't know exactly what it meant. It could be dangerous.

It could also be incredible.

"We can talk about it more later," Jude promised. "Now put on some clothes so we can go to breakfast."

"Better idea," Anton countered, stealing another kiss. "We stay here, you take *off* your clothes, and we—hey!"

Jude chucked a shirt at Anton's head. Begrudgingly, Anton slipped it on.

"Today's a big day. We don't want to be late," Jude told him.

"Why? What's happening?" Anton asked, pulling on a pair of pants.

Jude smiled. "It's King Hassan's coronation."

56

HASSAN

"ARE YOU SURE ABOUT THIS, HASSAN?" KHEPRI ASKED, HANDS LINGERING ON Hassan's collar as she pinned a gold scarab to his brocade jacket.

Hassan looked down at himself. "I think it looks good."

Khepri's mouth tilted into a wry smile. "Not the clothes."

He caught her hands. "I'm sure. This is what Herat needs. For the good of its future."

"There are many who will disagree," Khepri said.

"Do you?"

She didn't answer for a moment, looking down at their joined hands. "You know where I stand," she said at last. "Where I've always stood."

He kissed her knuckles. "I hope you will remember you said that when you're stuck sitting through your fiftieth meeting about tax law with me."

Khepri groaned, leaning her forehead against his shoulder.

"Where are your brothers, by the way?" Hassan asked.

"They're with Zareen," Khepri said. "Helping with some sort of light display."

"That worries me."

Behind them, the doors suddenly flew open.

"Hassan!" his mother cried. "Everyone's waiting for you in the throne room."

She paused at the threshold, her gaze locked on Hassan, eyes soft.

"What is it?" Hassan asked.

She stepped toward him and smoothed her hands over his shoulders. "Your father would have been so proud."

Hassan gave her a watery smile and stepped forward to embrace her as anticipation and nerves churned in his gut. He hoped she was right—that his father would be proud of who Hassan had become, and what he was about to do.

Zareen had done an admirable job with the lights, Hassan had to admit. Gold light shimmered from beneath the water that surrounded the pyramid-shaped dais. Sunlight streamed through the now open ceiling, illuminating the throne perched atop the pyramid. Even the painted falcon on the wall behind it seemed to glow.

Khepri remained at the edge of the moat as Hassan and his mother ascended the stairs up to the top of the pyramid, followed by the crown-keeper. It was tradition for a civilian, not of noble birth, to be chosen to carry the gilded box that contained the crown of Herat. For this sacred duty, Hassan had chosen a familiar face—Azizi, the refugee boy whom Hassan had first met in the agora of Pallas Athos so many months ago. He, along with the other refugees, had arrived back in Nazirah the night before.

Hassan smiled at the boy, his heart bursting with joy that he had managed to keep the promise he'd made to him. That he would make

Nazirah safe for him to return to. Azizi didn't quite smile back, trying his very best to look serious and solemn as he carried the crown reverently up to the top of the pyramid.

Hassan looked at the crowd within the throne room, which spilled out through the open threshold and down the many steps and into the central courtyard. It might even have stretched back through the crumbled palace gates and into Ozmandith Road.

But there, near the front, he spotted his friends: Anton, Jude, Ephyra, Illya, and Zareen. Hector's absence felt like a raw wound in his chest, but seeing the others' faces was a balm. Even Ephyra looked happy, smiling for the first time in days.

Hassan recalled, what felt like a lifetime ago, the dream he'd had of his triumphant return to Nazirah and his coronation. Standing up here now felt different than he'd imagined it. Back then, it had felt like it would be an ending.

Now, it felt more like a beginning.

Azizi opened the gilded box, and Hassan's mother lifted the crown into the light. Golden laurel leaves overlapped to form a circlet. This was the crown that had been worn by every monarch since the original Crown of Herat—the Relic of Mind—had been hidden away by the Lost Rose.

Hassan bent his head and allowed his mother to crown him. The crowd erupted into cheers and fell to their knees.

Hassan waited for the noise to die down and then stepped forward to speak.

"People of Herat," he said, his voice projecting over the crowd through the artificed scarab pin on his jacket. "It is an honor to be crowned as your king. My father sat upon this throne for over two decades. He died trying to protect this country from tyranny and zealotry, to preserve the legacy of light and wisdom bestowed on us by the Prophet Nazirah two thousand years ago."

Hassan paused to take a breath, his gaze finding Khepri in the front row of the crowd. The same feeling he'd felt the first time he'd ever set eyes on her washed over him again. A sense of purpose and drive. Like the beginning of something so huge he could not yet grasp it.

"I vow to serve this country for as long as I live," he went on, "but my reign as your king will end one year from today."

He paused as murmurs of confusion and dismay rippled over the crowd. He felt his mother shift toward him, but no matter how shocked she was she wouldn't dare try to interrupt him.

"During my one-year reign, I will be meeting with leaders and other citizens of Herat, from tradespeople and scholars to soldiers and farmers. Together we will devise a new system of governance that protects all people of Herat, a system that vests its power not in one monarch, but in the people themselves. A system that is not imposed upon our country by the forces of fate and destiny but that is freely chosen by its people.

"The Age of Darkness is over," Hassan continued. "The lighthouse has fallen. Dawn has risen. The Seif line is this country's past. It's time now for Herat to choose its own destiny."

The crowd seemed to hush as Hassan's speech came to a close. For a moment, he stood suspended in the silence, unsure if a riot was about to break out or he was about to be forcibly removed from the throne by his own mother.

Then, from the front of the crowd, a single voice let out a joyful holler.

Another joined it. Then another. Soon the whole crowd was clapping and cheering, throwing brightly colored scarves and paper into the air.

Thumping drums, jangling bells, and trilling horns accompanied the royal procession as it made its way through the throne room and down the stairs. Music players, dancers, and fire-twirlers strutted down the aisle as the crowd caroused around them.

Hassan let the celebration wash over him for a moment and then turned to descend. He stopped short when he saw his mother behind the throne, wearing a grave expression.

They stared at each other for a long moment.

"I must say, I wasn't expecting that," she said at last. "Though perhaps I should have."

Hassan didn't say anything, just waited for either her acceptance or her ire.

"The nobles will be angry," she said, a smile threatening to break through on her face.

"I can handle them," Hassan assured her.

She swept her gaze over him. "You know, I think you can."

He beamed at her, overwhelmed by a rush of gratitude.

She tilted her head toward the stairs that led down from the dais. "Go on. Your royal procession awaits."

With a last glance, Hassan descended the stairs and joined Khepri, her brothers, and Zareen, who comprised his royal escort. Together they walked into the crowd—the soldiers, the alchemist, and the last King of Herat.

57

EPHYRA

ON THE SEAWORN CLIFFS ABOVE THE CITY OF CHARITY, EPHYRA KNELT BEFORE the Navarro shrine and offered an oath.

The Pale Hand will never take another life, she vowed, bowing her head.

Jude knelt beside her, Hector's reliquary held delicately in his hands. He placed it on the shrine beside Hector's brother's reliquary, and beneath his mother's and father's.

"I always wondered what Hector's home was like," Jude said after a moment, looking around at the simple three-room house.

Ephyra closed her eyes, thinking back to the six months that she and Beru had spent in this house when they were young.

"It was warm," she said. "Crowded, when it was all six of us. But there was always enough to eat. His father had the loudest laugh I've ever heard. His mother doted on both her boys, and on me and Beru when they took us in. She'd always wanted a daughter, but she loved her sons fiercely. Hector worshipped Marinos. He had a temper, even back then, and Marinos was the only one who could calm him when he really got going. Well—Marinos and sometimes Beru."

Jude glanced at her and Ephyra met his gaze. "He risked his life for me," Jude said. "You all did. But Hector's the only one who actually lost his. And I just keep thinking—I have to do right by him. I don't know how, but I have to make it count for something."

"Make what count?" Ephyra asked.

"My life."

"We can't go back," she said, remembering Hector's words. "Only forward. We can't undo our choices. We can only make new ones. Different ones. But—for the record, Jude, I don't think a single one of us would've chosen differently. I don't think Hector would've. He loved you. Not perfectly, not infallibly, but he loved you."

Jude met her gaze, but he seemed lost in thought.

"Ephyra," Anton called from outside the shrine. His voice was even, barely louder than his usual speaking volume, but there was an edge of alarm that sent adrenaline spiking through Ephyra's blood. By the quick, worried glance that Jude shot her, Ephyra could tell he heard it as well.

They rushed back outside. Ephyra took two running steps past Anton and then stopped.

Dusk had fallen, turning the light an eerie violet-gray as the last vestiges of sunlight glowed between the sea and the sky. At the edge of the cliff, backed by the rays of dying light, stood the goddess.

"I came to pay my respects to Hector and his family," she said.

Ephyra's heart thrummed. It was so hard not to think of the girl in front of her as her sister. Hard to remember that it wasn't Beru meeting her eyes across the yard.

It had been almost two weeks since she had disappeared in the aftermath of their attempt to slay the creature inside her. Almost two weeks since Ephyra thought she'd never see her again.

Ephyra took another step toward her.

"We'll meet you back on the road," Anton said gently, taking Jude's hand and leading him away.

"Beru," Ephyra finally choked out. "Beru."

And then she was walking toward her swiftly, throwing her arms around her. Beru let Ephyra embrace her, one hand coming up to rest between her shoulder blades.

Ephyra felt something inside her break at the touch, tears spilling from her eyes.

"I'm going to do it, Beru," she said. "I'll save a hundred lives. And then a hundred more. As many as I can."

She wished, desperately, that Beru would go with her. That they could return to how it was, traveling from city to city together. But this time they'd help people instead of killing them.

As if Beru could read her mind, she pulled away from Ephyra and laid her hand on Ephyra's cheek. "You have to let me go."

"I know," Ephyra said through her tears. "I know."

She didn't know how it would be possible.

The goddess stepped back, and with a smile that was purely Beru, she vanished.

Ephyra stared at the spot where she had disappeared as night consumed the sky, the first stars glimmering against the darkness.

She'd been losing Beru, over and over again, for almost half their lives, and it never got easier. Each time, it destroyed her. This time was no different.

But she would do what she'd never had the strength to do before. She would pull herself from the wreckage. She would gather the pieces that remained, and she would try to mend them into something new.

————————————

"So, this is it, then," Illya said, passing Ephyra her bag. "The beginning of your quest for atonement."

Ephyra frowned, taking the bag and hoisting it over her shoulder, with a glance back at the ship that was due to depart at any moment, with Ephyra on it. Illya had insisted on accompanying her to the marina. Jude and Anton had said their goodbyes earlier that morning.

"Are you mocking me?" she asked Illya.

"Never," he said. Then, offhandedly, he added, "I could go with you, you know."

She looked up at him in surprise. "Really?"

"If you wanted," he said, his gaze resting on her face like a caress.

She did want it. Too much, probably. She let herself consider it, for a moment. Not having to be alone. Having Illya with her. Illya, who had seen the worst of her and stayed despite it. Illya, who loved her and asked for nothing in return. It would make everything easier, if he was with her.

And it was that, perhaps, that made her decide. "I want to say yes."

"But?"

"I can't," she said. "I . . . think I need to do this on my own."

His smile was tinged with resignation. He'd known what her answer would be.

"What are you going to do?" She realized he hadn't told her his plans. And that she hadn't asked.

"Go back home, for a little while," Illya said. "Anton told me our grandmother is still alive."

"I thought you hated her."

"Yes," Illya replied. "I'm fairly certain she hated me, too. But Anton suggested it might help with—well, you know. Letting go of it all."

She knew how impossible a task that was. On impulse, she reached forward to cup his cheek. His eyes went wide, dark pupils swallowing his gold irises. She didn't think she'd ever touched him this tenderly.

"We'll see each other again," she promised.

He settled his hands at her waist and drew her close to him. "I know we will."

He kissed her. She could taste his longing, even after he pulled away.

"Don't want to miss your boat," he said.

"What?" She was still a little dazed from the kiss.

He nodded behind her, and she turned to find the boatswain waving a blue-and-white-striped flag, indicating their imminent departure.

Ephyra cursed under her breath, turning back.

"Illya—"

"Go," he said, a small, genuine smile lighting his features. "You can tell me next time."

With that promise ringing in her ears, she turned away and boarded the ship.

58

JUDE

JUDE SHIFTED THROUGH THE NEXT FORM OF THE KOAH SEQUENCE, HIS ARMS crossed in front of him, palms facing out.

It felt different than it used to. When he summoned Grace now, it was like calling out to the universe itself. Feeling the answer thread through his bones. He was still learning, still growing accustomed to this new form of Grace. But on mornings like this, it felt instinctive.

As Jude moved through the second half of the koah sequence, he became aware that someone was watching him.

"I'm in the middle of something," he said lightly, without looking behind him.

"I can see that," Anton replied, something warm and admiring in his voice.

"Well, unless it's urgent . . ." Jude said, shifting into the next stance that brought Anton into view. He leaned against one of the trees in the orchard, just watching.

Fairly certain that he knew what Anton's game was, Jude went back to his koahs as if he wasn't there. It had rained the past few days, and overnight the rain had frozen so that the frosted leaves of the orange trees glittered in the early morning sun.

"Jude," Anton said.

Jude breathed and moved through the next sequence.

"Jude," Anton said again, drawing the syllable out. "Are you done?"

Jude again did not reply.

Anton huffed out a breath, knocking his head back against the tree. "You'll be done *soon*, though, right?"

Jude finished the sequence and then stopped abruptly, spinning on his heel and stalking toward Anton.

Anton's eyes went wide, blinking at Jude as he backed him against the tree.

"You wanted my attention so badly?" Jude asked in a low voice, just this side of threatening. "Well, you have it now."

Anton flushed a pale pink that made his freckles stand out.

"I just thought"—his gaze flickered to Jude's lips—"that we could have breakfast, if you were done with your koahs."

"I think," Jude said slowly, "that you came out here so you could distract me."

Anton shivered. It was rare that Jude was able to fluster him the way Anton so easily and so often ruffled him. He planned to savor it.

"And you think you're charming enough to get away with it."

Anton aimed an insouciant little smile at him, tilting his face up toward Jude. "I *am* charming enough to get away with it."

"Are you sure?"

Anton nodded.

Jude leaned in, and Anton's eyes fluttered closed.

But before their lips could meet, Jude drew back. "You should learn a little patience."

Anton's eyes blinked open, his mouth pressing into a frown. "And you should be nicer to me, or I might leave you for Tuva."

"I feared this day would come," Jude said with a sigh. "It's his berry tarts, isn't it?"

As if on cue, Anton's stomach grumbled.

Jude laughed. "I guess so."

Jude took his hand and led Anton back through the orchard, toward the sound of the river and the cottage that sat on its banks. They had imposed themselves on Tuva once again and made the Lost Rose's former safe house their home for the winter. Between their journey to Charis with Ephyra and the trip up to Anvari to visit Lady Iskara, they hadn't had time to figure out where to point themselves before winter had made any kind of travel impossible. Luckily, Tuva hadn't minded the extra mouths to feed, and though spring was quickly arriving, still they lingered.

"There was a bit of news," Anton said as they passed the barren fields and crunched up the gravel path to the cottage. "Nothing urgent. Evander wrote again from Endarrion. He says things are improving— the newly elected council just convened their first session. And of course he asked again if we would come for the Moon Festival."

"What did you say?"

"I said we would discuss it," Anton replied.

It still felt odd to Jude, the idea that they could simply go wherever they pleased, that their obligations began and ended with the little garden plot outside of their cottage and the occasional letter from one of the only five people who knew they were here.

It wouldn't last forever. There were still remnants of the Witnesses causing trouble throughout the Six Prophetic Cities. There was this new form of Grace, which they had inadvertently created, and people who needed to be trained and taught how to control that power. There was the goddess, appearing in cities at random, seemingly to repair the damage the god had inflicted. There was a whole world, destabilized and crawling its way back from the brink of destruction.

But there were also people—people like Lady Iskara, like Evander, like King Hassan and Khepri, like Ephyra, wherever she was—who were trying to help the world heal. And for a moment, for now, it felt like Jude and Anton could take time to rest.

"There was also a letter from Kerameikos." The hesitation in Anton's voice was palpable.

The words hit Jude like a blast of cold air. He had written to Penrose over a month ago, to find out what had happened in the aftermath of Pallas's attack. And to tell them what had happened to Yarik.

"They're deciding what to do," Anton went on. "Whether the Order will disband or carry on. It seems some number of the Paladin have already left, including Annuka. She returned to the steppe, to join up with the Wandering City. Penrose said your input would be welcome."

Jude gripped Anton's hand tighter, looking off toward the peaceful flow of the river. With Anton's patient help, he'd slowly begun working through the tangled knot of feelings he had about the Order—his guilt, his anger, his grief. Some part of his heart would always live within the crumbled walls of the fort, but he didn't know if he was ready to go back there. If he ever would be.

"It should be up to them," Jude said at last. "I made my choice. Now they get to make theirs."

Anton drew their clasped hands to his lips, kissing Jude's knuckles. A benediction, a promise. That in this, he would follow Jude's lead.

They passed beneath the bent fig tree at the edge of the garden. The nest of mourning doves that Jude had spotted earlier that week were awake, cooing away to the sun. The sound filled Jude's chest with light, and he came to a stop, tugging Anton to a halt beside him just to enjoy the moment a little longer.

"This is what I would have wanted," he said.

Anton looked at him questioningly.

"A long time ago, Hector asked me what I would have wanted to do if the Prophets hadn't made me Keeper of the Word," Jude explained. The memory was a tender ache, as all his memories of Hector were now. "This is it. A house. A garden. Crickets to lull us to sleep, and birds to sing us awake. A home. And you."

"Well, you have me," Anton said, pressing a kiss to his cheek. "Now and always."

His gaze moved past Jude and his face suddenly lit up. Before Jude knew what was happening, Anton was pulling him into the garden.

"Look!" he said, dropping down into the dirt and leaving Jude with little choice but to follow. "The carrots I planted last week, Jude, look!"

Jude shifted to his knees, bending toward Anton as they both peered down at the dirt. There, between Anton's carefully cupped hands, two tiny green leaves had sprouted.

"It must have been all the rain," Anton said, awe creeping into his voice.

"I'm surprised they survived the freeze last night," Jude said. "They're so small."

"They're strong." Anton smiled down at the sprout. It was a soft, tender smile, usually reserved for Jude. "They'll grow."

AFTER

WINTER MELTED INTO SPRING. THE WORLD TURNED ON. THE GODDESS REBUILT the cities she had destroyed, but when that work was done she disappeared. According to some, she'd retreated into the Unspoken Mountains, at the edge of the world.

There were many who prayed to her to ease their suffering or forgive them their sins. She did not answer them, but in the last standing wall of the Temple of Pallas, there was a record, etched in stone, of her first and only sermon.

It went like this:

Do not search for me. You will not find what you seek. I leave you with no edicts, no laws. I will neither be your vengeful god, nor your benevolent ruler. Do not pray to me. Pray to one another. Take care of one another. Your fate is in your hands and the hands of those who build their lives beside yours.

If there is one thing I have learned from my time among you, it is this: Love can break the world, and make it into something new.

ACKNOWLEDGMENTS

There are so many people to whom I owe my deepest gratitude, but the first thank-you belongs to the booksellers, bloggers, and librarians who have championed this series, and to each and every reader who has picked up this book and found something to love. This series may be over, but it will never truly end as long as there are readers to discover it, and for that I am deeply grateful.

I could not have asked for a better partner to bring this series into the world than Brian Geffen, whose ability to steer these books closer to my own vision will never cease to amaze me. Thank you also, Starr Baer, Banafsheh Keynoush, Jodie Lowe, and everyone involved in the production of this series. I am endlessly grateful to the wonderful marketing, sales, and publicity teams at Holt Books for Young Readers and Macmillan Children's, including Brittany Pearlman, Molly Ellis, Allison Verost, Johanna Allen, Allegra Green, Julia Gardiner, Gaby Salpeter, Mariel Dawson, and many more. Thank you also to the brilliant minds of Mallory Grigg, Rich Deas, and Jim Tierney for the most gorgeous series design a girl could ask for. And of course to Jean Feiwel and Christian Trimmer for putting these books into the world.

To Hillary Jacobson and Alexandra Machinist: I am so grateful to have this dream team in my corner. Thank you also to Lindsey Sanderson and the rest of the team at ICM, as well as Roxane Edouard, Savannah Wicks, and the Curtis Brown team. Thank you also to Emily

Byron, James Long, and the rest of the team at Little Brown/Orbit UK, as well as Leo Teti, Umbriel Editores, and the incredible translators and publishing teams who have championed The Age of Darkness series across the globe.

Thank you to Janella Angeles, Erin Bay, Ashley Burdin, Alexis Castellanos, Kat Cho, Madeline Colis, Mara Fitzgerald, Amanda Foody, Amanda Haas, Christine Lynn Herman, Axie Oh, Claribel Ortega, Meg RK, Akshaya Raman, Tara Sim, and Melody Simpson. Your friendship, support, and humor have been absolutely essential to me, especially this past year. Thank you also to Swati Teerdhala, Patrice Cauldwell, Scott Hovdey, Laura Sebastian, and Sara Faring for every pep talk and check-in.

To my family: Mom and Dad for being the most supportive parents in the world. Sean, Julia, Riley, and now Theodore Wilder, you make my life so much better for being in it. Erica, it would be impossible to put into words how much this series owes to you and your eagerness to listen, brainstorm, and be the best sounding board and sister in the known universe. I'd resurrect a hundred evil dead gods for you, no question.

Nov

Kerameikos Fort

Endarric

N

Temple
of Pallas

W E

S

Pallas Athos

T H E   P E L A G O S

M e r a u   D e s e r t